PRAISE FOR *MARKED FOR REVENGE*

"In Swedish author Schepp's outstanding second novel, [she] sure-handedly brings her characters to unhappy life in a police procedural that lays bare the most sordid aspects of immigrant-related crime."
—*Publishers Weekly*, starred review

"Emelie Schepp is rapidly securing her place as the master of the ensemble police procedural novel.... Make time to read *Marked for Revenge* in one sitting. The pages just fly by." —*Bookreporter*

PRAISE FOR *MARKED FOR LIFE*

"Move over, Jo Nesbø." —*Fort Worth Star Telegram*

"A stellar first in a crime trilogy... Schepp couples an insightful look at the personal and professional lives of her characters with an unflinching multi-layered plot loaded with surprises." —*Publishers Weekly*, starred review

"A fast-paced thriller with a good blend of police procedural, the draw of a ninja-strong female lead, and enough adrenaline to make a good night's sleep a near impossibility." —*Booklist*

"This debut novel captivates the reader from the first moment and is impossible to put down."
—*Detective Magazine*

"A page turner you can't put down." —TV4

"Schepp captures you from the first page and never lets go. Gradually you are brought into an almost unbearable darkness where layer after layer of human evil is revealed. An impressive debut!"
—Cilla and Rolf Börjlind, bestselling Nordic crime authors

"One of the best crime novels I have ever read!"
—Anna Jansson, bestselling Nordic crime author

Also by

Emelie Schepp

MARKED
FOR
LIFE

MARKED FOR REVENGE

EMELIE SCHEPP

mira

mira

ISBN-13: 978-0-7783-3029-5

Marked for Revenge

Copyright © 2017 by Emelie Schepp

Translation by Suzanne Martin Cheadle

Recycling programs
for this product may
not exist in your area.

For questions and comments about the quality of this book, please contact us at
CustomerService@Harlequin.com.

www.Harlequin.com

Printed in U.S.A.

For Dad

MARKED

FOR

REVENGE

PROLOGUE

THE GIRL SAT QUIETLY, LOOKING DOWN at her bowl of yogurt and strawberries. She listened to the clinking of silverware against china as her mother and father ate breakfast.

"Would you please eat?"

Her mother looked at her imploringly, but the girl didn't move.

"Are your dreams bothering you again?"

The girl swallowed, not daring to lift her gaze from the bowl.

"Yes," she replied in a barely audible whisper.

"What did you dream about this time?"

Her mother tore a slice of bread in half and spread marmalade on it.

"A container," she said. "It was..."

"No!"

Her father's voice came from the other side of the table, loud, hard and cold as ice. His fists were clenched. His eyes were as hard and cold as his voice.

"That's enough!"

He got up, pulled her from the chair and shoved her out of the kitchen.

"We don't want to hear any more of your fantasies."

The girl stumbled forward, struggling to keep ahead of him as he pushed her up the stairs. He was hurting her arm, her feet. She tried to wrench herself from his grasp just as he changed his grip and put his hand around her neck.

Then he let go, his hand recoiling as if he'd been stabbed. He looked at her in disgust.

"I told you to keep your neck covered all the time! Always!"

He put his hands on her shoulders and turned her around.

"What did you do with the bandage?"

She felt him pull her hair aside, tearing at it, trying frantically to expose the nape of her neck. Heard his rapid breathing when he caught sight of her scars. He took a few steps back, aghast, as if he had seen something horrifying.

And he had...

Because her bandage had fallen off.

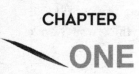

CHAPTER

ONE

THERE! THE CAR APPEARED FROM around the corner.

Pim smiled nervously at Noi. They were standing in an alley, in the shadows of the light from the streetlamps. The asphalt was discolored by patches of dried piss. It smelled strong and rank, and the howling of stray dogs was drowned out by the rumbling highway.

Pim's forehead was damp with sweat—not from the heat but from nerves. Her dark hair was plastered to the back of her neck, and the thin material of her T-shirt stuck to her back in creases. She didn't know what awaited her and hadn't had much time to think about it, either.

Everything had gone so quickly. Just two days ago, she had made up her mind. Noi had laughed, saying it was easy, it paid well and they'd be home again in five days.

Pim wiped her hand across her forehead and

dried it on her jeans as she watched the slowly approaching car.

She smiled again, as if to convince herself that everything would be okay, everything would work out.

It was just this one time.

Just once. Then never again.

She picked up her suitcase. She'd been told to fill it with clothes for two weeks to make the fictitious vacation more convincing.

She looked at Noi, straightened her spine and pulled her shoulders back.

The car was almost there.

It drove toward them slowly and stopped. A tinted window rolled down, exposing the face of a man with close-cropped hair.

"Get in," he said without taking his eyes from the road. Then he put the car in gear and prepared to leave.

Pim walked around the car, stopped and closed her eyes for a brief moment. Taking a deep breath, she opened the car door and got in.

Public prosecutor Jana Berzelius took a sip of water and reached across the pile of papers on the table. It was 10:00 p.m., and The Bishop's Arms in Norrköping was packed.

A half hour earlier, she'd been in the company of her boss, Chief Public Prosecutor Torsten Granath who, after a long and successful day in court, had at least had the decency to take her to dinner at the Elite Grand Hotel.

He had spent the two-hour meal carrying on about his dog who, after various stomach ailments and bowel problems, had had to be put to sleep. Although Jana couldn't have cared less, she had feigned interest when Torsten pulled out his phone to show pictures of the puppy years of the now-dead dog. She had nodded, tilting her head to one side and trying to look sympathetic.

To make the time pass more quickly, she had inventoried the other patrons. She'd had an unobstructed view of the door from their table near the window. No one came or went without her seeing. During Torsten's monologue, she had observed twelve people: three foreign businessmen, two middle-aged women with shrill voices, a family of four, two older men and a teenager with big, curly hair.

After dinner, she and Torsten had moved to The Bishop's Arms next door. He'd said the classic British interior reminded him of golfing in the county of Kent and that he always insisted on the same table. For Jana, the choice of pub was a minor irritation. She had shaken her boss's hand with relief when he'd finally decided to call an end to the evening.

Yet she had lingered a bit longer.

Stuffing the papers into her briefcase, she drank the last of her water and was just about to get up when a man came in. Maybe it was his nervous gait that made her notice him. She followed him with her gaze as he walked quickly toward the bar. He caught the bartender's attention with a finger in the air, ordered a drink and sat down at a table with his worn duffel bag on his lap.

His face was partly concealed by a knit cap, but she guessed he was around her age, about thirty. He was dressed in a leather jacket, dark jeans and black boots. He seemed tense, looking first out the window, then toward the door and then out the window again.

Without turning her head, Jana shifted her gaze to the window and saw the contours of the Saltäng Bridge. The Christmas lights swayed in the bare treetops near Hamngatan. On the other side of the river, a neon sign wishing everyone a Merry Christmas and a Happy New Year blinked on and off.

She shuddered at the thought that there were only a few weeks left until Christmas. She was really not looking forward to spending the holiday with her parents. Especially since her father, former Prosecutor-General Karl Berzelius, suddenly and inexplicably seemed to be keeping his distance from her, as if he wasn't interested in being part of his daughter's life anymore.

They hadn't seen each other since the spring, and every time Jana mentioned his strange behavior to her mother, Margaretha, she offered no explanation.

He's very busy, was always her response.

So Jana decided not to waste any more energy on the matter and had just let it be. As a result, there had been few family visits over the past six months.

But they couldn't skip Christmas—the three of them would be forced to spend time together.

She sighed heavily and returned her gaze to the man whom the server had just given a drink. When he reached for it, she saw a large, dark birthmark on his left wrist. He raised the glass to his lips and looked out the window again.

He must be waiting for someone, she thought, as she got up from the table, carefully buttoning her winter jacket and wrapping her black Louis Vuitton scarf around her neck. She pulled her maroon hat over her head and gripped her briefcase firmly.

As she turned toward the door, she noticed that the man was talking on his phone. He muttered something inaudible, downed his drink as he stood up and strode past her toward the exit.

She caught the door as it swung shut after him and stepped out onto the street and into the cold winter air. The night was crystal clear, quiet and almost completely still.

The man had quickly vanished from sight.

Jana pulled on a pair of lined gloves and set out for her apartment in Knäppingsborg. A block from home, she caught sight of the man again, standing against the wall in a narrow alley. This time he wasn't alone.

Another man stood facing him. His hood was up, and his hands were stuffed deep into his pockets.

She stopped in her tracks, took a few quick steps to the side and tried to hide behind a building column. Her heart began to pound and she told herself she must be mistaken. The man in the hood could not be who she thought he was.

She turned her head and again examined his profile.

A shiver went down her spine.

She knew who he was.

She knew his name.

Danilo!

Detective Chief Inspector Henrik Levin turned off the TV and stared at the ceiling. It was just after ten o'clock at night and the bedroom was dark. He listened to the sounds of the house. The dishwasher clunked rhythmically in the kitchen. Now and then he heard a thump from Felix's room, and Henrik knew his son was rolling over in his sleep. His daughter, Vilma, was sleeping quietly and still, as always, in the next room.

He lay on his side next to his wife, Emma, with his eyes closed and the comforter over his head, but he knew it was going to be difficult to fall asleep with his mind racing.

Soon he wouldn't be sleeping much at night for other reasons. The nights would instead be filled with rocking and feeding and shushing long into the wee hours. There were only three weeks left until the baby's due date.

He pulled the comforter down from his head and looked at Emma sleeping on her back with her mouth open. Her belly was huge, but he had no idea if it was larger than during her earlier pregnancies.

The only thing he knew was that he was about to become a father for the third time.

He lay on his back with his hands on top of the comforter and closed his eyes. He felt a sort of melancholy and wondered if he would feel different when he held the baby in his arms. He hoped so, because almost the whole pregnancy had passed without him really noticing. He hadn't had time—he'd had other things to think about. His job, for example.

The National Crime Squad had contacted him.

They wanted to talk about last spring's investigation of the murder of Hans Juhlén, a Swedish Migration Board department chief in Norrköping. The case was closed and Henrik had already put it behind him.

What had initially seemed to be a typical murder investigation of a high-ranking civil servant had turned into something much more, much worse. Something macabre: the smuggling of illegal refugees had led the team working the case to a narcotics ring that had, among other activities, been training children to be soldiers, turning kids into cold-blooded killers.

It was far from a routine case, and the investigation had been front-page news for several weeks.

Tomorrow, the National Crime Squad was coming to ask questions about the refugee children who had been transported from South America in shipping containers locked from the outside. More specifically, they wanted to talk about the ring leader,

Gavril Bolanaki, who had killed himself before anyone could interrogate him.

They'd be reviewing every minute detail yet again.

Henrik opened his eyes and stared out into the darkness. He glanced at the alarm clock, saw that it was 10:15 and knew the dishwasher would soon signal the end of its cycle.

Three minutes later, it beeped.

CHAPTER
TWO

HER HEART WAS POUNDING AND HER
pulse racing.

Jana Berzelius breathed as quietly as possible.

Danilo.

A wave of mixed emotions flowed over her. She felt simultaneously surprised, confused, irritated.

There was a time when she and Danilo had been like siblings, when they had shared a daily existence. That was a long time ago now, back when they were little. Now they shared nothing more than the same bloody past. He had scars on his neck the same as she, initials carved into flesh, a constant reminder of their shared dark childhood. Danilo was the only one who knew who she was, where she came from—and why.

She had sought out Danilo last spring to ask for his help when the shipping containers filled with refugee children began appearing outside the small harbor town of Arkösund. He had seemed helpful, even favorably inclined, but in the end he had still betrayed her. He had attempted to kill her—unsuccessfully—and then disappeared underground.

Ever since then, she had been searching for him, but it was as if he had vanished into thin air. She hadn't been able to find a single trace of him in all those months. Nothing. Her frustration had intensified in proportion to her desire for revenge. She daydreamed of different ways to kill him.

She had sketched his face in pencil on a white sheet of paper, drawing and erasing and drawing again until it was a perfect likeness. She had saved the picture, pinned it to a wall in her apartment as if to remind herself of the hatred she felt for him—not that she could ever forget it.

In the end, she had given up on her search for him and returned to her everyday life with the belief that she would probably never find him.

He was gone forever.

Or so she had thought.

Now he stood fifty feet from her.

She felt her body tremble and stifled an impulse to throw herself forward—she had to think rationally.

She held her breath so that she could hear the men's voices, but she couldn't make out a single word. They were too far away.

Danilo lit a cigarette.

The worn duffel bag lay on the ground, and the man with the birthmark was crouched down next to it. He pulled the zipper, exposing its contents. Danilo nodded and gestured with his right hand,

and both of them went with quick steps through the alley and disappeared down the stone steps toward Strömparken.

Jana clenched her teeth. What should she do? Turn around and go home? Pretend she hadn't seen him, let him get away? Let him disappear from her life yet again?

Silently, she counted to ten before stepping out of the shadows and going after them.

Detective Inspector Mia Bolander opened her eyes and immediately clapped her hand to her forehead. Her head was spinning.

She got out of bed and stood there naked, looking at the man whose name she had forgotten, who lay on his stomach with his hands under a pillow.

He hadn't been completely with it. For twenty minutes, he had paced the room and repeated that he was a waste of space and didn't deserve her. She had told him again and again that of course that wasn't true, and in the end she had convinced him to get into bed with her.

When he later asked considerately if he could massage her feet, she was too exhausted to say no. And when he had put her big toe in his mouth, she had finally reached her limit and asked straight out if they couldn't just fuck. He had gotten the hint and taken his clothes off.

He had also moaned loudly, licked her neck and given her hickeys.

That shithead.

Mia scratched under her right breast and looked down at the floor where her clothes lay in a heap.

She dressed quickly, not caring if she made noise. She just wanted to go home.

She'd only intended to make a quick stop at the pub. Harry's had had a Christmas-themed karaoke night, and the place had been packed with women in sparkly dresses and men in suits. Some had been wearing Santa hats and had probably gotten drunk earlier in the night at some Christmas party somewhere in Norrköping.

The man whose name she had forgotten had been standing at the bar, holding a beer. He seemed to be around forty and had straight, blond hair that was oddly styled—parted straight down the middle. She had seen a colorful skull-and-crossbones tattoo on his neck. He had otherwise been neatly dressed in a sport coat with overstuffed shoulder pads and a tie.

Mia had sat down a few stools away from him, fingering her glass and trying to get him to notice her. He finally had, but it took even longer for him to walk over and ask if he could join her. She had answered with a smile, again running her finger around the top of her glass. He'd finally understood that he should buy her another drink. Three pints of beer and two seasonal saffron-flavored cocktails later, they'd shared a taxi home to his apartment.

She could still taste the saffron. She went out in the hall, into the bathroom and turned on the light. She was blinded for a second and kept her eyes closed while she drank water out of her cupped hands. She squinted into the mirror, tucked her hair behind her ears and then caught sight of her neck.

Two large red hickeys featured prominently on the right side, under her chin. She shook her head and turned off the light.

She took his sport coat from the hook in the hall and rifled through the pockets. His wallet was in the inside pocket and only held cards—no cash at all.

Not a single krona.

She looked at his driver's license and saw that his name was Martin Strömberg, then she replaced it and put her boots and jacket on.

"Just so you know, Martin," she said, pointing a finger toward the bedroom, "you *are* a goddamn waste of space."

She unlocked the door of the apartment and left.

Jana Berzelius stopped at the top of the hill near Norrköping's Museum of Work and looked around. She couldn't see Danilo or the man with the birthmark anymore.

She surveyed all the street corners in front of her, but neither of the men were there. She didn't see another living soul, in fact, and was amazed at how deserted the industrial landscape could be on a chilly Wednesday evening in early December.

She stood there silently for ten minutes, watching. But she didn't hear a single sound or see the slightest movement.

Finally, she accepted that they were gone. She had lost him. The anger welled up inside her. There was only one thing to do now, and that was to leave, go home with the feeling of again having been tricked.

But what had she thought was going to happen? What had she been thinking? She shouldn't have followed him; she should just leave him alone and take care of herself.

There was nothing else she could do, really.

Walking along Holmensquare, she suddenly had the strange feeling that someone was following her, but when she spun around, the only thing she saw was a short man walking a dog off in the distance. She glanced up at the apartments along Kvarngatan and saw advent candelabras in many of the windows. The sky was pitch-black and still crystal clear.

Shivering, she pulled her shoulders up before continuing across the square and into the tunnel. Halfway through, she was again gripped by the feeling of being followed.

She stopped, turned and stared into the darkness behind her. She stood still, breathing quietly, listening.

Nothing.

She crossed Järnbrogatan with quick steps and rushed through the pink archway that marked the entrance to the Knäppingsborg neighborhood.

Then she suddenly heard a sound behind her.

There he stood, alone.

Thirty feet from her.

His chin was down and his jaw was clenched.

She met his gaze, dropping her briefcase, and prepared herself.

"JUST SWALLOW IT!"

Pim gave a start and met the man's eyes. He stood, leaning over the table with his face a few inches from hers. He was wearing a dark gray shirt with rolled-up sleeves.

She looked at the capsule in her hand. It was larger than a grape tomato and had more of an oval shape than she had expected. The contents were tightly packed in layers upon layers of latex.

Noi sat next to her and looked pleadingly at Pim, nodding almost imperceptibly in encouragement. *You can do it!*

They were sitting in a room above a pharmacy, the stairs to which had really been more of a ladder. A fan on the floor hummed from one corner of the room. Even so, it was hot and smelled musty.

She'd had no problem swallowing the tablet that neutralized her stomach acid. It had slid right down. But the capsule looked so huge, she thought now, pressing against the coating with her pointer finger and thumb.

The man grabbed her arm and slowly pushed her hand toward her mouth. The capsule touched her lips. She knew what she was supposed to do and her mouth instantly went dry.

"Open up!" he said between clenched teeth.

Pim opened her mouth and placed the capsule on her tongue.

"All right then, chin up and down the hatch with it."

She looked at the ceiling and felt the capsule drop far back on her tongue. She tried to swallow, but she couldn't. The capsule refused to go down.

She coughed it up into her hand.

The man slammed his fist onto the table.

"Where did you find this piece of garbage?" he said to Noi, who turned white as a sheet. "I can't afford idiots, do you understand that? Time is money."

Noi nodded and looked at Pim, who avoided meeting her gaze.

"Try again," Noi whispered. "You can do it."

Pim shook her head slowly.

"You have to!" Noi insisted.

Pim shook her head again. Her lower lip quivered and her eyes watered. She knew that she was lucky, that she should be happy that she had this opportunity. She wasn't used to good luck, but when Noi told her about the possibility of earning quick, easy money, her heart had leaped in excitement.

"Okay, that's it! Get out of here!" The man grabbed Pim's arm and pulled her to standing. "I have plenty of others who want to earn some cash."

"No! Wait! I want to!" Pim screamed, resisting. "Please, I want to! Let me try again. I can do it."

The man held her tightly. He glared at her for a moment, at her narrow, bloodshot eyes, red cheeks and compressed lips.

"Prove it!" he said.

With a bottle in one hand, he grabbed her jaw, forced her mouth open and squirted lubricant into her mouth three times.

He held up the capsule.

"Here," he said.

Pim took it and popped it into her mouth. She attempted to swallow. Poking it with one finger to move it farther back into her mouth, she only gagged more.

She grew more panicked.

She stuck the capsule down her throat again, thrust her chin up. But that only resulted in more gagging.

Her palms were damp with sweat.

She closed her eyes and opened her mouth, poking the capsule as far down her throat as she could.

She swallowed.

Swallowed, swallowed, swallowed.

Slowly, it slid down toward her stomach.

The man clapped his hands together and grinned.

"There you go," he said. "Only forty-nine left."

* * *

The first blow was aimed at her head, the second at her throat.

Jana Berzelius deflected Danilo's fists with her lower arms.

He was in a rage, darting from side to side, trying to land blows from every direction. But she fought against him, got her right fist up, ducked, jabbed with her left and then kicked. She missed but repeated the movements, quicker this time, striking Danilo's knee. His leg buckled slightly, but he kept his footing. She knew she had to make him lose his balance and fall, so she kicked again—this time at his head. But as she did, he grabbed her foot, wrenching it forcefully to the left. She was twirled around and landed flat on her back on the cold, hard ground. In almost the same movement, she rolled to the side, hands in defensive position, and jumped to her feet.

Danilo was standing completely still in front of her, waiting, his nostrils flaring and teeth bared.

He rushed toward her, throwing himself forward. At the same moment, she bowed her head, holding her fists in front of her face. Using all of her strength, she raised her foot and kicked in defense.

She hit her target.

As Danilo crumpled to the ground, she pounced on top of him and was about to put one knee on his chest when, with a primal roar, he threw his weight around so that they rolled together and he ended up on top. He sat astride her, punching her in the ribs with all of his strength.

Grabbing her hair, Danilo pulled her head toward him, lifting it from the ground. She tried to lift her upper body to lessen the pain, but his weight on her chest made that impossible.

"Why are you following me?" He leaned forward, hissing in her face.

She didn't answer. She was thinking feverishly: this can't happen, she couldn't let him win. She knew far too well what he was capable of. But she was trapped, her arms under his legs. She reached out with her fingertips, trying to find something to defend herself with, but there was only ice and snow.

An unpleasant feeling began to wash over her. She hadn't counted on ending up on the bottom. She had been intending to ambush him—she'd had the advantage from the beginning.

She clenched her fists and flexed her muscles, summoning all of her energy. Swinging her legs into the air, she drove her knees into his back. Danilo arched backward, losing his grip on her hair. She kneed him again and again, trying unsuccessfully to hook one leg around his neck.

He wouldn't budge.

He grabbed her hair again.

"You shouldn't have done that," he snarled, beating her head against the ground.

The pain was incredible. Her vision went black.

He slammed her head against the ground again

and again, and she felt how the strength ran out of her body.

"Stay away from me, Jana," he said.

She heard his voice as if in a fog, far away from her.

She didn't feel the pain anymore.

A warm wave washed over her, and she realized she was about to lose consciousness.

He raised his fist, holding it near her face without striking her. It was as if he was hesitating. Meeting her gaze, panting, he said something unintelligible that echoed as if in a tunnel.

She heard a shout that seemed to be coming from far away.

"Hey!"

She didn't recognize the voice.

She tried to move, but the pressure on her chest made it impossible. Fighting to keep her eyelids open, she looked straight into Danilo's dark eyes.

He glared back at her. "I'm warning you. Follow me one more time and I'll finish what I started here."

He held her face a half inch from his.

"One more time and you'll regret it forever. Understand?"

She did, but was unable to answer.

She felt the pressure on her chest release. The silence told her Danilo was gone.

She coughed violently and rolled to her side, closing her eyes for a long moment...until she thought she heard the unfamiliar voice again.

* * *

Anneli Lindgren laid a plate with two pieces of crispbread on the kitchen table and sat down across from her live-in partner, Gunnar Öhrn. Both worked for the county police, she as a forensic expert; he as a chief investigator.

Steam rose in wisps from their teacups.

"Do you want Earl Grey or this green tea?" she asked.

"Which are you having?"

"Green."

"I'll have that, too, then."

"But you don't like it."

"No, but you're always saying I should drink it."

She smiled at him and as she opened the tea bags, music came drifting in from Adam's room. She heard their son singing along.

"He seems to like it here," she said.

"Do you?"

"Of course."

She could sense Gunnar's anxiety in the question, so she answered quickly and without hesitation. It was the only way to avoid any follow-up questions. He was always nervous about everything, overthinking, analyzing, obsessing about things he should have let go of long ago.

"Are you sure? You like it here now?"

"Yes!"

Anneli dropped her tea bag into her cup and let it swell with hot water as she listened to Adam's voice, the music and lyrics he had memorized, and watched the color from the tea leaves seep into the water, counting the number of times she and Gunnar had lived apart but then together again. It was too many to remember. It might be the tenth time, maybe the twelfth. The only thing she could be sure of was that they had lived together off and on for twenty years.

But it was different now, she tried to convince herself. More comfortable, more relaxed. Gunnar was a good man. Kind, reliable. If he could only stop harping on every little thing.

He rested his hand on hers.

"Otherwise we can try to find a new apartment. Or maybe a town house? We've never tried that."

She pulled her hand away, looking at him without bothering to voice an answer. She knew the look on her face was enough.

"Okay," he said, "I get it. You're happy here."

"So stop nagging."

She sipped her tea, noting that there were approximately ninety seconds left of the song Adam was playing. One guitar solo and then the refrain three times.

"What do you think about the meeting with the National Crime Squad tomorrow?" he asked.

"I'm not thinking anything in particular. They can come to whatever conclusion they want. We did a very good job."

"But I don't understand why Anders Wester would come here anyway. I have nothing to say to him."

"What? That really sexy guy is coming?"

She couldn't help teasing him. There was something in his unnecessary worry, his jealousy, that she got a kick out of. But she regretted it immediately.

He glared at her.

"I'm only kidding," she said.

"Do you really think so?"

"That he's handsome? Yes, at one time I did."

She tried to look nonchalant, amused.

"But not anymore?" he asked.

"Oh, stop it," she said.

"Just so I know."

"Stop! Drink your tea."

"Are you sure?"

"Stop nagging!"

She heard the guitar solo. Then Adam's voice singing the refrain.

Gunnar got up and poured the contents of his teacup into the sink.

"What are you doing?" Anneli asked.

"I don't like green tea," he said, heading for the bathroom.

She sighed, at Gunnar and at the music she could barely stand. But she didn't want to end the evening with yet another argument. Not now, when they had just decided to try living together again.

She was already tired.

So tired.

"Hello? Are you okay?"

Robin Stenberg knelt down beside the woman

who was lying on the ground in the fetal position. The chain from his ripped jeans clattered as it touched the hard concrete. He saw she was bleeding heavily from the back of her head and was just about to poke her when she opened her eyes.

"I saw everything," he said. "I saw him. He went that way."

He pointed toward the river, his hand trembling.

The woman tried to shake her head.

"Ffff…ffeh…ehlll," she tried to say, her voice thick.

"No," he said. "You didn't fall. You were attacked. We have to call the police."

He got up and dug around in his cargo pockets, looking for his cell phone.

"Nuuuh…" she said.

"Shit, you're bleeding really bad," he said. "You need an ambulance or something."

He paced back and forth, unable to stand still.

"Shit, shit, shit," he repeated.

The woman moved a little, coughing.

"Don't…call," she whispered.

He found his phone and typed in the passcode to unlock it.

The woman coughed again.

"Don't call," she said again, clearer this time.

He didn't hear her as he typed in the emergency number. Just as he was about to hit the green call button, his phone disappeared from his hand.

"What the…"

It took a few seconds before he understood what had happened.

She had gotten up and now stood before him with his cell in her hand. Blood was dripping down from her head over her left ear.

"I said you shouldn't call."

For a moment, he thought it was a joke. But when he saw her threatening look, he understood that she was serious. He saw how she was examining him and despite being fully dressed, he felt almost naked.

Her eyes swept quickly over him, noting his black hat, heavily lined eyes, tattoo of eight small stars on his temple, pierced lower lip, lined denim jacket and worn-out military boots.

"What's your name?" she asked, more a command than a question.

"R-Robin Stenberg," he stammered.

"Okay, Robin," she said. "Just so we understand each other, I fell and hit my head. Nothing more."

In shock, he nodded slowly.

"Okay."

"Good. Take this now and go."

The woman tossed his cell to him. He caught it clumsily, stumbling backward a few steps and began to run.

It wasn't until he was inside his apartment on Spelmansgatan and had locked the door behind him that the magnitude of what he had just witnessed sunk in.

FOUR

THE INTERNATIONAL TERMINAL AT Suvarnabhumi Airport in Bangkok was swarming with people. Long lines wound around from every desk, and from time to time the clerks yelled out names of people who were requested to contact the information desk. The sound of suitcases arriving on the conveyor belt at baggage claim thundered through the hall.

Large groups were chattering noisily, babies were crying and couples were arguing about their travel plans.

"Passport, please."

The woman behind the check-in desk put her hand out.

Pim held her passport with both hands to hide the fact that they were trembling. She had been told not to panic, to relax, to try to look happy. But as the line in front of her got shorter, her anxiety grew.

She had fiddled so continuously with her ticket

that it was now missing a bit of the paper in the corner.

Her stomach hurt.

The nausea came in waves, and she wished she could just stick her finger down her throat. She wanted to spit—the amount of saliva in her mouth increased with every wave of nausea—but she knew she couldn't. So she swallowed, again and again.

Two lines away, Noi stood obsessively flicking her backpack strap. They avoided looking at each other, pretended they were strangers.

For now, it was as if they had never met.

Those were the rules.

The woman behind the counter tapped on her computer keyboard. Her hair was dark and pulled into a tight ponytail. The airline emblem was embroidered on the left pocket of her black jacket, underneath which she was wearing a white blouse with a Peter Pan collar.

Pim stood with one arm on the counter. She leaned slightly forward in an attempt to reduce the pain in her swollen belly.

"You can put your bag on the belt," the woman said, examining Pim's face. Taking a deep breath, Pim swung her suitcase onto the conveyor belt.

Nausea ran through her like an electric shock.

She grimaced.

"Is it your first time?"

The woman looked at her questioningly.

"Going to Copenhagen, I mean?"

Pim nodded.

"You don't need to worry. Flying isn't danger-ous."

Pim didn't answer. She didn't know what she was supposed to say. She kept her eyes on her shoes.

"Here you go."

Pim took her boarding pass and immediately left the counter.

She wanted to get out of there, away from the woman, away from her wondering gaze.

She didn't want to talk to anyone.

No one.

"Hey! Wait!" The woman behind the counter called to her.

Pim turned around.

"Your passport," she said. "You forgot your pass-port."

Pim went back and mumbled thanks. Clutch-ing her passport to her chest with both hands, she walked slowly toward security.

Alone again, Jana Berzelius sank slowly to her knees. The pain was excruciating.

She just wanted to close her eyes. Carefully, she touched the back of her head, feeling the wound. Her fingers were immediately covered in blood. She wiped them on her jacket and looked around. Her maroon hat lay fifteen feet to her left, next to her briefcase. She carefully crawled to it, feeling the hard ice against her legs, knowing she couldn't stay out here on the cold ground.

Then she noticed the bitter taste of metal. She spit and saw that it was red.

As red as the color of her hat.

She counted to three and struggled to her feet again. It felt like someone was stabbing her in the head, and the world was spinning. She supported herself with one hand on the wall of the pink archway.

She didn't yet have the strength to walk.

So she stood there, letting the blood run down her neck.

Pim was shaken awake by the plane flying through turbulence.

She clutched the armrests, breathing quickly. Nausea radiated through her body, causing her heart to pound even faster.

She craned her neck in an attempt to see Noi, who was sitting in a window seat seven rows behind her. The headrests were in the way.

The plane was quiet. Most of the passengers were sleeping, and the flight attendants had withdrawn behind the curtains. The lights were off, but here and there a reading light glowed above someone's seat. Some people were reading, others watching movies on the tiny screens mounted on the seat backs in front of them.

The plane shook again, this time more forcefully. Her palms were damp with sweat, and she kept her death grip on the armrests, closing her eyes and trying to focus on taking long, slow breaths.

Her stomach was aching.

She suddenly had the urge to go to the bathroom and glanced over the headrests toward the bathrooms at the rear of the plane. After a brief moment's consideration, she unlatched her seat belt and slowly stood. Walking carefully down the aisle, she gripped one headrest after another along the way to keep her balance.

Her stomach cramped up again, and she started panicking.

The plane's jerky movements made her sway and bump against the seats.

A quiet voice from the cabin crew encouraged all passengers to remain in their seats and fasten their seat belts.

Pim stopped, hesitating, but continued toward the bathrooms.

She had to go, there was no stopping it. No waiting, either.

Not even for a minute.

She stumbled forward and had just reached the back of the cabin when the plane suddenly dropped. She lost her balance and fell to the side, but she was able to keep herself mostly upright until she reached the door of the bathroom. Rushing in, she closed the door behind her and locked it.

The pain in her stomach was unbearable.

She opened the lid and looked into the toilet. The stink of industrial toilet cleaner and urine hit her in the face. On the floor lay damp, trampled, ripped hand towels. The white plastic faucet dripped, and she could hear the thunder of the engines clearly.

Pim gave a start when there was a knock at the door.

"Hello? I'm sorry, but you must return to your seat," yelled a voice in English.

Pim tried to answer, but her body crumpled in pain. She pulled down her pants and sat on the cold seat.

"Can you hear me? Hello?" the voice outside continued.

"Okay," Pim said.

Then she could say nothing more.

Panic had captured her in its iron fist. The pain in her stomach slowly sank farther down in her gut.

She held her breath, sitting absolutely still for thirty seconds. Then she got up and again looked into the toilet.

There it was. A capsule. Lying there in the toilet.

"I'm sorry, but you really have to return to your seat now! *All passengers!*"

There was pounding on the door and the handle jiggled up and down.

"Yes! Yes!"

Pim wiped herself, tossed the paper in the wastebasket, pulled up her pants and carefully reached her hand into the toilet to retrieve the capsule.

She retched when she saw the brown film on its surface.

Holding it under running water, she carefully

rubbed the rubber membrane with soap and water a few times.

She knew what she had to do now. She had no other option.

When the pounding on the door started again, she opened her mouth and placed the capsule on her tongue, tilting her head back, her panicked gaze fixed on a point on the ceiling.

She sweated profusely as the capsule slowly slid down into her stomach.

It was early morning when Jana Berzelius saw her reflection in her two-hundred-square-foot bathroom. She had managed to stumble home and pass out on her bed the night before. She decided to work from home today, having no desire to put in an appearance at the Public Prosecutor's Office, or risk questions or curious glances from colleagues or clients. She didn't want anyone to see her in the rare moments when she wasn't totally put together.

She rested her hands on the square sink mounted on a black granite countertop. There was no cabinet underneath, instead only a shelf with folded snow-white washcloths in two perfect stacks. The shower was enclosed with dark tinted glass and the showerhead came directly out from the ceiling. The floor was Italian marble, and the room also held two closets and a white bathtub. Everything was sparkling clean.

Jana stood there in a camisole and panties. Her skin was covered in goose bumps.

Her face was swollen and her neck ached.

She cleaned the wound on the back of her head, replacing the bloody bandage with a clean one.

She was thinking about Danilo. She had thought about him all morning. He had attacked her, abused her and again tried to kill her. The thought of it all made her tremble in rage. If that skinny Goth kid hadn't appeared, she might not be standing here— she might be dead.

Danilo had been vicious and brutal. He had had the advantage and had left her feeling completely powerless.

It was a strange and unpleasant feeling.

She shook her head and tucked her hair behind her ear, his words echoing in her head.

I'm warning you. Follow me one more time and I'll finish what I started here.

She tried to massage her aching muscles but gave up, letting her hand fall back to the sink.

One more time and you'll regret it forever. Understand?

The message was unmistakable. It was a death threat, and she was completely certain that he meant it.

But what was he so scared of that he would want to kill her?

He was the threat—a threat to her, her career, her life. So why did *he* want to kill *her*? He could destroy absolutely everything for her if he wanted— but as long as he stayed away from her, he was no threat. As long as she stayed away from him, she was no threat to him, either.

She shouldn't have followed him. *I have to keep him out of my life*, she thought, becoming aware that she stood at a crossroads. She had to make a decision.

She had nothing to gain from him. Next time, he would kill her. She knew that for a fact. She simply couldn't let there be a next time.

Never.

Never.

Never.

She'd made up her mind. He would never be a part of her life again. She was finally going to put her past behind her.

Her hands trembled against the cold, hard porcelain.

The walls were closing in on her, and she was having trouble breathing. She understood that letting him go was the most important decision of her life. It meant letting go of her horrific childhood, her past, and moving on with her life—but she had lived her entire life with the uncertainty of who she was and had just begun to find answers.

She looked into the mirror. Her eyes narrowed.

There is no time for hesitation, she thought, turning around and yelling as if Danilo were standing there. She hit the door, aiming again, kicking, screaming.

Panting, she sat down on the floor.

Her mind was racing. Memories of him washed

over her like a tidal wave. His face in hers, his ice-cold eyes, his hard voice.

I'm warning you.

"I have to," she whispered. "I don't want to, but I have to."

She got up carefully and repeated this again and again, as if to convince herself that she was making the right decision. Slowly she stepped back to the sink and forced herself to breathe calmly.

From now on, everything is different, she thought.

From now on, I'm done with Danilo.

GUNNAR ÖHRN AND COUNTY POLICE

Commissioner Carin Radler stood in front of the oval table in the police department conference room on the third floor. Gunnar glanced at the clock just as Detective Inspector Mia Bolander came into the room, almost ten minutes late for the meeting with the National Crime Squad.

"Sorry," she said, mumbling an inaudible explanation. She sat down at the table, avoiding Gunnar's tired look by fixing her gaze out the window.

He closed the door and sat down next to her.

Around the table sat Mia, Gunnar and Carin, as well as Anneli Lindgren, Henrik Levin and technician Ola Söderström. Mia noticed one more person in the room.

She guessed from his appearance that he was VIP brass.

"What about Jana?" she whispered to Gunnar.

"What about her?" he hissed back.

"She's not here?"

"No."

"Why not? Why should we have to be here if she doesn't have to?"

"Because we were told to be here."

"But she should be here. She was in charge of the preliminary investigation in the case, unfortunately."

"Unfortunately?" Gunnar looked at her. "Do you want me to call her?"

"No."

"Then be quiet."

Carin Radler cleared her throat.

"Now that we are all here, let me introduce the commissioner of the National Crime Squad, Anders Wester." Gesturing toward him, she continued, "He and I have had an internal conversation and I've called this meeting so that you will all be informed of what he has to say about the investigation that was carried out last spring."

"Isn't it better for us to spend our time working on new cases rather than closed ones?" said Gunnar.

Carin ignored him and sat down.

Mia smiled wryly. This was going to be interesting, she thought, her eyes drifting to Anders Wester. She examined his bald head, black-rimmed glasses and blue eyes. His lips were narrow and his face seemed relatively pale. His posture was less than impressive, with stooped shoulders and feet that pointed inward.

"Thank you," Anders began. "As Carin said, we

have already begun a discussion about the investigation you carried out last spring, and that is what I'm here to talk to you about today."

"Get on with it then," said Gunnar.

"It happens at times—" Anders straightened his shoulders a little "—that some districts attempt to lead federal murder investigations on their own, without the help of the National Crime Squad. Sometimes the outcome is good. Sometimes not so good. We have brought to Carin's attention the mistakes that were made in last spring's investigation."

The room was quiet. Everyone exchanged glances, but no one spoke.

Then Gunnar scratched his chin and leaned forward over the table.

"Come on, you can say it! You think we did a bad job," he said.

"Gunnar…" Carin said, holding up a hand to calm him.

"A mistake was made, yes," Anders replied.

"A mistake?" Gunnar said. "What do you mean, a mistake?"

"It's called a lack of cooperation. As you know, Gunnar, our purpose is to fight serious organized crime, and in order to carry out our purpose as professionally as possible, we have to cooperate on a national level. It sounds obvious, for most…"

"Listen. We did everything… There wasn't any more we could do."

"Except contacting us earlier. Playing special ops is not recommended. Not at the county level."

"What should we have done, do you think?"

"You should have brought us in much earlier, as I said."

"We let you take over."

"Yes, but even that didn't go according to plan." Gunnar chuckled.

"And whose fault was that?"

"Gunnar…" Carin gave him a look of warning. Mia stretched her legs out in front of her.

"Correct me if I'm wrong," Gunnar continued, "but we exposed a gang that had for many years been trafficking drugs via illegal refugee children. We captured their leader, Gavril Bolanaki, and everything was handy-dandy until *you* took over and started negotiating with Bolanaki."

"You know very well that he had important information."

"Oh, yes. I know that you were going to protect him in exchange for his information. Names of middlemen, pushers, places. But he never got around to revealing anything, did he?"

"No. Exactly. What are you getting at?"

"That your 'protection' didn't work very well. Admit it. You never got any information."

"His case is closed. He killed himself. There wasn't much more we could do there."

"Who told you he had information anyway? Bolanaki himself?"

"I am convinced that Gavril Bolanaki would

have been a resource for us," Anders said. "But as I said, that case is closed."

"Exactly. That must be a tidy way of solving an investigation. Say to hell with finding answers and just end it. It's obvious you are very competent in this kind of operation."

"Gunnar!"

Carin slammed her hand down on the table.

"Anders is claiming that we didn't do our job," said Gunnar. "But I disagree. We're the ones who got Gavril Bolanaki, and I think it's time to say it was *you*, Anders, who didn't do *your* job because *you* were supposed to protect him."

Anders smiled.

"That's funny. You don't understand what I'm saying, Gunnar. There is no 'you' and 'us.' The police are one single organization, and I hope you'll have learned this when the new authority takes over."

"Oh, yes, thank you. We know that the National Crime Squad is changing its name to the Department of National Operations. But we don't know anything more than that. We have no idea how the organization will look in detail."

"No, because it hasn't been fully decided yet," Anders interrupted.

Gunnar exchanged an angry glance with Carin, which Anders noticed.

"Maybe it'd be better if Carin explained it to you. Carin is very well-informed about the reorganization."

"But I am not?"

"You will be now, because unlike you, I choose to share the information I have rather than hiding it."

"How nice."

Anders stood behind Carin and rested his hand on her shoulder.

"Carin has been offered the position of regional police chief for Eastern Sweden, and has accepted. Over the course of the year, she will work together with the six other regional chiefs to finalize the details of the new organizational structure and create an action plan for 2015. At the same time, she will be finishing out her assignment here as county police commissioner until she steps into her new position at the start of the New Year."

Carin stood up, adjusting her jacket, and said, "We have a tight timeline and it will be quite a challenge. Replacing the twenty-one police districts with a single authority can't be done overnight. As I'm sure you know, we initiated the change in 2010, and now we're down to the final steps. I understand that you have questions, and I will try to answer them as best I can. Your participation in this process is important to me."

Carin nodded at the team sitting around the table. Henrik and Anneli smiled, Ola gave her a thumbs-up and Gunnar clapped cautiously.

"Well, congratulations," Mia said, her arms crossed.

Carin nodded in reply and sat down.

"Carin is right. Your participation and your opinions are important."

Gunnar sighed loudly. Too loudly.

Anders rubbed his hand across his balding head.

"You know what, Gunnar? I truly believe there are many advantages with the new Swedish Police Authority. But the greatest advantage is probably that the boundaries will be erased, that it will become easier to work together. Don't you think so?"

The farm fields were covered in snow, the white blanket taking on a blue cast in the growing darkness. Narrow paths led into the dense forest. Lights from houses and farms glimmered through the trees.

Pim sat with her head resting against the vibrating window on the X2000 express train between Copenhagen and Stockholm. The train had left Copenhagen at exactly 6:36 p.m. and would reach Norrköping in less than four hours.

She touched the passport stuffed into her waistband and felt a gnawing anxiety in her belly. She turned around toward Noi, who sat in the row behind her, arms hanging limp, mouth open. Her gaze was locked on a point far beyond the window.

"Are you sleeping?" Pim asked.

"No," Noi said, slowly.

"Are you sure someone is going to meet us?"

Noi didn't answer. She closed her eyes.

"Noi? Noi!"

Noi slowly opened her eyes again and continued

to stare out of the window. "I'm freezing," she said, closing her eyes again. Her head fell gradually forward until her chin met her chest.

"Who's coming to meet us? Noi? Noi!"

Noi slowly lifted her head back up to meet Pim's eyes.

Her pupils were awfully small, Pim noticed.

"What's going on? Are you feeling okay?" Pim asked.

"Nothing…sleep…" Noi slurred.

"Who's going to meet us? Can't you answer me?"

But Noi didn't answer.

Pim pulled her knees up to her chest and sat huddled on the seat, watching the landscape rush past outside. Apart from her anxiety over the drugs still inside her, she felt a different kind of uneasiness now. She remembered clearly the last time she had felt this way.

It had been just one month ago. She'd been sitting on the floor and looking at her dead mother's face. Her little sister, Mai, hadn't yet understood what was happening. She'd thought her mother was sleeping, because that was what Pim had told her.

But she hadn't been sleeping. She'd had the fever. Dengue fever.

Her mother had had bloodshot eyes and large bruises on her body. She'd screamed from the pain in her muscles and joints.

That one time, Pim had wished her father were

there. She'd wished him there so that she could be allowed to be a child again.

Just a child.

She had wished that a grown-up would come in and make everything right. But it had been pointless to even think about it, a fruitless hope. Her father had abandoned them long ago. He had a new family; he couldn't come to her aid then.

And when her mother had refused to go to the hospital, Pim's last hope had vanished.

"It's best for me to be here," her mother had said.

"But they can help you."

"Help costs money, Pim."

"But…"

"Promise me instead…that you'll take care of Mai." Her mother had coughed out the sentences while frantically clawing at her arm until the fluid-filled blister had popped.

"No… I can't do it myself!" Pim had said, starting to cry. "She's only eight years old."

"You're fifteen. You can do it."

Now Pim looked down at her hands, thinking of Mai and wondering what her little sister was doing that very moment. Was she sleeping? Did she feel alone or scared? But Pim was only going to be gone for five days, and soon, soon she would be home with Mai again.

Her lower lip started to quiver and she suddenly felt another, stronger pain—this one from the pills in her stomach.

I have to make sure I get home again, she thought.

* * *

Gunnar Öhrn sat at the desk in his office with his legs spread apart. He stretched his arms up and grunted when he felt the twinge in his shoulders. The pain went all the way up to what used to be his hairline. He felt too heavy and old, but he pushed those thoughts away. He didn't have time to worry about things like that.

Investigation reports were piled on the bookshelf behind him. He was going to start somewhere in the middle, being effective and focused, reading carefully to shake off this feeling of tiredness.

He picked up folder after folder, flipping through a couple of documents in each one, but hadn't gotten any further than this when there was a knock at the door. Anders Wester appeared with two coffee mugs in his hands.

"Did I wake you?" he said.

"What do you mean, wake me?" Gunnar asked.

"It looked like you were sleeping."

"I was just thinking. Since when is that forbidden?"

"This damn weather."

"I don't feel like talking."

Anders put the mugs on the table, sitting down in the chair across from Gunnar and resting his fingertips against each other.

"How is she?" Anders asked.

"Who?" Gunnar said.

"Anneli."

"That's none of your business."

"She looks tired."

"I'm not into small talk."

"I just want to know how she is."

"You shouldn't give a damn about her, do you hear me?"

"Calm down," Anders sneered. "I was just asking how she is."

"And I'm working."

Gunnar shifted his weight in his chair, feeling the sweat on his back seeping through the material of his shirt. He looked at Anders, who sat composed and still, hands now by his mouth, fingertips still pressed against each other. He had an expression of superiority on his face, a crooked smile visible at the corner of his mouth.

"Coffee?"

"Oh, are we going to take coffee breaks together now, too?"

"Here you go," Anders said, pushing the mug toward Gunnar, who looked at it with disgust.

"I don't understand how you can dare to come in here," Gunnar said.

"I value your opinions," Anders replied.

"You have nothing to do here."

"I hear what you're saying."

"To think that you have the balls to question our investigation."

"I'm doing my job."

"We're doing ours, too."

"Clearly not, because I'm here."

"There must be another reason you're here. I really want to tell you to go to hell."

"I know."

"But then I risk retaliation?"

"You might anyway."

"What do you mean?"

"What I just said."

"Are you threatening me?"

Anders continued smiling, rested his elbows on his knees and leaned forward.

"No, Gunnar. Why would I threaten you? I just want to make sure that you're all doing a good job here in Norrköping."

"I have worked in law enforcement my whole life. I know how to do a good job."

"Then I'll have to see that you do a better job, then."

"You can sit here, leaning in to seem more dangerous," Gunnar said, leaning back in his chair, "and you can say whatever you want. I'm still not going to listen."

"I hope you know what you're doing," Anders said.

"I know exactly what I'm doing."

"I don't think you do. It seems like you don't understand the importance of cooperation. That *we* are going to cooperate. Regional and National Crime Squads. Norrköping and Stockholm. You and me, Gunnar."

Gunnar didn't want to hear any more. Sweat ran

down his temples, but he didn't dare wipe it away for fear of showing Anders how upset he really was.

"Obviously, *we* will cooperate," he said, his voice dripping with sarcasm. "You and me. Anything else I can do for you?"

Anders stood up.

"No," he said, putting his hand out and giving Gunnar a firm handshake. Unnecessarily firm, for unnecessarily long.

And Gunnar responded.

Just as unnecessarily hard and for just as unnecessarily long.

HIS COAT SPARKLED WITH SNOWFLAKES.

Karl Berzelius stamped the snow from his shoes before he got into the taxi outside the Louis De Geer Concert Hall.

He raked his hand through his thick gray hair and straightened his coat underneath him.

Margaretha was already sitting in the backseat with her purse on her lap. She wiped her delicate eyeglasses with a tissue before replacing them on her nose and carefully folding the tissue and putting it back into her purse, closing it with a click.

"Fantastic," she murmured as the taxi swung out onto the cobblestones.

"What did you say?" Karl asked, looking out the window.

"The concert was fantastic. The best I've heard in a long time. Makes me happy."

"Yes, it is one of the most played pieces in the entire piano repertoire."

"I understand why."

"Rachmaninoff, hard to beat."

"Yes."

He looked at the snowdrifts. As the car turned to the right, he turned his gaze up to the garlands that hung over the street, watching the thousands of lights swaying back and forth.

"It's the second Sunday of Advent this week," Margaretha murmured. "And Christmas soon…"

She said it quietly, but he heard her.

"Yes? And what about it?"

She didn't answer at first, as if she were biding her time. Then came the question he had expected. "Maybe it's time to invite her over?"

He looked at his wife, saw how she was hugging her purse and knew that she was waiting for his reaction.

"For Christmas, yes," he replied.

"Or earlier, maybe even this Saturday so that we could…"

He held his hand up, signaling that he'd heard enough.

"Please, Karl."

"No."

"But I don't want to wait until Christmas, and I think it's a good idea if we…"

"She hasn't called."

"But I've called her."

He glared at her, making Margaretha hug her purse even more tightly.

"Have you spoken with her?" he asked.

"Yes, and you should, too. It's been a long time since you did," she said, adding his name. "Karl."

He cleared his throat.

"I don't want to hear any more," he said.

"So we should just leave her alone?"

"Yes."

"But I don't want to."

"That's enough! If you want to see her, do it. Invite her over. Do what you want! But leave me out of it!"

There it was again. The anger, irritation. He surprised himself with it. He heard her sigh but didn't care.

He turned his gaze back to the window.

Back to the swaying lights.

Jana Berzelius opened her inbox and glanced through new emails that she had received during the late afternoon. The first was from Torsten Granath, an invitation to the regional prosecutorial chamber's traditional Christmas dinner at the Göta Hotel in Borensberg. The next two were regarding a hearing about an assault at a pub, to be held at Norrköping's district court within a week. The last one contained a two-page document that had to do with an amendment decision in the Swedish Prosecution Authority statute book.

Twenty minutes later, she turned off her computer and walked slowly into her bedroom, taking off her clothes, folding them and putting them on a chair. She turned on the light in her walk-in closet and stood before the mirror that stretched from the floor to the ceiling. She pushed her long, dark hair to the side, letting it fall over her right breast.

She stood and examined herself for a moment, studying her arms, hips and thighs. She let her hand caress her shoulder, down to the curve of her back, her buttocks. Her whole body shuddered as she surveyed her bruises. They had darkened, and would gradually disappear—along with her thoughts of Danilo.

She pulled a drawer out, forcefully grabbed a silk bra and matching panties, flung them onto the bed and went into the bathroom. She showered quickly, put on the underwear and swept a thin bathrobe around herself.

In the kitchen, she poured a glass of wine, stood by the window and looked at the dense clouds. After taking a big sip, she held the cool glass to her temple. Leaving the window, she went into her office and unlocked the door to the secured inner room.

Standing on the threshold, she turned on the light and looked into the small secret space. Her gaze traveled across the bulletin boards, whiteboard, pictures, photographs, books and notes. Every detail of her childhood that she could find, she had recorded here. She carefully stroked her neck with her fingertips. She felt the uneven skin, the three letters that would never disappear, that were immortalized in her pale skin. *K. E. R.* Ker— the goddess of death.

Her eyes focused on the drawing in the middle of the bulletin board, attached with staples in every corner. It was a sketch she had drawn of Danilo after their encounter last spring. After all these years, she had searched for him then in his home in Södertälje.

Tell me instead what you as a prosecutor are doing in my place, he had said to her. He hadn't any idea who she was when she had suddenly appeared in his home.

I need your help.

He had laughed.

Oh, really? You don't say. How interesting. And what can I help you with?

You can help me to find out something.

Something? And what is this something *about?*

My background.

Your background? How could I help you with that when I don't even know who you are?

But I know who you are.

Really? Who am I, then?

You are Danilo.

Brilliant. Did you work that out all by yourself, or did you perhaps read my name on the door?

You are someone else, too?

You mean I'm schizoid?

Show me your neck?

He had fallen completely silent.

You've got another name written there, she had said. *I know what it says. If I guess right then you must tell me how you got it. If I guess wrong then you can let me go.*

We'll change the agreement a little. If you guess right then I'll tell you. Sure, that's no problem. If you guess wrong, or if I don't have a name on my neck, then I'll shoot you.

She had guessed correctly.

She took another sip of wine, went into the room, sat on the chair and put the glass on the desk in front of her.

She felt some sort of melancholy about what she had to do.

No one knew that she had a room dedicated to all of the unsorted memories of her childhood, and no one would ever know, either. She hadn't said a word about it to anyone. Not her father or mother. The room had been her own business and no one else's.

Last spring, she had gotten more answers about her background than she had wanted. She had found out about the man who had made her into what she was, into what she had been: a child soldier.

She still remembered his words: *From a crushed child you can carve out a deadly weapon. A soldier without feelings, without anything to lose, is the most dangerous there is.*

She was made to call him Papa.

But his real name was Gavril Bolanaki.

Now Gavril was dead, and from Danilo—or Hades, as was carved into his neck as a trafficked child—there was nothing left to gain.

She got up suddenly and started to pull the pictures of the shipping containers from the walls and folded them up. She ripped down the pictures of the house on the island outside Arkösund, where she had lived with Danilo and the other children. She put the photographs of mythological gods and goddesses into an envelope and piled the books about Greek mythology in stacks. She erased the notes from the whiteboard. She took empty boxes, lined them up along the wall in the bedroom, and put all of the pictures, books, photographs and notes in them. Finally, she took down the sketch of Danilo and put it on the boxes.

In the kitchen, she poured a new glass of wine and drank it standing up. Then she went back into the bedroom, opened her nightstand drawer and looked at the journals hidden there.

For a moment, she considered just leaving them there, but she regretted the hesitation and put them into the boxes, too.

After two hours, both the hidden room and one more glass of wine were empty.

With her finger on the switch, she looked around the room and realized that, without all of the materials of her investigation, the room looked remarkably naked.

She had cleaned up everything that revealed her background. It was meaningless to keep it. She should let it remain a secret, live her life as buttoned-up as the oxford shirts she wore in court.

She closed her eyes.

And turned off the light.

She stood still, listening to the sound of her heart pounding.

Her life would take another direction from now on, no longer driven by shadows from the past.

She felt a shiver go down her spine and wondered if it was relief she felt.

SEVEN

TRAIN ATTENDANT MATS JOHANSSON
kept his eyes looking out the window. The late
night's intense calm had settled in on the X2000
between Copenhagen and Stockholm. It was the
sort of quiet that made him relax.

He always longed for peace and quiet, which is
why he and his wife spent every summer in a little
red cottage in the middle of a forest in Småland.
The cottage had a white veranda, and they sat there
every warm summer evening and looked out at the
majestic trees and the emerald green lawn. They
puttered around in the garden each day, planted
carrots and tomatoes. But this time of year there
was nothing to do there, Mats thought. Not in cold,
harsh Sweden.

He saw the clock turn 10:12 p.m., knew that there
were ten minutes left before they would arrive in
Norrköping and went with calm, steady steps down
the aisle, keeping his balance as the train swayed.

When he opened the door to the fifth car, he saw

a young woman standing outside the bathroom. Her hair was dark, shoulder-length and glossy.

She was pounding on the locked door and yelling, turning toward the people sitting closest to her, but no one would meet her panicked eyes.

The train slowed down with wavelike motions, and the brakes squeaked lightly on the rails.

The young, desperate woman yelled again.

Mats went to her quickly, and when she saw him coming closer, she rushed forward and grabbed his arm. Speaking in a language he didn't understand, she dragged him to the locked bathroom door and gesticulated wildly.

He understood that something serious was going on.

The clock read 10:22 p.m. when he finally was able to force the door open.

He saw the toilet. To the left of it was a wall-mounted changing table. He stepped cautiously forward and saw a young woman propped up in a sitting position on the floor. Her fingers were bloody. Her face was pale and her lips were blue. Some sort of white foam dripped from her lower lip onto her chest.

Mats covered his mouth with his hands and stared in horror at the dead woman's body.

Mia Bolander reached for the cell phone that was lying on the table. She scrolled through the status updates on Facebook but was irritated, as usual, by all the people who had posted pictures of freshly baked cakes, Christmas decorations and things as idiotic as pictures of future vacation destinations.

How the hell do they have the energy? she thought, releasing her phone onto her lap.

She drew her hand through her blond hair and yawned, sinking into the sofa. She cast a glance at the fifty-inch television that she had bought on a payment plan last spring and sure, it was a great deal, but now she was behind on her payments. Two months, maybe, but as soon as she got her next paycheck, she'd rectify that, for sure. It kind of sucked, though, paying so much for a TV that was now almost a year old. She'd rather put the money toward a new one, and had seen an awesome one with a curved screen. If she had only been a little less impulsive last spring, she'd have bought one like that instead.

Mia wound a blond lock around her finger. She was tired and not satisfied with how the day had gone. Nor her life, for that matter.

She was turning thirty-one in two months and had discovered new wrinkles on her forehead and around her eyes. The skin above her breasts also seemed less tight and made a fanlike pattern when she wore a tight sports bra.

She tried to convince herself that she still looked good, but it didn't work. In spite of her regular workouts, with strength training three times a week, she didn't feel attractive. She never slept enough, ate at odd times and drank too much.

All wrong.

She spent money on unnecessary things and was always broke. She had a tiny apartment and only occasional relationships with men who seemed all but normal. The last one had seemed loving and tender, but as soon as they went back to his place, he had shown a sick interest in her feet. A foot fetishist.

He'd had a corny name, too.

Martin.

He had satisfied her, but she never wanted to sleep with him again. Not with someone who wanted to suck her toes.

That was crossing the line.

She had spent just over half her life finding out what a mature sex life had to offer. She had lost her virginity when she was fourteen and spent the rest of her teen years experimenting with horny classmates and older high schoolers. She had a heavy make-out session with a teacher at an end-of-the-year party when she was in ninth grade, had a threesome with two guys in a bathroom and had on one occasion given blow jobs to three heavy metal dudes at a house party. In her twenties, she had tried bondage with a tattooed man from Falun. She had dressed up as a flight attendant, a nurse and an innocent girl wearing a corset. Whipped and been whipped. Had sex at secret clubs and in public places. Her sex life required a constant stream of new men.

She was, therefore, not interested in a long-term relationship, and had never understood how someone could be with the same person year after year. She had sat in the police department cafeteria and listened to her female colleagues gush about how their male partners were wonderful, insightful, exciting, generous, warm and romantic one day, then bitch the next day about their bad habits and how they left beard hairs on the sink and shit-stained boxers on the bedroom floor for days. She had heard them say that they had met the man they wanted to grow old with, have children with, that he was The One. Mia had never felt that way. She didn't want just one.

She wanted many.

Preferably.

She looked out the window at the darkness outside. She rubbed her hands across her face and thought about brushing her teeth, but she felt too lazy and instead put her feet up on the table.

Her thoughts wandered to the two-hour morning meeting with the National Crime Squad. She'd had a hard time deciding in the last half hour if she should do something, say something. Anders Wester was an unpleasant man. He had criticized their work and been really hard on Gunnar. She had never seen Gunnar so irritated and tense.

But he had been the only one who had defended them, and the only one from the investigation who had said anything during the meeting. Maybe she should have said something, stood up for herself and her colleagues. But no one else had, either. It wasn't only her responsibility.

Carin could have been more assertive in the conversation. But she surely didn't dare, Mia thought.
Not having just received a new position—in the
new Police Authority, where everything would be
changed for the better and everyone would take part
and live happily-ever-after. What bullshit!

She lay down on the sofa, crossed her arms over
her head and stayed there for a long time before
picking up her cell phone.

She knew she shouldn't. She knew she'd regret it.

Still, she looked for Martin Strömberg's number.

But just as she raised the phone to her ear, someone called.

She saw from the display that it was Henrik
Levin.

"Yes?" she answered.

"You have to get down to the train station. Right
now!"

The X2000 to Stockholm with departure time
10:24 p.m. stood still on Track 1 at Norrköping's
Central Station. It had taken an hour to evacuate all
of the travelers and get them on a bus to Nyköping
where a regional train had been waiting to take
them to their planned destination.

All of the platforms had been roped off, parking
lot and building, too.

Henrik Levin stood at the police tape and
watched as Mia Bolander parked her wine-red Fiat
Punto at the intersection of Norra Promenaden and
Vattengränden. He waved when she got out of the

car. She pulled her white hat down over her ears and zipped her jacket all the way to her chin to keep out the cold.

"So what happened?" she asked, ducking under the tape.

"A young woman was found dead in a bathroom. Her name is Siriporn Chaiyen, Thai national. We found her purse with her passport and other possessions in it."

"How old?"

"Eighteen."

Henrik saw her raise her eyebrows.

"Come on," he said, showing her the way to the train and the bathroom in Car 5 where Anneli Lindgren crouched down with tweezers in her hand. The small room was illuminated with bright lights.

Henrik and Mia stood in the doorway and studied the dead woman. She was young, with a characteristically Southeast Asian appearance.

"A suicide?" Mia asked.

Anneli looked up.

"No…" she said, getting up from the floor. "At first glance, it looks like an epileptic seizure, like she asphyxiated. But exactly how she died, I'm not sure yet."

"So what are we doing here?"

"We can eliminate suicide," said Henrik. "And it's probably not an epileptic fit."

"Who found her?"

"A train attendant, Mats Johansson," Henrik said. "He is unfortunately in shock, but we were able to speak with him for a moment before he was taken to Vrinnevi Hospital. He said that he had been rushed by a crazy woman who had forced him to open the bathroom door. I know what you're going to ask next—who was that woman?"

"Yes. But what, don't I get to?"

"Well, you should, but I don't know the answer."

Mia gave him a questioning look.

"Why not?"

"She disappeared from the train."

"And where is she now?"

"No one knows."

IT SMELLED STRONGLY OF BLEACH IN the corridor of the National Laboratory of Forensic Science in Linköping.

Pathologist Björn Ahlmann looked up as Henrik Levin and Mia Bolander walked into the room. Björn stood at his stainless steel autopsy table with a serious look on his face. His eyes flashed a silvery blue.

The fluorescent lights cast their harsh light on the tiled walls, the double troughs and channels for drainage.

Henrik stood a bit from the table and observed the woman lying there. He thought how small and thin she looked. Above her breasts, her sternum was clearly outlined and her ribs stuck out under her smooth skin.

Her complexion was pale and her long black hair lay over her forehead and shoulders. It looked like she was gazing out into the room with a mixed expression of amazement and sorrow.

But there was no gleam in her small, narrow eyes.

"I saw the announcement in the paper. It was tiny, as if death doesn't interest anyone anymore," Björn said with a sigh.

"Everyone is probably too preoccupied with their own worries," Henrik said.

"How did she die?" Mia asked. "Do we know now?"

"You didn't have to come here to find out."

Björn passed the autopsy report to Henrik, who glanced expertly through the main points.

"As you see," he said, "the cause of death is asphyxia, a complete blockage of oxygen to the brain."

"So she suffocated?" Henrik asked.

"Yes. The result of an overdose," Björn said. "Heroin. She had fifty capsules in her stomach."

"Fifty?" Mia asked, whistling.

"Yes, you heard right. Fifty," Björn said.

"And the capsules?" Henrik asked.

"They've been analyzed," said Björn, pushing his glasses up his nose. He nodded toward the report. "Everything's in there."

Henrik contemplated the lifeless body. The nails on her fingers and toes were painted pink. He took a deep breath and felt depressed, as he always did when victims were young.

"Anything else you can give us?"

"No, there's nothing that sticks out. Besides that she was a teenager, fifteen years old."

"Fifteen? On her passport it said she was eighteen."

"I can only say what I know," said Björn, giving him a serious look. His glasses flashed as he turned toward the body again.

"Christ," said Mia. "Someone's using young women to smuggle. That's just shitty, plain and simple."

"She wasn't a young woman," said Henrik. "She was just a child."

It was hard to stretch out her legs enough as she ran up the steps, yet she increased her speed. Running the last bit quickly and easily, she slowed down toward the top, stopping and panting for a moment on the landing.

In her apartment, she did one hundred sit-ups. The back of her neck itched from sweat. Jana Berzelius pushed her hair to the side and stroked her fingers across the inscribed letters.

After a quick shower, she put on a discreet amount of makeup, though she had to do extra touching up in those places where her skin was still discolored. She looked at herself, turning first to the right and then to the left, checking to see if the bruises showed through the layers of makeup. She reluctantly dabbed on a little extra blush and decided that would have to do.

With her briefcase in one hand and her overcoat in the other, she went down to the basement. Her high heels drummed rhythmically as she walked quickly over the concrete in the garage. She unlocked her black BMW X6 from thirty feet away and placed her briefcase on the black leather passenger seat.

A shiver went down her back. She felt ready to work, again checking her face in the mirror, repeating to herself that no one would suspect anything through the makeup.

But she was still nervous. She hesitated a moment before pushing the start button and driving out of the garage.

Anneli Lindgren sat on the edge of the bed, her hair loose and not yet brushed. She opened her nightstand drawer and took out a pair of heart-shaped diamond earrings, weighing them in her hand. She carefully fastened them to her ears and stood, remaining there for a moment in her nightgown, gazing out the window. The wind rustled the frosty leaves on the trees. A rabbit bounded away, and she followed it with her eyes until it disappeared into a yard.

She lifted her hand to her ear, twisting one of the earrings and thinking about when she had received them. It was a long time ago now, during a period when everything had been different, free. She still remembered that time in his apartment, how she had looked at him with red, warm cheeks. He had opened a dresser drawer, taken out a plastic fastener and a soft whip, forcing her arms up over her head. She'd lain on the bed protesting, keeping her legs together, twisting away when he pulled her panties down. He'd hovered over her, kneeling, watching her attempts to get free. He had smiled when he began to caress her from her knees up to her upper thighs, smiled even wider when she had stopped protesting, spread her legs and let him enter her.

He had carried the package in his sport coat, then placed it on her naked stomach and said something that sounded like love. But she hadn't been looking for love—she had only wanted to quench her desire. For once, at least, she had been able to give herself up to the desire she felt for him.

For Anders.

"The meeting starts in ten minutes."

The door to the bedroom squeaked when Gunnar came in with a towel around his hips.

"Yep…" she said absentmindedly.

Gunnar laid his hand on her shoulder, and she felt the warmth from his damp skin. He gently caressed her neck, under her hair, over her right shoulder. She felt the shoulder strap of her nightgown slip off. When he then tried to caress her breast, she carefully pushed his hand away.

"What's wrong? What were you thinking about?" he asked.

"About you. And us," she said, leaving the window. "We have to get going. We can't be late to this meeting."

She opened the closet and grabbed the first shirt

she touched. She just wanted to get out of the bedroom without him seeing the blush on her cheeks.

The blush of shame.

Jana Berzelius entered the conference room on the third floor of the police station in Norrköping. She sat at the oval table and glanced furtively at the team that was already seated there. Anneli Lindgren was taking down important details about the dead woman from the train; Mia Bolander was drawing ten pointy flowers in the margin of her notes. Ola Söderström was adjusting the screen of his laptop. Gunnar Öhrn was sitting with his hands folded on the table.

"Ah, so you also had to show up?" Mia said without raising her eyes.

"Yes," Jana said, her head held high and her back straight. Her jacket was black, her skirt was knee-length and her hair was stick straight.

"But don't you prosecutors usually wait until we've done the heavy lifting? Or at least until we have a suspect?"

"Not all do," Jana said.

Henrik gave Mia a tired look, as if he wanted to tell her to skip the bullshit. She knew very well that preliminary investigations were led by the prosecutor if the victim was under eighteen years old.

"And not all come rushing into the initial briefing," Mia continued.

"No," Jana said. "But that's how it is to be *devoted* to your work."

"Thanks, I know what that means," Mia said, glaring at her.

"Well, then," Henrik said, tossing the autopsy report on the table, thus beginning his report on the preliminary examination that Björn Ahlmann had performed on the dead woman from the train.

"So you're saying she had swallowed fifty capsules of heroin and cocaine," Gunnar summarized when Henrik was done. Standing, he continued, "One capsule had begun to leak, and she died of an overdose. We're dealing with an obvious case of narcotics smuggling, right, Ola?"

"Yes," Ola said, opening the screen of his laptop. "The woman was a 'bodypacker,' a person who transports illegal narcotics within her own body. A courier, drug mule, pack mule…"

"Pack mule?" Mia repeated. "'Bodypacker' sounds more accurate."

"I agree," said Ola. "And that's one typical name. But despite the fact that drug mules are a well-known problem, it's hard to catch them. Every year, between sixty and seventy million people cross the Swedish border."

"It's like trying to find a needle in a haystack," Henrik said.

"Right. Many more mules get through than are caught. Customs largely works based on intelligence. Sure, they are always trying to find patterns in the *modus operandi*, but these drug mules crop up everywhere, frequently change their identity and come from all different countries."

"In this case, from Thailand," Henrik said.

"But she could just as well have come from Japan. Or China. Or Malaysia or something," Mia said, rubbing her nose.

Gunnar cleared his throat.

"Her passport was issued in Thailand, so we can assume that she is a Thai national. So, Ola, continue."

"Lots of mules come via budget flights from Spain. Often what happens is that vulnerable people are recruited in the Málaga area. But a lot also come from West Africa, Asia, Eastern Europe, Middle Eastern countries and South America. A lot of narcotics pass through Holland. Schiphol Airport has such a huge problem that the border police sometimes don't even arrest the drug mules. Instead, they just send them back on the next flight out. It is, as you might guess, a lengthy process to secure evidence against bodypackers."

Ola crossed his arms and rested his elbows on the table, continuing.

"If they are arrested, the police have to decide if the mules should be X-rayed at the hospital, then further decisions have to be made about whether the suspects should be kept under constant observation until they have answered nature's call. The swallowers have to use a nonflushing toilet, and then the jail guards have to dig around in the toilet to find the capsules and confiscate them."

"Sounds lovely," Mia said.

"We used to use an emetic to make them vomit.

The mules would take a huge dose and then after just a couple seconds, the proof would come up. It was effective, but the Swedish Prosecutor-General decided sometime in the nineties that it shouldn't be allowed anymore, that it violated human rights," Ola said.

Jana straightened up, saying, "From what I know, it takes about five days for the capsules to pass through the body."

"That's right," said Ola, "but it varies a lot. It can take as short as two days or as long as two weeks. Most use a laxative or enema, but not everyone has access to these, and it has happened that smugglers have died from injuries related to constipation. The most common cause of death, though, is leakage, as with our victim."

Ola closed his computer.

"But drug mules, or rather those who employ the mules, are constantly learning better ways to smuggle. It's not common to use cutoff rubber gloves or condoms anymore. Now, the capsules are machine-made, wrapped in multiple layers and coated with beeswax. Generally the mules are carrying between fifty and seventy capsules in their stomachs, and every capsule contains about ten grams of narcotics. The capsules are then divided into 'balls' of two-to three-tenths of a gram. One ball of heroin could cost one hundred fifty kronor on the street— a third of what it cost a few years ago."

"But experienced drug mules can smuggle more than seventy capsules, can't they?" Gunnar asked.

"Yes. Some mules swallow over a hundred capsules. Last year an Eastern European man was arrested at Copenhagen's Kastrup Airport. He had 1.2 kilograms of heroin and cocaine in his stomach. The street value was hundreds of thousands of kronor," said Ola.

"Denmark is also a common stop. They fly into Kastrup and then take the train over the Öresund Bridge into Sweden. I would dare to guess that this is what happened here," said Gunnar.

"I think so, too," said Ola. "The dead woman wasn't traveling alone. It's common that the leader of the operation will send a number of mules, because they figure that a few of them will get stopped by customs. If he sends twenty, for example, maybe eighteen will get through and he's made his money."

"Fifty percent, then," Mia said.

"No, not exactly. Eighteen of twenty isn't half. It's ninety percent," Jana corrected, fixing her gaze on Mia without moving a muscle in her face.

Mia clenched her jaw.

"I was talking about our girls! Two girls were sent, and one of them died, so only one got through. Half. Fifty percent. *Exactly.*"

"There could have been more mules on the train," Henrik said, clasping his hands around one knee.

Mia sighed.

"But we're focusing all of our energy on the female friend who disappeared. And we assume that she is also a mule," Gunnar said. "Otherwise she probably would not have run."

Jana nodded at Henrik.

"Were there witnesses?" she asked.

"Yes," said Henrik. "We have a number of passengers who have provided information."

"And the train attendant? Where is he?"

Henrik opened his mouth to answer, but Mia spoke up quickly.

"He's in shock."

"I didn't ask about his condition. I asked where he was," Jana said without looking at Mia.

"He's at Vrinnevi Hospital," she said curtly.

"Have you talked to him?"

"Only briefly. I'll question him after we're done here," Henrik said.

"If you're lucky," Mia said. "He's being treated. He might have to go to therapy, delaying the investigation even further."

Gunnar pretended not to hear her, walking instead to the whiteboard.

"According to the train attendant, the second woman ran straight out from the train, and this is confirmed by the security camera footage that Ola checked."

"Exactly," Ola said. "I studied the film from Central Station this morning. At exactly 10:23 p.m., a young woman runs off the train. Like the victim, she has Asian features, and I assume that she is the woman we're looking for. On the film you see clearly that she runs from Platform 1 straight toward the parking lot and then disappears into the darkness."

"So we have a picture of her?" Jana asked.

"Yes, not as clear a picture as I'd like, but I think it will help."

Ola leaned forward across the table.

"You can see that she's completely panicked," he said. "I mean, she's sprinting as fast as she can from the train. But what's strange is that she stops, looks at something in the dark, hesitates and then speeds up."

"As if she's trying to find someone?" Henrik asked.

"Yes, as if she's looking for someone," Ola said. "And at the same time you see red brake lights, like a car is slowing down in front of her."

"You think she jumped into a car," Henrik said.

"Yes, someone was probably waiting at the station, waiting for her and her friend. And we need to find out who that someone is."

"So the narcotics may have been destined for here, for Norrköping?" Jana asked.

"Well, that's a reasonable possibility," Henrik said. "We've seen signs that something is going on in the area when it comes to narcotics. Not least since Gavril Bolanaki disappeared."

"You mean that the market has increased?"

"Yes."

"Okay," said Gunnar. "As you all understand, these women are just pawns in a much larger game…" He leaned forward with his hands on the table and looked at the team. "We need to find the woman who ran. She could be our key into this whole operation. If we find her, we have a good chance of finding who was controlling her."

CHAPTER NINE

THE SOUND OF WAVES WOKE HER UP.
Her head was pounding, and Pim blinked a few times to clear her eyes. She sat up on the thin mattress and noticed that she had been covered up by a blanket. Next to her was a bucket with no handle.

How long had she been sleeping?

She tried to open her mouth but couldn't. Tape stretched from one cheek to the other. She wanted to rip it off, but her hands were bound behind her back with a coarse rope. She twisted and turned until she was breathless. Trying to take short quick breaths, she felt like she was going to suffocate.

She had felt like this before. Often, when they played, her little sister, Mai, had sat on her, held her hands tightly and yelled, *Try to escape, Pim. Try to escape, if you can!*

Then she had to fight to get free, to cast the weight off her chest. Mai had almost choked with laughter. It was just a game. But it wasn't now.

No part of this was a game.

The room had no windows. It was small, with a wooden floor and ceiling. It was cold and damp.

She thought about Noi and began to cry. She should have stayed with her, shouldn't have left her alone on the train.

She slowly pulled one leg up, shifted her weight onto her knees and sat up. Her eyes darted around the room, looking for a way out.

Where was she?

She had no idea.

And no one else had any idea that she was sitting there with her hands bound, her mouth taped shut, in a strange country.

Her legs shaking, she stumbled forward toward the wall, stood with her back to it and began feeling for something sharp.

Finally she found an uneven spot in the planks and immediately began to rub the rope against it. She pushed her back against the wall, up and down, to the sides, fighting and tearing to get the rope to break.

Jana Berzelius placed her notepad in her briefcase and left the conference room.

Outside the window, she saw snow falling heavily in the light gray darkness. She placed her hand on the shiny handrail and walked down the stairs from the third floor to the garage. The stairwell smelled like dust and Pine Sol. She stepped slowly, listening to the echo of her high heels and thinking about the investigation they had just begun. She was back to doing what gave her purpose—that meant something: a job, punctuality, achievement. She felt energetic and strong again. She wanted to focus on what lay ahead, on her future.

At that moment, her cell phone rang. She stopped, pulling it out of her pocket, but when she saw it was her colleague Per Åström she silenced it and put it away.

She had reached the first floor and was about to continue down the next flight when she stopped suddenly.

Through the glass door that led to the main entrance and reception area of the police station sat the thin, black-clad kid she had met the other evening at the entrance to Knäppingsborg.

Robin… Stenberg.

What was he doing here?

He sat with his elbows on his knees, one leg bobbing up and down with nervous energy.

She took a step forward, wanting to go into the reception area and talk to him, but a stronger impulse convinced her to instead leave the station.

Then Robin got up from the chair and was soon out of her field of vision.

She continued down the stairs, barely conscious of the fact that she was walking more quickly now that her thoughts were back at Knäppingsborg, seeing Robin's slim body, the panicked look on his face, the stars tattooed on his temple and his worried voice saying that he had to call for help.

That he had witnessed her violent encounter with Danilo gave her an uneasy feeling.

She pushed open the door to the parking garage just as a police car swung out from a parking space and disappeared in the heavy snowfall, its lights flashing.

Henrik Levin pushed the gray button that opened the door to the Psychiatric Clinic at Vrinnevi Hospital. They had hoped that someone would soon come forward with information that would help them find the missing woman, and he realized now that he had the most faith in the train attendant, Mats Johansson.

Henrik shook hands with Mats's doctor and exchanged a few words with him before being allowed into the patient's room.

A woman was sitting on the bed, and he met her brown eyes. She drew her hand through her curly hair before standing and quietly introducing herself as Marianne.

"I'm Mats's wife," she added, taking Henrik's jacket and hanging it carefully on a hook on the back of the door. As quietly as possible, she moved her chair closer to the bed, sat down and took her husband's left hand in hers.

"Mats," she whispered. "You have a visitor."

Henrik stood on the other side of him and observed his angular face, the wide mustache, the thin hair and pale skin. Mats's eyes moved under his closed eyelids.

"He's been dreaming a lot," Marianne said, smiling apologetically. "It's horrible, of course, to witness such a thing…and on his train, too… He's been rambling quite a bit."

"What does he say?" Henrik asked.

"Mostly nonsense, actually."

Marianne chuckled.

"I heard that," Mats said, opening his eyes. He lifted himself up on one elbow with a great deal of effort and looked at Henrik.

"Hi," Henrik said, putting his hand out. "I'm Detective Chief Inspector Henrik Levin. I need to talk with you, ask a few questions."

"Okay," Mats said, weakly shaking Henrik's hand.

"As I understand it, you found the woman in the train bathroom."

Mats nodded.

"Yes, I found her. She was lying in there…on the floor."

"Can you tell me anything else about it?"

Mats bit his upper lip.

Henrik took the close-up picture from the security camera out of his pocket.

"I'm going to show you a photo now, and I want you to look at it very carefully."

Mats sat up and looked at the photograph for a long time—at the black hair, the narrow eyes, the pale skin.

"Do you recognize this woman?" Henrik asked.

"This isn't the one you found in the bathroom."

Mats nodded.

"This is the girl who was standing outside the door, who ran away when I opened it. I couldn't stop her. I wanted to, but I couldn't. I had to stay with the girl in the bathroom. Noi, her name was."

"Noi? You mean Siriporn? The girl who died?"

"No..." Mats looked confusedly at him. "I mean Noi."

Henrik cast a glance at Marianne.

"Think carefully, Mats," his wife said.

"Was her name Noi?" Henrik asked.

"I don't know." Mats sighed. "But that's what she said, the other one, the one who ran away. When I came down the aisle, I saw her standing there, banging on the bathroom door. She was yelling 'Noi' again and again. I assumed that was the girl's name. And when I had opened the door, she ran away. I called out to her to stop, but she didn't."

Henrik thought for a moment.

"Where were they while the train was moving?"

Mats rubbed his eyes and raked a hand through his hair. He seemed tired now, weary of thinking, of remembering. He took a deep breath before he answered.

"Both were in Car 5, but they weren't sitting together. They were each in their own seat, one in front of the other, if that makes sense. There were plenty of open seats. The train wasn't full."

"How were they acting?"

Mats wrinkled his forehead as if he didn't understand the question.

"Were they nervous, uneasy, sullen, angry?"

"No, they mostly just slept."

"Where did they get on the train?"

Mats lay down with his head on the pillow and looked at the ceiling.

"They got on at the start, in Copenhagen."

"And they were heading for...?"

"Norrköping. That's why she screamed...why I needed to open the door. They were supposed to get off."

Mats paused, closed his eyes. Marianne stroked his cheek in an attempt to comfort him, but he turned his face away.

"I'll leave you to rest now," Henrik said. "Thank you for seeing me."

Marianne nodded in response.

Henrik met her gaze and saw that she was holding her husband's left hand in both of hers.

"So Anders is still in town?"

Gunnar Öhrn glared at Carin Radler, who was sitting in a visitor's chair in his office.

"Yes, and the next time you call a meeting, it'd be best if you let him know," she said, crossing one leg over the other. She bounced one high-heeled foot up and down.

"Or he'll make sure he's here in the building," Gunnar said.

"Which he's doing anyway after he's gotten settled in the hotel."

"Is it certain that he's staying here?"

"Considering that we have just had a case of narcotics smuggling fall into our laps, yes."

"He's not going to give up?"

"Anders has fought for many years to stop narcotics trafficking. It's thanks to his efforts that we've been able to arrest multiple central figures who control the different narcotics markets in Sweden. Just last spring, coordinated raids flushed out a huge gang in Gothenburg. Anders had comprehensive responsibility for the whole operation, and long prison sentences are waiting for those who were arrested."

"Yes, I'd heard that he got to show off in the newspapers."

Carin raised her voice.

"His war against drugs has given results, Gunnar!"

"And now he wants to do the job for us?"

"No, but he is extremely competent when it comes to questions of narcotics, which we can naturally benefit from."

Gunnar sneered. "So we're supposed to be best friends now?"

"You know that he's working hard for the new Police Authority, and I am, too."

"I understand your new role, but his?"

"He is running to be the National Police Commissioner, as I think you are well aware."

"So he's looking for more power, you mean." Gunnar rubbed his eyes.

Carin uncrossed and recrossed her legs, answering in a calm voice. "I know that you don't like him. But he is actually a good boss. Just like you."

"Cut the flattery. You and I both know that I may not be here long."

Carin sighed. "The problem with this reorganization is that we're faced with completely new, maybe even unforeseen, challenges, and that will require a lot from everyone."

"So who's to stay?"

"I can't answer that right now."

"Because you don't know?"

"I understand you're worried."

"I'm not one bit worried. But my colleagues are worried, and I don't know what I'm supposed to tell them."

"Tell them that we have a narcotics case that we have to solve. That's where our focus should be right now."

"In cooperation with Anders," Gunnar said with a sigh.

"Yes, in cooperation with Anders," Carin replied.

Mia Bolander came into the police station cafeteria, took a pear from the fruit bowl and stuffed two more into her pockets. It was really too many, but she knew she couldn't put them back once she turned around and caught sight of Henrik Levin and Ola Söderström. She rubbed the pear on her knit cardigan and sat down across from them.

Henrik removed the blue lid from his glass container, the steam from the red curry stew warming his face.

"That's a small lunch," Mia said.

"There wasn't much left after dinner last night."

"What, did Emma eat everything?"

"She's pregnant, you know."

"When's she due?"

"December 31."

"She'll have to keep her legs crossed tight for the baby's sake. It's no fun to have your birthday on the last day of the year, because then you're the last to get your driver's license or get into bars."

"No, it's…"

"And you have to ask your buddies to buy drinks for you."

"Right, of course." Henrik sighed. "But the main thing is that the baby is healthy."

"Everyone says that. The main thing is that the baby is healthy and has ten fingers and ten toes and develops a little faster than all the other kids. Just imagine how it is for people who have ugly babies. I mean, *really* ugly, not just the normal ugly."

"What do you mean, *people*? You mean, what if *I* have an ugly baby?"

"I wasn't talking about you."

"But I'm the one who's going to have a baby."

"Take it however you want."

Mia examined her pear.

"If we're being honest, though?"

"But aren't all babies cute?" Henrik asked.

"Parents say so, yes. But have you ever heard someone say, 'Oh, what an ugly baby'?"

"No, because there's no such thing as an ugly baby."

"No, it's because no one would dare to say so. But everyone has thought it at one time or another."

"But not everyone thinks that babies are ugly!" Henrik protested.

"Haven't you ever thought it?" Mia asked.

"No. Never."

"See, it's because you're a father. If you weren't, you would have. You agree with me, don't you, Ola?"

Ola held his hand up. "No comment." He wasn't going to join in Mia's fun.

"Wimp. You agree with me," Mia said.

"I don't even know what you're talking about," Ola said.

They all fell quiet. Ola broke the silence. "Going back to our previous conversation, Henrik, did that train attendant actually have anything to say?"

Henrik didn't have a chance to answer before Gunnar Öhrn came into the cafeteria and interrupted them.

"Mia!" he barked.

"Yes?" she said, turning around.

"I want to talk to you."

"Is that an order?"

"Yes. It's important. In my office in five minutes."

Mia sighed and took a bite of the pear.

* * *

Gunnar sat in his office and knew that as soon as he had given Mia the assignment, he should let Anders Wester know that a new witness had turned up at the train station. But it was hard.

He fiddled with his phone and pulled out Anders's number. It still felt unnatural having the National Crime Squad looking over his shoulder, as if their department had suddenly become a class of special needs kids with Anders Wester as their "normal" peer mentor.

He knew that if she could hear his thoughts, Anneli would say, *Knock it off! You're being childish!*

He began to type in Anders's phone number, but when he came to the last digit, he changed his mind and deleted it. He had absolutely no desire to talk to Anders, or to have anything at all to do with him, really.

Just then, someone knocked on his door. Mia stuck her head in. "You wanted something?"

Gunnar rubbed his hands over his face several times.

"Sit down," he said, pointing at the chair in front of him.

"What is it?" she said, sitting down.

"I just want you to interview a witness who was in the parking lot yesterday when the train with the dead woman rolled into the station. He says he saw a man. Find out what he saw. His name is Stefan Ohlin."

"Sure, sure, sure."

Gunnar took a deep breath.

"And one more thing."

"What is it?"

"Your attitude is a little, well, how should I say this. It's too much."

"Are you going to fire me or what?" Mia crossed her arms over her chest.

"No, I'm not going to fire you. But…you're sucking energy out of the group with your attitude, and I want you to get it together."

"Okay. I should shut up, you mean?"

"That's exactly the attitude I'm talking about."

"What do you mean? I'm just saying what I think."

"Well, stop doing that, then. Keep your opinions to yourself and focus on doing a good job instead!"

Mia didn't answer, just pursed her lips.

"This is how it's going to be," Gunnar said. "We have the National Crime Squad looking over our shoulders, and I want you to help me live up to their expectations. We can't give them any reason to question our work."

"Sure," Mia said, nodding slowly.

"Good. So then, I want you to start by interviewing this Stefan guy. Here's his number. He's a teacher at Vittra School in Röda Stan, the neighborhood with all the red houses, and wants us to meet him there."

"Henrik and I will go…"

"You go by yourself."

"Okay. I'll leave right away."

Mia got up and walked toward the door.

"And, Mia…"

Gunnar looked at her with a frown.

"Yes?"

"Show me what you've got. Please?"

"I will," Mia said with a wide, bright smile.

She looked happy, Gunnar thought. Way too happy.

Then he understood.

She had been telling him to go to hell.

With her smile.

Jana Berzelius did not seem to be in any hurry when she entered the Public Prosecution Office on Olai Kyrkogata 50, in the middle of downtown Norrköping. But in reality she was in a terrible state. She didn't know how to handle the fact that she had seen the skinny kid Robin Stenberg at the police station. Hadn't he understood that she was serious? The last thing she wanted was for the police to get involved.

She put her briefcase on the floor and stood behind the desk in her office without sitting down. She didn't want to sit; she just wanted to stand, wanted to escape the unpleasant feeling that Robin Stenberg was about to do something at the police station that wouldn't turn out well for her.

It was quiet on her floor. The only thing she could hear through the glass wall was a colleague's steps and the electronic hum of a printer spitting out copies of a report, a court order or some other document that was hundreds of pages long.

A photograph hung on one wall of her office. It showed a family standing on the steps of a large yellow summerhouse. Jana looked at the girl's eyes, meeting the gaze of herself as a nine-year-old girl, and remembered that day. The sky had been clear and the air dry and warm.

The sunshine had made the house stunningly gorgeous. Her mother always said that you couldn't imagine a more beautiful place. They had driven from Norrköping to Arkösund, walked down to the cliffs and looked over the sea.

Then it had been time for the family picture. The three of them, together. She'd been wearing a white dress and had stood unmoving on the stone steps in front of the house, her mother and father standing next to her. Her mother had stood still while her father stamped his feet impatiently, his voice stern, as always.

"Hurry up!"

"Just one last adjustment."

The photographer waved his hand, signaling that they should move closer to each other.

"Now smile, all of you! One, two, three."

Click.

"I want all of you to smile at the same time. One more time. One, two three."

Click.

"Are you happy now?" Karl asked.

"No, one more. Now we're smiling, come on

now, little girl, you, too—give me the prettiest smile you can."

But she didn't smile.

"Let's try again!"

"Wait!" her father said, turning toward her. "Why won't you smile, Jana?"

She didn't answer.

"If you smile," he said, "I'll buy you a toy. Would you like that?"

She looked at the ground, feeling unsure of herself. His voice was suddenly soft, his face so kind.

"What do you say?" he asked.

"What kind of toy?" she asked.

"Whatever you want."

"Really?"

"If you smile."

She had a strange feeling in her stomach. She thought that a smile would buy her what she wanted most of all in the whole world—a doll to hold tight at night, so she wouldn't feel so alone.

A doll, for a smile.

The photographer signaled again.

"Okay!" he yelled. "Now then. One, two, three!"

She smiled.

Click.

"There we go! That's it."

She had sat expectantly in the car on the way home. As they approached downtown, she couldn't keep it in any longer.

"Are we going shopping now?" she asked.

But her father had kept his eyes straight ahead the whole time.

"No," he said.

"But we were going to buy a doll…"

"I don't have time right now."

"You promised," she said quietly.

"I didn't promise it would be today."

She had tried to catch his eye but couldn't. Then she understood. His voice had been soft.

She had felt a small shudder pass through her body. She had been afraid that he would notice, afraid that he would see that she had learned how to tell when something was wrong. When something was terribly wrong.

Jana moved her gaze from the photograph to the window. Her hands were clenched into fists. That day, as a nine-year-old in the car on the way home from their summerhouse, she had learned not to trust anyone. If she wanted something, she had to rely on herself. There was no one else to do it for her. She couldn't leave anything to chance.

If she wanted to stop the gnawing sense of uneasiness in her body, she would have to find Robin Stenberg. Tonight.

 TEN

MIA BOLANDER PARKED OUTSIDE
Vittra School and walked through the gate into the
schoolyard. She was met by happy cries, running
children and flying snowballs.

Three little girls with their hats pulled down over
their foreheads came running toward her. Their
cheeks were red from the cold and snot was running down the upper lips of all three.

"Who are you?" they said in chorus.

"I'm Mia."

"Why are you here?"

"I'm meeting someone."

"Who?"

"A man who works here at the school."

"What's his name?"

"I can't say."

"Why not?"

"Because it's a secret."

"Why is it a secret?"

"Because it is. I need to know how to get to the third grade classroom."

"The yellow group is over there."

One of the girls pointed with her mitten toward one of the entrances.

Mia stepped inside and was met by the smell of the damp outerwear that hung lined up on hooks in the hallway. The floor was wet with melted snow. A hand-written sign instructed everyone to take off their shoes in the cloakroom. Mia ignored the sign, walked forward, turned to the right and took the stairs to the second floor.

She walked through the lounge, looking for the right classroom, and finally found it all the way down the hall.

The class was empty except for a man, a few years older than herself, who was standing in front of a whiteboard writing the day's lesson. She knocked on the door frame and walked in. She noticed the map of Sweden, the calendar and the colorful alphabet on the walls.

"Mia Bolander, police."

"Wonderful, great that you could come right now," the man said, introducing himself as Stefan Ohlin. "You had some questions?"

"Yes, about your testimony."

"Come in. Sit down."

Stefan pulled out a chair from a round table and gathered up the notes that lay on it.

"Group work," he said. "The yellow group is learning about the Bronze Age."

Mia nodded and looked at his reddish hair and beard, freckled face and hands.

"How long can we talk?" she asked.

"Fifteen minutes max. They're at recess now."

"I noticed. The playground is a lively place."

He was silent for a moment.

"So…" both said at the same time.

"I'm sorry. You start," Stefan said.

"Okay," said Mia. "You were at Central Station yesterday?"

"Yes. I was waiting for my wife, who was coming on the commuter train from Linköping just before eleven o'clock. She's also a teacher. At the university there."

"But you were there early?"

"Yes, I'd met a buddy who just had a kid and left their house around ten in the evening. Because we live a ways out, in Krokek, there wasn't any point in going home, which takes twenty to twenty-five minutes round trip, so I went downtown and waited."

"What time was it then?"

"Well, what would it have been, around ten fifteen or ten twenty, maybe."

Mia pulled out a small notebook, looking for a blank page to write on but didn't find one. All the pages were full of scribbles. She began taking notes on the brown cardboard back.

"Where were you parked?"

"Right in front of the taxi stand."

"And while you sat there waiting, what did you see?"

"Yes, that's the thing. There was a car parked right behind me, and a man sitting in it."

"Can you describe him?"

"I only got a quick glimpse."

"What kind of car was it?"

"I don't know."

"You don't know?"

Stefan thought, resting his chin on his hand.

"No, cars have never been my thing. But I would guess that it was a Volvo, an older model. Or a Fiat."

Mia wrote again.

"Color?"

"Dark. Blue, maybe."

"Hatchback?"

"No."

"License plate?"

"The thing with memory is that it only gets worse with age. I used to be so good at remembering things like that, but...maybe a *G* in the beginning, and a *U*. Or maybe vice versa."

"Any digits?"

"It started with a one, but then...no, I don't really remember. I think there was a four and a seven."

"Okay, so 147?"

"No, probably 174, I think."

"Good," said Mia. "Then we're only missing the letters. Tell me about the driver..."

"Sure. I left my car to go into the convenience

store. I wanted something sweet, I'm addicted to Daim bars, but anyway, when I walked into the shop, I ran into the driver, I mean, the man. He stood in the doorway with a lighter in his hand, as if he wasn't sure whether he should go in…"

"So he never went in?"

"No, not that I saw. But I bumped into him accidentally and he dropped the lighter."

Stefan glanced up at the clock on the wall.

"The children will be coming back soon."

"Okay, can you describe the man for me now?"

"Well, I wouldn't have hardly noticed him if he hadn't been acting so nervous, as if he didn't want to be seen. In any case, he was wearing dark clothes, had his jacket collar pulled up to his nose, was wearing a hat."

"Did he have a mustache? Beard? Light or dark hair?"

"He had dark hair. It was sticking out on the sides. I thought he looked foreign."

"What do you mean?"

"I don't know. Maybe it was his hair that made me think that. And his eyes."

"Which were?"

"Also dark."

"A dark-haired man, possibly foreign. How old?"

"Oh, hard to say. Around thirty, maybe."

"Anything else that stood out about him?"

"No…it was mostly that he was acting so nervous…but I hope I've been able to help anyway."

Mia closed her notebook.

"Your observations are very important to us," she assured him, getting up from the chair to leave.

"Wait!"

Stefan held his hand up in the air, smiling.

"GUV!" he said. "I just remembered the license plate. GUV 174."

"We have a description of a man who might have picked up the girl," Mia said into the phone.

Henrik Levin sat in his office with the phone to his ear. His gaze was fixed on his bulletin board as he listened to Mia tell about her meeting with the teacher at Vittra School.

"You're saying that we're looking for a foreign-looking man, with dark clothes and dark hair," Henrik said. "I know that this isn't going to sound good, but there are quite a few people who fit that description."

"I know," Mia said. "I'll check with the convenience store and see if they have a security camera, since he poked his head in there. Maybe we'd get a better description."

"That wouldn't be a bad idea."

"The teacher seemed a bit unsure, but ask Ola to search for license plate number GUV 174 or something similar. It should be a Volvo or Fiat, a dark color."

Henrik combed his hand through his hair and shifted his weight in his chair, feeling a pang of hope.

"Bye," Mia said, ending the call with a normal

closing. No swearwords, nothing cynical, no sighing. Just "bye." Henrik was almost shocked. What had happened to her?

"Did you get somewhere?"

Ola Söderström suddenly appeared, leaning against the door frame, smiling. His ears were sticking out from under his striped hat. He always wore a hat, no matter whether he was inside or outside, no matter what the season.

"Good thing you came by. I have some new information for you. First, I want you to look for a car with the license plate GUV 174."

"Okay," he said.

"Then, I have the feeling that the dead woman on the train, or rather, her passport, was fake. Björn Ahlmann said she was fifteen years old, but according to her passport, she was eighteen. And the train attendant thought her name was Noi, not Siriporn."

"But Noi isn't a given name, it's a nickname. It's common in Thailand, especially because first names can be so long."

"How do you know that?"

"My cousin married a Thai woman. They met in Phuket. Love at first sight. They just clicked."

Ola snapped his fingers.

"Even if the passport is fake, we shouldn't underestimate its importance," he continued. "I've sent a request to all of the airlines. I haven't heard anything yet, but we can still hope that her name is on the passenger list somewhere. It would be good to know where they came from."

"Both of their names should be on some list," Henrik said.

"If they flew on the same plane, that is. They may not have."

Ola scratched with his hand up under his hat.

"It might help that they looked Asian," he said. "I mean, more people would have noticed her, or them, on the train."

"Right," Henrik said. "If you don't find anything from the license plate, we have one relatively poor description of the man who was driving the car. Check it out, see if you can get anything from that. The capsules we found in the woman's stomach were supposed to be delivered to someone, after all, and I'm wondering who."

"I know where to look," Ola said.

"Great. So get to it."

The sound of the doorbell made Jana Berzelius jump up from the chaise lounge. It was late in the afternoon, and she went suspiciously toward the door. She wasn't expecting any visitors; she never had any.

She padded silently into the hallway and looked through the peephole. She clenched her jaw when she saw the face of her colleague, prosecutor Per Åström.

He rang one more time, then knocked, too.

Slowly, she turned the dead bolt, leaving the chain fastened.

"What are you doing here?" she asked.

"You haven't been answering your phone."

"I'm really busy."

"With what? Why are you avoiding me?"

Per threw up his hands.

"Look," he said. "We haven't seen each other in eight months…"

"We see each other multiple times every week at work."

"You know what I mean. I want to see you again. There. That's what I came here to say."

"Great," Jana said, closing the door and resting her forehead against it, eyes closed.

The doorbell rang again. And again. Short, quick buzzes as if a child were standing outside and wanted to come in.

She hesitated before opening the door again.

His eyes—one blue and one brown, characteristic heterochromia—met hers.

"One more thing," he said. "Would you have dinner with me tonight?"

"No."

"Great! Should we go to The Colander? The usual?"

"No."

"Eight o'clock?"

"No."

"Perfect! Should I pick you up?"

"No. I want someplace new."

Per looked confused, pulled at his blond hair.

"Are you sick?" he said.

"Just need a change. Let's go to Ardor, eight thirty. I'll meet you there."

Then she shut the door.

"I didn't find any car with license plate GUV 174," Ola said upon meeting Henrik Levin in the hallway. His arms were filled with file folders.

"As I suspected," Henrik said with a worried look. "Mia said that the guy seemed a little unsure. Or the plate could have been fake."

"Possible," Ola said, thinking for a moment. "It's too bad, though. This was the best tip we had to go on, right?"

"Yes, and we haven't gotten any more info from the street," Henrik said. "Our usual sources have been silent. Either they don't know anything or they don't dare say."

"Typical," Ola said.

"Yeah, but I still think something about it is strange. A young girl dies with her body packed full of narcotics—someone should have seen or heard something. It's not usually the case that someone hides their tracks so well. This is no amateur we're dealing with. They clearly have their eye on importing and distributing. Someone has to be willing to talk."

"*Had* an eye, you mean. Obviously something went wrong with the girl on the train."

"Absolutely, but as I said, they're calculating for some waste, as in all import/export businesses."

Ola held out the files.

"I did a little searching of my own and printed out all of the files on men with connections to drug trafficking. I thought someone must know something. Two of the files are thick as Bibles."

"Great," Henrik said, taking the files. "If we aren't going to get anything from the streets, we'll have to do our own digging."

In spite of the growing blister on her skin, Pim continued fighting to get the ropes around her wrists to snap. Even with the chill in the room, sweat was running down her back.

Suddenly she heard footsteps outside the door.

She hurried to the corner of the room, overturning the bucket in the process. She picked it up and huddled with her knees to her chest, taking short, silent breaths, sitting completely still, listening.

The door slid open and a man stepped into the room. He was wearing dark clothes, and his eyes were as dark as night. He put a plate of food on the floor.

Pim looked at the food, then pushed it away.

He stood in front of her, stared, and then in a single movement ripped the tape from her mouth. The pain was immense. She wanted to scream, but she was too scared to make a sound. She didn't say anything when he violently loosened the ropes around her wrists. She only rubbed one hand carefully against the smarting sore on the other wrist.

She heard him say something before the door closed behind him.

She carefully picked up the plate and looked at the sandwiches and plastic gloves. Only then did she think about the capsules that were still in her stomach.

She returned to the corner, picked up one of the sandwiches and forced herself to chew.

Touching one of the thin gloves, she looked at the bucket and knew what she had to do.

Henrik Levin turned slowly out of the general parking lot of the Ektorp shopping center. Next to him sat Mia Bolander in an oversize down jacket.

"He didn't say shit," she muttered, waving one of Ola Söderström's files in Henrik's face before tossing it in the backseat. She balanced the others on her lap.

"I don't get it. He's committed hundreds of break-ins and has been caught for possession a thousand times, and now he's on disability for a slipped disk. And he's not even thirty? And he's got five kids. Completely unbelievable. Completely fucking unbelievable."

"Yeah…" Henrik sighed.

"If they'd placed the camera at a smarter angle at the convenience store, we wouldn't have to drive around chatting with criminals," Mia said.

The afternoon traffic moved slowly down

Kungsgatan. A bus stopped in front of them and released a single passenger, who immediately jay-walked across both lanes. Henrik considered honking his horn, but changed his mind.

"Who's next?" he asked instead.

Mia flipped through a new folder, looking at the picture for a moment.

"Stojan Jancic," she read. "Born in Serbia. Was sentenced for, among other things, a felony narcotics charge after being arrested for selling a mix of Ecstasy and ketamine. Three years in prison."

She entered the address into the navigation system and closed the folder.

Twelve minutes later, they were there. Henrik made a U-turn across both lanes and parked in a spot reserved for visitors.

A streetlight flickered on when they got out of the car. The light stretched over a gravel field.

Stojan opened the door on the second ring. His hair was sticking out at all angles, his jeans were filthy and his T-shirt had large holes along the neckband.

"Come in," he said after Henrik had introduced them and their errand.

Mia was quiet and kept her hands in her pockets as they stepped into the apartment and sat at the kitchen table.

Henrik leaned against the kitchen counter and took a notebook from his pocket. He squinted out the gray-streaked window that faced the parking lot.

"Your tattoo…" he said. "Does it mean something?"

"No, well, yes, well, fuck. I don't know," Stojan said.

He sat across from Mia and rubbed his hand across his neck, over the large cross and the black letters above it that spelled "Respect."

"I mean, is it a sort of identification?"

"Well, it's not a gang tattoo, if that's what you're suggesting."

"We know you used to belong to a gang."

"But the tattoo doesn't have anything to do with that."

"M-16? Was that what you were called? Weren't you guys close to the Black Cobras?" Mia asked.

Stojan didn't answer, looking instead out the window.

"You got into things pretty early, didn't you?" she continued.

He looked at her. "Yes. I was eleven. Are you guys here to talk about that?"

"No, we want to talk about your cat," Mia said wearily.

"I don't have a cat."

"Exactly."

Stojan looked confused.

"Why do you want to talk about cats? I hate cats."

"Fuck cats, now talk."

"Oh, I get it, you were kidding, right? You knew I didn't have a cat."

"Oh, for fuck's sake… Come on now, genius, we don't have all afternoon."

Mia pointed to her bare wrist, as if to show that time was passing on a watch that wasn't there.

"Chill out, Christ!" Stojan said, leaning back. Then he shrugged his shoulders.

"Okay," he said, "I started early. Drank just as much as my dad."

"Was he an alcoholic?"

"He was a fucking idiot, that is what he was. Didn't give a shit about me. Then it went how it went. Didn't go well in school because they thought I was too much trouble, fought too much, talked back too much, so it was better to hang out with the gang. Better to get their attention than none at all."

"And the narcotics?"

"What about them?"

"You got caught for possession."

"I sold a little bit, I admit that. Everything happened so fucking fast. Tried a little new shit, hung out with new buddies. Looked for a place to sleep at night. Temporary places where people did drugs, fucked, slept, ate and shit. It didn't matter where I ended up, whether it was at a buddy's house or in a park, a stairwell or a trash room, as long as I got my fix."

"And now? Are you clean?"

"I've distanced myself from all of it. Some respected that, some wished me luck and others didn't say anything. But everyone has just let me be since then. No one's tried to get me to come back. It's as if they all know that I've made up my mind. I don't want to do that stuff anymore, want to do something else with my life."

"Like what?"

"Go to school. For economics, maybe."

"So when did you get clean?"

"Three years ago."

"And how are you supporting yourself right now?"

"My cousin has a little shop, a kiosk, so I help him sometimes. It makes the days pass. It's hard, but it works."

Stojan stuffed his hands between his knees.

"It's sick, you know…" he said. "No matter how shitty it is to be addicted, you still crave it sometimes, wish you were back in that time when you just hung around town. I see users in movies or TV shows and start craving a fix. Know what I mean?"

"We know." Mia sighed.

"I take it that the market has changed since you got clean," Henrik said.

"It's always changing. New networks crop up, they're strong and fast." Stojan looked down at his hands.

"But just tell me now," he said.

"Tell you what?"

"Why you're here. You want something, right? Pigs always want something."

"We've heard there's been some talk," Henrik said. "Can you confirm that?"

"'There's been some talk'?" Stojan said, sneering again. "You'll have to be more specific than that, man."

Henrik glanced at Mia.

"We know that something's going on," Henrik said. "*The market* is getting nervous."

"Something's always going on," Stojan said. "But don't think that I know anything about it, 'cause I don't."

"But you know what would happen if you knew and didn't tell us."

"You can't make me say anything."

"But I can make you come down to the station with me."

Stojan was quiet for a second and then said, "Okay, I'll save you the work of taking me down to the station. All I can tell you is that there are rumors of a guy, someone who goes by The Old Man, who's driving things, managing them. But no one knows who he is, no one's met him. He's like a shadow, really."

"And how do you know about The Old Man?"

"I told you, there are rumors."

"What else have you heard?"

"I know just as much as anyone else. Not much, I mean. And you didn't hear this from me, either. Right? I'm no snitch."

That's exactly what you are, Henrik thought.

CHAPTER ELEVEN

JANA BERZELIUS WRAPPED A TOWEL around her body and went into her walk-in closet to select clothes for the evening. She cast a glance in the mirror at the bruises and saw that they were still dark.

She dressed quickly, buttoning her blouse with careful fingers in a gliding movement. Her pants were slimming, her jacket cropped.

In the bathroom, she washed her face and applied moisturizer and a discreet amount of makeup. As she put on lipstick, she suddenly felt nervous for her dinner with Per. It was both safe and scary to see him one-on-one again. Safe because she knew him. But scary because there was so much he didn't know. So much he didn't need to know. So much that hiding it all was difficult.

She thought about their last dinner.

It was more than eight months ago. She remembered his inquisitive face, his endless anxiety-inducing questions about what was wrong. It felt like he wanted to crawl right under her skin. She couldn't do it, felt suffocated and in the end had just gotten up and left without an explanation. He seemed to respect that. He hadn't followed her, called or anything; he had simply let her be. She hadn't needed to explain anything, but then again, she shouldn't have to, either. She shouldn't have to do anything for him.

Now she looked at the clock. One hour left before dinner, which gave her plenty of time to pay Robin Stenberg a visit. She picked up her phone, searched the web with lightning-fast fingers for his address and found it quickly.

She lifted her purse and opened it. Hidden under a false bottom was the knife. She didn't need to touch it, just confirm that it was still there.

Thirty seconds later, she left her apartment, started her BMW and drove out of the garage. She could hear her own breath as she approached Stenberg's address.

She parked and took the knife out of her purse, placing it against the small of her back before she got out of the car, then crossed Spelmansgatan 62 in spite of the "Don't walk" sign.

The seat belt caught in the car door. Mia Bolander opened the door again and pulled the belt over her lap.

"Who are we talking to next?" Henrik asked, turning the heater to high and holding his frozen hands up to meet the warm air flowing from the vents.

Mia picked up the two folders that lay on the dashboard, opened the one on top and looked at the picture. "What the hell? It's..."

"What? Who?" Henrik asked.

"No one."

"Do you know him?"

Clearly not, she thought, glancing through the file. She felt her cheeks flush and sincerely hoped that Henrik hadn't noticed it. She saw *possession* and *sale of a controlled substance*, just like the others. He'd been caught and served two years in jail when he was twenty-one. Still, she couldn't believe it. Toe-sucker Martin was a junkie.

A fucking, goddamn junkie.

"Just drive," she said, irritated, entering the address into the navigation system as if she didn't already know the way. It was a pointless game; she had already revealed herself. Yet she continued playing.

Henrik got out of the car first. She dillydallied, looking at herself in the vanity mirror, taking her hair out of her ponytail holder and combing her hands through it. She took a deep breath and prepared herself.

Martin Strömberg opened the door right away.

Mia stood behind Henrik and signaled that Martin shouldn't let on that he knew her.

That he "knew" her in the most intimate way.

Still, he nodded in recognition.

"We're here to ask you a few questions," Henrik said.

"This late? About what?"

"Let us in," Mia said with a knowing look.

"Sure, sure, come in then. Let's sit in the kitchen, why don't we?"

"The living room is better," she said, stepping past him. She looked around the room quickly to make sure none of her things were lying about the room.

She sat down on the sofa, moving a pillow from behind her back. Martin sat down so close to her that she immediately moved a few inches away.

"We want to talk to you about the narcotics market here," Henrik said, still standing at the entrance to the living room. "We understand you were arrested for cocaine."

"I can't deny that."

"Do you still do drugs?"

Martin hesitated for a moment. "Sometimes you fall back into it for a moment. But even alcohol is a drug. Coffee was thought to be a drug when it first came to Sweden, you know."

Henrik sighed and took his notebook out of his jacket pocket.

"Yes, well," he said. "Yesterday, a girl was found dead on board a train. In her stomach were a whole lot of capsules containing heroin and cocaine."

"Oh, Christ," Martin said, drawing his hand through his greasy hair. "But what does that have to do with me?"

"We are hoping to reap the benefit of your impressive knowledge of the drug market here in town," Henrik said. "What channels are most active and all of that."

"But it changes constantly."

"Exactly, and we've just heard that a rumor is circulating about a new man who is controlling the drug trade here," Henrik said.

"What's his name?" Martin asked, looking up at Henrik.

"We were hoping you could tell us that."

"I have no idea who you're talking about."

"We're talking about The Old Man."

"The Old Man? That's his name?"

"Seems so."

"Doesn't ring a bell. Sorry."

"Are you sure?" Mia said, looking at Martin with a tired expression.

"Yes…"

"Completely certain?"

"Okay, okay. Maybe I've heard of him."

Mia perked up, locking her gaze on him.

"In what context?" she asked.

"I don't remember."

"You have to tell us if you know something," Henrik said.

He looked at Martin, saw that his eyes were searching for hers, saw his grin and her flushed neck. He sighed again.

"From what I understand, you haven't always been very reliable," he said instead.

"No," Martin said. "I tried to find shortcuts, but they only led to dead ends."

"And now?"

"As I said, sometimes you fall back into old habits, but now I've found a new drug. The best one of all."

"Oh, really?"

"Love."

Mia felt the warmth of his breath. It made her nauseous.

"Great," Henrik said.

"Love is wonderful. The most wonderful thing we have."

Mia felt like she was going to throw up. She couldn't listen to any more of this.

"Okay," Henrik said, with an expression that said he wasn't sure if this man was messing with him or not. "We won't keep you any longer. If you hear or see anything about The Old Man, you'll let us know, right?"

"Of course I will. If for nothing else than your sake, Mia."

Mia didn't say anything as they walked back to the car. She couldn't think, could only kick the snow to vent her irritation and anger. She was angry at the cold evening, her worn boots and tight jeans, angry at everything that bothered her, at everything ugly and excessive.

She put her seat belt on and crossed her arms over her chest. She looked at Henrik.

"Martin and I... We..." she began.

"You don't have to explain," he said.

"Good. Because I'm not going to be seeing him again. Ever."

The guests' conversations around the large dinner table drowned each other out. Karl Berzelius raised his glass, but no one heard what he said.

"Cheers to a pleasant evening," he repeated, tasting the wine. He signaled the two young female servers to open another bottle of Clos Saint Jean Deus Ex Machina, but they didn't notice him snapping his fingers. Instead, they disappeared out of the hall with their serving platters on their shoulders.

Karl turned toward Margaretha, who was talking with the man sitting next to her. She had left her silverware resting on her plate, where the venison had hardly been touched. He attempted to get her attention so that she might call the servers back, but the conversation clearly required all of her attention.

"I must congratulate you…" a voice came from the other side of the table.

Karl raised his eyes and saw Herman Kanterberg raise his glass in his direction. Karl was swirling the wine in his glass, breathing in.

"You must be so proud!" Herman said.

"What do you mean?"

"Your daughter's successes."

Karl took his cloth napkin and slowly dabbed the corners of his mouth.

"Does she have the same ambitions you had?"

"I can't speak for her."

"If she continues at the same rate, she could become Prosecutor-General." Herman turned his head toward the other guests, lifted his glass and nodded. "Cheers to hard work, my friends. It is the only path to success. There are no shortcuts."

"Hear, hear!" came a shout.

"Cheers!" came another.

The glasses clinked over the table.

Karl's glass remained on the table. He looked down at his plate, noticing the reflection of the lights in the silverware.

"What's wrong, Karl? Don't you agree?" Herman asked.

He didn't answer, instead folding his napkin and letting the question die out by slowly getting up and leaving the table. He felt dizzy from the alcohol as he walked down the hallway, past the many rooms. He heard the muffled sound of laughter from the dining room when he came into the kitchen, which smelled strongly of red wine sauce.

The girls stood at the kitchen counter, setting out the dessert plates in three parallel rows.

He didn't have the energy to filter himself. His voice was hard.

"Go and serve more wine. Now!" he commanded.

The girls immediately disappeared from sight.

Alone in the kitchen, he decided he would hire different staff for the next dinner party. Over the years, he had built up a large and impressive circle of friends, and they expected only the best service. He couldn't employ just whatever bungling idiots happened to come along.

With his hands shaking, he hung his jacket on the back of a chair. The collar of his white shirt was damp with sweat. He drew his hand through his thick gray hair and listened to his guests' glasses clink against one another.

He knew that he should go back to the dining room, but instead he picked up a bottle of wine, opened it and took three big gulps. Nausea hit him immediately and he leaned over the sink and vomited.

"Karl?"

He heard Margaretha's voice far away, traveling through the walls.

He heard a door close and small, quick steps pass over the floor. Her voice became clearer as she came closer.

"Karl?"

Suddenly, the kitchen door opened. "Karl? What are you doing in here? Come back now, the guests are wondering where you are."

"I'm coming," he said without turning around, avoiding her quisitive gaze.

"Hurry, please."

"I said, I'm coming!"

He didn't feel like covering up his irritation. It felt good to release the anger, even though it was really toward... Jana.

He looked down at his hands, remembering the

first time he'd let them touch his adopted daughter's cheek. She was nine years old. They were late to dinner at the Swedberg's house, and Jana came slowly down the stairs of their house in the wealthy Lindö neighborhood.

He and Margaretha were waiting for her. She was wearing an evening gown; he was in a tuxedo, his overcoat over one arm. His hair was combed back and his face clean-shaven.

"Hurry up now," he said to his daughter, moving her hair to the side and seeing that the bandage was no longer there. He saw the three distorted letters.

"Why did you take the bandage off? Didn't I tell you that you always have to hide that? Always cover it up?"

She didn't answer, looking directly in his eyes.

"You're making me crazy. What about this don't you understand? You have to hide these scars. Always! What you have on your neck is ugly. Disgusting!

"And stop staring at me like that. Stop it, I said!"

But she kept staring. "Can't you hear me?"

His face grew red.

"That's enough!" he screamed, grabbing her arm. He dragged her up the stairs to her room.

"You're going to learn to do what I say. Do you understand?"

She still didn't react.

Then he slapped her, right across the face.

Hard.

But she just looked at him with her dark eyes.

He hit her again. And again.

"What's wrong with you? Why aren't you crying?"

Another slap, even harder.

"Cry, for Christ's sake!"

Jana didn't cry.

But he did.

Karl was jerked from his thoughts when the door closed again and Margaretha's footsteps disappeared down the hall.

He was alone in the kitchen and stood there for a few moments, rinsing the sink clean. He wiped his mouth a few times, took a gulp of wine and wiped his mouth again.

Taking his jacket from the chair, he returned to the dinner with a controlled smile.

Shit, what a racket. Fucking neighbors from hell.

Robin Stenberg let the movie he was watching play while he got up to get some Coke from the fridge. There were only a few ounces left in the bottle, and what remained was completely flat.

His downstairs neighbors were being loud again. Every weekend was the same. Screaming, crying, a howling dog. Sometimes it went on for an hour, sometimes all night long.

With the taped-up remote control in his hand, he increased the volume on the TV, raised the bottle to his lips and gulped the last bit down.

Just then, he stopped. He heard something else. He froze, soda still in his mouth, and listened.

Swallowing slowly, he muted the TV, put the bottle on the ground and listened again.

"Shit, shit, shit," he said, getting up.

Listening carefully, he went into the hallway and froze when he saw that the mail slot was open. He closed it with his foot and stared at the door. An unpleasant feeling made him reach his hand out and try the handle. He was astonished to find it was unlocked.

"What the fuck?"

He knew he'd locked it. He had checked that it was locked—a few times, even.

He opened the door, first slowly, then quickly swinging it wide open. The stairwell was dark. He heard his neighbors' voices much more clearly out here. Angry, cruel words echoed against the cold, bare walls.

He quickly closed the door again, bolted it for security's sake and stepped back into the apartment. He glanced to the right into the kitchen and saw nothing unusual, yet he couldn't shake this unpleasant feeling. How could the door have gotten unlocked?

He bit his piercing, pulled it back and forth through his lip, quickly and nervously. He checked the bathroom to confirm that it was empty, too. Looking at the flickering, silent television in the darkened living room, he saw the light from the screen disappear before returning just as quickly. He sensed that the apartment was somehow suddenly different. It was as if the air had a different density, as if someone else was there. He looked behind the door and in the closet.

He found nothing, but he still couldn't shake the unpleasant feeling of being watched.

"There must be thousands matching the description of the man at Central Station," Mia Bolander said. "But I don't think our man is in this pile. Unfortunately."

"That's what I told you," Henrik Levin replied.

"And now I've told you," she said, warming both hands around her coffee cup. She had a ham and cheese baguette in front of her.

"Okay, I admit it," she said a moment later. "The tip from that teacher was worthless."

It was late in the evening, and Café Fräcka Fröken was empty. They were taking a break after all of the questioning. Both were turned toward the picture window that faced Skvallertorget, where bicyclists, motorists and pedestrians usually combined into a sort of organized chaos without yield signs or traffic lights. Now, the cold had scared off the residents; the sidewalks were empty except for a few people who hid inside thick layers of clothing and longed for warmer climates.

"And nothing new about the girl who disappeared from the train, either?" Mia asked.

"No. I just hope she's inside somewhere warm," Henrik said. "No chance she'll make it otherwise. She'll freeze to death in just a few hours the way she was dressed."

"But she seems to have been picked up," Mia said. "Someone is keeping her somewhere, to make sure she delivers. Then they'll let her go. If we're lucky, we'll find her in some airport somewhere. Or Central Station."

"If she hasn't already crossed the border," Henrik said, concealing a yawn.

Mia nodded, taking two bites of her sandwich. A sunflower seed fell from the baguette to her plate.

"And The Old Man, then?" Mia said between bites. "Whom everyone knows of, but no one has heard or seen? The name itself, The Old Man, sounds like a sick longing for the father they never had when they grew up. I doubt he even exists."

"Of course he exists," Henrik objected. "Something's going on, someone has taken over the market…"

"So you buy it? About The Old Man?"

She took another bite of her sandwich.

"Yes."

"Why is that?"

"As I said, a lot is going on right now."

Mia wrinkled her forehead, took a sip of coffee and took her cell phone from her pocket. She had received a text, and Henrik noticed that she smiled as she read it.

While she responded, he looked around the café. A woman in a dark blue sweater and skirt sat hunched over with her hands in front of her face. A man sat next to her with his arm around her shoulders and looked like he was trying to comfort her.

An older man in a beige overcoat stood talking on the phone, his face stony.

"I think Gavril Bolanaki was taken out," Henrik said quietly.

"Really?" Mia said, putting her phone back in her pocket.

"Yes. I think he was silenced. You know what people think of snitches."

"They're worthless."

"Exactly. And it's very possible that there's a power shift going on in the narcotics world. Or more accurately, when Gavril disappeared, someone else took over."

"The Old Man?"

Henrik nodded, drinking the last of his coffee.

"The case with Gavril is closed, in any case," Mia said, picking up the sunflower seed from her plate and popping it into her mouth.

"Which is even more strange," Henrik said, putting his cup back on the table.

"Why is that?"

"No reason. Forget it."

"No, tell me. You think it's all related?"

"Maybe."

"Don't beat around the bush, Henrik. We're colleagues, for Christ's sake."

"I'm not. I think that Bolanaki was silenced by someone, and we still don't know who. And I don't like not knowing. I want answers, but we may never get them."

"No, not now anyway, because it seems to be pretty hushed up."

"Exactly. No one's talking," Henrik said, deep in thought.

Mia pushed her plate away from her and stood up, jacket in hand.

"It's late," she said. "Let's be done for today, okay?"

"Sounds like a good plan," Henrik said, yawning.

"Do I have anything in my teeth?" she asked, smiling widely.

"No."

"Good. See you tomorrow then. And thanks for the sandwich, by the way."

"You're welcome," Henrik said. "Don't you want a ride home?"

"I'm not going home," she said, waving over her shoulder before disappearing through the door.

What was she doing here, really? She shouldn't have come. She should turn around, leave Robin Stenberg alone. Shouldn't let the aggression and her nervous instincts take over.

The stairwell was mercifully dark as Jana Berzelius stood unmoving outside Robin Stenberg's apartment.

She swallowed, closed her eyes for a moment and went back down the stairs.

The night air cooled her body as she stepped back onto the street. The snow crunched slightly under her feet. She stood still for a few seconds, looking around. She breathed deeply, feeling her body relax.

The snow on the sidewalk was so trampled that no one would be able to follow her footprints. No one would know she'd been here.

She remained standing for fifteen seconds and listened to the stillness of the cold winter evening. Then she continued back to her car, under the cover of shadows and darkness, keeping a watchful, sweeping eye over her surroundings.

She saw that it was getting close to eight thirty and hastened her steps.

Per Åström looked at the clock for the second time. Three minutes left before they were supposed to meet.

He nodded a greeting to an acquaintance who came through the entrance to The Lamp Hotel and its restaurant, Ardor. He shivered and stamped his feet. Under his green jacket, he wore a shirt and loosely tied tie, black dress pants and polished shoes. The red rug he was standing on was wet with melted snow. The flames from the outdoor candles danced in the wind.

He looked at the clock again and saw that it said eight thirty. Just then, he heard the sound of high heels. Jana Berzelius came toward him, her back straight and head held high.

"I didn't think you were going to come," he said.

"You thought wrong," she said.

Per smiled and bowed deeply. "After you."

They went into the packed restaurant. The reserved table stood under the large silver lamp. Jana immediately sat down, laid the cloth napkin on her lap, took the menu from the server and glanced at the select few entrées listed there.

Per ordered a bottle of red wine.

"I prefer white," Jana said.

"But I was thinking of having meat."

"Me, too."

"Okay, then we'll have white instead," Per said to the server, laying his menu to the side and looking at Jana.

"What is it?" she asked without looking up from the menu.

"It just feels good to see you again."

"Don't get sentimental now."

"I can't promise anything. Maybe I'll make a scene, here and now."

Jana raised one eyebrow, still not looking at him.

He smiled teasingly and glanced quickly at the menu, deciding quickly.

The server returned with the wine, poured two glasses and stood with her hands behind her back.

"I'll take the entrecôte," Per said.

"The same for me," Jana said.

"Good choice," said the server, taking the menus. "How would you like it done?"

"Medium rare," Per said. "And you?"

He nodded toward Jana. She met his gaze.

"Same here," she said.

"I thought you preferred yours rare."

"Not today."

TWELVE

OFFICER GABRIEL MELLQVIST SET THE emergency brake, opened his car door and got out.

The call had come in at 8:34 a.m. from a woman named Sussie Anander. She had been completely hysterical, screaming at the emergency operator. Now she stood there silently in the stairwell as Gabriel came through the door. He nodded at her but didn't stop, leaving her with his colleague Hanna Hultman as he continued up the stairs, taking two at a time. He smelled cigarettes and trash and heard loud, upset voices from the first floor. He ran up to the fourth floor, not bothering to use the loose handrail.

It was not the first time Gabriel had answered a call knowing someone was seriously hurt or even dead. Not infrequently, parents were the ones who suspected that their son or daughter was in trouble, that they were lying unconscious or unable to call for help. Sometimes it was a false alarm and the person in question had knowingly avoided contact, ignored phone calls or for various reasons ignored their loved ones, who then became unnecessarily anxious. But Gabriel had also found young women who had cut themselves so badly that they had bled to death, or women who had been abused so severely that they died, or men who had attempted suicide. And been successful.

Gabriel heard the sound of sniffling and then Hanna's calm voice from below. He listened for a moment before putting on the gloves he kept in his pocket, reaching forward and turning the door handle. The door swung open softly.

He stepped inside. Everything was quiet and still. The upset voices were no longer audible. He saw three pairs of shoes, a lined denim jacket and a guitar case in the entryway. He closed the front door behind him, wiped his shoes on the mat and went into the apartment. The drapes were closed and it smelled musty. The apartment was silent.

He continued across the floor.

First he saw a TV sitting on a low table, its screen black. Then he saw the young man with eight black stars on his temple.

Gabriel could have believed he was sleeping if it weren't for the deep cut around his neck.

Pim moved toward the door, but she couldn't quite reach it. The ropes still restricted her movement. Fingers trembling, she felt along the wall, searching for cracks, loose boards, anything that might help get her out of this room.

She searched around the dark steps that led to an upper floor, picked off small splinters from the floor, felt along the door frame.

A little bit of light trickled in from somewhere outside the room. It was the only thing preventing her from sitting in complete darkness.

She had to hurry. The last time she received food, she had only had five minutes to eat the dry bread before the man returned.

She felt along the floor with both palms. When she reached the bucket, she paused, sitting, staring at the capsules that lay there in the disgusting muck.

Then she continued to search the floor, as far as the ropes allowed her, and finally found a hatch. She tried to pull it, but it was stuck. Her fingers slipped before she could get a grip on it.

Then she heard the sound of a car, and the footsteps, the determined footsteps, outside the door.

She crept back to the corner, sank down and tried to make herself as small as possible. She felt her body trembling.

The door flew open a moment later, revealing the man, who came in and walked straight toward her. He grabbed her arm.

"Did you eat?" he asked in English, looking at her plate.

She began kicking and screaming, yelling that it hurt, that he should let her go, leave her alone. But he didn't listen, instead pulling her to the bucket and counting aloud. He tightened his grip on her arm, and she knew why.

There were only twenty-three capsules in the bucket.

"Please," she said. "Let me go."

"Go?" he said with a sneer. "Where would you go? You're not going anywhere."

"I want to go home…"

He laughed loudly in her face.

"Home?"

"Please, please, let me go."

"You know what? You're not going home. You're stuck here with me until you've delivered the goods."

"But I have to go home, I have a little sister who…"

"Sorry," he said. "To disappoint you, I mean."

She noticed the door was open and saw the cold, frozen ground outside.

She started hitting in an attempt to get away. She pulled his hair, tried to scratch his face. But the ropes around her wrists made it impossible.

She threw herself backward with the weight of her whole body to free her arm from his grip. She screamed as loud as she could, kicking again and again. He let go. She saw her chance and began running—but she'd forgotten about the ropes and violently jerked to a halt when the ropes became taut.

She crumpled in front of him, silent.

"You're not going anywhere," he said.

Picking up the empty plate, he said something she couldn't understand before disappearing through the door.

She watched as he closed it. The only way out.

Henrik Levin ended the conversation with a sigh. Yet another murder.

He sensed he was being watched and looked up. His daughter, Vilma, stood next to his bed, looking sad. Her hair was disheveled and her cheeks red.

"Daddy," she whispered. "I think I have a fever."

"Come here," he said, letting her crawl in under the covers. She lay snuggled up against him and he felt her warm skin next to his.

He laid his hand on her forehead.

"You don't feel like you have a fever."

"Can't you check with the thee-mometer?"

He smiled at her pronunciation, climbing carefully out of the bed. He opened the bathroom cabinet and took the digital thermometer from its case.

Vilma was sitting up in the bed when he returned. She poked her mother.

"No, no, no," he whispered. "Let Mommy sleep."

"I'm awake," Emma mumbled, her face pressed into her pillow.

"Now let's see."

Henrik put the thermometer in Vilma's ear, waited until it beeped and read the number.

"No fever," he said. "How lucky."

"But I think I do have one."

"Do you want to have a fever?"

"Yes!"

"Why is that?"

"Because then you can stay home with me."

He hugged her, kissing her forehead.

"Mommy is home with you," he said.

Emma had rolled toward them in the bed and was looking at him with sleepy eyes.

"When do you have to leave?" she asked.

He looked at the clock and saw that it said eight o'clock.

"Right about now."

"When will you be home?"

"I don't know. Some things have come up that I have to take care of."

"'Some things'? Yesterday you said that you were just going to work for a couple hours, and it was a lot more than a couple."

"It took longer than I thought… I'm sorry…"

Henrik combed his hand through his hair, conscious that he had just done the one thing he shouldn't do. He shouldn't apologize for needing to do his job. Instead he should be telling his wife that a young man had been found dead in his apartment, and *that* was why he needed to do his job. But he couldn't say that, not with Vilma right there.

"Listen, I really need to spend extra time at work today, too."

"You always need more time. But think about us! We need more time, too."

"What do you mean, more time?"

"With you. We want to be with *you*."

He sighed heavily, knowing that it was a compliment. Maybe that was why it was so hard. He felt like he was deserting them.

"But it's a difficult time right now."

"What does that mean?" Vilma blinked at him.

"Go and play in your room for a little while," Henrik said, setting her feet on the floor.

"Can't you let someone else work today?" Emma asked when Vilma had disappeared through the open door. "It's not supposed to be like this, is it?"

"Like this?"

"With you working every weekend."

"I don't work every weekend. Have you said that to Vilma?"

"That you work a lot? No, she's big enough to understand that herself."

"And you understand that I can't just have someone else do my work, right?"

Emma laid her arm over her forehead and closed her eyes.

"I thought we were going to go out and buy a stroller," she said.

"What's wrong with the old one?"

"It's five years old."

"But it still works."

"Barely. I saw a white one I like. At Babies "R" Us."

"When did you go there?"

"Last weekend."

"Without me?"

"You were working."

Henrik got out of bed and quietly got dressed. He stood for a moment and looked at Emma, who had turned her back to him. He was just about to say *I love you* when the cell phone rang again.

Jana Berzelius sat in her kitchen, looking at a bowl of yogurt with sliced melon and pineapple. She wasn't hungry and pushed the bowl away, turning her gaze toward the morning news on her Mac-Book.

It was quiet in her apartment, but she heard sirens in the distance. Through the large windows she saw lights on in the surrounding apartments. The street below was lit like a Christmas tree.

When she had come home from her dinner with Per the previous night, she found she couldn't sleep. Her thoughts were racing and had kept her up.

She wondered if she would ever be able to tell anyone who she really was.

There had been a moment during dinner when she could have told Per, but the moment had quickly passed. She had stopped herself and couldn't for the life of her imagine how he would react if he had known that just minutes before they met, she had been on her way to a young man's house to…

To what?

She sighed, knowing she couldn't keep this up anymore.

Just a few days earlier, she vowed to stop caring about the past and focus only on the present. She had to follow through on this decision and not allow herself to be led by aggression and instinct. No more.

That was enough.

She got up and went into her bedroom, looking at the boxes with all of the notes, pictures and books that were stacked against the wall. She didn't want anything to do with them anymore. She couldn't imagine just throwing it all away, though. At the same time, she couldn't keep it all in her home. She had to get it out, away from her apartment. Now. Immediately.

She went back to the kitchen, picked up the bowl and emptied it into the sink. Instead of eating, she would start the day by looking for a good place to store everything. She pulled her MacBook toward her and opened Google.

People were already milling about Spelmansgatan 62. The area around the building was roped off, and officers had begun searching the surrounding area and nearby buildings.

Henrik Levin crouched down and looked at Robin Stenberg, who lay dead against the wall. Anneli Lindgren pointed the lamp toward the body, picked up his arm and inspected it.

"Fully developed rigor mortis," she said.

"So he's been dead for a while," Henrik said.

"I'd guess around ten or twelve hours, but could be less."

Henrik followed Anneli's methodic procedure. He had always liked watching as she worked so systematically, photographing crime scenes, finding clues and carefully following protocol.

He got up and looked around. He saw no direct signs of a break-in or a struggle in the room.

"Are you finding anything?" he asked Anneli.

She shook her head just as Mia Bolander appeared in the doorway.

"And what do you make of this?" she said to Henrik.

"That whoever did it knew him."

"Why do you think that?"

"His wallet is still here. Cell phone, too. Aside from the gash on his neck, there's nothing to indicate that this is a crime scene. It's remarkably clinical. This isn't a typical murder. I…"

Henrik stopped short when he saw a number ticket on the floor from a take-a-number machine. It was in the corner, folded in such a way that he could see the first few letters. He put on gloves before picking it up.

"I'll take that," Anneli Lindgren said, holding out a plastic evidence bag.

Henrik dropped the ticket into it and looked around again. He had an uneasy feeling that they weren't going to find anything important in the apartment. No fingerprints, no DNA. No mysterious telephone calls or testimonies from the neighbors, either.

"It could be revenge for something he did," Henrik said. "Who is this guy? Anyone we know?"

"Not really," Mia said. "But he's not completely clean, if you catch my drift."

"So what do we have on him?"

"Narcotics misdemeanors."

Henrik sighed.

"For his own use, or for selling?"

"I can't speak to that," Mia said. "But it feels really shitty to have this on our plates right now. You and I should work on something else today."

Henrik didn't answer. He was looking around the room for potential hiding places where Robin may have kept his drugs.

After two hours, he gave up and decided to go down to the station. Once there, he poured a cup of coffee, and as he took a sip, he received confirmation from the technicians.

No drugs.

No traces of anything.

That clinched it. Whoever had been in Robin Stenberg's apartment yesterday evening was no amateur. But the question remained: *Why* had that person been there?

THIRTEEN

JANA BERZELIUS ACCEPTED THE bronze-colored key, signed the storage rental contract and paid the rent for the entire year in cash. The property owner, Stig Ottling, thanked her for her patronage and wished her good luck.

"The building is a little shabby, but the attic storage is fairly clean. Well, actually, I haven't been there in six months. But it should be good enough for storage. The building will be renovated, but not for a few years," he said apologetically, and launched into a long harangue that there was a great desire among the city's residents to develop the area where the property stood, to attract more businesses, to establish themselves in the area, and to create attractive spaces to foster the tourism industry. This would require building more restaurants, creating commercial space, light-filled offices. But also residential apartments.

"Yes, but it will take time, as I said, so you can use the storage space however you want. There are hardly any other renters, just a music club, an old pool hall, things like that. Did I give you the key?"

Jana nodded, thanked him, and leaving the apartment in Kneippen, drove directly to the industrial district and Garvaregatan 6.

The storage space was surprisingly small.

But she recognized it. It looked exactly how it had been presented in the ad. The wooden bench and the filing cabinet with a padlock. The light yellow concrete walls.

It smelled damp, musty and stuffy.

She put the box she was carrying on the floor, thought better of it, and placed it on the wooden bench instead. She felt a thin thread against her neck and swept away the remains of a spiderweb with her hand.

She took a deep breath and convinced herself that the small space would be enough. There was no other storage space for rent, not near her apartment, and definitely not on such short notice.

She got the rest of the boxes from her car and lined them up on the bench. She noted that she would have to get plastic bins of some sort because the boxes would surely absorb the moisture.

Then she heard it.

A sound, as if someone were knocking.

She froze, holding her breath and listening.

There it was again. Someone knocking.

It was Saturday afternoon and the building

seemed empty. No bands rehearsing, no association meetings. No residents—the place was too run-down for that. But someone was knocking.

She went to the door and listened. She heard it again. She waited a few seconds, then walked with quick, silent steps out of the storage area and stopped at the stairs, trying to figure out where the sound was coming from.

But there weren't any other doors on that floor.

She took another step down the stairs. And one more.

The knocking became quieter. She went back up to the storage area and stood against the wall across from the door, pressing one ear against the cool concrete, holding her breath.

Knock. Knock. Knock.

It was coming from the pipes. Someone or something was knocking on them.

She went down the stairs and out onto the street. She looked in the windows but saw only darkness. She held her breath, listening, and had the feeling that the whole building in front of her was also holding its breath.

Maybe I was imagining things, she thought.

At that very moment, she got a text from Per asking if they could get together for coffee. Realizing she was now hungry, she answered him immediately.

With a determined gait, she left without noticing the shadow moving slowly inside one of the windows of the building.

* * *

He heard her puttering about in the kitchen. Margaretha had been at it all morning. The aroma spread through the house. Like a gas, it had filled its container, reaching into every corner, permeating the clothes, fabrics, curtains. The smell of a freshly baked cake coming out of the oven. The smell of anxiety.

Karl Berzelius closed the door to his office.

He couldn't sit still. The only thing he could think about was that Jana was coming today, and that didn't feel right.

He tried to focus on one of the paintings on the wall, but it was like the color had been suddenly sucked out of it, black horsemen in a gray landscape.

The painting next to it was just as colorless. Three faces immortalized in oil. He tried to remember when it had been painted.

Searching through his memories, both light and dark ones.

Some consciously repressed, others erased by alcohol.

But then he saw tiny, minuscule glimpses of color. Red, green, brown. Swirling around each other. Autumn leaves dancing in the wind, against a clear blue sky. And he remembered the day they were walking around Stockholm. They had eaten at the Grand Hotel, walked along Strandvägen, gone into shops and looked at furnishings and china.

And a necklace.

It had been resting in a red box in the middle of a display window, all by itself.

He had gone into the shop and bought it, and had it engraved with both of their initials: *to JB from KB*. He had put it around her neck and said something apologetic to her, something that really could be taken as nonchalant, that couldn't be taken as a declaration of love. Or maybe he hadn't said anything, he couldn't remember now. Margaretha had laughed, at the purchase, at the occasion or lack thereof, happy that he was finally showing some affection for their daughter. It was as if all of his feelings lay in the glittering, expensive necklace that now encircled her neck.

Jana's neck.

But she didn't smile. Not then, not ever.

It was as if she couldn't.

He looked at the painting again, seeing the narrow line on her face. It was a smile that said everything and nothing. A practiced smile that had stuck, glued on her lips. He searched his memories, every moment he could remember, but could not come up with a single time that she had smiled spontaneously, eyes sparkling, dimples showing.

He was gripped with sorrow; it felt like a claw around his neck. He swallowed a few times to make it release.

Then there was a knock at his office door. Margaretha came in holding two mugs.

"I don't want any glogg," he said.

"I know, that's why I made some coffee for you."

She smiled and the color returned to the room. He loved his wife's smile, wished she could smile all the time, wished he could tell her that.

"You look pale. Are you feeling well?" she asked.

He swallowed again. The claw was still there around his neck, squeezing harder now.

He took the coffee and slurped it. Standing silently, he looked at her.

"I baked a saffron cake," she said.

Karl turned his gaze toward the snow-covered trees.

"She's coming at four o'clock."

"I know."

"Will you join us?"

"No."

"Why not?"

"I have a meeting."

"At that exact time?"

"Yes."

Margaretha looked at him dejectedly.

"What exactly did she do to you?"

He didn't answer. A crease appeared between his wide, gray eyebrows.

"Regardless," she said. "It's possible to leave the past behind, you know."

No, it's not, he thought, turning his head away as the first tear trickled down his cheek.

"What's that?"

Per Åström wrinkled his nose when Jana Berzelius placed a tray on the table before him, revealing mineral water, two chicken salads and a covered plastic cup containing a green smoothie. They had taken the last available table at restaurant Asken. On the table sat a wide pillar candle, its three wicks lit festively. The air was warm and heavy.

"A vegetable smoothie," she said.

"It looks like bile," he said.

"Do you want a taste?" she asked.

"And risk all those healthy side effects? No, thanks."

Per took the mineral water and a salad while Jana looked out the window at the people walking around. Many had their hands full of shopping bags, and it seemed that the Christmas shopping season was under way.

"It's better in the summer, don't you think?" Per asked.

"Maybe," she said, beginning to poke around in her salad.

"There's so much more to do."

"Like?"

"You're kidding. You can lie in the sun, have a picnic, go boating, go in the water…"

"Go in the water?"

"Yes, you know—to cool off."

"The only water I go in is my shower."

"You're hopeless." Per sighed. "Don't your parents have a summerhouse on the coast?"

"Yes."

"Don't you ever go swimming there?"

"No."

"What do you do there, then?"

"Enjoy the peace and quiet."

"But it's never quiet on the coast in the summertime. I mean, with the noisy motorboats, screeching gulls, drunk tourists…"

"But not during the winter." Jana put the straw to her mouth and drank her smoothie. She met Per's gaze. His eyebrows were drawn down over his different-colored eyes. He looked serious.

"What?" she asked.

"I'm seriously considering suing you," he said.

"Am I accused of something?"

"Lack of legal excuse. You haven't given me any reason for your absence that can explain why you have failed to appear at dinners or other friendly gatherings over a time frame of several months."

"But that does not preclude that there could be a valid reason," she said. "And if I am not mistaken, the consequence of legal excuse is that a cause is removed from the list, or that the cause is postponed until another time. And I believe, your honor, that yesterday was such a time that the cause could be taken up again; that is, the dinner was carried out. And in consideration of the fact that I chose to meet you again today, this should in some way be deemed good enough. Happy?"

"Happy. I still can't stop feeling a little curious about your 'legal excuse,' but we'll have to take that up another time," he said. "Unfortunately, I'm in a bit of a hurry. You can be thankful I was able to meet you."

"But didn't you call me?"

"Doesn't matter."

"You mean that I'm the one who should be thankful?"

"Something like that."

"Yet you were the one who wanted to meet?"

"I'm incurably overly optimistic where time is concerned."

"Is it contagious?"

"Temporarily, maybe."

Jana cocked her head to one side.

"Where are you hurrying off to?" she asked.

"Work," Per said. "I got a new case. The police suspect murder. The victim is a young man in Navestad."

"In Navestad?"

"Yep. Name is Robin Stenberg, just twenty years old."

"What?" Jana exclaimed. She coughed and spilled her smoothie all over the table.

"I'm sorry," she said, wiping her mouth with a napkin. "I swallowed wrong."

"Do you know anything about it?" Per asked, looking at her closely.

"No, nothing at all, I just… Did you say murder?"

She took another napkin and began wiping the table, feeling her pulse increase.

Per leaned over the table, watching Jana's hand as she wiped the last specks, and lowered his voice.

"Yes. His mother found him in his apartment. His throat had been slit. Crazy, right?"

Jana nodded slowly. She heard Per's voice as if it were far away, heard the murmuring of other people around her, but she felt a compact silence inside her.

The flames from the candle flickered as two people walked past their table.

"Hello?" Per said. "Are you listening?"

Jana licked her lips and cleared her throat.

"What do the police think happened?" she forced herself to ask.

Per looked at his watch.

"I'll know that in ten minutes, and I'm sorry, but I really have to go now. I'll talk to you later, okay? And I don't mean in a few months."

Jana nodded.

"Oh, and," he said, pointing to her chest, "you have something on your shirt."

Jana looked down and saw the green spot on her blouse. She wiped it with a napkin but it stubbornly remained.

CHAPTER

FOURTEEN

GUNNAR ÖHRN KNOCKED ON THE TABLE with his pointer finger and looked at the team sitting before him in the conference room. Henrik, Mia, Ola and Anneli were all looking at him and the whiteboard on which he had written three points.

"It seems that…" Gunnar began before he was interrupted by Per Åström coming into the room.

Per made an apologetic gesture and sat down at the table.

Gunnar rubbed his hand over his hair. "It seems," he said, "that someone we have yet to identify was able to, without any witnesses, enter the young man Robin Stenberg's apartment and take his life. Judging from the injuries, the perpetrator used a knife, though no murder weapon has been found in the apartment or the surrounding area. But the technical investigation is still in progress."

He flipped through the report on the table.

"The victim was found dead in his apartment

this morning. The call came in at 8:34, and officer Gabriel Mellqvist arrived on the scene at 8:55. We have no leads at this time," Gunnar said, looking up from his glasses.

"None at all?" Per asked.

"No," said Anneli. "Not because the apartment had been cleaned, but because we still haven't found any reliable trace of any other person. Whoever did this was a very methodical killer."

"The perpetrator leaves the apartment and disappears without anyone having seen or heard anything," Gunnar said. "There's a cellar door to the building that could have been used as an escape route, but that assumes that the perpetrator had a key."

"But is there anything that suggests that door was used?" Henrik asked.

"No, but as I said, the technical investigation is still in progress."

"And what do we know about the victim?" Per asked.

"He was a student, taking some courses at the university here in Norrköping," Henrik said.

"Does he have a record?" Per asked.

"Yes," Henrik said. "Possession of a controlled substance."

"And he lived in Navestad," Mia said, "where we've had to straighten out a few things. They seem to have their own justice system."

"Who are 'they'?" Henrik asked.

"The gangs. Threats and extortion are routine

out there. And you said yourself the victim may have known the perpetrator."

"Yes, I think that we can start with that theory," Henrik said. "In any case, it was an incredibly precise incision around the victim's neck, which means that it was carried out by someone who was comfortable using a knife. The murder seems well-planned. There were no other stab wounds to the body. The goal was to kill, plain and simple."

Everyone sat quietly for a moment.

"Career criminal, in other words," Gunnar said. "And the victim wasn't in a gang?"

"There's nothing to suggest that, no," said Ola. "But we do know that he was fairly politically active. Left-wing activist, maybe."

"Extreme left-wing?" Per asked.

"I don't know," Ola said. "I'll check him out thoroughly. We've confiscated his computer."

"Check it immediately after this meeting," Gunnar said.

"I will," Ola replied.

"Do we know if he was still using drugs?" Per asked.

"Unfortunately not," Henrik said. "But we'll have to check that out, too. It's very possible that he was still using, that the murder was a drug-related dispute of some sort…in the underworld, that is."

"Or a debt," Mia said. "Maybe he owed someone money, couldn't finance his drug problem."

"Henrik and Mia," Gunnar said. "You continue to survey the territory around the narcotics trade in town, maybe revisit the people you've already talked to. Check the criminal network."

"As I've understood it," Henrik said, "Gavril Bolanaki controlled a large piece of the market. But otherwise it's primarily the motorcycle gangs that are dominant here."

"That's true," Gunnar said. "They've steadily built up influence based on fear and violence, and they're using that to control the narcotics trade and to employ extortion against business leaders within, for example, the hospitality industry. But there are many more networks than just them."

He quickly counted them: Red & White Crew, Black Cobra, M-16, Gypsy Bloods, Asir, the Berga Gang, Berga Boys, Outlaws and Bandidos.

"These networks primarily attack each other because they are competing for the same market. We've seen this numerous times. In March of 2011, a man was stabbed in an apartment on Bråbogatan. Later the same evening, downtown, another man was shot in the leg. Four men were arrested, but they were released due to lack of evidence. One of them was said to be the leader of the Black Cobras. In June that same year, gunshots were fired outside the Deli pub, and that was Black Cobras attacking members of the Outlaws. The district court acquitted all of the defendants, but on appeal one of the men connected to the Black Cobras was sentenced to five years in prison for attempted murder."

Gunnar held his finger up in the air.

"But..." he said, "the problem is that new constellations are appearing all the time. People group themselves according to a certain gang membership, ethnicity or family tie. The configuration of the gang becomes incredibly complex, and here in town there are, as we've talked about, indications that a new leader is on the verge of rising to the top—it's tense out there right now.

"I think we would have had a good bird's-eye view of all of it if we'd been able to keep Gavril Bolanaki alive," Gunnar said.

"Bolanaki?" Per asked.

"Jana's case," Henrik said. "Bolanaki was the brains behind one of the narcotics syndicates that we as yet knew nothing about…"

"…that was using child soldiers. Now I remember," Per said. "He was murdered, right?"

"We still don't know what happened to him," Henrik said. "The National Crime Squad claims that he committed suicide. But regardless, he's dead."

"What happened to the market when he was gone?" Per asked.

"And why isn't more being done to stop the development of the market? Why aren't more people being prosecuted?" Mia said.

"You probably know the answer to your own questions," Gunnar said. "No one wants to say anything. They've got each other's backs. You can ask, but no one knows anything."

"Exactly what's happening with The Old Man," Henrik said.

"Yes, exactly," Gunnar said. "You've mentioned him before. What do we know about him?"

"I've already told you," Henrik said.

"But you haven't said anything," Gunnar said.

"That's just it," Henrik said. "That's because there isn't anything to say. Everyone's keeping their mouths shut. And why do people keep their mouths shut?"

"Because they're scared," Mia said.

"Exactly," Henrik said.

"Okay," Gunnar said. "But if we're going to focus on Robin, how are we going to find the perpetrator? Who should we talk to?"

"Mia and I will start by questioning Robin's mother, Sussie Anander. She wasn't in any condition to answer questions this morning."

"And I'll take the computer, like we said," Ola said.

"And you guys keep me updated about what you find," Per said.

Henrik and Ola nodded.

"Good," Gunnar said. "We have to be effective. We'll learn everything we can about Robin. It's probably like you already said, Henrik, that the murderer was close to him. Check out all of his friends, enemies, girlfriends, parents, relatives, everyone. I want this to end up in the pile of quickly solved cases."

"Excuse me, can I get you anything else?"

The server focused her large blue eyes on Jana

Berzelius, who sat with her gaze fixed on a point far outside the window. Her salad was still untouched. Per's plate and mineral water were still there even though he had left more than an hour earlier.

She saw the young woman out of the corner of her eye.

"Otherwise perhaps you could leave the table for other guests?" she said.

"I'm leaving now," Jana said, getting up.

The server immediately began clearing the table. Jana buttoned her jacket, pulled on her gloves and wound her black Louis Vuitton scarf twice around her neck. Then she walked straight out into the cold, standing for a moment with her eyes toward the sky.

Snowflakes whirled outside picture windows, around lit shop signs and along the sidewalks.

The streetlights glowed like frosty lanterns. People were everywhere. Three women stood talking with each other, laughing loudly and opening their shopping bags to compare their recent purchases.

Jana's long, dark hair rustled in the wind and was swept in front of her face.

Her hands were clenched.

Robin Stenberg was dead.

Murdered!

Why?

It must be sheer coincidence that Robin was murdered after having happened upon her and Danilo at the entrance to Knäppingsborg. But why? Who could feel more threatened by what Robin had seen than she?

Danilo?

She tried to force herself to stop, but her thoughts remained with him and the fact that she had been at the scene of the crime the very night it had occurred. Her heart was pounding loudly when she finally began walking.

Henrik Levin pushed up his sleeves before sitting down next to Mia Bolander in the kitchen on the fifth floor of a Ljura neighborhood apartment building. He looked at Sussie Anander, who stood leaning on the stove with her fingers wrapped around a cigarette. She looked like a woman on a downward spiral, but maybe he was just looking at a grieving mother.

He knew he'd soon be asked the most difficult question, the one that no parent ever wanted to have to ask: *Why did someone take my child from me?*

After the usual formalities, Henrik explained that they hoped she would be able to help shed a little light on this horrible situation. She remained silent. The only sound was the squeak of a chair, the weak hum of the fan over the stove and a sigh. Henrik was also silent, waiting for Sussie's first words.

She slowly exhaled the smoke, wiped her nose with the back of her hand and tapped the ash from her cigarette into a glass jar.

"Did he have socks on?" she asked quietly.

Her chin was angular and her eyebrows drawn

on. She was wearing black jeans, a brown T-shirt and silver rings on all of the fingers of her left hand except her thumb.

"Why do you ask?" Henrik said.

"The floor in his apartment was cold, you know, so I had told him he should always wear socks. And I don't remember, was he?"

Although Sussie spoke in a calm voice, he noticed a constant tremor in her head. She tightened the gold-colored lid on the glass jar.

"Yes," Henrik replied.

"Good."

She remained at the stove, holding the jar as if she were never going to let it go.

"Can you tell us a little bit about Robin?"

She talked about his childhood and adolescence in great detail—his personality, his mediocre performance in school. When she came to his moving out, she grew quiet.

"He moved out at a young age?" Henrik asked.

"Yes, four years ago," Sussie answered. "He was only sixteen, but he needed a change of scenery, a new beginning."

"A change of scenery from what?"

"From me, maybe. From life? I don't know."

She sighed heavily.

"Before that, he would sometimes be gone for several days in a row. He always did what he wanted."

"Where would he go?"

"Anywhere," she said.

"Any siblings?" Henrik asked.

"No," Sussie said with a sad expression, setting the jar down. "He was an only child. He liked being alone—completely alone, I mean, with his thoughts. He didn't like talking."

She shrugged her shoulders, took a deep breath.

"I didn't know what I should do. I called a psychologist once, but Robin didn't want to go. He wasn't of age yet, but even so, I couldn't do anything. Typical teenage rebellion, people said. I felt so helpless, you know? In the beginning, I'd go out and look for him, and I often found him where local bands practiced, but he would never come home with me. He said he was better off without me, so I stopped looking. I let him be. In the end, he moved out."

"He played guitar?" Henrik asked.

"Yes. How did you know that?" Sussie replied.

"I saw a guitar case in his apartment."

"He loved playing. He'd been playing for a long time. He was good."

Sussie dried a tear. Her mascara was running and was now smeared onto her cheek.

"Did he play in a band?" Mia asked.

"No, but he liked to hang out at the rehearsal space, where the others played."

"Where is that?"

Sussie thought for a moment. Her hands were trembling as she fished out another cigarette.

"There have been a few over the years. In the industrial district, for one, and at different clubs and such, but lately he'd been spending a lot of time at the community arts center."

Henrik nodded to Mia as if to say they would start at the arts center after leaving Sussie's apartment.

"What were his friends like? Was he particularly close to anyone, did he have any enemies?"

Sussie had put the cigarette between her lips, but the lighter wouldn't spark. She tossed it onto the counter and took a new one from the cupboard.

"He didn't have friends or enemies, from what I know. He just had his guitar. And his computer, of course," Sussie said, exhaling smoke toward the ceiling. "He was always sitting there staring at it."

New tears trickled down her cheeks.

"Sorry," she said.

"You don't need to apologize," Henrik said, looking at her exhausted face, her dry, pale lips.

"When did you last see Robin?" Mia asked, waving her hand in front of her face and coughing a little to show that she didn't like sitting in the smoke-filled kitchen.

"A week ago," Sussie said.

"How did he seem then?"

"Himself."

Sussie shook her head, swallowing.

"On Saturdays I usually swing by with a little food—a loaf of bread, some butter, other milk-free things. He was kind of a—what's it called?—veggie-something."

"Vegan?" Mia asked.

"No, vegetarian," Sussie said. "He started with that when he was only thirteen. That's typical, I've heard. A sort of revolt, but it was nothing compared to how he reacted when Jesper died. His father. Cancer everywhere—stomach, lungs... He had ten tumors in his head, can you believe it? They couldn't do anything. All we could do was watch."

Henrik sat quietly, struck with strong compassion for this woman who had lost both her son and her husband.

"How did Robin react to that?" he asked in a calm voice.

Sussie twirled her cigarette against the inside of the glass jar.

"Robin has never been much of one for talking, like I said, but when Jesper died, I couldn't talk to him at all. But I wanted to talk, so that was hard. And then when I found the bag, I'd had enough. I just couldn't do it any longer."

"The bag? Do you mean drugs, that he started doing drugs?"

"Yeah, first alcohol and tobacco. Then cannabis. I have no idea how he got his hands on all of it, but when I noticed the heroin, I finally understood it was serious. I mean, heroin is for serious addicts. Not for kids like my Robin. I wanted to stop it, right away."

"So you called the police?"

"Yes. I know it was wrong of me, but..."

"I don't think it was wrong," Mia said. "I think it was the best thing you could have done."

"You reported him a year ago," Henrik said. "Do you know if he continued to abuse drugs?"

"No, but I assume he did. I can't even think about it right now, I…"

Sussie fell silent, her eyes filling with tears.

"When you arrived at Robin's this morning with the food," Henrik said, "did you see anything unusual?"

"No, he was just lying there, he…"

Sussie shook her head, sniffling, one hand pressed against her forehead.

"You have a different surname than Robin, is that right?" Mia asked when Sussie had composed herself.

"Yeah. I happened to meet a new man, Peter," Sussie said. "Or, well, we met even before Jesper died. Robin wasn't too happy about that, as you can guess. But what the hell was I supposed to do? I couldn't just sit there and rot while I waited for Jesper to die. I had to think about myself a little bit, too."

"When did he die?" Mia asked.

"Six months ago. Peter and I got married right after. Jesper said that he wanted me to be happy, so…"

"Did Peter get along with Robin?" Henrik asked.

"They didn't see each other often," Sussie said, putting her cigarette out and wrapping her arms around her body. "Honestly, I don't really think men are my thing," she added.

"Why not?"

"Peter's not in the picture anymore, if you get what I mean. He doesn't like conflict, so he left, the idiot. We're getting divorced now."

Sussie's eyes filled with tears.

"But it's okay, it's okay…" she said to herself.

"I've been sitting here and listening to you," Henrik said. "You've been through a lot in such a short time…"

"Yeah…" she said.

"And I think you need some help. Do you want me to help you with that? Find someone you can talk to?"

Sussie sighed.

"No, but I thought I would call my mom."

"Call her now, and we'll make sure someone waits here with you until she comes."

Sussie nodded and went out into the hall. Henrik heard her talking on the phone.

"'Shed a little light,'" Mia said, chuckling.

"What?"

"You said that to Sussie, that you hoped she could help *shed a little light* on this horrible situation."

"Yes, and? Don't people say that?"

"No, Henrik, they don't."

"Yes they do."

"In the fifties, maybe, but not anymore. They just don't. Trust me."

Henrik didn't want to think about what had been said during their conversation, but instead was thinking more about what *hadn't* been said. He thought about Sussie, that not once had she asked that awful question. And Henrik knew he shouldn't feel this way, but he was glad—almost grateful—that he didn't have to give the equally awful answer: *I don't know.*

Gunnar Öhrn stood at the window and looked out over the street. He thought about how he had worked as a policeman his entire adult life. When he was asked twenty years ago if he wanted to become the head of the division, he couldn't refuse. He had moved to a larger office, a more comfortable chair, bigger bookshelves. And when he finally sat there in his new space, he realized that without knowing it, the whole time he had dreamed of becoming the boss. But what was he going to do now? When the new organization was standing there, knocking on the door? Was there anything else to reach for, or would he just dream of being done?

He sighed without being conscious of it and lifted his gaze. He looked at the offices and apartments in the neighboring building, his gaze lingering on windows of bedrooms and living rooms, and he sighed again. Maybe he expected something that wasn't going to happen, maybe he'd been naive when he had hoped that he would be chosen to oversee the Eastern region instead of County Police Commissioner Carin Radler.

He turned toward his desk, sitting down and looking into his water glass. He heard footsteps echoing down the hallway, then voices before Anneli came in through the door.

"It's time for lunch," she said.

"Yes," Gunnar said, barely audible.

"Are we going to eat?" she asked. "I'm hungry."

He didn't answer at first, and Anneli shut the door behind her, taking a couple steps toward him.

"You're brooding over something. What is it?"

"Nothing."

"Yes it is. I know you."

"No."

"But I can tell that there's something, and I don't want to have to drag it out of you every time. Now just tell me!"

Gunnar picked up his glass, closed one eye and looked at the water with the other.

"I don't like that he's here," he said.

"He's the head of the National Crime Squad. He's supposed to be here."

"That's not why."

Anneli sighed, crossing her arms over her chest. She sighed again.

"Remember that I said it didn't mean anything."

She lowered her voice so she wouldn't risk her colleagues hearing them through the walls.

"It was a long time ago, you know that."

"But I think about it anyway," he said, putting the glass down.

"You and I weren't even together then."

"Doesn't matter."

"Yes it does."

"No it doesn't. I don't like that type of guy."

"Oh, now you can just go…"

"I just don't like the thought that he…"

"That he what?"

"Nothing."

"Just say it!"

He met her eyes and understood that she was mad. He was scared, consumed by a feeling of inadequacy, that what he was wasn't enough for her.

"I'm sorry," he said, reaching out his hand. "It's just really difficult to have him looking over my shoulder all the time. What do you say to pizza for lunch?"

Anneli released her arms to her sides, shaking her head at him.

"Sure," she said through clenched teeth.

He smiled and reached his hand out to her, expecting her to put her hand in his.

But she didn't.

Henrik Levin and Mia Bolander could hear music as they approached the front door of the community arts center.

Henrik knocked on the door to the large recreation center that housed a concert hall, art gallery and café, but realized that it was pointless because no one could hear them.

Instead, he tried the doorknob, opened the unlocked door and walked in.

Kulturhuset in Norrköping was a creative meeting place for young people. The building was furnished with pieces from across the decades. A moss green living room set from the sixties, armchairs from the seventies, a bright yellow wall from the eighties. In the corner of the concert hall, a stage rose twelve inches from the shiny gray sealed concrete floor. A band comprised of four young women was standing there now, and Henrik thought they were playing an original song until they arrived at the refrain. Only then did he realize they were playing Soft Cell's "Tainted Love."

Henrik and Mia wandered farther into the building, trying to get away from the loud music.

They found a man with a bushy beard and a thin black cloth wrapped around his dreadlocks sitting at a table. He was wearing two tank tops and necklaces made from wooden beads, and his hands were wrapped around a cup of coffee.

"We're police," Henrik said. "We want to ask you about Robin Stenberg."

"Who?" the man asked.

"Robin Stenberg!"

The man shook his head.

"Ask the café!"

Four people sat around a table, talking in low voices, when Henrik and Mia entered Café Manala. A young woman stood behind the counter, transferring freshly baked cookies from a tray onto a platter.

She had blond hair, a low-cut shirt and a tattooed sun on her neck.

"I'm Lisa," she said when Henrik had introduced

himself. "May I offer you a cardamom cookie? No eggs or dairy. It's completely vegan."

Henrik shook his head, as did Mia.

"We're here to ask about Robin Stenberg," Henrik said without needing to shout this time. "Do you know him?"

"I wouldn't say I *know* him. He comes here a lot, almost every Sunday," she said, continuing to stack the cookies on the platter.

"Did he practice here?" Mia asked.

"No, but he likes to hang out here," Lisa said.

"Any particular reason?" Henrik asked.

"Every Sunday we have open jam. We call it Band Camp," Lisa said. "Everyone who wants to can come."

"Do you know who Robin hung out with?"

She suddenly looked at them suspiciously.

"Did he do something?"

"Probably not," Henrik said. "But we're trying to find out who he hung out with."

"I have no idea. There are usually so many people here. Everyone hangs out with each other, really. Sorry."

She shrugged her shoulders and smiled apologetically.

"So can you give us some names?"

"I can't, but you can probably get some from Josefin, who organizes Band Camp. You can call her."

Her arms were cramping up.

Pim felt her skin being torn, warm blood dripping from her little finger to the floor. It hurt—so much. She had rubbed large sores on her hands, wounds that had grown over the hours she had spent grinding the ropes up and down on the small, sharp edge she had found on the wall behind her.

The pain had caused her to say a short prayer that the ropes would break, that she would be able to get away. But no one heard her prayer.

Her movements became weaker and weaker. Up and down. Up and down. In the end, she simply couldn't do it any longer.

She closed her eyes and felt the pain as she pulled her hands up one last time.

And felt the ropes suddenly release.

FIFTEEN

IT WAS FOUR O'CLOCK IN THE AFTER- noon, and the dark gray clouds hung like a heavy blanket over the wealthy Lindö neighborhood. The windshield wipers fought to keep the windshield free from slush. Jana Berzelius watched the black, slushy road in front of her.

She parked her car on the wide driveway and walked up the path to the front door. Ringing the doorbell, she took a step back and waited.

She heard slow steps coming from inside the house, and after a moment the door opened.

"Hello, Mother," she said. Margaretha was wearing an apron and gripping a checked kitchen towel so hard that the veins and ligaments were visible under her pale skin. Her eyes were blue and sparkled merrily; she appeared calm.

"Jana," she said, her laugh lines drawing together behind the thin bows of her eyeglasses. "I'm so glad you could come."

She spoke slowly but smiled happily. She reached out her hands and gave her a hug.

"Come in," she said. "I just have to check on the glogg."

Margaretha disappeared into the kitchen.

Jana hung up her coat and put her shoes neatly on the shoe rack. The scent of saffron greeted her.

She walked down the hall and poked her head into her parents' bedroom. She didn't go in, just looked around at the white walls, large bed, comforter and pillows.

The closet was open, displaying hangers hung with suits, shirts and pants, carefully grouped according to season and color. Every item of clothing was clean, pressed and precisely placed on a hanger. The hangers were all exactly two inches apart.

It felt strange to be home again.

She went back out into the hall, conscious of all the sounds of the house. Ticking, creaking, tapping, humming.

There were clattering sounds from the kitchen.

She went slowly up the stairs and through the hallway to her childhood bedroom. Everything seemed untouched, preserved from when she still lived at home, as if time had stood still since then.

She continued to her father's office and opened the door, exhaling in relief when she saw it was empty. She stepped in and looked around at all of the binders, cabinets and drawers. Various reports, shareholder newsletters, statements of accounts and minutes lay on his desk.

She went across the room, opened a cabinet and took out a white binder. It was in its usual spot on the left—she knew this because she had taken it out so many times before. Her father never knew, though; she only went in when he wasn't home.

She opened the binder and looked at the certificate of her adoption. It had yellowed a bit; it was over twenty years since she'd become a Berzelius, after all.

She remembered the day she had sat in the hallway at the social services office, her eyes locked on her hands lying in her lap.

Now and then, she would raise her hand to touch her neck, where the large bandage was taped.

"Don't do that, honey," Beatrice Malm, the social worker, had said when she came out of her office.

"But it itches," she said.

"Let it itch, then. Just a little while, until they get here."

Beatrice looked at the clock on the wall.

"This is going to be really great," she said in an attempt to calm her. But how she said it made Jana's heart pound harder.

Then they arrived. The man walked in front, the woman three steps behind. His lips were pressed together firmly, but she had a wide smile on her face.

"This is Karl and Margaretha Berzelius," Beatrice Malm said, looking at her.

She slid down from the chair without looking at them and mumbled a greeting.

"And the papers?" Karl asked.

"Everything is in order. Classified, as you requested."

"Great."

Karl turned on his heel toward the elevator.

"Come, sweetheart," Margaretha said, reaching out her hand toward the little girl. Jana didn't dare at first, hesitating for a long time before taking her new mother's hand. It was cool and gentle.

They walked down the hallway and into the elevator.

She lifted her hand toward her hair, but forced it back down when she met the social worker's eyes through the open elevator doors.

"Take good care of her!"

Those were the last words Jana heard before the elevator doors closed again.

Only then did she lift her hand up all the way and scratch.

The scratching was the first thing her father had noticed, the first annoyance, she thought as she closed the binder and returned it to the cabinet.

She saw a red box on the left side of the table. She opened it and looked at the necklace resting within it. She remembered receiving it as a gift long ago, far too long ago. *To JB from KB.*

She looked at it for a long time, reaching inside

to touch it, hesitating at first, then lifting it out and watching it swing from her fingers.

She fastened it around her neck and felt the cold chain against her warm skin.

Just then, she heard her mother call from the first floor.

"Jana, where are you?"

She lifted her hand at first to take off the necklace, but she changed her mind and left it on.

She left the room, the red box sitting on the desk, open and empty.

"Didn't she answer?"

Mia Bolander sat in the passenger seat next to Henrik. Her blond hair stuck out from under her hat. Her cheeks were red, and her hands were wedged between her thighs to warm them.

"No," Henrik said as he heard Josefin Ek's voice mail pick up for the second time.

"Try again, then."

"We'll try again later. She's probably busy with tomorrow's Band Camp. Let's head back to the station instead," he said.

He started the car and drove away quickly from the arts center—a little too quickly, and the car began to slide into the oncoming lane. He regained control and braked carefully. They stopped at a red light.

He sighed heavily.

"How's it going?" Mia asked.

"It's fine."

"And how's Emma?"

He sighed again, thinking about her. He thought about her all the time even though he tried not to because it made him feel guilty.

"She's good, too," he said automatically. "What about you?"

"I'm sort of at a crossroads…" she began.

"About what?" he asked.

"Whether I should go for it or not. With Martin, I mean."

He sighed, thinking how much he disliked being dragged into her personal life.

"But you've only seen each other once, right?" he said.

"Twice, actually. I slept with him last night, too."

"But, Mia, you shouldn't…"

"If you're going to give me a lecture, you can just shut up."

She watched the cars driving in the opposite direction, following them with her gaze.

"But you think, I mean… Is it serious between you two?" he asked.

"I don't think so, but *he* seems to," Mia said.

"He's actually *said* it?" Henrik said, flinching.

"What do you mean?"

"That he loves you?"

"Not exactly, but that's how he's acting."

"Have *you* said it?"

"That I love him? For Christ's sake, I'm not one to say it first."

"How do you feel about him?"

"I might as well. Go for it, I mean."

"But you can't just think like that."

"What do you mean, 'think like that'?"

"Honestly, Mia, Martin Strömberg is not exactly a mother's dream for her daughter… We've just questioned him for being, well, who he is."

"But you're forgetting something. Maybe I'm not looking for my mother's dream for me."

"What *are* you looking for, then? A criminal?"

She looked at Henrik in all seriousness.

"You are so boring, Henrik. But okay, I'll forget about him then."

"Of course you should. You'll find someone else. Someone better, Mia."

"Maybe," she mumbled as the light turned green.

In the last few miles before reaching the coast, he was filled with a sort of inner peace that allowed him to lighten up on the gas. There was no reason to stress right now. The drug mule might need a few extra minutes to release the last of her delivery.

He drove somewhat more slowly past the snow-covered fields and the leafless trees. He felt the wheel tremble when the wheels met the ice-covered edges of the road.

He rested his head on the headrest and smiled, thinking it was time to snuff her out, to make room for someone else.

A quarter-mile from the coast, he turned off the headlights. He didn't want to risk anyone noticing them. Him, really. All it would take was one nosy local and the whole operation would have to move.

It was a problem that the moon was shining far too brightly. It worried him.

Go behind a cloud, for fuck's sake, he thought with his gaze turned toward the large, stubborn celestial body that shone blindingly white high above the tops of the spruce trees.

Finally, he got out of the car and stood still with his arms at his sides, listening and watching for any sign of life. Then he began walking toward the building. With long strides, he trudged through the ankle-deep snow, keeping the whole time in the shadows of the trees, hidden from the moonlight.

It's time, he thought, just before he noticed the footprints outside the structure.

Before he noticed that the footprints weren't his.

The wind increased, as did the falling snow.

Henrik Levin wanted to go home, take the kids to the park and go sledding. He knew they would be jubilant in the untouched, white blanket of snow that waited for them on the little hill behind the house.

It would be fun for him, too, sitting on the Snow Racer and speeding down the hill, the wind and cold on his face.

But he didn't get up out of his chair. It was as if he were looking for a reason to stay.

He thought about the Thai girls. Shouldn't they find out more about them? Two more entered in the statistics for narcotics crimes. Two more in unsolved cases.

And then he thought about Robin Stenberg.

He pulled out the pictures and the list that Anneli had compiled after going through Stenberg's apartment. He skimmed through the neatly written list, everything from bed linens to the contents of the refrigerator, thinking that there should be a clue in it somewhere. Something that should tell them what this was all about.

He heard a quiet knock and looked toward the door. There stood Mia, her jacket hanging over one arm. She stepped into the room, leaned against the wall with her head cocked to one side.

"You look deep in thought," she said.

"I'm thinking about Robin. It's strange that there's not a single trace of a perpetrator," he said. "It must mean that it was a premeditated murder. And if it was premeditated, there must have been a clear motive. And if there was a clear motive, we should be able to figure it out. I don't get it…"

"I agree," Mia said. "But I'm sure it has to do with his drug addiction."

"Yeah…"

It was quiet in the room for a moment.

"And then there's the Thai girl…" he continued.

"The one who died from an overdose?"

"Yes, her, too, but I'm thinking more about her friend, the one who disappeared from the train. We really needed to find her. But I think, as I've said before, that it's too late now. She's probably already

delivered the goods and gone home to Thailand…"
Henrik sighed.

"Not yet," Mia said. "I think she's sitting on a
toilet somewhere here in Norrköping and trying
to shit."

Henrik sighed again.

"I hope you're right and that we can find her, because I think something bigger is going on."

He nodded toward the window.

"What do you mean, 'bigger'?"

"It just feels like something different is happening now…and our sources haven't cracked it yet."

"We have the National Crime Squad here."

"I know, but still, I'm a little scared…"

"Scared?" Mia said. "What are you scared of?"

"That there's something insidious going on that
we don't understand. We don't have all the pieces
yet."

Pim ran as fast as she could into the forest, toward the darkness where the trees stood close together. The snow had covered the paths and the
stones and had erased all contours of the landscape.
Every step she took created a deep, revealing foot-
print.

She jumped over a fallen branch, slipped and fell.
She stood quickly and listened. Her heavy breathing tore apart the silence and formed small clouds
in the cold air. She tried to muffle her breath, but
the sound was replaced by that of her heartbeat
pounding in her ears.

With jerky movements, she wrenched her body in all directions, trying to see if anyone was chasing her. But the darkness distorted everything in the same way it had amplified her panic over hearing the sound of the man's car.

Suddenly, she saw a beam of light off to her right. It flashed and then disappeared just as quickly. It reappeared after a moment. She peered into the darkness, trying to figure out where the light was coming from. It reappeared again, pulsing between the tree trunks and disappearing, reappearing, pulsing and disappearing. The light was as rhythmic as a heartbeat slowly pulsing its last beats.

Suddenly, she heard a twig snap. The footsteps in the snow grew closer.

She didn't dare stand still any longer, turned on her heel and ran as fast as she could.

She was running for her life.

"Can I give you a little more?" Margaretha Berzelius held up the pitcher of glogg. Small saucers and bowls stood on the table, filled with raisins, almonds, gingersnaps and blue cheese. In the middle, on a silver tray, stood a saffron cake with white icing and gold pearl sugar. Jana looked at the careful table setting, held out her mug and let her mother fill it. She held it to her lips, taking a sip.

"Is it cold?"

"No."

Her mother sat across from her, refilling her own mug, too.

"You're lying." She smiled.

"Only so you don't have to warm it up again."

Margaretha slowly cut into the saffron cake, putting a piece on Jana's plate and then a piece on her own. Instead of eating, though, she just looked at Jana.

"Are you sure you're feeling well? You look worn-out."

"No, I feel fine."

Jana met her gaze and felt tense. She wasn't really comfortable talking about her private life. It was as if the words were blocked inside her, caught in her thoughts. It was easier to hide behind the neutral jargon of a career woman. Keep things short, concise and impersonal. Only talk about work.

"You haven't been here in a long time," her mother said.

"I know."

"Why don't you call more often?"

"I haven't had time. Besides, it's awkward now with Father."

"I wish you would."

"Why didn't you tell me that sooner?"

"You wouldn't have listened anyway," her mother said.

Jana didn't respond. She fixed her eyes on a single point out in the garden. She thought she saw something move, but it was hard to make out any contours in the dense afternoon darkness.

"Where's Father?" she asked, still looking out the window.

"He had to go to a meeting."

Jana nodded, thinking it was unnecessary for her mother to say he "had" to go. There was nothing her father "had" to do. He made all of his own decisions. He had chosen to have a meeting. *Chosen* not to see her.

"How is work?" her mother asked.

"Fine," Jana said, looking at her.

Margaretha straightened her back, picked up the silver spoon and ate a bite of cake.

"I heard that you're in charge of the investigation of the dead woman on the train."

"Who did you hear that from?"

"Jana, you know he's always been interested in what you're doing."

"She died of an overdose."

"Yes, I heard that, and that her friend is gone."

"She disappeared, yes."

"You can't find her?"

"We don't know where to look."

"So awful, the whole thing," her mother whispered.

They fell silent. Jana looked out the window again and saw it was completely still now. She thought about the missing girl from the train. She had probably, like her dead friend, been exploited by a drug trafficking ring by swallowing capsules filled with drugs. Just as she herself had once been exploited by being made into a child soldier, forced into the game surrounding the drugs, the same drugs that the Thai girls were smuggling in their bodies.

The more she thought about it, the more her neck itched.

She was just about to push her hair to the side to scratch it but paused when a question popped into her head. It was one of the many questions she had never asked her mother.

"Why did you adopt me anyway?"

Her mother froze, food still in her mouth, looking at her. She sighed and slowly laid her silver spoon on her plate.

"Because we wanted a child so badly, of course. And I was getting older," she said, smiling.

"But why did you make it a closed adoption?"

"How do you know that?"

Jana thought she heard the front door opening and closing.

"I have to go," she said quickly, getting up.

"Jana?"

She got up from the table and went out into the hall without answering. Her mother followed her, and Jana was acutely aware of her gaze as she located her shoes on the shelf by the door.

"Please, can't you stay a little longer?"

Jana glanced at the glossy, carefully shined shoes. She saw the wet spots on the rug and guessed it had been her father coming home. But he wasn't alone—a pair of thick-soled, steel-toed boots stood there, too.

She turned toward her mother.

"Goodbye, Mother."

"Will you come for Christmas? You can, can't you? For my sake?"

Jana hesitated, her hand on the door handle.

"Okay," she said, "but only for your sake."

She smiled her practiced smile and stepped out of the door.

Henrik Levin walked with his hands in his pockets, looking at the row houses and the advent candles in all of the windows. The evening was dark and cold. The snow crunched under his feet.

He unlocked the door and took off his shoes. Emma's and the children's shoes were gone from the shoe rack, and their jackets were missing, too.

He pulled his hand over his mouth, stood for a moment, looking at the white stroller standing in the hallway. He reached out with both hands, gripping the handle and rolling it back and forth.

There was no price tag, but it looked expensive.

He turned on the light in the kitchen and read the note on the table. "We're at my mom's."

He flipped absentmindedly through the pile of advertisements that lay next to the note, then opened the refrigerator and looked inside. He pulled out cheese, butter and ham.

He toasted two pieces of bread but left them sitting in the toaster even after they were done. He stood with his gaze toward the dark garden, watching the strings of Christmas lights swinging in the branches of the apple trees as they swayed in the wind, saw the kitchen reflected in the dark glass and thought again about Robin Stenberg.

There was something about it that he just couldn't shake.

As he lifted the sandwich to his mouth, he realized what it was.

It didn't necessarily mean anything, but he immediately put the food back into the refrigerator, wiped the counter, put on his coat and left.

The long twig bent against his body and broke in the middle. He continued running, his eyes locked on the deep tracks in the snow.

It was too easy. She didn't have a chance.

After running around a large boulder, he stopped, closing his eyes and listening. He first heard only the gurgling of a river, but he focused his concentration and heard the vague sounds ahead of him. The crunching of snow, the quick, desperate footsteps.

She wasn't far from him now.

He smiled, opening his eyes and beginning to run again.

The door of the police station opened with a squeak. The stairwell was quiet, almost peaceful.

Henrik Levin leaped quickly up the stairs, opened the door to his office, turned on the light and stepped in. He looked for the crime scene evidence log of Robin Stenberg's apartment, but he couldn't find it.

His cell phone rang.

The unexpected sound made his adrenaline start pumping.

"Yes," he answered quickly.

"Where are you?"

Emma spoke in a low voice.

"I'll be home soon."

"When is soon?"

"It's…soon."

"In a half hour?"

"I hope so."

"Are you at work?"

"Yes. I'm just checking something."

Henrik could hear the kids in the background, Felix and Vilma. They were calling for Emma, asking if they could watch a movie.

"Okay," she said, and was silent for a moment. The children's voices were calling again, begging for a movie, insisting on watching it right that very minute.

"I see that you've been home," she said.

"I was, but came right back."

Emma was quiet again, as if she was waiting for him to say something. Then he remembered.

"The stroller is great. Beautiful, and so white."

"Thanks."

"I have to hang up now."

"Okay. We'll see you *soon*, then," she said.

"Yes," he said, adding: "I love you," but she had already hung up.

He put his phone back in his pocket and continued searching. Turning on the desk lamp, he tried to point it in the right direction with one hand while searching with the other. He finally found Anneli's inventory among all of the papers, skimmed through it all again and finally found what he was looking for: the contents of Robin Stenberg's refrigerator.

Just as I remembered, he thought.

Sussie had said that her son was a vegetarian. Then why had he had a package of ham in his fridge?

He heard the bathroom door close and lock.

Karl Berzelius went through the corridor and listened to his own footsteps on the floor. He wasn't exactly preoccupied, but he did not feel completely focused, either, when he stepped into his office to prepare for the secret meeting that was about to take place—a conversation with a good friend, just the two of them, and everything that was said would remain in that room. Just like it always had.

The vein pulsed in his right temple when he saw the little red box on the desk. He walked toward it, trying to keep calm, to breathe. He knew that his daughter had just visited. No, not his daughter, *Jana* had visited.

And she had clearly been in here.

The thought irritated him.

What had she done? What had she seen? Why had she been in here?

He glanced in confusion at the bookshelves, papers, binders and files, feeling the anxiety and angst now like a weight on his chest.

He blinked a number of times, trying to keep calm, but he couldn't erase the worried crease on his forehead.

What had she been doing in here?

He looked at the red box again. The lid was open, and it was empty.

When the bathroom door opened and he heard footsteps in the corridor, he took three long strides forward, took the box and threw it in the wastebasket next to the desk. Then he sat down and prepared for the conversation that could now begin.

 SIXTEEN

THE RIVER WAS SEVERAL YARDS WIDE.
The sound of its rushing water drowned out all other sounds. She couldn't hear branches snapping anymore. Pim turned around several times, well aware that he could catch up with her at any time.

She looked down at the dark, swirling water, hesitating.

Then she stepped into the water.

It was the only way for her to conceal her movements.

The water reached up to her knees. It was so cold it made her bones hurt, yet she began running again. She ran upstream with long steps, raising her knees high as if she was trying to escape the icy water under her. But it splashed everywhere and her clothes were soaked all the way to her waist.

She swept aside the branches that hung over the water, continuing on despite feeling like she couldn't manage to run as quickly now.

She couldn't feel her feet anymore.

In her next step, her foot landed wrong and she fell onto her stomach in the water. The water coursed over her, so cold that she thought her heart was going to stop.

Then she heard it. A branch snapped.

She stared into the darkness, listening again. Her fingers were becoming numb as she climbed onto the river's edge, but there she found a heap of large rocks. Teeth chattering, she crept behind it.

She heard another branch snap, closer this time. He was coming after her, and he'd probably heard her splashing.

She pressed her back against the rocks, drew her knees up to her chin and wrapped her arms around her legs.

Tears pressed against the backs of her eyelids, but she forced them back.

Voice mail again.

This time, it was Mia's voice encouraging him to leave a message.

Ola, on the other hand, had answered on the first ring, and Henrik Levin already heard him approaching in the corridor. He was practically running. Was he really that excited?

"Hit me," he said, sitting immediately with his computer on his lap.

Henrik pointed to the table where the report lay open.

"Well, like I said, Robin Stenberg was a vegetarian, yet there was a package of ham in his refrigerator. Maybe not earth-shattering information, I know…"

"No, I've heard more exciting things in my life…"

"But he had supposedly been a vegetarian for many years, so unless he suddenly converted back to eating meat again, I think someone else was living in the apartment with him. And I want to find out who. Our knowledge of his private life is pretty poor, but you've gone through his computer, right?"

"Absolutely, and everything is documented. He had a number of accounts on social media. All of them are private, but on Twitter he gave the email address Eternal_sunshine@gmail.com. And he's consistent online."

"What do you mean?"

"He uses that email address prefix remarkably often as a username. He just really likes Eternal_sunshine."

"Great. Search for everyone who has chatted with Eternal_sunshine."

"I already have. I've gone through all the names, but the thing is, there are so many—like Ilovebeethoven, soonerorlater, cyberfrog, cheesecurl, moltas666, phantomsmurf…"

"You can't get any regular names from these nicknames?"

"Oh, yes, of course I can. But that takes time and we're not even sure any of these people knew Robin… It might be a little unnecessary…"

Henrik sighed just as his phone rang.

"Mia?" he answered.

"Uh…no, this is Josefin Ek. You had been looking for me. I'm sorry I haven't had the chance to call sooner, but I was running a Christmas concert and I only just now saw that you called."

"Yes," Henrik said, "I was looking for you because I know you work at Kulturhuset."

"That's right."

"And that you are responsible for Band Camp on Sundays."

"Yes?"

"Do you know Robin Stenberg?"

"Yes, I do. Or, well, I did. I heard what happened to him. How horrible." Josefin grew silent.

"I understand he used to come to the community arts center?" Henrik said.

"Yes, he came here a lot," she said.

"On Sundays, too?"

"Mostly on Sundays. Band Camp is actually an open rehearsal space for girls."

"Only for girls?"

"Yes."

"So what was he doing there?"

"He came along when Ida was playing."

Henrik raised his eyebrows.

"Who is Ida?"

"His girlfriend."

"Girlfriend?"

Henrik got up, combing his hand through his hair.

"What's her last name?"

"Something starting with E… Ekberg, Ekstedt, Ekström…"

Henrik took a few steps across the room, stopping and turning toward Ola, who had turned his computer screen toward him. A young blonde girl with her hair in a ponytail was smiling at him.

"Eklund," Ola said. "Her name is Ida Eklund."

The tracks ended at the river's edge.

He looked in both directions, trying to figure out whether she had run upstream or downstream.

He chose not to follow the water's current and went parallel to the river. With his hands cupped around his mouth, he called her name a few times.

The moon was almost directly overhead, but he wasn't cursing it anymore. Far from it—he was thankful for the bright light that forced its way through the evergreen branches and lit up the snow, making everything around him light gray. Yet he still didn't see her.

He called again.

Out of the corner of his eye, he caught sight of something big—but it was just a deer that sprang up and disappeared in the darkness of the forest.

He watched the startled animal until he couldn't see it any longer and its hopping footsteps become ever weaker. Finally, he only heard the gurgling sound of the water; everything else was still.

But the realization that she, like the startled deer, had also disappeared in the darkness made him so angry that he screamed.

"Get out here for fuck's sake, you whore!"

He saw that his hands were shaking, and clenched them even harder. She couldn't have gotten far, he thought. She couldn't have gotten very fucking far.

He smiled when he thought about how little clothing she had on. *She'll be begging to come back*, he thought, and continued to walk along the river.

Jana Berzelius lay in her bathtub and absent-mindedly watched the foam floating around her. She hadn't taken off her necklace before getting in the warm water. Now she ran her fingers along it and thought about her mother, who had confirmed that the adoption had been closed. But why had they chosen to make it impossible for her to find out her true parents?

The water began to feel uncomfortable, too warm, oppressive.

She reached her hand down and gripped the wineglass that stood on the floor, swallowing the cold white wine in tiny, tiny sips.

Her thoughts wandered to her father. He had his priorities and always put work first. All these years, he had made sure to have the right people around him, and as a result, he had an enormous circle of friends. Sometimes he held large parties at the house in Lindö, sometimes more intimate dinners. There were also frequent meetings.

Because of this, she hadn't been surprised to

see a strange pair of shoes in the hall at his house. What did surprise her was that they were steel-toed.

There should be few among his friends, if any, who wore steel-toed boots.

She wondered who it had been, this person he hadn't bothered to introduce.

Small beads of sweat formed on her forehead.

She let the water out but remained sitting in the tub, watching the water level sink, watching how the suds stuck to her skin.

She emptied her wineglass, leaned forward and hugged her knees to her chest as the water dripped from her nipples.

Her recently warm flesh became cold, and it felt liberating.

Henrik Levin looked at the picture again, meeting the gaze of the girl with the blond hair. She had freckles and squinted toward the sun. She had pushed her oversize sunglasses up onto her head like a headband.

"You found her?" Henrik said.

"It wasn't hard to find her," Ola said. "There are a lot of chats where Robin was talking to someone called idaaa_star. She had sent a picture of herself under the title Miss U. And as you know, kids like to hang out on social media like Twitter, Instagram, Snapchat and Kik."

"Not Facebook?"

"No. Most people on Facebook are between

thirty and forty, like you. You have an account, right?"

"No," Henrik said.

"What?" Ola exclaimed. "You must be joking."

"No, I'm the type who avoids that sort of thing."

"How many of you are there?"

"More than you think."

"Surely, but I'd think you're an endangered species."

"I'm not sure about that. But soon they're going to shut down the whole internet, just wait and see."

Ola guffawed.

"Okay, whatever. I've looked at all of the Idas I could find on these social media sites that *modern* people are using, and I've found an Ida Eklund that had the picture from the chat as a profile picture on Instagram."

"Do you have her address, too?"

"260 Emil Hedelius Street."

"Thanks," Henrik said. "I wonder if she knows what happened, and why she hasn't called us if she does."

"Didn't Robin Stenberg's mother know about her?"

"She didn't say so if she did."

"What's your plan now?"

Henrik looked at the clock. Almost six.

"I have to try to find Ida. Do you have a telephone number?"

"Just a second…" Ola said, typing on his computer again. "From what I see, there's one registered phone number."

"Give it to me," Henrik said, putting in the numbers that Ola read to him and raising his phone to his ear.

"Straight to voice mail," he said. "I'll go to her place and try to get Mia to come with me."

Henrik looked at the clock again. *Mia should be here by now*, he thought, dialing her number. He had tried to reach her a number of times without any luck. To his surprise, she answered on the first ring.

"Time to work," he said in a chipper voice.

"Why is that?" she mumbled.

"We're going to go talk with Robin's girlfriend."

"He didn't have a girlfriend, did he?"

"In any case, we're going to go talk with a girl named Ida. Right now."

"But… I have to change."

"Okay. I can pick you up."

"But I'm not at home."

"What do you mean, not home? Where are you?"

Her stomach cramped up when she heard the scream. It was so close. *He* was so close.

Her body shook uncontrollably. Pim couldn't feel her feet anymore. Her fingers, either. She rocked back and forth in an attempt to get some warmth back into her legs.

She heard footsteps and tried to pull her legs in

even more, making herself as small as she could behind the rocks.

The footsteps were close now, but suddenly they faded and she couldn't hear him anymore.

Was he waiting? Trying to trick her?

She sat completely still, hardly daring to breathe.

She waited for five minutes, then stood up on unsteady legs. Hidden behind tree branches, she began to walk again. She took one step at a time, carefully and as quietly as she could, listening the whole time for sounds, branches snapping.

When she had gone one hundred steps from the rocks, she began to run. Her feet drummed against the snow. She didn't feel the cold anymore and ran straight ahead, knowing that at some point, the forest had to end. At some point, she had to reach something that wasn't white and cold.

Something that wasn't snow.

Mia Bolander flung her down jacket in the backseat and sat in the car with a sigh. She looked out through the windshield, at the snowplow moving back and forth in front of them.

Henrik tried to catch her eyes.

"What?" she asked.

"I thought you said you weren't going to see him anymore."

"And?"

"Nothing, I just…"

"Can't a person change her mind?"

"Of course."

"Well, then."

They drove in silence through Norrköping in the falling snow. Henrik kept both hands on the steering wheel to prevent the car from drifting when they went through the roundabout at Klockaretorpet.

A wooden gnome smiled kindly at them as they rang the doorbell at 260 Emil Hedelius Street.

The door opened, revealing a man in jeans, long hair reaching down his back. Henrik introduced himself and shook his hand.

"I'm Magnus," the man said.

"We're looking for Ida."

"What did she do?"

"We just want to talk to her. Does she live here?"

"Yes."

"Who is it?" came a voice from inside the row house.

"Is she home?" Henrik asked.

"Magnus? Who is it?"

They heard footsteps on the stairs before a woman appeared. Her body was cloaked in a floor-length cardigan. Her eyes were red, her cheeks sunken in.

"Henrik Levin, police," Henrik said. "This is my colleague, Mia Bolander."

"I'm Petra," the woman said. Henrik tried to steel himself against the look in her eyes, but he couldn't. He saw it. *The panic.*

"Yes, well," Henrik said. "We're looking for Ida.

You can relax, she's not a suspect or anything. We just want to talk to her."

"She isn't home," Petra said.

"Do you know where she is?"

"She's at…a friend's."

Henrik heard it now. *The fear.*

"Can I ask…" he began, meeting Mia's gaze. She had the same thought, the same question on her lips.

"What is her friend's name?" Mia finished for him.

"Well…" Magnus started, laughing nervously. "We don't really know."

"You don't really know?"

Magnus took a deep breath.

"Well, this is all so new… The only thing we know is that he calls himself… What was it, Petra?"

"Eternal_sunshine…"

Henrik swallowed.

"May we come in?"

Jana Berzelius's hair was still dripping water from her shower as she sat on the sofa with her MacBook on her knees. She spent most of the next two hours searching online. Her search broadened in a number of different directions because she wasn't completely sure what she was searching for. A few different questions kept nagging her. The first was why her adoption had been shrouded in secrecy.

The general rule in Sweden was that all public

governance should be open for review by the general public. This principle formed the foundation of Swedish democracy. Some information, however, needed to be kept confidential, such as sensitive information about personal circumstances. Within social services, the rule was that confidentiality was required for information about individual relationships, therefore it wasn't so unusual that an adoption would be closed, she decided, lifting her computer from her lap and allowing it to cool slightly.

She laid it back on her knees and returned her hands to the keyboard.

The second question that bothered her was about her father's perpetual preference for his work. Information on this issue was easy to collect. She found newspaper articles from 1991 in which he cropped up in connection with the police making a crackdown on a thirty-six-year-old man who was suspected of financial crimes. When the police searched his row house for his ledgers, they found one hundred kilograms of narcotics under the stairs. The thirty-six-year-old and another man were prosecuted on a felony narcotics charge. According to the prosecutor, Karl Berzelius, there were clear connections between the two men and "they can now expect many years in prison for possession and intent to sell."

Karl Berzelius's career as a prosecutor was straight as an arrow. According to a graph in one newspaper, he had won almost every single case he

took on during the early nineties. He was also pro-
filed, as Prosecutor-General, in an editorial piece
about promoting positive administration of justice,
a debate that was initiated by the bar association.
The background of the initiative was a development
in recent years that resulted in the tone between
prosecutors and defense attorneys at trial becoming
strikingly aggressive. This had become particularly
obvious in certain legal cases that had garnered
great media attention, like for example "The Goal
of the Game," where a network in Nyköping had
been conducting, among other things, illegal gam-
bling and collection using violence and extortion as
their chosen methods. One of the accused men had
claimed the whole time that police and prosecutors
had been out to get him and that the investigation
had been manipulated, that they had held back important proof and failed to follow clues that would
have led the investigation in a different direction.
The Court of Appeals' verdict stated that there was
no proof to support these claims and that "the involved authorities had carried out their duties in an
objective and lawful manner."

Jana put her laptop aside and thought that her
father hadn't only had a straight-as-an-arrow career path. It had also been incredibly successful.

Almost too successful.

When he had gone back and forth along the hill
for more than an hour without seeing a single sign
of life, he gave up. Filled with frustration, he went
back toward the building.

The mule had run straight out into the forest, away from the building, and had gotten away. He was furious and whipped the ropes against the wall.

No one could get away. Ever.

That was rule number one.

He thought feverishly, taking out his cell phone but halting at the last second.

It wasn't time to call yet. There was nothing to report. He had already lost a whole delivery this week and had too much against him.

Now the other mule had run away, too, and still with two capsules in her. The delivery wasn't assured. So what would he say at this point? That things hadn't worked out—again?

He didn't make the call.

It was that simple.

He was responsible for the numbers. No one other than he knew exactly how many capsules she had swallowed. He could lie and say that she had only swallowed 48. He could also lie a little more and say that she was already taken care of—snuffed out, dead.

It was a dense forest, after all.

And really fucking cold.

The kitchen was new, with oak countertops and white cabinets, a stainless steel refrigerator and two ovens. The chandelier hanging from the ceiling was adorned with ten half-burned candles.

"Ida isn't answering now, either," Magnus said, setting his cell down on the table. "Just voice mail."

He met Henrik's gaze, swallowing.

"Does she usually screen her calls?" Henrik asked.

"Sometimes. When we've had an argument, she doesn't usually want to answer."

"Do you argue often?"

"Not any more than usual with a teenager…"

"But why do you want to talk to her?" Petra asked. "What did she do?"

"She hasn't done anything," Henrik said calmly.

"Is it this boy then? Did he do something?"

"The young man who calls himself Eternal_ sunshine is actually named Robin Stenberg," Henrik said, taking a deep breath. "This morning he was found dead in his apartment."

"Dead?"

Petra covered her mouth with her hands.

"I'm sorry, but I can't say any more than that," Henrik said.

"And Ida?" Petra asked anxiously. "Did something happen to Ida?"

"We…" Mia began.

"Is she okay?" Petra interrupted. "She's okay, right?"

Henrik lifted his gaze.

"We have no reason to think otherwise. But we need to get ahold of her, of course."

"How is it that you didn't know what her friend's real name was?" Mia asked.

"As I said, it's a completely new thing," Magnus said, sighing. "Ida met this guy in a chat room recently, and we talked about it just yesterday. We didn't think it was a good idea for her to stay overnight with someone we've never met. I mean, she's only sixteen years old. We think it's appropriate to at least meet him."

"So you had an argument about it?" Mia asked.

"I just said what I thought," Petra said. "And when she didn't come home yesterday, we started calling her, but she wouldn't answer."

"How do you know that he calls himself Eternal_sunshine?"

"I saw it on her cell phone yesterday," Petra said. "I was going to hang some laundry in her closet and just when I went in, her phone dinged and I… well, I looked. They say you should keep an eye on things, they say that, you know, on TV, so…and it said 'Eternal_sunshine'…and so of course I had to ask her about it… Who saves a friend's name like that, 'Eternal_sunshine'? At first I thought it was a company or a sect or something…"

"And you think that it was a new relationship," Henrik began, "but from what we know, they've been seeing each other for a while, at Kulturhuset and possibly other places…"

Silence fell across the table. Magnus cleared his throat.

"Yes, they certainly could have been seeing each other without us knowing. You can't know everything all the time. For us, it became a problem when she wanted to sleep over at his place…"

"We were scared that she was being taken advantage of in some way…" Petra said. "There are so many strange people online…"

"But if we now think that she didn't go to Robin Stenberg's yesterday," Henrik said, "where else would she go, do you think? Do you have any idea at all where she could be?"

"No," Magnus whispered, his eyes empty.

"Where is my Ida?" Petra said, raising her voice.

"We'll begin looking for her," Henrik said. "But I ask that you really think carefully about where she might be. Could she have gone to a friend's, or is there anywhere else she could be?"

Magnus turned his head away when Petra started to whisper to herself.

"Ida, my little Ida…"

"We're going to do everything we can to…" Henrik began.

"Please," Petra interrupted. "Tell me she's okay."

Henrik's jaw muscles clenched.

"She's okay. Say it. She has to be okay."

"We're going to find her," Henrik said calmly, giving Mia a look that said he needed help.

"Say she's okay. Say it," Petra insisted.

"I know we'll find her," Henrik said.

"Say it!"

Henrik looked down, not wanting to meet Petra's desperate look. His thoughts spun around in his head faster and faster until he couldn't think anymore. He felt the words coming and was helpless to stop them.

"She's okay."

CHAPTER

SEVENTEEN

A SNOWPLOW SPED THROUGH THE sparkling winter landscape. Christian Bergvall sat in the cab. White snow whirled up behind him, tinted orange by the flashing warning lights before disappearing into the darkness at the side of the road. Sparks flew as the plow met the hard asphalt.

Now and then he saw glimmering lights in the forest as the headlights were reflected by the eyes of the forest animals. Christian wondered if he was seeing deer or moose. He knew that it wasn't wild boar—their eyes didn't reflect light, making them difficult to spot in the dark.

But he also knew that the wild boar population was increasing every year, that it wasn't going to be possible to stop the spread of this animal. Or the accidents they caused.

The first time Christian hit a wild boar, he was in his Volkswagen Passat. He had made two serious mistakes. The first was driving far too fast, which made the impact unnecessarily hard.

The second was that he had immediately stopped the car after the accident to check on the animal. The wild boar had lain down, but it had still been conscious. It had gotten up and attacked. Wild boars have large tusks that are sharp as knives.

He had paid for that mistake with thirty-seven stitches on his leg.

When Christian came out of the curve on Highway 209 toward Brytsbo, he was going fairly quickly. The thunderous sound of the plow filled the cab as the snow was scraped up from the ground and swept to the side.

He felt fatigue setting in and starting humming to keep himself awake for the last two hours of this late shift.

Suddenly, he saw a shadow and braked as quickly as he could.

Someone was on the road.

Christian pulled to the side of the road, turned off the plow and got out of the cab.

She had to say it.

Or maybe it was better to leave his apartment and never come back again, never answer her phone again. Maybe in spite of everything, it was better to go home—alone.

Mia Bolander had never liked being alone. She always preferred the company of others—at work, in her free time, in bed. But to keep things going with Martin Strömberg just so she wouldn't have to be alone was not a good idea, not good at all.

It would be better to find another guy, or rather a man. She wasn't made for relationships longer than one-night stands. That's just how it was.

But just now, she didn't want to think about what she should say to him, how she should say it to end things with him, to break up.

They lay in his double bed, naked. Mia's head was resting on his chest.

"You're so quiet, Mia," he said. "You look almost secretive. Are you with the secret service?"

He chuckled as if it were the first time he'd said that. "And I can't stop laughing," he continued. "You looked so funny when you and your colleague came to my door."

He was laughing now, way too loud.

"I know. You've said," Mia said.

"I wish I'd gotten it on camera…"

Then it was as if he realized what sort of mood she was in.

"Mia, are you upset? This is no time to be upset—it's almost Christmas, and if you're really good, really happy, Santa will bring you presents. What *do* you want for Christmas, by the way?"

She lifted her head from his chest and looked at him to see if he was serious or not. "Nothing," she said.

"Nothing?"

"Nothing!"

She laid her head back down, looking at his unusually large nipples and the hair growing around them. Glancing around the room, she looked at the nearly empty bookshelf, the dust in straight lines where the CD cases had stood. Now they were spread across the floor after having been played multiple times during the night and into the morning on an old stereo with two enormous speakers that looked like black towers in the corner of the bedroom. She never thought she would survive a night of Ace of Base, but on the other hand, she also never thought that she would date a man who liked sucking on toes, either.

She definitely needed to break up with him.

"A sweater, maybe?" he said. "Or earrings?"

"I don't like earrings," she said, sitting up.

"Tell me what you do like, then."

"Not earrings."

"No?"

"No."

"But you have to want something."

"No."

She looked at him and felt the irritation growing. What they had between them wasn't real. And now she regretted that she had come to this jabbering idiot in the first place, wished that she'd had enough sense to let it go. She didn't feel comfortable with him. He wasn't the right one at all, actually—not for her, not now, not at any time in the life she wished for.

He had done that moaning thing again, loudly, and despite that she had yawned during the act, he hadn't let that stop him—he'd just continued on top of her, inside her, and she had had the urge to stick her fingers in her ears so she didn't have to hear him anymore. That fucking irritating sound. She had wanted to scream at him to stop for Christ's sake, that it would be better to sleep than to waste time on what they thought they had in common—which was nothing.

"I've already bought something for you," he said.

"What did you say?"

"I've already bought something for you, I said."

"What is it?"

"You'll have to wait and see."

"Tell me what you bought," she said.

"Something nice."

"Like?"

"I can't tell you or it won't be a surprise."

"I don't like surprises."

"But I do."

"You can give me a hint, then."

"Nope," he said, getting out of bed.

He went into the bathroom and locked the door.

She got up, pulled her shirt over her head, put her hair in a ponytail and tugged on the roller shade so it would open. Although it was morning, she was met by darkness.

She pulled her jeans from under the bed and noticed a bag lying there with a black box in the bottom. It was a big, black box inscribed with the name of a boutique, and she knew that name stood for exclusive watches.

She listened for sounds from the bathroom. It was quiet, he hadn't flushed or run water in the sink, so she knew she had a little time to see what was in the box. She jerked the lid off.

Her mouth fell open when she saw the watch. It was small and really, really beautiful. She touched it, wanting badly to put it on her wrist right away, to feel how it felt to have such an expensive watch on her arm.

The toilet flushed. She hurried to put the box and bag back under the bed, pulled on her jeans and went out into the hallway. He was leaning against the door frame with his arms crossed. She saw he was completely naked, his entire goddamn package hanging between his legs.

It doesn't get any worse than this, she thought, struck by the realization that she really wanted to get out of this.

"So you're already on your way to the next case, Miss Policewoman?"

"You have to quit while you're ahead."

He laughed and fluttered his eyelids as if he were trying to flirt.

She put on her jacket, opened the door and looked at him. "You're crazy, you know that?" She forced a smile, shut the door behind her and hurried down the steps. She took a few deep breaths as she walked across the lawn, shoving her hands in her pockets and swearing—over the fact that she had wanted to break up but couldn't, not today and not now.

Not before Christmas.

Or more precisely, not before she'd gotten that watch.

* * *

Her hands were shaking, her body shivering.

Had she been dreaming? Not the usual dream anyway. Not about the violence and the spurting blood. Not about the scarring and the voice screaming at her. Not about the hands holding her tightly, hitting her so that she would learn to bear the pain and not give up, learn to be the deadly weapon she was supposed to be.

That Gavril Bolanaki had trained her to be.

And that she had indeed become.

Jana Berzelius opened her eyes, looking straight out into her bedroom. She heard the silence and breathed deeply.

She must have been dreaming—she had heard someone say her name. Or had it just been a sound in her apartment?

She straightened her fingers and looked at her palms for marks from her fingernails, but there were none. So it was as she had thought. It hadn't been the usual dream.

Raising herself on one elbow, she touched her necklace and decided there wasn't any reason to go back to sleep. Best to get up.

She reached for her phone and saw a missed call from Henrik Levin. Already?

She sat up, hit "Call Back" and waited for him to answer.

"Henrik," he said.

"You called. What's up?" she asked.

"I'm sorry for calling so early, but we've found

the woman who had disappeared from the train.
Everything points to that, at least."

"Is she alive?"

"Yes."

"I'm on my way."

The chair creaked as Henrik Levin sat down
beside Mia Bolander in the Intensive Care Unit of
Vrinnevi Hospital. Both looked at the woman who
lay with a slightly vacant expression in the hospital bed. They had no trouble recognizing her face,
which they had studied in photographs from the
security camera at Central Station.

A male interpreter was also sitting in the room;
he had been called in to ensure there were no mis-
understandings during the conversation.

The room was filled with hissing and ticking
sounds from the machines monitoring her respi-
ratory rate, pulse and heart rhythm.

Just then, there was a careful knock at the door
and Jana Berzelius stepped in. She quickly greeted
Henrik and Mia and sat down next to them.

It could be intimidating to be surrounded by two
police officers, a prosecutor and an interpreter, so
they decided that Henrik would lead the conversation. It was important to build trust.

"You haven't begun yet?" Jana whispered to
Henrik.

"No, I've been waiting a little."

The woman coughed, and Henrik looked from
the bandage around her wrists and the dressed

wounds on her arms, to what he could see above the blanket of the abrasions and bruises that covered her body, to the IV in the crook of her arm.

Her general condition was poor, the doctor had said. She had a high fever but her body was shivering as if she were still suffering from hypothermia as a result of the freezing winter night.

The doctor had explained that three of her toes had signs of frostbite. They might have to be amputated, but the doctor didn't want to make the call yet. The spread of necrosis was difficult to determine and they wanted to wait before making the decision.

The woman lay straight with her arms by her side above the blanket. On the table next to the bed was a glass of warm water that the nurse helped her drink before she would allow the two police officers to ask their questions.

"The door is locked?" the woman asked. "Is it? Have you locked it?"

"You are safe now," Henrik said calmly.

The woman shook her head as if she didn't believe him.

"We're here to help you," he said, nodding at the interpreter to begin. "But we have to understand where you've been and what you've been through."

"I don't know," she said. "I have no idea. I was sitting in a cold room, it was so cold…"

She began to cry. Henrik exchanged glances with Jana, pausing to let the woman catch her breath.

"This room you're talking about," Henrik said. "Do you know where the room is?"

"I don't know," she said with confusion in her voice.

Henrik saw that she was moving her legs under the blanket. He repeated that she was safe and that everything would be okay. She looked him in the eyes without replying.

"What is your name?" Henrik asked.

She looked down.

"Pimnapat Pandith, but I go by Pim."

Henrik leaned back in his chair, letting his arms rest freely on the armrests. He noticed that Jana was writing in a notebook.

"Your friend…" he began, waiting as Pim began to cry again. "You came on the train from Copenhagen?"

Pim nodded slowly.

"What were you going to do here?"

"We were going on vacation…"

Henrik crossed one leg over the other.

"Yes," he said. "We're very sorry about what happened to your friend, and I don't mean to make you upset but…we know that she had approximately fifty balls of heroin in her body, and we assume that you…"

"Her eyes…" Pim interrupted. "Her pupils were so small, so terribly small. She said she wanted to sleep on the train, she wanted to sleep, and I couldn't wake her up. She didn't wake up."

Pim's body shook with sobs, making the IV tube swing.

Henrik waited a few minutes, giving her time to compose herself.

"What was your friend's name?" he asked when she was breathing more calmly.

Pim hesitated for a moment, coughed and looked up.

"Siriporn."

"Siriporn Chaiyen. Is that right?"

"Yes," Pim answered.

"That's what it said in her passport. But her passport wasn't legitimate, so I think her name was something else, I think it was Noi. Am I right?"

He saw that Pim's gaze wandered.

"She went by Noi."

"And what was her real name?"

"Chaniporn," she mumbled, moving her hands under the blanket.

"What was her last name?"

"I don't know."

"Who provided you with the passports?"

"No one…"

Jana looked like she wanted to ask a question but stopped herself.

"Because your friend's passport was fake, it is probably best that we ask you again what your name is," Henrik said.

"I told you," Pim sniffled. "My name is Pimnapat, and I go by Pim."

"And what name was written in your passport?" Henrik said, not giving up.

"That's what it said. Pimnapat."

"Are you sure?"

"Yes."

Jana wrote something in her notebook again. Henrik rubbed his nose while he thought.

"So if we check with the airline, we will find a Pimnipat on a flight from…"

Henrik didn't finish his sentence.

"We understand that you want to be left alone," he said, "but we have to talk with you in detail over the coming days, and even if it's unpleasant, we have to ask you questions right now. But you don't need to be scared. Nothing is going to happen to you."

Pim closed her eyes, biting her lip. Her eyes flitted back and forth under her eyelids, making her short black eyelashes tremble.

"He's still hunting me, isn't he?" she whispered.

"Who?" Henrik asked.

"He's hunting me," she said.

"Who's hunting you?" Henrik repeated. "Is someone hunting you?"

"No. I don't want to, I don't want to…"

"You're not in danger," Henrik said quietly.

Pim sighed, opening her eyes and looking at the interpreter.

"But we have to…" Henrik said. "What was supposed to happen when you came to Norrköping?

Was someone meeting you, or were you supposed to get in touch with someone?"

Pim didn't answer.

"But you knew that Noi was supposed to make this 'delivery'?"

"No, I didn't know anything. We were going on vacation…"

"To Norrköping?" Mia exclaimed skeptically. "You traveled from…wherever you traveled from, to take a vacation in Norrköping?"

Henrik glared at her.

"Yes," Pim said.

"And who did Noi get this job from?" Henrik asked.

"I have no idea."

"Okay." He decided to change his approach. "Can you tell me anything about where you were? It was a room, you said."

"It was so cold in the room…"

"What else? Was there furniture?"

"Water. There was water everywhere."

"Water. Was it running water? Waves?"

"Wood…and two stories."

"There were two stories?" Henrik said.

"Yes."

Jana wrote in her notebook again.

Pim's voice cracked. She pulled her hands up and put them in front of her face.

"So much snow," she cried. "I was running through the snow. He was hunting me. I was able to get away. He'd tied me up."

"Why had he tied you up?"

"So that I wouldn't run away."

"Was there any other reason?"

"No."

"But it wouldn't be that he wanted to make sure that what you had swallowed came out in a secure location?"

"I didn't swallow anything. Noi had. I was just traveling with her."

Pim took her hands from her face and began fingering the blanket.

"When can I go home? I have a little sister who's waiting for me."

"Where is she waiting?"

Pim fell silent.

"We have to know where you live."

She remained quiet.

"You'll have to stay here for a while," Henrik said.

"No, I have to go home," Pim said. "But he has my passport! I want my passport!"

"Calm down, we'll help you get home. But first you have to tell us the truth, all of it. We want to know what you were going to do here in Sweden and who held you captive..."

"I don't want to go back there," Pim said. "I just wanted to get out of there, and I tried to help her, but I couldn't. I had to run."

"You wanted to help Noi?"

"I didn't want to leave her, but I had to. I had to leave her."

"Listen to me," Henrik said in a calm voice. "Who were you forced to leave? Do you mean Noi, on the train?"

"No, the girl sitting in the room."

"What do you mean by 'the girl'? You say 'the girl'—what do you mean?"

"She was with me."

"In the room where you were held captive?"

"Yes."

"There was another girl there?"

"Yes."

EIGHTEEN

GUNNAR ÖHRN PULLED THE GOLD-colored chain hanging from the desk lamp. The green shade gave off a dim light.

He sat down at the desk and looked at the advent candelabra that stood there. It was red with seven candles, with small plastic wreaths at the base of every candle.

It was Second Advent. The countdown to Christmas was in full swing.

He moved his gaze to the computer in front of him, meeting his own reflection in the black screen. He hardly recognized himself. Gray and pale. Bags under his eyes.

Unkempt hair.

When was his last haircut?

He had forgotten, maybe because he was tired. Maybe because he was old. He didn't know which.

He heard a knock at the door and watched it swing open. Suddenly he was standing there, that idiot. But he didn't come in, just lingered in the doorway with one hand on the doorknob and a sneer on his face.

"What smells?"

"What do you mean?"

"There's something…"

Anders Wester lifted his nose in the air, sniffing like a damn hunting dog.

"Oh, I know. It smells like gingerbread."

"And?"

"Are you sitting here in your office pigging out?"

"No. Anneli bought new soap."

"So now you're walking around smelling like gingerbread. That's one way to spread Christmas cheer."

"Just stop."

Anders sneered again. He remained in the doorway, rubbing his hand over his bald head.

"So we've had a breakthrough?" he asked.

"Clearly."

"But you weren't the ones who found her?"

Gunnar clenched his teeth, inhaling through his nose.

"She was found by the slowplow driver on Highway 209."

"Where is she now?"

"At the hospital."

"And where has she been since she ran from the train?"

"It's very unclear. She isn't really at home in these parts, if I can say that. But we hope it will become clearer over the course of the day. We're questioning her now."

"And the perpetrator? What are you planning to do about him?"

"You sound like a journalist. Are you writing an article or what?"

Anders let go of the doorknob, crossing his arms over his chest.

"I just wanted to know what you're thinking."

"We're having a meeting in an hour."

"Good. Make sure you do."

"I just said we're going to."

"And I just encouraged you to."

"I don't care about your encouragement."

Anders sneered again, placing his hand on the doorknob and closing the door before opening it again.

"Hey, Gunnar," he said. "Try a different scent next time. Gingerbread doesn't suit you."

Pim looked up at the ceiling, feeling a chill pushing into her skin from the IV fastened in the crook of her arm. At the same time, she felt the warm tears running down her cheeks and into her ears. The nurse held out a tissue, but Pim was too weak to take it. Henrik exchanged glances with Jana and Mia.

"Can you describe the girl?" he asked carefully.

Pim listened as the interpreter asked her the question.

"Can you describe her for us?"

"She screamed when I left her. I didn't want to leave her, but I had to get out of there before he came back… I had to leave her."

Pim closed her eyes, remembering how the girl had looked up from the steps to the upper level. She sat still and quiet, only her eyes moving, silently telling of the shock, panic, fear she must have felt. Pim had seen her face; they'd looked right at each other.

"Can you tell us any more about her? Did you speak to each other?"

The only thing she heard was the hissing and ticking from the machines. Pim couldn't bear to keep her eyes open. She blinked but only saw darkness.

She heard the policeman breathing, quickly, nervously, but his voice was calm when he repeated the question.

"Can you tell us any more about the girl?"

Pim opened her eyes, shaking her head.

"She was so scared," she said, her lips trembling. "She cried all the time…"

Pim's voice cracked. She was thinking about how she had run through the deep snow. She didn't want to experience that frozen feeling again. She just wanted to go home to the warmth, to the sun and to Mai. The police shouldn't keep her any longer. She didn't have anything in her anymore. The last two capsules lay in the forest somewhere.

"Do you remember her name?" he asked.

"I don't know," Pim whispered.

"Was it Ida?"

Henrik received a questioning glance from Mia. Pim didn't answer.

"Now we should let Pim rest for a while," the nurse said, drying the tears that ran down Pim's cheeks.

Henrik chose not to listen. He pulled out his cell phone, flipped through pictures until he found one of Ida Eklund. Her eyes were big and blue. Her long blond hair lay in a tangled braid over one shoulder. She was smiling at the camera.

"Is this the girl who was with you?"

Pim squinted at Henrik's phone.

"I don't know," she said in a barely audible whisper. She turned onto her side and pulled the blanket over her head.

"Look carefully," Henrik said.

But Pim didn't say any more. She had turned in on herself.

It was freezing cold outside when Henrik Levin, Mia Bolander and Jana Berzelius stepped out of the main entrance to Vrinnevi Hospital. Mia immediately hunched her shoulders in an attempt to get warm.

"Hey, where did you get Ida from?" Mia asked. "How would she be mixed up in this? Are you totally out of ideas, Henrik?"

"Wait, start from the beginning," Jana said. "Who is Ida?"

"Yesterday, we found a young man murdered in his apartment."

"Robin Stenberg? I heard about it from Per Åström."

"Exactly. And we thought at first that Robin was alone, single, but apparently he had a relationship with a girl named Ida Eklund."

"I'm freezing to death," Mia said. "Do we have to stand out here for this?"

"And Ida is missing?" Jana said.

Henrik nodded.

"To make a long story short, Ida had told her parents that she was going to stay the night at her boyfriend's house, which the parents didn't like because they'd never met him. Ida chose to ignore her parents' disapproval, and we assume that she slept at Robin's the night before last. We haven't yet confirmed it, but we're proceeding from that assumption right now."

"Hello?" Mia said, wrapping her arms around herself but getting no reaction from the others.

"So she might have been there when Robin Stenberg was murdered?" Jana said, feeling the hair on her arms stand up.

"Like I said, we don't know anything for sure yet, but yes, it is entirely possible that Ida was in the apartment when Robin was murdered."

Jana's thoughts whirled around in her head. She didn't meet Henrik's or Mia's eyes, held her pale face pointed toward the ground, on the snow.

"But why would Ida have been in the same place

as Pim?" Mia said, shivering. "And how would she get there in the first place? Because of Robin Stenberg? Isn't it a bit of a long shot to believe that a sixteen-year-old high school chick and a twenty-year-old vegetarian have anything to do with this drug case? Use your brain, Henrik."

"It is a long shot, I know. But considering that Robin had had problems with drugs, it is possible that he could have had contact with our man. And now, when Pim talked about another girl, I had to ask if it was Ida."

"That's great, really. Now give me the car keys."

"Are you that cold?" Henrik asked.

"Yes. Not everyone can afford high-tech, name-brand gear," she said, glaring at Jana.

Henrik pulled the keys from his pocket and gave them to Mia, who immediately set off for the parking lot.

"I'll wait in the car," she shouted over her shoulder.

Jana followed her with her gaze, gripping her briefcase so hard that her knuckles whitened.

"You believe that this Ida witnessed Stenberg's murder?" she asked.

"Yes," Henrik said.

"So where is she now?"

Jana turned her gaze to Henrik, looking straight into his eyes.

"That's what we need to find out," he said, meeting her gaze.

HENRIK LEVIN LIFTED HIS GAZE WHEN Anders Wester came into the room and sat at the table where Gunnar, Mia, Ola, Jana and Per were already seated.

"Are you going to be presenting any suspects today?" Anders asked, his eyebrows raised.

"No, we haven't gotten that far yet," Henrik said with uncertainty in his voice, looking at Gunnar.

"And yet you have no less than two representatives from the prosecution here already," Anders continued, looking at Jana and Per.

Per stretched a little uncomfortably, but Jana didn't move a muscle.

"We may collaborate here in a way that you aren't familiar with," Gunnar said. "On the other hand, we aren't used to having National Crime in the room, either. But thank you for pointing that out and welcome to the meeting. Shall we begin?"

Gunnar turned toward Henrik.

"Yes, well, last Thursday night," Henrik began,

"Pimnapat Pandith, whom we can call Pim, arrives in Norrköping by train with her friend Siriporn Chaiyen. Siriporn, who also goes by Noi, dies of an overdose. Pim is in shock and runs from the train where a man in a car is waiting for her. According to what she herself has told us, she is taken to a room, which she describes as cold and located near water. It might be an abandoned summer cottage, a shed or a boathouse of some sort."

"But a boathouse wouldn't necessarily have two stories, would it?" Mia interrupted. "I'd be more inclined to believe it was an abandoned cottage or something."

Henrik nodded and continued, "In any case, Pim is able to escape from the room or cottage and is found by Christian Bergvall, who calls the emergency number. She's now receiving care at the hospital. We will keep her there, and we've put a guard on her because she is likely sitting on important information that someone doesn't want us to know."

"We hope to question her further," Jana interjected, "above all on the question of the man who picked her up at the train station."

"What do we know about who she was working for at this point?" Anders asked.

"At present, not much," Henrik said.

"But we are working on it," Gunnar added quickly.

"How, if I may ask?"

"The plan is to continue questioning Pim, of course," Jana said.

"Yes," Henrik said, "but we have also gotten a description of the man who picked her up. We've also gotten hits on the dead woman's passport, isn't that right, Ola?"

Ola leaned forward, his knit cap pulled partially back so that it resembled a pointy mountaintop on his head.

"Thai Airways confirms that Siriporn Chaiyen was on a plane from Bangkok that landed at Kastrup Airport in Copenhagen on Thursday morning."

"And Pim? Or, I mean, Pimnapat?" Mia asked.

"That's more difficult," Ola said. "Not one single name began with 'Pim.'"

"But she could have come on a different flight," Henrik said.

"Or she could be lying," Mia said. "Her real name might be there."

"How were the tickets booked, do we know?" Jana asked.

"The ticket," Ola said. "Only one ticket was booked in Siriporn Chaiyen's name."

"Online?"

"Via a travel agency in Bangkok."

"And payment?"

"No information, so probably cash."

Ola pulled his hand over his cap.

"It would have been easier if we'd had her passport," he said. "But sooner or later, we'll find out her name."

"I wonder about that," Henrik said. He wasn't at all sure that Pim would tell them of her own accord.

"But what has she said so far about the drug smuggling?" Anders asked.

"She's quite unclear about that," Jana said.

"I agree," Henrik added. "But she thinks that the man who picked her up at the station had made a mistake regarding her and Noi. She claims that she was only traveling with Noi to keep her company… that she never had anything to do with drugs."

"And what do we think about that?" Anders asked.

"Doubtful…" Henrik said.

He paused for a moment.

"Okay, if we don't have any more questions for the moment about the Thai women, I thought we could shift to case number two. Robin Stenberg," Henrik said, flipping through his papers. "He was found murdered in his home yesterday, and the perpetrator or perpetrators are still on the loose. The technical investigation has just been completed and…what should I say, nothing of value has been found. A pack of ham in a vegetarian's refrigerator is our best clue at the present moment. We also know that Robin was convicted of possession of heroin and that this could be a connection to the case with the Thai women."

"Isn't that drawing a hasty conclusion?" Anders asked. "Connecting the murder of Robin Stenberg to narcotics smuggling?"

"We are making no assumptions here," Gunnar said.

"Well, at least there's *that*," Anders said, smiling.

"But we haven't yet gotten a clear answer to the question of whether Robin Stenberg was still using drugs," Per said.

"No, not yet," Henrik said. "In which case, what we do know is that Robin Stenberg had a close relationship with a sixteen-year-old girl, Ida Eklund, and that she happens to be missing since Friday evening. A lot points to her being at Robin Stenberg's apartment on Friday evening."

Henrik again paused.

"Might she have something to do with the murder?" Per asked, leaning forward.

"Of course," Henrik said. "But because of how the murder was committed, I don't think the perpetrator was so young. I believe we're dealing with a professional murderer here. But that's just my own conclusion."

"Yes, and you believe instead," Mia said, "that Ida Eklund could be the girl that the Thai woman claims to have been imprisoned with."

"But what points to that?" Gunnar asked.

Henrik gave Mia a tired look.

"So far, nothing," he said. "It was just something that struck me when we were talking to the Thai woman. One girl is missing, while in another place, a girl pops up…"

"So Ida Eklund could really be in a completely different place?" Gunnar asked.

"Yes, absolutely," Henrik said. "And she could be staying away of her own accord."

Jana looked up from her notepad.

"Still no trace of her, then," she said.

"No," Henrik said, shaking his head.

"Okay, but if we go back to the Thai woman, this Pim," Anders said. "The place, or this room, what does she say about it?"

"Hardly anything," Henrik said, walking to the large, detailed map on the wall. A red dot marked where she had been found on Highway 209.

"She was on foot, and she had likely been moving fairly slowly. It's hard to believe that she could go faster than about two miles an hour, considering how frozen and stiff she probably was."

With a ruler, Henrik had already measured the maximum distance in relation to that pace, marked it south of the red dot and, using a large compass, he drew a large circle.

"She mentions water," Henrik continued, "which means that within the primary search area, we can concentrate on searching along the coast. We'll begin on the north shore near Marviken, Viddviken and the other areas near there."

Henrik pointed to the map again.

"We should find the place she was kept captive in this area. We have patrols searching there right now."

"How many buildings are there in the area?" Per asked.

"We're working on finding out," Henrik said, sitting down. "But since we don't know much about the place right now, what do we know about the perpetrator? That he had a car with a fake license plate, was wearing dark clothes and has dark hair."

"Nothing more than that?" Gunnar asked.

"No," said Henrik.

"Then we should call a press conference," Gunnar said.

"And ask the general public for help in finding the man?" Henrik asked. "I don't think…"

"Do you have a better suggestion?" Gunnar asked.

"But don't we have enough to go on for now?" Henrik asked. "I just mean that more tips could lead us in the wrong direction. We already have people searching in the area where the Thai woman was found."

"Or it could lead us in exactly the right direction. Someone must have seen something, either at the train station or out on the coast. We aren't hunting ghosts!"

Gunnar sat with his elbows on the table and buried his face in his hands.

"Right now, only the Thai woman knows who he is," he said.

"But she's not talking," Mia said.

"Then we'll have to make sure she does," Gunnar said.

"So now we finally have something in common," Per Åström said to Jana Berzelius when the other team members had left the conference room.

"I don't follow you," she said.

"The investigation."

"We don't know that yet. There's no established connection between the Thai women and Robin Stenberg's murder."

"The drugs?"

"That's too weak right now."

"Well, you're lucky then, because if there is a connection you just might have to see me more often," Per said.

"I'll take that as harassment toward a colleague," Jana said, studying Per as he took his short green jacket from the chair. She wondered why he so stubbornly wore that hooded jacket that was far too sporty for this environment. It would be much more appropriate for the ski slopes in Åre.

"What do you think? Here or in town?"

"What's that?"

"Lunch. You have to eat, I have to eat, so we might as well eat together, right?"

Jana gave him a tired look.

"What?" he said, hands out to the sides.

"Nothing," she said, pulling her coat over her shoulders.

"In town is better, right? It'd be good to get out of here. In the station cafeteria, people might see us together, and I don't want that. They might get ideas, think we're together or some other horrible thing."

Jana put one hand on her hip, tilted her head to the side and looked at him, his wide, irritating grin.

"Come on!" he said, laughing.

"Where should we go?"

"We'll decide on the way," Per said.

They walked out of the police station and were met by whirling, glittering snowflakes. It was colder now and Jana wrapped her arms around herself.

"Sushi?" Per asked. "Or McDonald's. I end up eating there fairly often."

"Then it'd be good to have a change of pace, right?" Jana said. "There's a good Thai restaurant in Old Town."

They walked up Kungsgatan, alongside men and women with strollers and a few joggers. They passed a beggar holding out a paper cup, shaking the coins inside in hopes of attracting attention. They turned left onto Sandgatan and continued over the bridge, passing three men in thick overalls leaning against the black railing with long fishing poles in their hands. The snowflakes had formed a white blanket on their shoulders and knit caps.

Per talked the whole time. She directed the conversation to him and his work, which wasn't hard. When he asked questions, she gave short answers, then either returned the question or was quiet. She hadn't planned to have lunch with anyone that day, but when she walked along in the falling snow with Per next to her, she realized with astonishment that her thoughts of Robin Stenberg and Ida Eklund slowly faded and that Per was actually quite good company.

* * *

Henrik Levin got out of the car and inhaled deeply, thinking that winter didn't smell as much. What did snow actually smell like, though?

Mia walked next to him, texting with Martin Strömberg.

"You can put your phone away now," Henrik said as he rang the doorbell. They were standing outside the Eklunds' row house and heard the bell ring melodically inside the house.

After a moment, Petra opened the door, a smile on her face. When she saw Henrik and Mia, she took a few steps backward in the hall.

"Come in, come in," she said, happening to catch a jacket that fell from its hanger on the coatrack to the floor. She picked it up, laughing as she replaced it on the hanger.

"It's Ida's jacket," she said. "Sorry, I'm just so happy she's home again!"

She gestured with her hand, repeating that they should come in. Henrik and Mia followed her through the hallway and into the kitchen, where Petra set out coffee cups and invited them to sit at the table. Just then, Magnus entered and said hello.

"Ida, the police are here now," Petra called. Ida came into the kitchen immediately, pulled up the zipper on her hooded sweatshirt and sat between her parents. They looked at her, but she avoided their eyes. Her eyes were red and swollen from crying.

"My name is Henrik Levin, and I'm the detective chief inspector. This is my colleague Mia Bolander," Henrik said.

"I haven't been hiding, if that's what you think," Ida said impatiently, as if she had already explained this many times.

"We don't think that," Henrik said. "But we are wondering where you've been."

"I stayed overnight at a friend's."

"Whose name is…?"

"'Whose name is…'" she muttered sullenly, crossing her arms over her chest. "I was at Sofia's, who else?"

"Sofia is clearly also a new friend we didn't know about," Magnus explained.

"But you don't need to know everything, either," Ida said with a sigh.

"And Sofia can confirm that you were there?" Henrik asked Ida.

"Yes, she can," Ida said. "Her mother can, too." Petra nodded.

"That's right," she said. "I've already talked with both of them. Sofia seems conscientious and smart."

"What does that have to do with anything?" Ida said.

"Nothing, I just…" Petra fell silent, then sighed and met Henrik's eyes. At the same time, Mia's cell phone rang. She looked at it before pushing the button to ignore the call.

"As you know, we're here to talk about Robin Stenberg," Henrik said. "You were a couple?"

Ida rested her elbows on the table and laid her chin in her hands.

"Maybe," she said.

"Were you or not?"

"We were, and we weren't."

"Ida," Magnus said, "can't you just answer properly?"

"Yes, okay, we were together."

"How long had you known him?"

"Like, four months."

Her eyes had again filled with tears. Magnus laid his arm across his daughter's shoulders, but she shook it off.

"Do you know if Robin used drugs?" Henrik asked.

"I think so."

"What?" Petra said, turning toward Ida. "Dear Lord, not that, too."

"Why do you think that?" Henrik asked.

"He wrote a few songs about it. You just kind of know."

"But did you ever see him under the influence?"

"No, but I wasn't with him all the time."

"Do you know who else he hung out with?"

"No, but he liked to hang out at the community arts center and other rehearsal spaces like The Bridge and stuff."

"The Bridge?"

"Down in the industrial area somewhere."

Henrik nodded.

"Have you tried drugs yourself?"

Ida shook her head.

Petra looked at her for a long time.

"Really! I haven't!"

"Is it true that you were at Robin's on Friday?" Henrik asked.

"Yes."

"When were you there?"

"Like when did I get there and stuff, or what?"

"Yes."

She dried her eyes with one arm.

"You left the house at four…" Petra began.

"I can talk for myself, can't I?"

"Yes, of course. I just wanted to…"

Ida fell silent, her lips tightly closed.

"So you left the house here at four o'clock?" Henrik asked.

"Yes," Ida mumbled, "and I went to Robin's."

"What did you do?"

"The usual."

"Which is?"

"Just, like, hang out. Watch movies and stuff."

"Did you notice anything unusual over the course of the evening?"

"Well, I wanted to go out and do something, but he didn't want to. He's usually always the one nagging to go out, but on Friday he didn't want to. He, like, refused."

"And what happened?"

"I went out by myself. Who wants to sit there moping around on a Friday night? I don't, so I left.

It was around eight, maybe eight thirty, I don't remember exactly. I…"

Ida's lip trembled. It was as if she had suddenly become aware that Robin was actually dead.

"I was really irritated, thought he was being boring by wanting to sit inside the whole time."

"How did he react to that?" Henrik asked, hearing Mia's cell phone ring again.

"He said that I could go out however much I wanted as long as he didn't have to. He was so, I don't know, so strange those last days. He didn't even want to go to the grocery store. He did it, but he was, I don't know, just strange."

"In what way?"

"He was in a hurry, wanted to rush all the time."

"Was there any reason for him to be like that?"

Ida lowered her gaze, thinking for a moment, then nodded slowly.

"Yes…" she said, hesitating. "It was like he was scared."

"Of what?" Henrik asked.

She swallowed, thinking. Henrik continued; he wasn't going to let her go now, not when she seemed so close to revealing something more, maybe even an answer.

"He never told me," she said.

"Do you have your own idea about what could have made him scared?"

Ida's lips trembled again, but she regained her composure and the hard, defiant look in her eyes.

"Ida," Magnus said. "You have to tell if you…"

"Yes! I know. But I don't know… He said that he'd seen something."

"When did he say that?"

"When he came home on Wednesday. I was there waiting for him and when he showed up, I thought he seemed a little strange, so I asked what it was. That was when he said that something had happened…"

"What sort of something?"

"That's what I don't know! He never said what it was. He just sat in front of his computer and then went to the window, tilted the blinds, looked out and then closed them again. He did that a lot. Then I got tired and went home. He was just as strange on Friday."

"And you have no idea?"

Ida shifted uncomfortably in her chair.

"Yeah, well, so…he bought sometimes…from some older guy, and I thought it maybe had to do with that…"

"What did he buy?" Henrik asked.

"But, Ida, what did he buy?" Magnus echoed.

"It was just a little that he, like, smoked…"

"Were you ever with him when he met up with this older guy?"

"No, never…"

"Okay," Henrik said calmly as he collected his thoughts. "But if we go back to Friday, you left Robin's apartment around eight or eight thirty?"

"Yes, I went out to the bus. The bus stop is just across the street."

"Did you see anyone in the stairwell or in the general area?"

"I didn't meet any *drug pushers*, if that's what you're wondering," Ida said sarcastically.

"But you didn't observe anything else?"

"Observe?" she repeated. "Well, I saw…"

She stopped when Mia's cell phone rang again.

"Sorry," Mia said. "I have to take this." She got up from the table and disappeared into the hallway. Henrik heard her answer, "Hey, Martin."

He sighed, turning back to Ida.

"Tell me, what was it you saw?"

"What I saw when I was standing there was a woman walking away from the building, or maybe she was just walking past, I have no idea. I noticed her because she was so, like, well dressed. She didn't really fit in there, if you get what I mean."

"Explain it to me."

"Well, it's not often you see people like her in the area."

"Ida, now, you're being mean toward the people who live there," Magnus said.

"But how can I explain it, then? Okay, she looked like a rich bitch, is it better to say that? She had straight glossy hair, a totally gorgeous scarf and then a fucking huge BMW that she hopped into. I'm going to have one like it when I move out."

"Then maybe it's time for you to start saving your money," Magnus said.

"Why? Maybe I'll win the lottery or something, or find a sugar daddy, you never know."

"No…" He sighed.

"And you're sure it was a BMW?" Henrik asked.

"Completely. You don't see cars like that in that area. But maybe I shouldn't say that, either?"

Ida's voice stuck in her throat.

"Did you see the license plate of the BMW?"

"No, it was too far away."

"And did you observe anything else?"

"Well…" She sighed. "I was watching that woman, like, the whole time. But after she'd driven away, I saw a man leave through the door of the building."

Out of the corner of his eye, Henrik saw Mia appear in the doorway.

"From Robin's building, I mean," Ida said. "And…the man got into a car that was parked there on the street."

"What did he look like?" Henrik asked.

"He had dark hair, dark eyes."

"Do you remember anything about the car he got into?"

"It was a dark color, that's it."

"Type?"

"No, it was just a normal car, like a Volvo or something."

Henrik felt his heart starting to pound in his chest. He glanced at Mia and saw that she was thinking the same thing. A dark Volvo. Could it be the same car that was at the train station?

Ola Söderström worked quickly over the keyboard, searching again through Robin Stenberg's computer. He had previously checked Robin's private conversations and now, when he went through all of the cookies, he found sites with social protest commentary.

Ola sat in his room at the police station with his feet up on the desk, eating chips directly out of the bag and bobbing his head in rhythm with the music streaming out of the Bluetooth speaker to which his iPhone was connected.

Under the username Eternal_sunshine, Robin had written a number of comments and articles and had even started a debate on the site *Stand Up for Human Rights* that highlighted people who protested and "exposed the hidden plans of governments, big business and their bureaucracies." Eternal_sunshine had commented on a journalist's article about the Nobel Prize winner Aung San Suu Kyi. He had even expressed his opinions on an article about the struggle for freedom in East Timor, which had been violently occupied by Indonesia.

Ola wiped his greasy hands on his jeans, dropped his feet to the floor and pulled the keyboard closer.

He continued to skim through the cookie files and found a thread started by Eternal_sunshine that was only a few days old. He read quickly through the discussion, which was published in the gossip forum Flashback. It was about an assault.

An assault that had happened in Knäppingsborg.

They drove in silence most of the way, which didn't bother Henrik. But it clearly bothered Mia.

"Are you upset or what?" she asked.

"I'm not upset. I just think it was unnecessary for you to answer your phone when we were in the middle of a conversation with Ida Eklund," Henrik said, gripping the wheel. "Really unprofessional, if you ask me."

"Maybe it was important."

"What *we* were doing was important."

Mia glared at him.

"But you were still there."

"You know what I mean."

"Okay, I'm so fucking sorry then."

She pursed her lips and turned her face away, looking out the car window. When the Christmas song playing on the radio had ended, she turned toward Henrik again.

"Tell me, then."

"What should I tell you?"

"What I clearly missed during the questioning that made you so upset."

"I'm not upset."

He pulled his hand across his face before he continued, "Ida said that she saw a dark man driving a car…"

"That was probably a Volvo. I heard that. Was there something else that came up, or what?"

Henrik thought about the woman Ida had described and felt the uneasiness come creeping into his chest. It was a strange coincidence that bothered him more than a little bit. Should he tell Mia that Ida had described a woman with a large, shiny

BMW, a woman who bore an uncanny resemblance to Jana Berzelius?

He hesitated. It would only raise unnecessary suspicions if Jana hadn't been the woman Ida saw on Spelmansgatan in Navestad.

"No, not really," he said. "Nothing else came up."

"Well, then," she said. "So I didn't miss anything."

They drove on in silence, which didn't seem to bother Mia anymore. But now it bothered Henrik.

It wasn't in her briefcase, or anywhere.

Jana Berzelius looked at Per Åström, who took the bill from the server at Sing Thai restaurant.

Round lamp shades hung from the ceiling, and there were yucca plants and gold statues and figures in every window.

"Do you remember if I had my scarf on the way here?" she asked, looking around the chair, lifting the white tablecloth and checking under the table.

"No, you didn't," he said.

"I had it yesterday, when I went to the police station."

"You must have forgotten it there."

Jana looked at her watch.

"Did we have to *walk* here?" she asked.

"Are you stressed?" Per said. "It's Sunday."

"I hadn't planned on a two-hour lunch. I have to be in court tomorrow."

"Little bit of prep to do, then?"

"Yes."

"But can't you get your scarf tomorrow?" he asked.

"My car is parked there, too, so I have to go back anyway."

She finished her water and got up. She watched out the window as a car spun its tires trying to get up the hill, finally getting traction and disappearing from view.

"I know what you're thinking," Per said.

She turned toward him.

"Impossible," she said curtly, pulling the belt of her coat tightly around her waist.

"No, seriously," he said. "I know what you're thinking. And I agree, we should take a taxi back."

Before she could answer, he had pulled out his cell phone.

She took her briefcase and stood just outside the door of the restaurant, noticing a cigarette butt lying on the ground outside. The flattened, wrinkled yellow filter and the dirty cigarette paper being gradually dissolved by the wet snow.

"It will be here soon," Per said when he came out.

"Good," Jana said, her gaze still locked on the cigarette butt.

"So you're saying that Robin Stenberg witnessed an assault last Wednesday?"

Henrik Levin pulled his hand over his chin, feeling the stubble scratch against his fingers. He looked at Ola's energetic face. Mia was nibbling on a gingersnap and held four more in her hand.

"Yes," Ola said. "I found Eternal_sunshine on the crime forum Flashback."

"And you're sure it's him? Anyone could call themselves Eternal_sunshine, couldn't they?"

"No, that's not right. Forums like this allow only one user to have a certain username. The IP address matches, too—the comment comes from his computer. It is Robin, without a doubt."

"What does he say?" Henrik asked.

"Here," Ola said, passing a sheaf of papers to him and Mia. "Read for yourselves."

Henrik took the papers and sat on a stool to begin reading. The thread had begun at 11:42 p.m. Wednesday night.

Robin had written:

[Anyone know anything about an assault tonight?]

Two minutes later, there was a response from someone who called himself Redflag.

[What assault? By Swedes?]

[Knäppingsborg. Entrance to Järnbrogatan. A man and a woman.]

[Rape?]

[Didn't seem like it. No one saw or heard anything?]

[A man in a hoodie and dark clothes, maybe a leather jacket or something. Sitting on top of a woman hitting her. No one saw or heard anything? Someone must've been near there around 10 at night.]

There was an answer from Nothingtolooose.

[How do you know all that? Were you the one doing the assaulting r wat?]

[No. But someone must've seen something.]

Donotdo wrote:

[Must have been your typical love quarrel. Silly to make such a big thing out of it.]

[What "big thing"?] Robin wrote. [If you think it's normal to get beat up, I have to wonder what your relationships have been like.]

Donotdo: [I'm of the belief that there isn't a single woman who is completely innocent. She must have provoked him in some way that meant she deserved it.]

Nothingtolooose: [Are you crazy r wat? Since when does a woman deserve to be beaten up, regardless of whether she provoked her man? If a man doesn't have big enough balls NOT to hit his woman, he should be locked up for good.]

Donotdo: [I sense you're a woman?]

Nothingtolooose: [Whatever.]

Robin wrote: [He ran away.]

Nothingtolooose: [Weak bastard.]

Redflag: [If we were to give a percentage of possible suspects, we could divide them into two piles. 1. Unknown suspect. 2. Suspect with connection to the victim. I hope the woman recovers and that the idiot that did this ends up behind bars.]

Redflag: [I'd put a twenty on it being an ex-boy-friend that beat her.]

Golddigger: [Not finding any info. Nothing in the media. Smells fishy.]

Nothingtolooose: [Talk about a troll.]

[No.] Robin wrote. [It's true.]

Redflag: [Bullshit. Stuff like this has been made up before and the story actually sounds really un-likely, but never say never, I wasn't downtown to-night so actually have no idea.]

[But I was there. I saw everything.] Robin wrote.

Redflag: [You saw everything go down?]

Robin: [Yes.]

Redflag: [Tell us more details then.]

Henrik looked up at Ola, who was still standing in the room. He sat like that for a moment, looking at Ola's face, his gray knit cap with hair sticking out around his ears, waiting for Mia to finish reading.

"He didn't write any more?" she asked.

"No," Ola said. "But he obviously saw something that bothered him."

"Have we gotten a report on this?" Henrik asked, waving the papers.

"No," Ola said. "I checked, but no one filed a report."

"Okay," Henrik said.

"And that's too bad," Ola said, "because it would have been better if Robin had spent his time com-ing to us with this information rather than wasting time asking around on a forum like this."

"But wait, maybe he did," Henrik said, flinging the papers onto his desk as he got up and walked toward Anneli's office.

She placed her purse in its usual spot next to her desk. Anneli Lindgren sat in her office chair, read through a few emails that had just arrived, then closed her eyes and slowly rolled her head in a circle, realizing how tense she was.

Then she felt a warm hand on her neck. Fingers encircling the stiffness, fingers that slowly began to massage it away.

"God, that feels great," she said without opening her eyes.

She moaned when the pressure against her neck grew firmer. Gunnar had always had a special ability to find where her body was sore and he never tired of massaging her; he continued until the tension had broken up.

She hadn't heard him come into the room, but now she thanked the powers that be for his presence. Maybe he'd seen her through the doorjamb, had seen how she'd rubbed her own neck and knew she needed a helping hand.

She smiled and opened her eyes, and looked at the face reflected in her computer screen.

It wasn't Gunnar!

"What do you think you're doing?" she hissed, twirling around in her chair.

"Relax a little," Anders said ingratiatingly.

"Stop that," she said.

"You seemed to like it."

She felt herself blushing and turned her back on him again.

"I thought you were someone else," she said. "I want you to leave."

"Are you sure?" he asked.

"Anders, go. Now."

He didn't answer. Instead, she felt how the chair rocked slightly—he had leaned forward, was holding his face close to hers, whispering in her ear, "See you later… Anneli."

She heard his footsteps across the floor, the door slowly closing. The feeling of his fingers on her skin remained.

She was irritated. Irritated that he had taken the liberty of coming into her office and coming on to her. But mostly irritated that he had been right.

She had liked it.

"Pull yourself together," she said to herself. "Pull yourself together, right now."

A quick nod. Nothing more. That was how Henrik Levin greeted Anders Wester when they met in the hallway outside Anneli's office. Henrik knocked quietly before opening the door.

"Come in," Anneli said brusquely, staring at him.

Then she averted her gaze and began shuffling the papers around on her desk.

"Am I disturbing you?" he asked.

"No, of course not."

She turned back to him and smiled. "What can I do for you?"

"I need your help," he said. "When we searched Robin's apartment, we found a ticket with a number on it there, right?"

"That's right," she said, turning toward her computer. "Do you want to see it?"

"Absolutely."

It didn't take long for the number ticket to appear on the screen. "Welcome to the Police Station" was written in capital letters at the top of the folded white paper.

"I had actually intended to talk to you about that," Anneli said. "As you can see, he took the ticket out of the dispenser on Friday at 10:41 a.m."

"So he was here then," Henrik said, "the same day he was murdered."

"Yes."

"That's so strange, because Ola checked and there's no record of him being here."

CHAPTER

TWENTY

PIM LAY PROPPED UP IN THE HOSPITAL bed with her arms crossed over her chest. Her wounds were clean and bandaged, but the pain in her toes had become worse, spreading up into her leg. The skin had turned dark in places.

She had contracted pneumonia in connection with the chill and had consequently been moved to a small room in the Isolation Ward, Ward 20 at Vrinnevi Hospital.

She had to lie in the room by herself with the irritating buzzing sounds of the machines around her. Her body was heavy, like she was being pushed down into the mattress.

She looked around the room, thinking of her little sister, Mai, and feeling panic wash over her because she was still here in this cold land. Slowly she folded back the blanket, heaving her legs out of the bed and coming to a seated position. She sat like that for a moment, catching her breath and trying to wiggle her toes.

She shivered as her bare feet touched the floor. She tried to stand but collapsed. Lying on her back on the floor, she stared at the ceiling for a moment before rolling onto her side, grimacing at the pain but rising to her knees. Supporting herself with the bed frame, she pulled herself up and stood for a moment on shaky legs.

She closed her eyes and collected herself. She listened for sounds outside the door but didn't hear anything, no steps, no voices.

She took one step forward.

And one more.

She felt her strength come back and took two more, and then two more. She reached the door and opened it. The chair where the guard usually sat was empty and the hallway was deserted, not a nurse in sight.

So she began to run. She ran as fast as she could toward the glass doors. She was out of breath after only a few steps, but she continued running on her shaky legs.

A voice called out after her.

"Hey!"

Twenty more steps to the end of the hallway.

But where was the elevator?

Her naked feet drummed against the floor, her gown flapping against her skin.

Ten steps.

Out through the door.

No elevator!

Just a dead end.

Then she faltered, tried to catch herself with her hands against the wall but crumpled to the floor. She was about to try to stand again when she saw the guard coming toward her with a cup of coffee in his hand.

"Hey, where do you think you're going?"

She didn't protest when he took her back to her room. The only thing she was thinking about was that if she ever had the chance to run away again, she would run in the opposite direction.

Henrik Levin studied the image of the man who pulled the numbered ticket from the dispenser and gripped it in his hand. He was wearing jeans and a shirt and had a brown leather jacket that was many sizes too big—that or it was very heavy, judging from how it hung from his shoulders. The man sat down, looking at the display that had just changed.

"Now serving number 918."

The man's lips moved, and it looked like he was counting how many other people were before him in line.

Henrik turned his gaze to the counter and received an affirmative look from the short-haired female receptionist when he came forward.

"What can I help you and your colleague with?" she asked.

"Were you working here last Friday?" Henrik began.

"Yes," she said, taking off her headset.

"Do you know if a young man named Robin Stenberg was here then?"

"Yikes," she said, her face becoming worried. "It's impossible to remember the names of everyone who comes in here."

"He was here in the morning," Henrik said. "Around 10:30."

"Okay…" she said hesitatingly, still looking worried.

Henrik surveyed the waiting room and was met with a number of questioning looks from stressed visitors wondering why the next number wasn't appearing on the display. What was taking such a long time?

An older woman with purple hair had just gotten up and taken a few steps forward, as if she were ready to pounce as soon as the number changed. She was presumably next in line.

"Robin Stenberg had black hair and eight stars on his temple," Henrik said. "Does that ring a bell?"

"Oh, then I think I know who you mean," the receptionist said, smiling. "He came up and said that he had something to tell us about. I asked if he wanted to report something, but he answered that he just wanted to talk with someone. I asked if it was urgent, and he said no. So I suggested that he call the nonemergency police number, but then he got angry and said he really needed to talk to someone right away. At that point it became urgent, of course."

"What did you do?"

"I took him into an interrogation room."

"With whom?"

"Axel Lundin."

"Is he here now?"

"He's off today."

"You don't have his telephone number?"

"Wait," she said, reaching for a list.

She quickly wrote the number down on a piece of paper and gave it to Henrik before putting on her headset again, saying, "I should probably take some customers again."

"Thanks for the help," Henrik said just as the display changed.

"Number 919," called the receptionist, and Henrik heard the purple-haired woman clip-clop over the floor.

Five minutes later, Henrik was back in his office, his chair squeaking as he sat down. He turned his computer on and searched the system. If Robin Stenberg had come into the police station to file a report, the police clerk Axel Lundin should have recorded it as an affidavit. Once entered, an affidavit couldn't be taken back or deleted. It was archived in the system for all eternity. He stared at the screen.

Ola had been right.

There was no affidavit from Robin Stenberg.

Strange, he thought.

Henrik picked up the phone and dialed Axel Lundin's number. It rang twice.

"This is Axel."

He sounded relaxed.

"Hi, this is Henrik Levin, we're colleagues. I work as detective chief inspector and I need to talk to you about…"

Click.

Henrik stared at his cell phone. The conversation had ended. He called again but didn't get an answer.

Strange, he thought. Very strange.

It had taken Ola thirty seconds to find Axel Lundin's address. It had taken Henrik Levin twenty minutes to find a parking spot.

He called Axel one last time, but there was no answer.

The building didn't have an intercom system, only a number panel to unlock the door. Just as Henrik pulled on the door handle to see if it might be open, an older woman came out with a long-haired Chihuahua in her arms.

She put the dog down.

"Excuse me," Henrik said.

"Yes?" said the woman, looking up at him.

"I'm looking for Axel Lundin. He lives here, right?"

"Yes," the woman said, peering at him. "And who are you?"

"I'm his colleague…"

"Then you've just missed him…" She looked down the street. "But that's him there, standing over there by the car."

"Thank you," Henrik said. "Thanks for your help."

Axel had already had enough of a head start to get into his car, so Henrik turned abruptly and ran quickly back to his own, and began pursuing Axel and his silver Porsche through town.

They drove past the university campus, then slowed down and turned right on Sandgatan toward the industrial district. Axel parked on Garvaregatan, jumped out and disappeared through door number 6.

Henrik looked at the run-down façade, got out and peered through the dark windows. He couldn't make out much. What was Axel doing here?

Henrik suddenly felt freezing cold. It was afternoon by now and he hadn't had anything to eat or drink in hours. On his way back to his car, he stopped in his tracks when he saw a sign over the entrance to number 6.

Even though it was broken, he could still make out the letters. "The Bridge."

He quickly pulled out his cell phone to call Mia to ask her to come quickly, but her line was busy.

"Maybe I'll see you in court tomorrow," Per Åström said as Jana Berzelius shut the door of the taxi.

She had been forced to listen to Christmas music the whole way. The radio station had boasted in a jingle that they were going to play it nonstop until Christmas Eve. She couldn't imagine anything worse.

She turned her collar up and looked at the building that housed the police station.

It had already begun to grow dark, and she could see lights on in a number of windows. In just one hour it would be dark—at just three o'clock in the afternoon.

She had no problem with the darkness, quite the opposite. She appreciated it, felt comfortable and safe in it.

An older couple was walking down the sidewalk some distance from her. Otherwise, the street was empty. She went in through the glass door, into the warmth. Slowly she ascended the stairs to the third floor and entered the conference room and looked around for her scarf.

It wasn't there.

She crouched down, searching everywhere a second time.

But no scarf.

Then she went back through the hallway, checking Henrik's office. He wasn't there. But in the next room, Mia sat with her feet on the desk and her phone pressed to her ear.

Jana leaned against the door frame. Mia didn't sound like herself. She was talking with a silky, unnatural voice and Jana heard something akin to *I miss you* before Mia pulled her phone from her ear and looked toward the door.

"Can't a person talk in peace? What do you want?"

"I just wanted to ask if you've seen my scarf. It's black. Louis Vuitton."

"Haven't seen it. Ask someone else."

Mia turned away and put the phone back to her ear. "Sorry," she said to the person on the other end of the line.

Jana continued down the hallway. She nearly ran into Ola, who came rushing past her. He stopped outside Mia's door and Jana heard him tell her to hang up.

"You have to call Henrik. He's on his way to a building downtown…"

"What happened?"

"Just call him. He's down in the industrial district, Garvaregatan 6. He'll explain…"

Jana gave a start at the address. She felt an icy chill run down her spine and up the back of her neck, then all the way down to her fingertips.

Garvaregatan 6!

She stood still, waiting for Ola, who was now on the way back to his office.

"Where did you say Henrik was? I need to talk to him about something."

"He's looking for a man whom he clearly thinks is in town somewhere."

"Thanks, good to know," she said in a controlled voice.

The last thing she wanted was for the police to search the building.

She pulled open the door to the stairwell and ran down the stairs, slipping along the way but recovering quickly. She leaped down the last few steps before emerging in the parking garage and heading diagonally over the hard, cold cement. She saw a group of three patrol officers and went past them toward her car.

There was a loud bang as she stepped on a sewer grate, and the sound made her speed up. She walked as quickly as she could, then ran the last few yards to her car.

She started her BMW X6 and stepped on the gas.

The hunger and tiredness gnawed at him.

Henrik Levin sat in his car on Garvaregatan and waited for Mia Bolander to appear. With one hand on the steering wheel, he intently gazed at the building. He saw a movement out of the corner of his eye and watched a magpie take flight. Following the bird's fluttering, he leaned forward and saw it disappear behind the roofline.

His stomach growled and he began feeling around in the compartment on the bottom of the driver's-side door. He found only a napkin. Then he looked in the glove compartment, but only the owner's manual was there. He felt around in the pockets of his coat and jeans—not so much as a piece of gum. Finally, he lifted the hinged lid between the seats and rustled around in the pens and receipts, looking for anything edible. He was completely unaware that a woman was quickly nearing the area at that very moment.

And that woman was not Mia Bolander.

Jana Berzelius had parked a couple blocks from Garvaregatan and was now running over the Järnvägsbron bridge, keeping her eyes on the ground. She stayed in the shadows as much as she could.

She knew she should turn around, but instead she yanked open the door at number 6. Ignoring, the elevator, she pumped her legs up the stairs toward the attic. Dust whirled with every step she took. She realized she was acting out of panic. What was she going to do here?

To move the boxes was impossible without someone seeing her. Throwing them away was out, too. She felt cornered.

What if they searched the whole building?

Three stories up, she heard voices. She stopped, listening. Two men talking, their speech slurred.

At least they weren't police.

The men fell silent and raised their eyes as she approached up the steps. They stood close to each other, leaning against a wall that had been carved with names and slang for genitalia, sharing what seemed to be a beer can. One had light blond hair and blue eyes; the other was dark with a scar across his cheek.

Jana looked at the ground, hoping that they wouldn't pay her any attention. But it was pointless to think that was possible.

"Well, would ya look here," the blond man sneered, standing in her way. "Where's a little chickie like you going?"

"Let me pass," Jana said.

"I own this stairwell," the man said. "I own everything here, just so you know. And if you want to get past me, you're gonna have to pay."

"Let me pass," Jana repeated.

"If you pay."

He came closer, and the stink of sour sweat forced its way into her nostrils.

"I'm not going to pay."

"Then I'll make you," the blond said. Jana noticed that he took something from his pocket. She heard a clicking sound as he popped the blade from the shaft of a jackknife.

She felt the familiar calm wash over her as she slowly raised her head and looked the blond man in the eyes.

"Let me pass," she repeated. "I will hurt you if you don't let me pass right now."

The blond man took a step backward, holding the knife and jabbing it toward her. He sneered with narrow, threatening eyes.

"Watch yourself," Jana said, following the man's jerky, arrhythmic movements.

"Or what?" he said. "You'll spit on me? Scratch me with your painted nails?"

"I'll take the knife from you and kick your knee out."

The blond man laughed.

"Do you hear that, Mogge? She's going to kick my knee out. Now I'm scared. *Woooo!*"

"Make her shut up, the little cunt," the dark man said.

"What did you call me?" Jana said.

"Little cunt. You like that, dontcha?"

The blond man stepped forward. The attack came quickly; Jana saw the light reflect on the blade and ducked.

"This is your last warning," she said. "Put the knife down."

"I'm gonna make you shut up," the blond said, and Jana twisted to avoid another lunge.

She stretched out her fingers and then didn't need to think consciously anymore. Everything happened quickly; she was acting on instinct. The moments followed one after another with lightning-quick reflexes.

She bent the blond man's wrist and used her other hand to help redirect the movement, then wrenched the knife out of his hand and into hers. She shifted her weight and kicked sideways toward his knee. As he doubled over, she shifted her weight again, twisted her body and kicked once more.

The man fell backward and lay unconscious on the ground.

Jana turned her gaze to the dark man who now stood with his back pressed to the wall. She twirled the knife between her fingers and threw it. The tip slid through his hand and buried itself deep into the wall behind him. Blood gushed onto the ground. The man howled when he realized that he was stuck to the wall.

Jana walked toward him and stood close.

"You probably shouldn't faint," she said. "If you faint, your whole hand will be sliced by that knife and for the rest of your life, you'll have a scar that's much worse than the one on your face. But if you stay standing, it won't require more than a couple of stitches."

Then she turned and continued running up the steps, toward the storage area in the attic.

The large building at Garvaregatan 6 appeared empty and deserted from street level. The windows were just as black as the sky above. Henrik Levin and Mia Bolander stood next to each other outside the door.

"Are we really going to go in?" Mia asked, shivering.

"Yes, we are," Henrik said, pulling the door handle. It was locked.

"Why would anyone store their stuff here? There doesn't seem to be a soul around. We have other things to do, Henrik. Come on."

"I saw Axel Lundin go in here…"

He stopped short when he heard a howl. They looked at each other. "Let's take a look around. I'll go right, you go left."

He heard her footsteps disappear behind him. The gravel crunched under his feet, until he turned the corner and the soft snow muffled the sound of his movement.

He continued past a doorway that was spray-painted with some illegible message. He noticed a weak light in one of the basement windows, then a shadow moved.

He moved more quickly, searching for a way in. He turned and went back toward the doorway. There was a window with its pane broken out. It was narrow, but it was a way in. He wormed his way inside, cursing as the sharp glass jutted out like knives around the window's edges, ripping his jacket to shreds.

Thirty seconds later, he found himself on the basement floor. It was pitch-black until his eyes adjusted and he could finally make out the contours in the room.

It smelled musty from old piss. A damp T-shirt lay on the floor, along with toilet paper rolls that had flattened from the dampness, empty beer cans, cigarette butts, empty cigarette packs and a used condom. It looked like a homeless encampment, a place to use drugs and sleep before moving on to a park or maybe even a hospital bed.

Henrik listened quietly.

A sound...like knocking.

He continued in its direction, but regretted having split up with Mia. He took out his phone and whispered his position, asking her to come. Just as he put his cell into his pocket, he heard the sound of breaking glass.

Then through a door he could see the rest of the basement, a long hallway with doors on both sides. Everything was bathed in a dim light.

Now he also heard murmuring voices and could tell a number of people were in the building. From a door opening farthest from him he could make out a pale face that stared directly at him with wide-open, scared eyes.

"Axel, I just want to talk to you," Henrik said.

The man took a step back.

"Stand still," Henrik said. "I just want to talk."

Instead the man slammed the door. Henrik heard quick steps across the floor and knew that everyone was fleeing. He fumbled for his cell phone and requested reinforcements as he ran after them.

The door creaked as Jana Berzelius unlocked her storage space and stepped inside. Her eyes scanned the small room. The wooden bench, the wall closet with the padlock open. The pale yellow walls.

But…where were her boxes? The boxes that contained evidence of her secret past.

It took a second for her to comprehend that the bench was empty; the boxes gone.

The shock and confusion made her suddenly short of breath. Her thoughts whirled around in her head, and she broke out in a sweat. Her back, palms and forehead became damp. She shut her eyes tightly, hoping that the boxes would be there when she reopened them. But they weren't.

She was having a hard time collecting her thoughts.

On the floor lay a sketch of a face. Danilo. The one she had drawn herself.

It wasn't there by coincidence. It was a greeting.

She closed her eyes, sank to the floor and put her face in her hands. Danilo had come into the storage space and stolen her journals, her secret journals, her most important belongings.

But how had he known that she was storing everything here? Had he been watching her?

She got up suddenly and examined the door, but there was no indication of a break-in. He had probably picked the lock.

She stood in the middle of the room, feeling naked. She had never before felt as vulnerable and powerless as she did in this moment. He had everything in his hands, proof of a past that could cost her her whole career, that could cost her everything. Absolutely everything.

But what did he want with the boxes? Were they his insurance that she wouldn't do something he didn't like?

She looked at the sketch.

She thought about her decision to keep him out of her life, to move on. Now she again stood at a crossroads.

The decision was easy this time. She had previously fantasized about his death, but not anymore. Now she began to plan it.

He was going to regret having started this.

* * *

Henrik Levin didn't like the dark but forced himself not to think about it as he ran through the basement hallway, his gun drawn in pursuit of those who were fleeing.

He opened the door at the end of the hall and saw a sofa in the corner, a dirty mattress on the floor and a pool table in the middle of the room.

No one was there. The footsteps had disappeared.

He listened, then went into the room. He had the sudden feeling of being watched. He turned around, sweeping with his gun, and scratched the wall with its muzzle. He swung around again, holding his breath, but didn't see anything other than the dimly lit basement hallway.

A blue light shone in through the barred windows, and Henrik knew that reinforcements had finally arrived.

Gravel scraped against the floor as Jana Berzelius opened the door and stepped out into the stairwell. Through the window she saw two police cars and a horde of officers converging on the street below.

They must have found something, she thought. But *she* didn't want to be found. Not here.

She had to find another way out.

She quickly turned back into the storage space.

She knew she had to hurry, had to figure something out. She probably only had a few minutes before her escape route would be closed off.

The police officers immediately dispersed to all floors. Henrik Levin heard their loud footsteps on the floor above him. He was standing in the room with the billiard table and was just about to go out when he heard a sound. A metallic sound, like a steel pipe being dragged against stone.

It was coming from next door.

He went slowly out into the hallway with the pistol pointed in front of him and positioned himself with his back against the wall. He looked carefully through the doorway and suddenly saw Axel Lundin standing there, in the middle of the dark room, ready to attack. But it wasn't a steel pipe—he was holding a crowbar in his hand and was only three long strides away from Henrik.

Axel's eyes had a vacant, disturbing look, and his whole body swayed back and forth.

"Drop the crowbar!" Henrik shouted, showing himself.

Axel took a step forward. Henrik stumbled backward into the hallway. Axel advanced, swinging the crowbar at him, forcing him to take several steps backward.

"Drop the crowbar, for fuck's sake!"

The command came from Mia Bolander, who had entered through a doorway behind the man and was now standing with her feet firmly planted and her pistol pointed at his head.

"Drop it, I said!"

* * *

Jana Berzelius stuffed the sketch of Danilo into her pocket, pulled the bench away from the wall and opened the only way out, a hatch in the ceiling.

With both hands, she heaved herself up into the crawl space above the ceiling, closing the hatch behind her without a sound. She wriggled forward, searching for an opening and finding a large ventilation shaft. She kicked the sheet metal forcefully. It gave immediately, exposing a hole to the roof.

She went feetfirst out onto the slippery roof. She was just about to take a step forward when she nearly lost her balance; something was holding her back.

Her coat had gotten caught in the hole from the ventilation shaft. She wriggled out of it and jerked and pulled until it finally came loose.

Then she disappeared without a sound across the roof.

Henrik Levin crouched down under the pipes in the ceiling and headed back into the room where he had encountered Axel Lundin, who was now being taken by police cruiser into custody.

They had also found two drunk men in the stairwell, where one of them had been in the process of pulling a knife out of the other man's hand. After a brief hearing, they were now being sent to social services.

Mia coughed. She was right behind Henrik, pinching her nose with her fingers to escape the smell of mold and dried urine. In her other hand, she held a flashlight.

The floor was uneven and shards of glass crunched under the soles of their shoes. It was bitterly cold.

"It was right here," Henrik said, pushing the door in front of him. "This is where the light was coming from."

Mia went in, flipping the light switch to no avail—the naked lightbulb in the ceiling didn't turn on. Someone had broken it. She swept the beam of her flashlight across the floor. The room was empty except for glass, gravel, newspapers and flattened paper food containers.

"Let's look in the other room," Henrik said, heading for the door.

"Wait," Mia said, pointing the light toward one part of the cinder block wall, holding it completely still on one of the blocks.

"There," she said, indicating a block on the left before kneeling by it.

It was sticking out slightly, and below it was a small pile of dust and tiny pebbles. Mia laid her flashlight on the floor and tried to get her fingers around the brick, but couldn't get it to budge. Henrik tried as well, also unsuccessfully.

"It's got to come out," she said.

She picked up her flashlight, pointed it at the block and began pounding.

"This was probably why Axel had the crowbar,"

Henrik said as he began to stamp his feet impatiently behind Mia.

"Come on, now," he said as the block began to move.

Finally, Mia got hold of it and pulled it out. With a crash, the block fell to the floor, revealing a large hole.

She shined the light in.

There lay a number of well-packed bags.

All filled with small white balls…

"Totally crazy," she said.

CHAPTER TWENTY-ONE

WHEN MIA BOLANDER OPENED THE CAR door, she noticed a dog tied next to a fence. It held up alternating paws in an attempt to escape the cold ground under its feet. Its cropped tail wagged and it looked at her with desperation in its eyes, then it began to whimper as if to get her to untie the leash. She thought how in a certain way she felt similarly. She felt just as bound up because of an exclusive fucking wristwatch. But she coveted it, the watch. She would wear it 24/7; she just had to come up with a way to get Martin to give it to her before Christmas.

She cast a glance at the wrapped package on the passenger seat and thought that she would have to get Christmas presents for her mom and brother, too. But with what money? She didn't know. Had no idea, actually. What would she be able to spend? Thirty? A hundred, maybe? A hundred wasn't that much, really. The problem was that she didn't have that kind of cash.

She saw her face reflected in the rearview mirror, inspected it and hated the swollen features and the reason she looked that way. She hated the shame that was written on her forehead, her cheeks, in her eyes, the shame over never being able to afford anything.

Irritated, she got out of the car, slammed the door and walked along the shoveled walkway that led to the white house.

A gust of wind made a hammock sway in the yard and she drew the cold air deep into her lungs while waiting for the front door to open.

"Welcome," Stig Ottling said.

Mia looked at the plastic entry rug on the floor and the white walls with light green trim.

"Do you live alone?" she asked.

"Now I do."

Stig gestured with his hand.

"Come in," he said. "Keep your shoes on if you'd like."

"If you say so," Mia said.

"Thirsty?" he asked, going into the kitchen.

"A glass of water would be great," she said, following him.

Stig opened the refrigerator and took out a pitcher with water.

"Cold and refreshing," he said, placing a glass on the table.

Mia sat down and took a sip, noticing that it had absorbed some other taste. Possibly onion.

"This is about your property at Garvaregatan 6," she said.

"Yes, you said that. I prefer to use the old name for the building."

"Which is?"

"Nyborg's Wool Factory."

"Okay. Now, it so happened that two junkies—men, I mean—claim that they were attacked by a woman in your *wool factory*. According to them she was on her way up the stairs. So I'm wondering first of all what this building is used for."

"Oh, nothing much happens there these days. I'm just waiting for approval from the zoning board on the building plans. We plan to renovate, make space for apartments and such. But the process takes time. So it earns basically nothing right now."

"You mean it's empty?"

"I used to rent rooms and such, but not anymore."

"But you already have some tenants, right?"

"Well, it isn't like I don't know that the Wool Factory is used by squatters and addicts, but there's not much I can do about that right now."

"Otherwise is the building empty? No *legitimate* renters?"

"No, they're hard to come by. I've tried to rent out space as storage areas in the attic to cover some of the costs—it's relatively clean—but that hasn't been easy. A few days ago, a woman actually wanted to rent one of the spaces."

"Strange that anyone wanted to rent there," Mia said. "Do you remember her name?"

"Not off the top of my head. She was a lovely little thing. Wore leather gloves. If I were only twenty years younger…well, maybe forty."

"I believe you," Mia said. "Can I see the contract?"

"Of course, of course. I'll go get it," Stig said, leaving the kitchen.

Mia stayed behind, staring into her water glass and thinking how she hated these routine visits.

Stig came back with a rectangular black binder and placed it on the table. He flipped through papers and rental contracts, stopping halfway through.

"Wait a second," he said, starting over. He ran his finger over the names and dates. Page by page, property by property.

"It's in here, the name you're looking for. It starts with a *J*, that much I remember."

Stig flipped through more pages.

"Here it is. Here's the name you're looking for."

He turned the binder around to face Mia and pointed to the corner with his finger.

"JB," he said. "Jenny Bengtsson."

Henrik Levin's shoes stuck to the vinyl floor as he moved his legs. He studied Axel Lundin. The first thing he noticed was the birthmark on his hand, then the wide furrow on his forehead. He had dark hair, dark eyes.

He hadn't slept enough, he thought, because when he sat there with Axel Lundin in front of him, he couldn't help but think about how his appearance didn't only match the man who had been seen at Central Station last Thursday evening, but also the person Ida Eklund had seen outside Robin Stenberg's apartment Friday night.

Next to Axel sat his lawyer, Peter Ramstedt, playing with his gold-colored cuff links.

Axel told Henrik that on Friday evening, he had been at home at his apartment. Henrik was unsure whether he should believe him since he had no real alibi.

"And Thursday evening, around ten, where were you then?"

"Probably also home."

"Probably? You didn't happen to find yourself at the train station?"

"I was at home."

"Okay," Henrik said, looking down at his papers. "But then maybe you can say why you were at Garvaregatan 6 yesterday?"

"Why?" Axel asked. "You clearly figured it out for the most part."

Henrik swallowed repeatedly in an effort to stifle his irritation. He felt such a strong disgust for the sleazy lawyer sitting before him that he wasn't sure how to manage the interrogation.

"I'm going to ask you the same question again and again until you give me an answer," he said, as controlled as possible.

"What do you want, Henry boy?" Peter Ramstedt asked, tilting his head to the side.

"Axel here is under arrest for threatening a police officer and possession of a controlled substance," he said.

"We know that," Peter Ramstedt said.

"I had to defend myself," Axel began. "I thought…"

He put his face in his hands and sighed heavily.

"You thought what?" Henrik asked.

"I thought you were someone else."

"Like who, then? Tell us."

"I don't want to talk to you."

"Well, that's the thing," Henrik said. "I have a very strong desire to talk to someone who can help me solve an investigation."

"I didn't have anything to do with any murder."

"Investigation, I said. Who said that it had anything to do with murder?"

Axel looked down.

"Okay, so maybe we should start there," Henrik said. "Do you know who Robin Stenberg is?"

"No."

"You've never met anyone named Robin Stenberg?"

"No, not that I know of."

"According to our information, he visited Bryggan often."

"But I don't usually meet my…"

"Your what? Your clients? What were you going to say?"

Axel shook his head, his gaze still focused on the table.

Henrik leaned forward, tapping his fingertips together. He was having a hard time sitting still.

"Did you know," he said, "that there are people who make sure evidence is destroyed or disappears? Sometimes it's pure ignorance, as for example when an officer contaminates the scene of a crime with his DNA. That's incredibly frustrating."

Axel lifted his head, blinking twice.

"What are you getting at?" Peter Ramstedt asked.

"What's even more frustrating," Henrik said, his jaw clenched, "is when proof or information is concealed. For us officers, it's important, of course, to secure evidence, or gain access to information, as quickly as possible. It's difficult to do a good job if you have obstacles in your path. A colleague you can't trust, for example."

"Now I'm really not following," Peter said.

"Your client is an officer of the law!"

"Yes, but…"

"On Friday, a young man named Robin Stenberg walked into the police station. He came here because he wanted to talk to someone. He talked to you, Axel."

Henrik's voice was hard. He took a deep breath to calm himself, repeating to himself that he had to keep his emotions from controlling the conversation; had to refrain from showing that he thought Axel was a disgrace to the entire police force.

"What did he want to talk about?" Henrik asked.

"I don't remember," Axel said and looked down at the table.

"So you admit that you talked to him?"

"No, I just meant…"

"Robin wanted to report an attack, isn't that right?"

"Yes…" Axel said slowly.

"Robin wanted to report an attack. So he gave an account of all of the details to you, went home and the next day was found murdered in his apartment. Maybe his murder could have been prevented if an affidavit had been filed. But you never filed one, did you, Axel?"

"Now, that's quite a stretch," Peter Ramstedt said.

But Henrik wasn't listening. He was looking at Axel, who now looked scared. But it wasn't the same fear that he usually saw in those who were taken in for questioning. Axel wasn't scared of the letter of the law; he was scared for his life.

"How did you know?" he asked quietly.

"We found a numbered ticket with the Police Authority's logo on it in his apartment. The receptionist at the station confirmed that he had been there, and that he had talked with you."

Axel's eyes darted around.

"What did Robin want to tell you? And why did you conceal the affidavit?"

"Maybe I was wrong, but I didn't think it was important. I didn't think he seemed trustworthy."

"So you just ignored it?"

"It doesn't matter now, does it?"

"You know that it does. All interactions have to be documented. Why didn't you document his visit?"

"In the first place, it wasn't an attack. He had seen a man and a woman fighting, and I thought he had too little information to be of use…"

Henrik leaned forward and clasped his hands on the table.

"Do you recognize this woman?"

He laid out a picture of Pimnapat Pandith.

"No." Axel shook his head, looking at the picture again. "No, no, no. Who is she?" he asked, looking at Henrik.

"I want you to tell me that," Henrik said.

"But I have no idea!" he insisted.

The room fell silent. Axel looked down at his hands.

"Right now, we're searching your apartment," Henrik said. "We will probably find a whole lot of answers to our questions there. But what do you say, isn't it better to tell us everything yourself? Come on now, let's take everything from the beginning. So you have 'storage' at Garvaregatan 6?"

TWENTY-TWO

JANA BERZELIUS OPENED HER PURSE and pulled out the knife, weighing it in her hand. She swung it back and forth where she stood in her apartment hallway. First slowly, then more quickly. The sharp blade sliced through the air.

She had a hard time taking in the enormity of the implications that Danilo had taken her notes and journals and left a message in the form of a sketch she herself had made of him.

It was incredibly humiliating.

What did he want?

She reached forward with her empty left hand, then made a quick attack with her right, and one more. She balanced her weight, counted to three and made another attack, directly followed by a kick. A new hold on the knife, a new attack. Her movements were agile, practiced, and would be extremely effective against an opponent.

Sweat was dripping down her forehead when her cell phone suddenly rang. Per Åström's voice was a bit hesitant, as if he didn't know quite what words were going to come out.

"Well," he said. "I happen to have an extra ticket to the hockey game tonight...the White Horses against..."

"I don't like hockey," Jana interrupted, still holding the knife in her hand.

"I know, but I thought..."

"So you know that I'm going to say no."

"Yes."

"Then why are you asking?"

"You have to take chances in this life. You don't have to watch the game. You could just eat popcorn," Per said.

"I'm actually already doing something else tonight."

"Like what?"

Jana fell silent, unable to come up with a white lie.

"Another time, then?" he said.

"I have to be in court in an hour," she said, looking down at the floor and letting her hair fall forward into her face.

"Anything interesting?"

Jana sighed, his questions irritating her.

"I don't have time to talk now, Per. But it's about an assault at a bar."

"On the subject of assaults," he said, "did you hear that we found a potential motive for the murder of Robin Stenberg? The murder may not have had anything to do with his drug use. He had apparently witnessed a fistfight between a man and a woman in Knäppingsborg, or, well, some type of assault anyway."

Jana took a deep breath, feeling her heart beat even faster. She gripped the knife.

"How do you know that?"

"Robin wrote about it."

"Wrote about it? What do you mean? Where?"

She knew that she asked too quickly, was too eager. She closed her eyes, clenched her teeth.

"Online," Per said, "on the Flashback forum. Ola found Robin's posts there. And we've also found Ida Eklund."

"Yes, that much I heard. Has she said anything?"

"Like what?"

"Has she?"

"Now you're certainly curious. If you come with me to hockey tonight I'll tell you more…"

"No, tell me now."

Per took a deep breath.

"Ida was at Robin Stenberg's on Friday evening, and she said that she saw a woman and a man outside the apartment when she was leaving. But why are you asking? Are you thinking of taking over the investigation now? Should I be nervous?"

"I think you should be more worried about who's going to go with you to the hockey game."

"So you haven't changed your mind? The popcorn at Himmelstadslunds Arena is fantastic."

"Goodbye, Per."

She ended the conversation, went into her office,

put the knife on the desk and woke up her computer. Her fingers danced quickly across the keyboard, a little too quickly—she kept mistyping and had to go back and delete, and she realized she was letting her mind race from one thought to the next.

Moving her fingers more slowly, she typed Flashback and hit Enter.

She was met by a sketch of a black-and-white cat with a cigarette hanging from the corner of its mouth. She flipped through various subjects like Computers and IT, Crime and Criminal Cases, and Celebrity Gossip. She used the search field to find Robin Stenberg's posts.

But the search returned zero results; there were no posts by Robin Stenberg.

She began to search by every keyword she could think of that could be connected to her and Danilo. No results found.

She started over again, finding a thread about a woman who had been assaulted by two men in Stockholm. The post had received sixty-three replies, and many of them knew who the perpetrators were.

She clicked on the search field, wrote assault and battery in Norrköping and got a number of hits. Finally, she saw the hit she'd been looking for.

She sat for a long time, reading the thread about the so-called assault in Knäppingsborg.

Under the name Eternal_sunshine, Robin had written everything online. It was all there. Laid out for the whole world to read. About her, about Danilo.

But she exhaled, because no one had seen anything, no one knew anything. The only witness was Robin Stenberg, and he was dead.

She picked up the knife and replaced it in her purse.

Anneli Lindgren stood on the threshold to the kitchen in Axel Lundin's apartment. The appliances were new, countertop polished to a mirror shine. The whole place looked high-end, like it was lifted from the pages of an interior decorating magazine.

She went into the kitchen and began opening the drawers, going through every saucer, bowl and plate. She opened the refrigerator and removed the food, looking in every jar, bottle and package. She cut open the freezer bags of stir-fry vegetables and the special Swedish sausage and potato hash called *pytt-i-panna*. Then she walked into the large, open living room decorated in gray and white tones. A sectional with a chaise lounge, a flat-screen TV mounted on the wall, a lamp arcing over a rectangular table with a white top and silver legs. Multiple side tables with drawers.

She pulled out each of the empty drawers and shone a flashlight from beneath each to look for any hidden doors or crannies.

She pulled up the plants and examined the pots, but found only dirt.

. Then she stood in the middle of the room, processing everything.

She examined the walls and the light in the ceiling. She bent down and looked across the floor, but found nothing out of the ordinary—just an empty, worn duffel bag in one of the corners.

She instead turned her gaze to the large bookshelf, pulled a chair up to it and began to search for anything that might be hidden behind the books. She went through it shelf by shelf, stacking the books on the floor after paging through some of them. After thirty minutes, she put the last book back on the shelf and noticed that all of them were about sports.

She sighed, looking around the room again.

As she got down from the chair, she landed wrong and her ankle buckled. She screamed and sank to the floor. Sitting there on the floor, massaging her hurt ankle, she looked into a small room resembling an office. On the floor stood an extra-large external hard drive. She wouldn't have thought much of it if it hadn't been for the back panel sticking out slightly. It was as if someone had unscrewed it but couldn't quite get it in the right place again.

There were endless reasons to use an external hard drive, like as a backup copy of an internal one or to store important information that could be jeopardized through online activities, or for downloading sensitive information, or large files such as music, photos or films. Her gut told her that Axel

Lundin had a completely different use for his external hard drive.

She fetched her tools and unscrewed the back panel. But there was no sign of the bags of drugs she had expected to see. The hard drive was just a single empty shell.

And was a perfect hiding place for Axel Lundin's money.

It took twenty minutes to find Jenny Bengtsson's apartment on Odalgatan.

The door opened just seconds after Mia Bolander had rung the bell.

"Yeah, whaddya want?"

Mia was struck with the thought that Stig Ottling had terrible taste when it came to women. She surveyed Jenny up and down—yellow aviator glasses, multiple necklaces around her neck and shiny, dark brown hair. The hair made Mia smile faintly, because that was the only thing that matched the description Stig Ottling had given. *"A lovely little thing," my ass.*

"Jenny Bengtsson?" Mia asked.

"Yes…"

Jenny looked skeptically at her, holding her hand on the door handle as if she were ready to close the door in Mia's face. She peered over Mia's shoulder to see if she was alone or not.

"I'm a police officer," Mia said quickly, showing her badge.

"Okay…?" she said questioningly.

"I called you, but you didn't answer."

"Oh, was that you? I don't usually answer calls from blocked ID numbers or ones I don't recognize."

Mia stuffed her badge back in her pocket.

"I need to talk to you," she said. "Is this a good time?"

"Sure, I'm just studying for an exam."

"I need to talk to you about a storage space."

"Okay...?"

Jenny's eyebrows rose behind the frames of her glasses.

"Can I come in?"

"Well, I haven't cleaned or anything. But sure."

She stepped aside and Mia came in, closing the door behind her. She decided to conduct the interview in the hall.

"As I said, it's about a storage space you rented."

"What about it? Was there a break-in? Ugh, I hate that you can never just have things left in peace. Three weeks ago some idiot pinched my bike. It was new. Even had a basket. It cost me five hundred kronor extra just to insure the thing."

"No, this isn't about a break-in."

"No?"

"I was just wondering if you've been there yet."

"What?"

"Have you had the chance to go to your storage space?"

"Of course I have. What sort of question is that?"

Mia smiled sourly.

"When were you there last?"

Jenny took a breath, thinking.

"Two weeks ago, maybe."

"What?"

"Yes, two weeks ago. What's the matter?"

"Wait a minute…"

Mia scratched her head, then took out the rental contract she had gotten from Stig Ottling.

"But you rented the storage space this past weekend, on Saturday."

"No… I've had the storage space the whole time."

"Is this not your signature?"

Jenny looked at the signature that Mia was holding out and began to laugh.

"No, I don't write like that."

"But you have a storage space on Garvaregatan?"

She laughed again.

"No, I don't."

"So you don't abuse drugs?" Henrik Levin said, looking suspiciously at Axel. It had gotten hotter in the interrogation room.

"No," Axel said. "Never have."

"How have you been able to resist?"

"Don't know. I've never tried anything, not even a cigarette. Don't want to subject my body to that shit."

"Instead you subject others to it," Henrik said, "and make them addicted."

"No, I don't."

"No? So what is it you are going to do with all of these balls of heroin, then?"

"I don't know what you want, but you can't prove anything."

"I don't think I need to prove anything, because you're already up to your neck in it. You're going to prison."

"Says who?" Axel said.

"Yes, says who?" Peter Ramstedt echoed, raising his eyebrows.

"Say the men we found with you, Axel, at Garvaregatan."

"They haven't said anything," he said curtly.

"They've spilled everything," Henrik lied. "So, yes, you're going to prison, and, as a police officer, you know the more you cooperate, the milder your sentence will be."

Axel bit his lip repeatedly. Henrik continued, "I've seen a lot of different types of hiding places. Once, a man had hidden his things in a heating pipe that was covered in insulation. He'd poked out a little insulation around one coupling and created a little nook. We would never have found it if he hadn't forgotten to sweep up the bits of insulation that fell on the floor. There were also a ton of fingerprints, exactly like there were on your hiding place."

Axel Lundin wrapped his arms around his body. He had suddenly turned white as a sheet.

"We found a number of empty areas at Garvaregatan and when you were searched, you had multiple bags of heroin balls in your pockets. Why is that? Were you going somewhere?"

Axel didn't answer.

"Did you get spooked when I called yesterday?"

Peter Ramstedt chuckled.

"Can't you stick to relevant questions?"

"The question is relevant. I believe that your client became so frantic when I called him that he immediately rushed to his hiding place to clean out everything that was in there."

Axel squirmed in his seat but remained silent. Henrik waited a moment before asking the next question.

"It also seems relevant to ask who is providing you with the drugs," he then said.

"Why do you ask?"

"You've maybe heard about the woman we found on the train a few days ago?"

Axel looked stressed.

"I don't know anything about what happened before that. I don't want to know, either. The only thing I care about is that the stuff gets to me in time."

"But you might care about it if I say that the woman died because of what she had in her stomach?"

"I know that she died, but I didn't have anything to do with that. It's none of my business."

Axel stretched out his palms.

"Whose business is it, then?" Henrik said.

Axel squirmed in his seat again.

"If it isn't me, it's someone else. I'm... I'm, like, a nobody. Just an insignificant little shit, like this..." Axel held up his thumb and forefinger, a half inch apart. "This is how tiny I am in the big picture. Get it?"

"So whose business is it? Tell me now, Axel. Come on."

"It's his! He's out there," Axel said, pointing with his hand toward the window. "He's completely fucking crazy, no conscience whatsoever."

"Who are you talking about?" Henrik asked, but Axel continued with his hand toward the window.

"You can't fucking let me go now," he said.

"There's not much risk of that happening."

Peter Ramstedt looked like he wanted to object, but Axel spoke up first.

"It'd be a death trap for me out there," he said. "He's never going to let me go. He'll come after me."

Henrik Levin took a deep breath, then spoke in a calm voice.

"Who is going to come after you?"

Axel's shook his legs nervously. He didn't answer.

"Listen," Henrik said. "We're going to go through everything. Your phone, your friends. We will find the person you're talking about."

"I hope for your sake that you don't," Axel said. "Anyone who does, dies."

"Did you think that it was him coming for you in

the basement on Garvaregatan? Was that why you started threatening me with the crowbar?"

"No, I've never met The Old Man."

"What did you say?"

Axel looked perplexedly at Henrik.

"What?"

"You said The Old Man."

"No."

"Yes, I heard you say The Old Man. Do you see that tape recorder on the table over there? That'll prove you said that exact name."

Axel covered his face with his hands.

"Who is The Old Man?" Henrik asked.

"No one." Axel sighed.

"Who calls him The Old Man? Why do people call him that? Is it an older man?"

Axel didn't answer.

"Sooner or later, you're going to have to answer these questions…"

"You don't understand…" he said, shaking his head dejectedly.

"What don't I understand? Was it The Old Man who murdered Robin?" Henrik asked.

Axel began laughing nervously.

"No, you don't understand—he doesn't exist. No one knows who he is—no one!"

Axel closed his eyes and put his hands over his mouth.

"Don't talk, don't talk, don't talk," he muttered.

The lawyer rested one hand on Axel's back, told him to calm down.

"I can't say anything," Axel said, "because I know how those people are, what they do, and I've heard them talk about how they do it."

"Now you're talking about *them* again. If we're going to have a chance of stopping these people, you have to help us find them. Not *protect* them."

Axel looked at Henrik, stamping his feet under the table even more quickly.

"Come on," Henrik said. "Give me names now."

"What's in it for me?"

"Just answer the questions. Who murdered Robin Stenberg and why? Who told you not to document his report?"

Axel swallowed, wringing his hands.

Henrik listened to the chair creaking from Axel's nervous movements.

"Answer me now," Henrik demanded.

Axel met his eyes and mumbled, "Okay, I can give you a name."

"Say it."

"You can look into…"

"Say it."

"You can look up Danilo Peña."

MIA BOLANDER DIDN'T UNDERSTAND
any of it. She stood with Stig Ottling in the storage space at Garvaregatan 6. Or the old cotton factory or whatever it was he wanted to call it.

Someone had stolen Jenny Bengtsson's identity and signed a year-long rental contract. Why? Why this particular building?

She swept her gaze over the closets, walls, floor and wooden bench, then took out her phone and photographed the space from different perspectives. She examined the door, the ceiling. "This wasn't exactly what I was hoping for," she said to Stig on their way back to the car. "An empty storage space, I mean. Can you come with me down to the station and we'll write up a proper report? This is a document forgery, after all."

"Yes, of course," he said.

They got into the car, and while Mia backed out from the parking spot, her thoughts wavered back and forth. *Why would a person rent a storage space under a false name? To hide something?*

But it was empty. Not one single box, no glass showcases or porcelain figurines, no fake Christmas tree or bicycle. None of the usual stuff people kept in storage spaces. There wasn't anything there at all.

On the other hand, the renter didn't seem to be the normal type. Had he or she just not had the chance to use it yet? What was the intended purpose? Stolen goods, maybe?

The only lead was those two idiots who claimed they'd been beaten up by a woman—who would want to admit to that?

But maybe they were telling the truth, despite both being partly disabled and significantly under the influence?

Maybe there was, in spite of everything, an elegant woman out there who knew how to handle a knife.

Anneli Lindgren turned her head when she heard the outside door slam.

Anders Wester came in wearing a brown sport coat, white shirt and steel-toed shoes. He stood behind her, arms crossed, and thoughtfully observed her movements as she placed stack after stack of kronors in white plastic bags.

"Look what I found," she said without looking at him. "This is a sick amount of money."

"Congratulations," Anders said. "Have you counted it?"

The way Anders was watching her made her skin crawl.

"What are you doing here?" she asked.

"Someone has to protect you."

"That's why I have colleagues outside the door."

"In here, I mean. Someone could be hiding in a closet. Or under the bed. A criminal lives here, don't you remember?"

Anneli snorted and got up, walking past Anders as if he wasn't there and putting the bags of money into her bag.

Then she went into Axel's bedroom, searching through pants, T-shirts and button-downs. She pulled out his underwear drawer and sorted through every single item on the bed.

"Are you hoping to find another stash in here?" he asked.

He had followed her and was standing just a few yards from her as he looked her up and down.

She didn't answer, turning back to her work.

"Oh, I'm just teasing you, Anneli. Sorry. You know that narcotics is my area. That's why I'm here."

He took a couple of long strides into the room and stood close behind her, wrapping his arms around her waist and breathing in the scent of her hair. She tried to twist out of his grip, but he slid his hands up anyway and squeezed her breasts.

"This also used to be my area," he whispered, letting her go.

She whirled around and met his intense gaze, but the words seemed to vanish from her throat. She turned back to the work of sorting underwear.

"You shouldn't be here," she said.

"Shouldn't I?"

"No."

"Tell me to leave, then."

She didn't answer, didn't turn around, not wanting him to see her flushed cheeks.

Then she felt him near her again. He was panting more deeply. His hands found their way back to her breasts, down to her hips, pushing her thighs apart. She was just about to open her mouth to beg him to stop.

"Just be quiet," he said, pulling her shirt over her head.

"So, we have a name to go on?" Gunnar Öhrn said, closing the door to the conference room.

Henrik Levin stood leaning against the table. Mia Bolander sat in her usual place.

"Yes," Henrik said. "Actually, two names. First of all we have Danilo Peña, whom Axel Lundin named. We're starting to look into who this Danilo is. I've got people working on it. Hopefully we'll soon have a picture of him, too."

"Good," Gunnar said. "And the other name?"

"During the course of the investigation, we've

come across the name 'The Old Man' a number of times."

"Oh, right. What do we know about him?"

Henrik cleared his throat.

"Still nothing, actually. He's like a ghost."

"And this Danilo and The Old Man can't be one and the same?" Gunnar asked.

"Might be," Henrik said, "but I have a feeling they're two different people."

"There's always someone behind the curtain, some mysterious type, but then it always turns out to be some everyday villain," Mia said.

"But it feels as if this is a new type of leader, a sort of brain of the operation, that we haven't encountered before," Henrik said. "No one will say anything, no one has met this Old Man, no one really knows who he is. Yet everyone seems terrified of him."

"Axel didn't want to say, either?" Gunnar asked.

"He seems scared, as I said," Henrik said.

"Of course he is. All snitches are scared."

"And Robin Stenberg seemed scared for his life," Mia said.

"There's something with that assault and battery. He saw something he shouldn't have seen," Gunnar said. "And he presumably wanted to have some sort of confirmation of it. That's why he started the thread on Flashback. Then he maybe was threatened, and finally made that police report."

"And had the bad luck of ending up with Axel Lundin…" Mia said.

"Whom he maybe knew already…from The Bridge," Henrik said.

"We have to get Axel to tell more," Mia said.

"That'll be difficult," Henrik said. "He's more scared of The Old Man than of us."

"But it's not completely impossible that Axel is the man from Central Station *and* the man outside Stenberg's apartment."

"But he's no murderer."

"You can't just say that like we have any proof of it…"

"Axel is at the bottom of this food chain. We want the higher-ups, The Old Man."

The room fell silent.

"Have any of you thought that The Old Man could be a woman?" Mia said.

"What makes you think that?" Gunnar asked.

"It's just a thought. Maybe a sidetrack, but there's a mysterious woman who has cropped up in the building at Garvaregatan 6."

"You mean the woman with the knife who the vagrants said stabbed one of them in the stairwell?" Henrik asked. "But is that even true?"

"I don't know if they're telling the truth. But she really scared the shit out of them."

"Interesting," Gunnar said. "Could it be the same woman who was seen outside of Stenberg's apartment?"

"Yes, we know she can handle a knife," Mia said.

TWENTY-FOUR

THE COFFEE IN HENRIK LEVIN'S MUG quivered as he drove over the icy, uneven road. He noticed the white veils of snow that had drifted over Gamla Övägen. An envelope containing two color copies lay on the passenger seat. One was a photo of Danilo Peña. The other was a photo of Axel Lundin.

Henrik parked the car and, carrying the envelope in his right hand, walked through the hallway of Vrinnevi Hospital.

Pim sat on the edge of the bed, turned toward him. Her black hair hung over her face. She looked so tiny; her body slender and pale.

Henrik walked in and greeted her.

"I heard you tried to run away," he said, waiting for the interpreter to translate.

"I just wanted to go home," Pim said, quietly.

"You will be able to go home, but first I want to ask for your help," he said. "Last time I was here, you talked about a girl. Do you remember that?"

She nodded.

"What did she look like?"

"Like me," she whispered. "But she had a big scar on her forehead."

Pim pointed at her own forehead, at her hairline.

"Did she go there with you?"

"No, she was already there."

"She was already there?"

"Yes, on the upper floor."

"Think really, really carefully now. Do you remember her name?"

Pim scratched her arm, thinking for a moment.

"Her name was Isra."

"Did you talk to her?"

"Not much," Pim said. "She cried when he pulled the tape from her mouth and when he went out, I asked her what her name was, but I didn't dare talk any more with her because if he heard us talking, he would definitely have hurt us."

"In my hand, I'm holding photographs of two men. I want you to look at them and say if you recognize either of them."

Henrik took the pictures out of the envelope and placed them in front of Pim.

"Look carefully. Do you recognize either man?"

Pim looked hesitantly at the photos as if she were scared for what she thought she might see. In the next second, her hands flew to her mouth.

"Him!" she screamed, pointing.

Her eyes were filled with fear.

Henrik picked up the picture she had pointed

to. He studied the man with the dark hair, brown eyes, chiseled face.

"Was he the one who held you captive?" Henrik asked.

"Yes," Pim said.

"And you're completely certain?"

"Yes…"

Henrik looked at the picture again, shuddering as he met the man's gaze. He picked up the phone and first called Gunnar Öhrn, then the prosecutor in charge of the preliminary investigation, Jana Berzelius.

Jana Berzelius stepped into the district court in Norrköping soberly dressed in a slim-fitting black jacket and matching slacks. Her blouse was creamy white with a round neckline. She had selected pointy-toed high heels by Yves Saint Laurent.

A female voice came over the speakers calling all parties and agents to Courtroom 2, where the court was conducting a hearing of case B3980-13 regarding an assault at a bar.

She double-checked that her cell phone was silenced and saw that Henrik Levin had called.

She stepped to the side and listened to the voice mail just to be safe. It was a short message, but what he said made the room spin.

"I thought it'd be good to let you know that we've made some progress in the case with the Thai woman. First of all, we've gotten the likely name of the girl who was in the room with her. We think it's Isra. Second, we know with a fair amount of certainty who the man was who picked Pim up at the train station and held her captive. Pim picked out a photo of a man named Danilo Peña and…"

She didn't hear any more after that. Her eyes darted across the walls and doors and the people sitting in the courtroom. She slipped out, punched in the code to a conference room, rushed in and put her hand in front of her mouth to stifle a scream. Her chest began to hurt, but she listened to Henrik's voice mail one more time.

"…picked out a photo of a man named Danilo Peña and…"

She threw her phone against the wall and a large crack appeared on the screen. She sat down, trying to breathe calmly, to think, but she couldn't. She got up again, trying to find a way out of the panic that gripped her.

Had it been Danilo who'd held Pim captive?

She heard the summons over the loudspeaker again and left the conference room. She was breathing just as heavily when she returned to the courtroom. She felt like being there was a huge waste of time now. She had to protect herself, her life.

Far off she heard the district court judge, together with the chairperson, begin by greeting everyone, introducing the three lay judges as well as the law clerk. Jana wasn't listening, though; all her attention was focused on the closed door. She was solely focused on one person now—Danilo.

"The Swedish Prosecution Authority is represented by Prosecutor Jana Berzelius," he said, introducing the defendant, the plaintiff and their respective lawyers, as well as the counsel for the injured party.

Her heart was pounding in her chest. Her gaze was still locked on the doors.

"At the prosecutor's request, we have called the witness Samir Ranji, who has been informed of the summons and from what I understand is waiting outside these doors. I don't believe there is anything in the way of holding the main hearing today."

"Yes, there is," Jana said, standing. "Chairman, I must request that we adjourn the proceedings."

Henrik Levin stroked the fingers of his right hand over one eyebrow, back and forth in a slow rhythm, and thought about how odd it was that Axel Lundin had given them the name of the man who had held Pim captive. Everything hung together. Robin Stenberg had led them to Axel Lundin, who now led them to Danilo Peña, the mysterious, dark man… Would he lead them to The Old Man?

He looked at his cell phone and began thinking about Jana Berzelius again. He was puzzled, unsure of how he should handle Ida Eklund's revealing that she'd seen a well-dressed woman with a large BMW outside Robin Stenberg's apartment the night of the murder. But why would Jana have been there? Jana, of all people!

The funny thing, or maybe not so funny, was that it was completely possible that the same well-dressed woman had been in the stairwell on Garvaregatan yesterday. There, the woman had more than proven that she knew how to use a knife—if the vagrants weren't just hallucinating, that is.

He thought he'd have to blame hallucinations when he considered the possibility that the well-dressed woman was Jana. There had to be other well-dressed women in the Norrköping area who drove dark BMWs. Jana Berzelius must have a doppelgänger.

He tilted the computer screen a bit to the right and googled her name. Numerous articles popped up where she had spoken about court rulings.

"What are you doing?"

Henrik twirled around and saw Mia Bolander standing in the doorway with her jacket in her hand.

"Just checking a few things," he said, attempting in vain to close Google.

"Why are you searching for Jana?"

When he met Mia's gaze, he felt the uneasy feeling again creeping into his chest and knew that he couldn't keep the truth from her any longer.

He sighed, as if to show her that he truly thought this was tough.

"I've received a difficult witness statement…"

"What is it?"

"It was when we spoke with Ida Eklund and you disappeared to take that call…"

He told Mia what had been bothering him, that there was a possibility that Jana had been on Spelmansgatan on the night of the murder, outside Robin's apartment.

"Why didn't you say something earlier?"

"I…"

The gnawing uneasiness was there again. He shuddered.

"Henrik," Mia said calmly. "This all sounds totally ridiculous, but why haven't you said anything?"

"I don't know. You also think that it would be completely ridiculous if she'd been there…but I don't know. I was waiting to confront her about it, but she seems to be avoiding us…"

"You *have* to tell the rest of the team," Mia said.

"I know, but there's one more thing…" Henrik looked at her, the worry plain on his face. "Ida's description also matches the one that the vagrants on Garvaregatan gave of the knife-wielding woman, right? And Robin's murderer used a knife with a surgeon's precision, if I can describe it like that…"

Mia stared at him.

"Jana Berzelius?" she said, beginning to giggle. "Have you checked if she's a former knife-thrower?"

"No, of course not."

"But seriously, Henrik. Do you really think that stuck-up priss-pants Jana is some sort of hit woman? I think it's time for you to go on paternity leave now."

She examined him.

"Besides, it's serious to withhold information about a case."

"Of course. I know that."

"I wouldn't have thought you'd do this," she said, grinning again. "You could be reported for this."

"Exactly. So don't say anything."

Mia looked out through the window.

"Seriously, Henrik, what do you gain by *not* saying anything? This could be seen as harboring a fugitive."

"Wait a second, now," Henrik said. "You've been grinning this whole time. Obviously you don't believe it, either. She might not have been anywhere near Robin's apartment."

Mia nodded, thinking.

"But now that you say it, she's always been so fucking…bizarre in some way."

"No, she hasn't."

"No?"

"No. I don't think so, at least."

"Oh, *now* I get it," Mia said.

"What?"

"You like her."

"Yes, I like her as a prosecutor. Nothing else."

"There must be more to it, because you're trying to protect her."

"Knock it off. I'm not trying to protect her. I just haven't had the chance to talk to her."

"Oh, really?"

"What's much more bizarre to me is that you seem so happy to be able to accuse her."

"The strangest part is that you aren't keeping the

rest of us informed of what you're thinking during the investigation. It's not really like you, Henrik."

"Listen. According to Ida, a woman was in the area when she left Robin's apartment. The description could very well fit Jana, but there is also a very, very, very strong possibility that it was some other woman Ida saw. Not Jana Berzelius. There must be other pretty women who drive dark BMWs, don't you think?"

"Pretty? You think she's pretty, and that's why you're protecting her?" Mia exclaimed.

"Now you're just being a pain."

"What do you mean?"

"I can't reason with you. Do you think, in complete seriousness, that Jana could have murdered Robin Stenberg?"

"No, but…"

"No. Exactly. It's precisely that reason that I don't want to disclose my every thought to you. You are only interested in the simplest solution. That's dangerous, Mia. You know that loose assumptions have no place in serious investigations."

"Neither do emotions," she said.

"Can't you just go now?"

"I am. I'm actually not going to work any more today. We've worked all weekend, so I thought I'd take off."

Lovely, he thought about saying, but she was already gone. He sat alone in the room with the feeling that he shouldn't have said anything to Mia about Jana Berzelius.

He shouldn't have said anything at all.

TWENTY-FIVE

PER ÅSTRÖM LOCKED HIS EYES ON THE ball. It made a loud smacking sound when it met his tennis racket. A straight, two-handed backhand, right at the baseline.

He moved quickly to the right, following the ball's movement over the net with his eyes, and moved again. Another smack as Johan returned the ball. Per crouched further and found his center of gravity, moved again and swung. Forehand cross. His blond hair swung to the side, his forehead damp with sweat.

He had been playing for an hour, and only he and Johan remained in the tennis hall. Both had ended their planned matches but had felt too restless to go home, so they'd spontaneously agreed to play a match together. The night had gotten late and the other courts were empty. Outside, large, fresh snowflakes whirled down from the dark sky.

Johan held up his hand, saying he had to be done

for the day. They met at the net and thanked each
other for a good match.

"Do you dare play me again?" Per asked.

"Of course. Tomorrow, same time?"

"That could work. I'll call you, Johan…"

"…Klingsberg."

"Right. Klingsberg, it was."

Per collected his water bottle and tennis balls
and stuffed them into his bag. He heard the door
slam after Klingsberg.

He went into the locker room and was greeted by
warm steam. The mirrors were fogged up.

Water was running from the nozzle of one of
the showers. Someone must have forgotten to turn
it off, Per thought.

He put his bag down on the bench and went into
the shower, reaching out his hand and turning the
faucet until the water stopped.

He went back to the bench and sat down, pulled
off his sweaty shirt and reached into his bag for
his cell phone.

No missed calls.

No messages.

He dried the sweat from his temples with his
shirt, wiping it slowly back and forth, finding himself lost in thought. He had called her yesterday
to ask if she wanted to go with him to a hockey
game. He'd also called her in the morning and left
a message to ask if she wanted to have dinner with
him. She hadn't called back. He interpreted her
silence as a no, and now he had found out that

she had adjourned the hearing because a new witness had incidentally cropped up in the case of
the assault at the bar. She wanted to have time to
question the witness before the hearing could be
revisited. Nothing strange about that, of course,
but the fact remained that she still hadn't called
him back. Maybe he'd been too pushy? She could
at least have said so.

He picked up his cell and typed her number
again.

"Hi there."

Mia Bolander smiled at Martin Strömberg's confused look and thought about how he looked really
unattractive when he raised his eyebrows like that.

"What do you have behind your back?"

"A surprise."

She winked at him.

"Aha," he said, laughing. "Come in."

Mia stepped into the apartment, noticing the
smell of cigarettes, and began taking off her boots.

"Don't look," she warned.

"I'm not looking," Martin said, holding his hands
over his eyes.

She stood in the hall with her eyes on Martin as
she took off her jacket.

"You're looking!"

"No!" He laughed, shaking his head. "But I hear
rustling."

She saw that his tight T-shirt had dark patches
of sweat in the armpits.

"Here you go," she said, holding out the package she'd been hiding behind her back. "Or maybe I should say Merry Christmas."

"But it's not Christmas yet."

"I couldn't wait."

Martin squeezed the package.

"It's soft," he said. "What could it be? A hat? A pair of socks?"

"Open it and find out."

"Not before I fetch your Christmas present."

Mia went into the living room, tense with excitement, and sat on the sofa. When Martin came back, she could hardly contain herself any longer. He showed her a square package. She reached her hand out to take it, but he couldn't help teasing her.

"Do I get a kiss?"

"Give me the package," she said, still holding her hand out.

"A little kiss?" he said, fluttering his eyelids.

Mia smiled sourly at him and held his gaze until he surrendered the package. She opened it carefully, trying to enjoy the feeling of opening the most valuable present she had ever received, that she'd probably ever receive.

"A scarf! Thanks, Mia."

Martin wound the black scarf around his shoulders.

"Do you like it?" she asked.

"Of course! Absolutely. But what does LV mean?"

"Louis Vuitton."

"Ah. But isn't that, like, a women's brand?"

"No, it's for guys, too."

"Oh, it's really too much."

Mia removed the wrapping paper and looked at the box in her hand briefly before quickly taking off the lid.

Now it was her turn to look confused.

"An egg cup?"

"I know, it's not much…and now you've given me such a nice Christmas present…"

Mia put the box down, refusing to touch the pink porcelain cup that read "Have an egg-stra good morning!"

"You can exchange it for a blue one if you want," Martin said. "Or green."

"What happened to the watch?"

"The watch? What watch?"

"The watch you bought, the one under your bed! Who did you give that to? Who?"

"Now, just calm down!"

"Are you seeing someone else?"

"No! For Christ's sake, it was for my mom. Were you snooping around my place?"

Mia got up and went into the hallway.

"Wait! Mia, where are you going?" Martin said, following her.

She hurried to put on her shoes, grabbing her jacket and opening the door in one movement.

"You know what?" she said in a tired voice, turning toward him. "You can go to hell."

* * *

The black shirt rustled as Jana Berzelius pulled it over her head. She stood in the hallway and tied her shoes, then flipped through the closet to find a dark tailored jacket.

She moved methodically, a woman on a mission. She had only *one* choice now, one path to follow. Danilo wasn't at his home address in Södertälje.

An hour ago she'd been on Svedjevägen in the Ronna district of Södertälje. She had walked past the high-rise apartment buildings with their green, blue and orange balconies. She'd stepped through the door to building number 36, taken the elevator up to the eighth floor and carefully, silently, approached his apartment door.

She had stood in that exact spot a couple of times over recent months, with the hope that at some point, he would be home. But the apartment had always been empty. And now the name on the door had been removed. Danilo didn't live there anymore.

Now there was only one person who could know where he was.

Only one.

She picked a thin, black knit hat out of a drawer and pulled it snugly over her head. Her gloves felt tight; she opened and closed her fists to soften the leather.

She nodded hurriedly at her reflection in the hall mirror before closing the outer door to her apartment. She ran quickly down the steps, pulled her hat farther down over her forehead and pushed her hands deep into her pockets.

Henrik Levin stopped the car outside the garage and walked slowly up to the front door of his town house in the southern district of Norrköping called Smedby. He sighed over the thought that they hadn't gotten further with Danilo Peña. Officers had been in place at his registered address in Södertälje but had only found an abandoned apartment. It was obvious Danilo hadn't lived there in a while. All the rooms were empty. No furniture, only a braided rag rug in the hallway and a mattress in the living room.

Henrik's keys rattled as he laid them on the hall table. He kicked off his shoes, took a deep breath and smelled the familiar scents of home. His head was spinning as he went into the kitchen. He fumbled toward the counter, went to pick up a glass, knocked it over, picked it up again and filled it with water. He drank in large gulps and breathed deeply, collecting himself.

In the same moment, he heard the bathroom door open. He turned and saw her standing there, hair sticking up, her eyes questioning.

"How's it going?"

He didn't answer at first, taking a few steps forward and embracing her. He inhaled the scent of her nightshirt, felt her fingers against his back, pressed harder against her large, round belly.

She let go first, stepping back and examining him.

He met her gaze and only then realized how tired he was.

"I…" he began, but then didn't know what else to say. He locked his eyes on the floor and felt like it was rocking.

"Henrik?" she asked.

"Yes?"

"How are you?"

"Fine…"

"You're lying."

"A little."

Emma smiled.

"Tell me," she said.

"I'd rather not," he said, noticing how her lower lip thrust forward.

"Come," she said.

"Where are we going?"

"To the sofa. I thought we could sit for a while."

Henrik smiled, put his hand in hers and let her lead him.

TWENTY-SIX

IT WAS QUIET IN THE HALLWAY.

The doors to the hospital ward were locked, and the number to the nurses' station stood on white placards for those who wished to gain entry.

The scent of disinfectant wafted throughout the building and got caught in Jana Berzelius's clothes as she walked the halls with silent steps.

She kept her eyes on the vinyl floor, following the tracks of bed wheels.

Her hat covered every strand of her hair.

When the elevator doors opened, she ducked behind a column, pretending to be waiting for someone. An orderly pushed a bed past her, an old man lying in it. Before the doors could close, she was inside the elevator, pushing the button for the Isolation Ward, standing where she would largely avoid being caught on the security camera above the monitor. When the mechanical voice welcomed her to the correct ward, she first confirmed no one was in the hallway before stepping out of the elevator.

She stood next to a locked glass door and waited. After five minutes, it opened and two nurses in white came out. The automatic door hummed loudly over her head as she slipped through. She stayed near the wall the whole time, glancing furtively around for any movements.

She heard voices and saw a light on in a room farther down the hall.

Taking a firm grip of the handle, she opened the door of the first patient room she came to and stepped in. She immediately scanned the two beds but didn't see the person she was looking for. She slowly opened the door to the hallway and looked out. She saw another door open; a smiling nurse exited and then turned toward the room again.

"Just tell me if you need another electric blanket," she said before disappearing down the hallway.

Jana stood still, waiting for just a moment, then moved quickly. She opened the door the nurse had just closed, went in and stood in the light shining from the hospital bed.

The young woman lay on her side, her back toward Jana.

"Hi, Pim," she said.

Anneli Lindgren closed the front door carefully, took off her jacket and noticed her tired face in the hall mirror. She went directly into the bathroom, thoroughly washing her hands twice. She sniffed her arms, but no longer detected his smell on her skin. She tugged at the wrinkles in her shirt and then noticed for the first time the bulge in her pants pocket.

She swore when she realized what she had forgotten. She pulled a transparent bag holding her underwear from her pocket. She had intended to throw them away on her way home! What was she supposed to do with them now? She considered the wastebasket, but instead hid the bag far under the towels in the bathroom closet. Then she released her hair from the hair tie and wrapped her hair into a new bun before going into the kitchen.

She looked for Gunnar, but he wasn't there. She noticed a flickering light from the bedroom and knew the TV was on.

"Hi," she said, casting a glance at the TV. "What are you watching?"

"A movie."

"I see that, but what's it called?"

"Something with 'hunt.'"

"You don't have the sound on?"

"No, sometimes the silence is nice."

"Is Adam sleeping?"

"Don't know. He's in his room."

Anneli stood there for a moment, following the action on the screen.

"Aren't you going to bed?" Gunnar asked.

"Soon. I was thinking about eating something first. And taking a shower."

"How did it go today?"

"It went well."

"And with Anders?"

"What do you mean?"

"You and Anders were in Axel Lundin's apartment."

"How do you know that?"

"I'm the lead investigator, if you haven't forgotten. Did you work well together? Help each other out and such?"

"Now you're being silly."

"I'm just wondering."

"You're making a much bigger deal out of this than it is," she said. "Stop bringing him into everything all the time."

"It's hard not to."

Anneli swallowed, sitting down on the edge of the bed. She had just noticed Gunnar's new haircut.

"You got your hair cut," she said.

"Yep. I got a walk-in appointment on the way home."

"It's nice."

"I shouldn't have done it."

"Why not?"

"It was unnecessarily expensive. I could've spent the money on something else. But it's too late for that now."

Anneli sighed and stood up.

"I…" she began. "I was going to eat something."

"Yes, you said that."

Gunnar turned off the TV and the room went

dark. He lay on his side and pulled the comforter far up over his shoulders.

"Aren't you going to finish the movie?" she asked.

"No."

"Why not?"

"I already know how it ends."

Anneli stood there for a minute, shifting her weight to the other foot, silently and slowly.

Then she turned around and left the bedroom. In the kitchen, she took out two pieces of crispbread, decided against the usual smear of butter and put three slices of cheese on each. She sat down at the table to eat but realized that she wasn't hungry anymore.

She got up and tossed the sandwiches in the garbage. She went into the bathroom instead to shower.

For thirty-eight minutes.

"What are you doing here?" Pim asked in English, her eyes wide. "Municipal Council" was written in pale letters on her shirt, above her left breast. She stared at Jana Berzelius with fear in her eyes.

"Don't be afraid," Jana answered in English as well. "I just have a question for you."

"About what?"

"I have to ask… The man who held you prisoner…"

Pim turned quickly onto her side with her back to Jana.

"Listen to me. This is important!"

But Pim didn't answer.

"I need to find him, and you are the only one who knows where I can find him."

"I've already told you everything I know."

"Then we'll go over it all again."

"I don't know where he is."

"But you know where you were."

Pim suddenly said something in Thai.

"I didn't understand what you said," Jana said.

"I said that I don't want to talk to you."

Pim quickly raised her hand to the emergency call button. Jana reacted instantly, throwing herself forward and blocking Pim's arm just two inches from the button. She twisted it and put her other hand over Pim's mouth.

"Don't do that again," Jana said, meeting Pim's panicked eyes. "When I take my hand away, you're going to tell me exactly where you and the man I'm looking for were. Okay?"

Pim swallowed and nodded.

Jana slowly removed her hand from Pim's mouth but maintained her grip on her arm.

"I don't know…but I heard…water."

"Okay," Jana said.

"It was cold."

"And?"

"That's it."

"And there was another girl named Isra in the room?"

"Yes."

Jana thought for a short moment.

"This man who kept you, did he whip you?"

Pim looked up at Jana with confusion on her face.

"No."

"Did he scratch you?"

Another, even more confused expression.

"No."

"Do you cut yourself?"

"No!"

"Then I'm wondering…" Jana said, taking hold of Pim's arm again, examining her arm and hands, "how you got these big scratches. Show me your neck."

Pim leaned her head to the side. The sores on her neck were a jumble of lines and crosses. Some were deep, others were wide.

"I think you were somewhere surrounded by branches. And that when you ran away, you were scratched by all of the branches. Is that right?"

Pim flushed, pulling her leg under the comforter.

"I don't know how to get there," she said quietly.

"But it's enough if you describe it."

Pim bit her lip, took a deep breath and finally began to describe a boathouse, a stream and a strange light.

And a deep forest.

THE WIND BIT THEIR CHEEKS.

Roger Johnson, a professional fisherman, nodded to his father, Sture Johnson, and looked out over the sea. He felt the boat being rocked by the waves and saw a lot of fish on the sonar, but he continued farther out in the Arkösund archipelago toward where the net had lain overnight.

Roger's fishing career had begun with poaching under the instruction of his father. Sture only had fishing rights to Baltic herring, and it was perfectly clear that other fish were not included. But Sture didn't care in the least.

There were also rules for what should be counted as private versus open waters. Simply stated, the law said that the water in the Östergötland archipelago was largely private and belonged to the properties on land. Open waters generally began a thousand feet from the farthest islands. But Sture didn't care about that, either. Sture and Roger therefore spent many nights poaching fish, both with illegal nets and illegal methods. They caught lots of fish: salmon, pike and perch by the ton, which they then sold for very good profits.

"Slowly now!"

Roger signaled with his hand, leaned over the rail, reached out to grab the float and lift the line. He pulled the net in bit by bit, trying to shake the fish free into the boat, but let the ones that had gotten stuck fast sit there until they got back to land.

Roger worked patiently, coaxing the lines past gills and fins. He pulled in more of the net but stopped when he suddenly saw something strange in the water.

He pulled again but had to really fight against whatever it was, pulled and pulled, more and more eagerly with each tug.

Then he recoiled.

He felt a strong sense of nausea as he realized what he was looking at.

In the net hung a dead woman.

The wall reverberated from the blow.

Jana Berzelius hit it again. Two, three, four times.

She felt anxious, impatient. She tried to dampen these feelings by striking out, but she still couldn't relax. Something was haunting her, hunting her, taking up altogether too much space in her mind.

She had to find Danilo before the police did.

She whirled around, striking straight out into the air with both fists, aimed her foot and kicked, then again. She visualized him standing before her with his head down and his gaze dark. She hit harder, meeting only air but seeing in her mind's eye that she made contact. She worked her right fist, left fist, a kick. Raised her left knee, then quickly kicked with her right leg, aimed at the wall, kicked again.

Bang.

Bang.

Bang.

She stopped and sat on the floor in her bedroom, panting, with her arms around her knees.

She had to find him. Had to find where he was holding his drug mules captive.

She looked at her hands and thought back through her conversation with Pim. She pondered the strange light Pim had talked about that looked like a spotlight that reached far in between the trees.

She would begin searching along the coast, and knew a place where she could start that was near Highway 209, heading toward Arkösund.

Her parents' summerhouse.

She gathered the necessities from the bathroom and brought them into the bedroom. She folded a few changes of clothes, clean underwear and socks, and stuffed it all into a backpack.

Then she took the knife and weighed it in her hand before placing it against the small of her back. She picked up the backpack and laid it on the floor in the hallway.

The last thing she did was to take one last look

around her apartment. She had the feeling that she wasn't going to return to it for a while.

Then she closed the door, went quickly down the stairs and left Knäppingsborg without looking back.

CHAPTER
TWENTY-EIGHT

PER ÅSTRÖM TURNED OFF HIS ELEC-
tric shaver and listened. Yes, that was the doorbell
ringing. He put the shaver back on its charger and
left the bathroom. In seven long strides, he was in
the foyer. The doorbell rang again. Henrik Levin
stood in the stairwell, a large rip in his jacket.

"I know it's early," Henrik said, "but I knew I
had the best chance of catching you here at this
time."

"What's this about?" Per asked.

"You know Jana Berzelius, right?"

"Yes, of course I know her," Per said, fidgeting.

"How well do you know her?"

"Why are you asking?"

"Do you know her as a colleague or as a friend?"

"Colleague."

"Your neck is flushed."

"What is this? Some sort of interrogation?" Per
asked.

"No. But people usually flush around the neck

when they're self-conscious. Or their eyes dart around. You're doing both. So I'll ask again. How well do you know her—as a colleague or as a friend?"

Per looked both ways in the stairwell.

"Come in," he said, showing Henrik into the apartment and gesturing toward the sofa. "Please, have a seat."

But Henrik went past the sofa and stood by the floor-to-ceiling window.

"What a view," he said.

"Yes, I always know exactly what's going on outside the nightclub down there."

Per nodded toward the street corner below at Sankt Persgatan and smiled.

Henrik met his cheerful gaze but looked serious.

"I'm here to ask you if you know where Jana Berzelius is. I was just at her apartment and knocked on her door, but she didn't answer. And I haven't seen her in a while. She also hasn't answered my phone calls, which is a little strange because she's leading an investigation right now and is usually much more available than she has been. So I'm wondering, have you talked to her?"

Per shook his head.

"I don't know how I should say this," Henrik continued, "but we've received some information in the murder of Robin Stenberg and I really have to get ahold of her. Because you're in charge of that investigation, I thought…"

He fell silent, turning his gaze out through the window again.

"I get the feeling that this is something that not many should know about," Per said, trying to catch Henrik's eyes.

"What makes you say that?" he said.

"Otherwise you wouldn't have come to my home so early."

"Okay… Ida Eklund says she saw a woman who fits Jana Berzelius's description outside Robin Stenberg's apartment on Friday, at the exact time of the murder," Henrik said slowly, watching Per's reaction. But he didn't react at all how Henrik had anticipated. He began to laugh.

"What's so funny?"

"We're talking about a colleague here, not a suspect!"

"I know," Henrik said, wearily.

He sat on the sofa, leaned back and studied the blond prosecutor sitting directly across from him. His different-colored eyes looked simultaneously sharp and friendly.

"Besides," Per said. "She has an alibi."

"How do you know that?"

"Because I was with her on Friday."

"Are you…" Henrik began. "I mean, do you… and she have a relationship?"

Per laughed again, loudly and long this time.

"Jana isn't really the relationship type. I've never seen her with a man, or even heard her mention one."

"A woman, then?"

"Haven't seen her with a woman, either. She prefers men, I know that much."

"So you're just friends?"

"That's probably a good way to say it. We've talked a lot, had dinner together and such. We are colleagues, as I said."

Henrik sighed.

"Okay," he said. "But I still have to talk to her."

"Don't you believe me?"

"Yes, of course. You had dinner together. At what restaurant?"

"Ardor. You can call them. We had a reservation."

"You know I have to."

Per was quiet for a moment.

"May I ask…" he said. "Has this Ida Eklund actually identified Jana, picked her photo out of a lineup?"

"No, not exactly. But her description of the woman could very well be of Jana…"

"But have you shown Ida pictures of Jana?"

"No."

Per looked puzzled.

"Has more come out in the investigation? Something that actually points to her having anything to do with Robin Stenberg?"

"No."

"So why are you investigating her?"

"I'm not investigating her."

"No? You're here asking a bunch of questions."

"I'm just trying to get some confirmation."

"That she could be a suspect?"

"No, exactly the opposite."

"Now I don't understand at all."

"Confidentially…" Henrik said.

"Yes?"

"…this is always my starting point when it comes to Jana Berzelius. She's my colleague, too, and I think she's an excellent prosecutor."

"Great," Per said, "then we agree on that. But that you're here," he continued, "feels…"

"Uncomfortable?"

"If it gets out that we've had this conversation…"

"No one knows that I'm here," Henrik said.

"But you know that this doesn't look good?"

"Absolutely."

She had awoken to the sound of a door closing but remained lying in the fetal position under the warm comforter.

She had tried to avoid him all night long. He'd done the same. They had lain on their respective sides of the bed with their backs to one another. Both wide-awake, without breaking the silence.

Now Anneli Lindgren got out of the bed and looked out the window at the snow drifting down from the ash-gray sky. She saw the thick white carpet that covered the road, the tracks from a cat that had traipsed diagonally across the street, the drifts that had formed by the mailboxes.

A shiver made her skin break into goose bumps

all over her body. The apartment felt cold, as if the windows had been opened to air it out.

She went to Adam's room and saw him still sleeping, mouth open, and knew she should wake him up. But she decided to let him sleep a little bit more.

The floor creaked loudly under her bare feet.

Just when she reached her hand out to open the bathroom door, she heard Adam's alarm go off on his cell phone, how he shifted under the comforter to turn it off. Then it was silent again.

She turned on the light and stepped into the shower. She showered quickly under the warm water, letting the water rinse her body clean. She was thinking of yesterday, of Anders.

Stepping out of the shower, she wrapped a towel around herself and opened the door to the cabinet. She reached her hand in behind the towels, but didn't feel the bag with her underwear in it.

She stuck her hand in again, feeling back and forth, pulling all of the towels out onto the floor and shaking them.

Still no bag.

She felt an icy sensation creeping up her spine and heard a strange moaning sound escape from her throat.

She froze when she heard a faint knocking on the door.

"Mom?"

Threatening, steel-gray clouds loomed over Norrköping. Henrik Levin looked up at them before entering the police station. He quietly greeted Gunnar Öhrn, who sat at his desk with a troubled look on his face.

"This other girl that Pim talked about, what are we doing to find her? Nothing! We're just standing here twiddling our thumbs!"

"Gunnar," Henrik said calmly. "We're doing what we can. We have a hot name to work with... Danilo Peña."

Gunnar wasn't listening. He snorted.

"That girl might not even exist. I almost hope Pim was lying..."

"I believe she exists," Henrik said. "And I believe that if we find Danilo, we'll find her."

"So why haven't we found Danilo?" Gunnar asked.

"He doesn't have a criminal record."

"But he must have done something, or had something done to him. You don't become a criminal and a drug dealer out of the blue, not of the magnitude all this suggests."

"Maybe we need to start over, come up with new ideas..."

"*Start over?* We can't start over. As you said, we have the name of a man who very well could be, one, Pim's captor, two, Robin Stenberg's murderer, and three, the spider whose web is the drug scene in Norrköping," he said, holding up his fingers as he spoke. "Now isn't the time to back off!"

Gunnar rubbed his hands over his face.

"And where is Jana for all of this?"

"I don't know."

"Well, shit."

Gunnar sighed and relaxed his shoulders.

"I'm sorry, Henrik," he said. "But why is this going so slowly?"

"Someone must have warned Danilo Peña that we were onto him," Henrik said. "Because if he doesn't live where he's registered, where *does* he live?"

"Good question."

Gunnar sighed and rocked slightly in his chair.

"You're a good detective," he said, adding, "unlike some others."

"Is there anyone in particular you're thinking of?"

"Mia, of course. I'm sorry, but she's a threat to the team."

Gunnar leaned forward over his desk and looked at Henrik with sad eyes.

"Anders has his eye on us, Henrik. I don't want him to take over. You're *my* team. That's how I want it."

"But he's only here temporarily."

"And has already ruined enough."

"I don't understand…"

"You don't need to, either."

Gunnar paused, wiping the sweat from his forehead with his palm and drying it on his pant leg before continuing.

"It feels like this organization is upside down.

And it will be even worse when the new reorganization has taken effect."

"Are you nervous?" Henrik asked.

"For the future, yes. Certain administrative positions don't exist in the new authority."

"So you don't know what position you'll have?"

"Or if I'll have one at all. The planning committee has been very clear that everyone on the lower rungs of the organization will keep their ranks and salaries. None of them are at risk for becoming unemployed, so that's some security in any case."

"Sure."

"But it would be good if you knew who was going to be your boss next year."

"What does Carin Radler say?"

"Nothing. What can she say?"

Henrik shrugged his shoulders.

Gunnar rested his hands on his knees.

"We'll just have to wait and see," he mumbled. "For now, I'm making the decisions, and I'm sure as hell going to see to it that we reel this investigation in nice and easy."

"Good," Henrik said. "So how do you want to do that?"

Gunnar let his gaze wander around the room and then out through the window.

"We've put out the APB on Danilo internally. Now I want to ask the general public for help."

At the same moment, his cell phone rang. He let it ring three times before he answered.

"Yes, what is it?"

Then he stood, his face suddenly strained.

"What the fuck did you say? What do you mean, 'dead'?"

He was hanging completely still, his arms hanging slack at his sides. His face was pale, his eyes wide-open.

Mia Bolander and Henrik Levin stared at Axel Lundin's body. They weren't allowed to go into the cell. The scene was supposed to be left intact.

Mia attempted to register the details of the scene, but she could hardly tear her eyes from the man who had hanged himself.

The small room was tiled and had windows with metal blinds that couldn't be adjusted. In a corner of the floor lay a blanket and pillow, which every inmate was given.

There was graffiti on the ceiling and on the inside of the door.

Axel Lundin had a shirt and a pair of boxer shorts on. His boxers had a large dark spot on them, and on the floor underneath, a puddle of urine had formed.

"Fucking weak if you ask me," she said, putting her hand on her hip. "Committing suicide, that is. I've never understood why someone would want to do that. It's like they don't want to take responsibility, right?"

Henrik didn't answer, just took a deep breath in through his nose.

"And the reason this guy said *sayonara* must be that he snitched and then felt guilty," she continued.

"I don't think there was space for a guilty conscience in him," Henrik said, glancing up at the ceiling, at the pants looped like a noose around Axel's neck. "There was only one thing in his head, and that was fear. He said that he didn't want to be released, remember?"

"Why wouldn't someone want to stay in this cozy place. Especially when you get a whiff of the wonderful scent from the drunk tank. Yum, really."

"Stop it now," Henrik said. "Call Anneli instead and ask her to come here."

"Better if you do."

Mia turned her back to Henrik and began walking with determined steps toward the exit. She heard Henrik's cell phone ring and noticed the stunned tone in his routinely short sentences. She stopped, turned and looked at him.

"More work," he said, pale as a sheet, when he'd hung up.

"What is it?"

"More bodies. Unfortunately, I think we've found the third girl."

CHAPTER

TWENTY-NINE

THE SNOW LAY COMPLETELY UN-
touched around the house and reached all the way
to the windowsills.

Jana Berzelius felt around under the flowerpot,
fished out the long, narrow key, inserted it into the
wooden door and opened it.

It opened with a small creak.

It was a large, manor-like structure with a yellow
façade and white trim. Wide stone steps led up to
the white double door. The house was far from any
neighbors and majestically placed right by the sea,
near Grunsöströmmen. The area was full of summer cottages and the occasional year-round home.
It was nearly five hundred feet to the nearest neigh-
bor, and they weren't home. Almost one thousand
feet to the cottage beyond that. From here, then, she
could work undisturbed in her search for Danilo.

She stepped in and let the door close behind her,
listening carefully as she stood in the dark foyer.

She took a few steps into the drawing room and

saw the armchair with its back toward the balcony. She thought about how he always sat there, every summer, with the newspaper in his hand. That was how he'd been when she was young, at least.

A memory flickered past, came back and insisted on her attention. It had been her first summer in the house. She'd been nine years old and had sat behind the armchair with her back against the brown leather, sitting back-to-back with her father, listening in secret to the adults talking. Her father had gotten a visit from an unfamiliar friend, and her mother had been running errands in town.

She had had to pee, so terribly that she could hardly hold it. She'd been just about to get up when she'd heard her father becoming upset.

"She's got to go," he said.

"That won't work. You know that."

"If I'd only known…"

"You don't like surprises?"

"Not like this."

"You were the one who said yes."

"Did I have any choice?"

"You know very well that this was the only solution."

Her father fell silent.

"How long does she have to stay?"

"Ask your wife. I'm positive she would be very disappointed if she didn't get to keep her beloved daughter."

"Don't call her that."

"Daughter? Yes, that's how I think of her. You should, too. You should get used to it."

"Never."

It was silent for a moment. Her father shifted in the chair, the leather creaking under him.

"Answer me now. How long does she have to stay with us?" he asked.

"Forever."

"You can't be serious!"

"You don't want me to tell your wife why you have the girl living with you, do you?"

"I don't like your tone."

"I just want to be sure you're aware that there is no alternative."

Jana clenched her legs together, no longer listening to the conversation. The only thing she felt was panic over the possibility of peeing her pants.

"Listen now, Karl. We have an agreement."

"What happens if I break it?"

When she heard the scornful laughter, she pressed her lips together, closed her eyes and wished she hadn't hidden there. Now she felt nothing other than the pain in her gut, heard nothing other than her soundless whimpering, thought about nothing other than her desire to get up and run to the bathroom.

"Listen, you have to take care of her now. That's the best thing you could do. For all parties," the other man said.

"You don't understand. She's wild," said her father.

"Rein her in, then."

"She's violent."

"I should fucking think so, with what she's been through. But she doesn't know why she's that way. She has no idea, Karl, and the violence will dissipate over time. You simply have to learn to like her. She's yours now. Your daughter."

She heard her father gripping the leather of the chair.

"And the boy?"

"We have him under control."

"What will happen to him?"

"We haven't decided that yet."

"And she remembers nothing about what she's been through? Not even him?"

"As I said, she doesn't remember anything, Karl."

"But if they meet?"

"They'll never meet. Believe me, their paths will never cross."

She made a last attempt to hold it, but she couldn't any longer. She wanted to run, run from the living room to the bathroom, away from here, away, away.

"I think we need a stiff one," her father said, getting up and going to the cocktail cabinet.

She took that opportunity to leave, slipping quickly away, not wanting to be seen, keeping her eyes on the floor and not looking back, not even once. She didn't even know who her father was talking to.

She'd never really thought about it.

Until now.

* * *

Anneli Lindgren looked out the window of the backseat of Henrik's car. Henrik and Mia sat in front of her.

She rubbed her eyes, feeling exhausted after working in the cell with Axel Lundin's body for two hours. Now she was on her way to Arkösund, to another shift with yet another dead body. But this time it was a young woman found drowned in a fishing net.

She leaned one elbow against the window, looking at the ring on her finger, the inexpensive ring that Gunnar had bought for her when everything was new, when they had been together for only a month. A smooth gold ring, no stones, no engraving or burnished edges.

But she had worn it all these years.

She had loved it, loved that idiotic ring on her finger.

What have I done? she thought, sighing.

She felt someone watching her and met Henrik's eyes in the rearview mirror.

"Tired?"

"Yes," she said softly.

"Did you find anything?"

"Nothing of interest, besides the money. I took a few samples, but I don't know, there wasn't anything other than Axel's own prints, unfortunately."

"I was thinking more about the holding cell he was in. You just came from there, right?"

"Yes," she said, looking down, running her fin-

ger along the camera case she had next to her. "I…
I took a sample from Axel's… I mean, I took a
number of samples. I think he committed suicide,
plain and simple. There was a lapse in security…"

"You think?" Mia said skeptically. "You don't
sound completely sure."

They fell silent, and the sound of the heat flowing from the vents filled the car.

"Well…" Anneli continued. "As you know, ho-
micide detectives like us as well as other police officers who might be present at the scene of a crime
must register their fingerprints and DNA."

"Yes?"

"There was one thing that bothered me, so I did
a quick search. But right now it's still incomplete."

"How incomplete?" Henrik asked. "It was what
he had under his fingernails, wasn't it?"

"Yes. I found skin cells and fiber fragments
under Axel's fingernails."

"Who were they from?"

Anneli swallowed again.

"It's too early to say," she said.

"Oh, just say it!" Henrik said.

"You can tell us," Mia said.

Anneli looked down at her lap.

"No," she said, touching the camera bag again.
"There's a chance it's not correct. I don't want you,
either of you, to draw any hasty conclusions. I've
sent the samples to the National Lab."

"What the hell!" Mia complained, disappointed.
"Don't you trust us?"

"Of course I do, but it's unnecessary to let something like this come out and then have it turn out to be incorrect."

"Well, make sure the lab puts a rush on it, then," Henrik said.

"Yes, of course," Anneli said, looking out the window again.

She didn't want to meet Henrik's eyes again. She knew she'd always been a terrible liar.

A map. She needed a map.

Jana Berzelius opened the app on her phone and clicked to a digital map of Bråviken and the Arkösund archipelago. The crack in the screen made it difficult to see. She guessed that the cell coverage along the coast wouldn't be the best, either, and knew she needed a paper map. There had to be one somewhere in the house.

She spent twenty minutes searching through cupboards, desk drawers and bookshelves. She looked through the secretary desk in the drawing room. No map.

She stood in the kitchen and drank a large glass of water. She dried the glass and returned it to the shelf before resuming her search on the second floor.

She entered the library. The room was more than four hundred square feet. One long wall was dominated by a built-in bookshelf from floor to ceiling, with a mix of fiction, biographies, nonfiction and about fifty binders with documents spanning her father's entire professional life, like souvenirs from his fantastic career.

The opposite wall was occupied by a sofa and armchairs and a large desk that was placed so that anyone sitting there would be facing the rest of the room. The floor creaked as Jana walked toward the desk, which was tidy, with a few papers stacked in a pile and some pens standing in a mug. She flipped through the papers absentmindedly, looked around and shook her head resignedly.

Then the binders, sorted by year, caught her eye. The first was from 1989. Her search for a map momentarily forgotten, she was overcome by curiosity and pulled out one of the binders and laid it on the desk. She opened it and began flipping through the legal proceedings it contained. She was about to close it and put it back when she noticed that her father had made private notes in the margins. The cursive penmanship was tiny and difficult to make out.

Mia Bolander stretched unconsciously in the seat, turned toward Henrik and hoped that he would meet her questioning gaze. Why should they accept that Anneli was keeping information from them? Now, when even Henrik had begun keeping quiet about things, she felt like she was being left out in the cold.

"But we can't fucking work like this!" she blurted out suddenly.

"What are you talking about?" Henrik said.

"I thought we were supposed to be working together. But if people aren't saying what they've found, how are we supposed to know if we're all going in the same direction?"

"Let it go," Henrik said firmly.

They fell silent.

"So we have a drowned girl?" she said instead, just to have something to say and to break the awkward silence. She was no longer sure of her relationship with Henrik.

"Yes," he said. "Probably the girl Pim was with. She was found by two fishermen."

"Her name was Isra, right?"

Henrik nodded.

"When was she found?"

"Seven o'clock this morning."

"But they didn't call us until 8:30?"

"There's no cell coverage out there…"

"They didn't have an emergency radio on board, a VHF radio?"

"Clearly not."

It fell silent again.

They drove past Östra Husby and on to Vikbolandet where the fields lay hidden under deep, white snow. The narrow road became even narrower. Over a half hour later, a large parking lot appeared. They got out of the car and walked toward the pier. It smelled of fish and seawater.

It was the boat farthest away. The fishermen had placed a tarp over the dead body to protect her, or maybe so they wouldn't have to look at her.

Anneli gave the camera to Mia and pulled thin gloves over her hands before crouching down. She took the camera back and photographed the boat. Mia and Henrik stood behind her. This was Anneli's domain; they were simply observers. Anneli leaned forward, carefully turning back the tarp. The woman's body lay reclined, her legs stretched out. Her clothes were torn and soaking wet. Her skin was as white as snow, but there were small sores on her hands, and around one wrist was a larger, wider wound. Her hair was dark and hung in wisps over her face.

Anneli photographed her from every conceivable angle.

"I need to photograph her face," she said, looking at Henrik, who took a step forward. Her voice had been quiet, but the small nod she gave him said that it was an order. Mia watched him pull on gloves, step into the boat and carefully brush the girl's hair aside.

"Look," Henrik said, pointing to her forehead.

Mia leaned forward and peered at the girl's forehead once, twice—there was no scar.

"This isn't Isra," she said.

Henrik Levin stood on the pier, his phone pressed to his ear, his eyes looking out over the sea. The wind tore at his jacket. He listened to Gunnar Öhrn's irritated voice. Gunnar rarely lost his temper. He was known for his composure, but over the course of this investigation, he had been anything but calm.

"How can you be sure it's not her?" he asked.

"Pim described Isra in quite a bit of detail. She said, among other things, that Isra had a scar on her forehead. The girl we found hasn't the slightest hint of a scar. This is another girl."

"But maybe Pim was wrong," Gunnar said.

"I don't think so," Henrik said.

Gunnar sighed heavily.

"Why do I have the feeling that this drowned girl doesn't exist?"

"What do you mean, doesn't exist?"

"That we aren't going to be able to identify her."

Silence again. Henrik thought about these victimized girls. Unidentified girl with Asian features and a fake passport dead on a train. Unidentified girl with Asian features found dead in the water. And Pim, Asian girl with a fake passport who had been able to flee from her captor. Three Asian girls in one week.

And then there was a fourth, unidentified, with a scar on her forehead, who went by the name Isra.

"It seems like they're in the process of getting rid of the girls," Henrik said.

"And that's why we have to take down this operation," Gunnar said.

"I'll see to it that this girl has Björn Ahlmann for the autopsy."

"Yes, definitely. Do we know how long she's been in the water?"

"Anneli thought just a day or so."

"Then there's no doubt anymore," Gunnar said.

"About what?"

"That we have to hold a press conference. We have to inform the public before people start writing and speculating too much about all of this."

Jana Berzelius had already spent almost an hour looking page by page through the court proceedings of the cases that were archived in her father's binders. She sat on the floor with some of the binders spread out around her. Her father had gathered information carefully and systematically. In the binders, over a hundred court cases were documented, from 1989 on. Most were represented by Prosecutor, then Prosecutor-General, Karl Berzelius. Some of them she had read about on the internet and had felt a certain pride over. She'd been quite simply impressed by her father's successes in the courtroom.

But what she saw in the margins bothered her. With a red pen, he had written small notes. Maybe it was only absentminded doodling that he'd done while he contemplated something. It was hard for her without being familiar with the cases and in such a short time to understand what his notations meant.

The clock was ticking.

She didn't have much time to work with and closed the binders she had in her lap. She knew she should be concentrating on finding Danilo instead.

Focus!

Through the dormer window, she saw the snow whirling around.

She listened to the wind howling outside, feeling satisfied by the promise that they would see each other again, she and he. She would take back her journals and her most valuable possessions. And then she would silence him. Silence the only one who knew who she actually was. Silence him for good.

She got up, leaving the binders on the floor, and continued looking for a map.

CHAPTER

THIRTY

GUNNAR ÖHRN CLEARED HIS THROAT, closed his eyes and said a quick prayer that there wouldn't be any intrusive questions from the press, but he knew that was like praying for a summer without rain.

Press Officer Sara Arvidsson leaned forward toward the microphone on the podium in front of her, and the murmuring in the room quickly died out.

"We've called you to this live-broadcast press conference because we are looking for a man named Danilo Nahuel Peña, whom we have reason to believe is a person of interest in the murder of twenty-year-old Robin Stenberg in Norrköping last Friday."

Sara paged through some papers, cleared her throat and continued. "Danilo Peña appears in this photo. He has dark hair, is thirty years old and six feet tall. We believe he is traveling by car, probably a Volvo, with the license plate number GUV 174."

"Is he the only suspect?" asked a man in the first row.

"It is too early to say anything about that, but because of the circumstances, we are eager to get in contact with him."

"What is the connection between him and the victim?" called a red-haired woman from the back of the room.

"We cannot say anything more at this time," Sara said.

"Do you have a motive? Do you know why Stenberg was murdered?"

"At this time, we are not free to discuss details about the ongoing investigation."

"There was a death at the jail today—what's being done about that?" asked a man with a mustache.

"What happened is incredibly tragic, of course, for the victim's family as well as our staff. An investigation is in progress involving that murder as well, and as we speak an internal investigation is also being conducted."

"But how could such a thing happen?"

"I'm not at liberty to say anything about that case. That is something the investigation will be looking into."

"How did he die?"

"I'm not going to say anything more about the circumstances surrounding that case. The press conference we've called today is about Danilo Nahuel Peña, whom the police are searching for."

The murmuring resumed, and Sara gestured for the reporters to be quiet.

"So this Danilo," said the man with the mustache. "Was he related to Robin Stenberg?"

"We don't believe so."

"Does he have a criminal record?"

"No. But we are releasing his name and picture now because we believe that he may be dangerous to the general public."

Per Åström examined the lunch menu at the restaurant Enoteket as he stood in line to order.

Three patrons in suits sat huddled together, eagerly discussing a data system that was to be delivered to a client in a week. Per couldn't avoid hearing their conversation and hardly noticed that it was his turn to order.

"What would you like?" called the man behind the counter.

He ordered the fish special of the day to go, paid with his card, found a table near the register and sat down to wait for the food to be ready.

Looking out the large glass windows near an inner courtyard, Per thought about Jana Berzelius. He picked up his phone and called her, but there was no answer. It was the fourth time she hadn't answered. She hadn't been in touch with Henrik, either.

Where in the hell was she?

When they called his name, he picked up the white

paper bag that contained his lunch. Jana's apartment wasn't far away, so he decided to swing by.

A vague anxious feeling grew in his stomach as he locked his bike out front and jogged up the steps. He knocked on her door three times, rang the doorbell three times, too, and even called out her name. But no one opened the door.

He got his bike and walked it over a snowdrift that was growing out of control between the sidewalk and street. He shook off the snow that had gotten stuck in his front wheel and pedaled vigorously. He swerved to avoid two blonde women with strollers, downshifted, increased his speed again and rode diagonally across Drottninggatan toward the Public Prosecution Office.

Outside the entrance, he parked his bicycle and then punched in the door code. He ran up the seven flights of stairs with the paper bag in his hand, hoping she would be in her office.

Jana Berzelius searched every little nook and cranny in the summerhouse before finally catching a glimpse of a framed nautical chart in one of the guest rooms. She carefully unhooked the frame and took out the yellowing nautical chart, placing it on the floor in the room.

The land map on her phone clearly showed a dense forest and houses all along the coast of Arkösund, which lay farthest out on Vikbolandet in the Norrköping archipelago. The community was on a promontory, surrounded by miles of coastline.

The boathouse where Pim had been held had to be around there somewhere.

If she could find it, she would almost certainly also find Danilo.

She felt a shiver run down her spine and examined the map on her phone again.

Pim had mentioned a stream, and Jana began to draw lines on the nautical chart to mark all of the watercourses. But she soon realized that there were far too many lines, and that it was going to be impossible to find the stream that Pim meant.

She began again, making a new marking of all the wider, larger watercourses right near the coast. She counted ten of them.

She zoomed in on the map on her phone and tried to see if there were any visible boathouses along the watercourses, but it was impossible— what she saw could just as well be cottages or storage sheds.

She took a step back and looked at all of her markings. Most of them were on the north side, but the police had already searched there and had come up empty-handed.

Then she saw the yellow cone-shaped areas on the chart.

In the same moment, she realized that the strange light Pim had seen, sweeping and rhythmic, must have come from the lighthouse at Viskär.

Jana moved her gaze to the markings she had made on the southern coast. The light from the lighthouse could reach quite far, but it would be strongest around Kälebo. There were a number of different buildings to choose from there, but she smiled as she realized only two of them were both near a watercourse and right on the water.

She rolled up the chart, left the guest room and searched for a flashlight. She felt the sharp weapon against her lower back as she descended the stairs with quick steps.

It was possible that Danilo was in one of those buildings.

The chance was remote, of course, but she had to pursue it.

Henrik Levin found a napkin in one of his desk drawers and blew his nose loudly. He sat in the chair in his office and stared straight ahead. His gaze fell on an old article about the Gavril Bolanaki case that was still hanging on his bulletin board.

On the surface, at least, the drug market had seemed calm until Bolanaki disappeared. Now it was total chaos. People were being exploited and their bodies brutally dumped. The outright ruthless operation was no longer being hidden. The question was how many girls were involved.

Henrik thought about the dead girl on the train and the dead girl in the fishing net. About Pim, who was able to get away, and the girl who may still be in miserable captivity. He thought about the almost clinical murder of Robin Stenberg, who had come to the police in spite of being scared, and of Axel

Lundin, who—also probably scared—had apparently taken his own life.

But no one knows who he is. No one's met him. He's like a shadow.

So many victims, and everything pointed in one direction—Danilo Peña.

Henrik ran his hand through his hair as he reviewed all of the facts in the case, the cases, in his mind, as he had already done a hundred times before. Isra, whom Pim had been captive with, was out there somewhere; they had to find her before she, too, was dumped into the sea.

His thoughts locked again on the drowned girl. He pulled out his phone and called Björn Ahlmann, the medical examiner, who answered on the first ring.

"Björn, it's Henrik Levin. I need your help. Call me when you have the drowned girl's body in front of you."

"She just got here, but I haven't had a chance…"

"There's something I need to ask you about."

Per Åström opened the door of Jana Berzelius's office. The room was immaculate. Papers in neat piles, the spines of binders in straight lines, everything clean, spotless, not a speck of dust.

She wasn't there.

He turned his gaze to the photograph on the wall. He had seen it before, but hadn't thought much about it.

He took a step forward, examining it more closely now.

There was something about the photo, something that made him frown, but he couldn't pinpoint exactly what it was. Maybe it had to do with the people in the picture. He stared at their eyes, their stiff facial expressions. A man, a woman and a child. Karl, Margaretha and Jana Berzelius.

He thought about the pictures of his own family taken when he was little, of himself, his parents and his two siblings. They captured laughter, delight, happiness. A hundred pictures of the same birthday, taken from every possible perspective, with balloons, cakes and presents. First days of school, last days of school. Playing in the park, at vacation destinations, in a sea, in a pool, on a beach. With a bicycle, on roller skates, on ice skates. On skis and kick sleds. His life was documented, immortalized, archived in billions of pixels. And then he thought about the photograph in front of him. A photograph that simply lacked any life at all. Why had she chosen to put it on the wall?

Per guessed that Jana was nine or ten years old in the photograph. Her hair was black as a raven's feathers, straight and well-groomed. Her hands were at her sides, and she was wearing a white dress and black, shiny shoes. Her lips were closed, but Per could still detect a light smile. Her eyes were deep and dark.

She stood in the middle, in front of her mom and

dad. In the background was a white double door, wooden with carved details.

He took a step forward and examined the door to what he assumed was the Berzelius family's summerhouse.

Then he turned and walked out of Jana's office and stopped the Chief Public Prosecutor midstep.

"There's big trouble," Torsten said immediately.

"Legal?" Per asked.

"No, marital. The missus wants a new dog. I think we could stand to wait awhile, since we so recently had to say goodbye to Scamp. But maybe it's just as well to go along with it, for the sake of keeping the peace. Anyway, what's weighing on you, young man?"

Per took a deep breath and said that he hadn't heard anything from Jana since she adjourned her hearing in the district court.

"I've been to her apartment, too, and she isn't answering her phone."

"Maybe she's sick."

"Then she should have called in..."

"I can see that you're concerned."

"I just thought it was strange of her to suspend a hearing. It's not really like her."

"If something had happened to her, her father would have told me," Torsten said.

"You know him?"

"Karl and I have regular contact, yes. Karl is of the old school. He's always formal, and he likes checking in."

"Checking in?"

"He just likes to stay apprised of what his daughter is doing."

"You mean how she's performing?"

"Yes, maybe that's the right word."

Per stroked his chin with his hand.

"Does he have a reason to keep an eye on her?" he asked.

"What do you mean?"

"Does she neglect things?"

"No, you know Jana. She's somewhat reserved, but she's a fantastic prosecutor. Almost more competent than her father. But don't tell him I said that."

"So what is he worried about?"

"Karl likes control," Torsten said, "and that's why I think that if anything had happened to Jana, he'd be the first one to know. If I were you, I'd talk to him."

Through doors and walls, Henrik heard his colleagues' voices, humming computers and the rumbling HVAC system. Far, far away, he heard a train horn. He was holding his phone up to his ear again.

"So what did you want to ask?" Björn asked.

"Do you have the body in front of you?"

"Do you even need to ask?"

"Does she have wounds on her arms?"

"Yes, but that's normal," Björn said. "Dead bodies in the water tend to be found in a characteristic position with the head, arms and legs downward and the back elevated, the legs usually bent at the hips. Decomposition begins in the head because of blood collecting in the cranium—the head can exhibit injuries received from scraping the bottom because of the movement of the water. Similar injuries can be seen on the arms and legs."

Henrik looked at her pale, thin arms in the photograph in front of him.

"But," he said, "on her left wrist is a larger, or rather, wider wound."

"Correct."

"Could that have been caused by chafing from something else?"

"And you're getting at…?"

"When we found Pim, she had wounds, both scratches and large lacerations. She also had wide wounds, like red ribbons, around her wrists that were caused by the ropes that she'd been tied up with. Is it possible that the victim in the picture also may have been bound by the wrists?"

"Yes, that's totally possible."

"Okay, thanks. I just wanted to have that confirmed," Henrik said, getting up. He darted out into the hallway, past a confused Ola, into the conference room and up to the large, detailed map on the wall, and put his finger on the round circle that marked where Pim had been found.

"What are you looking for?" Ola said from the doorway.

"Where was the drowned girl found?" he said.

"You mean the girl who—"

"Just tell me where she was found!"

Ola disappeared from the doorway and came immediately back with his laptop, which he placed on the table. He cast a glance at his computer screen and then stood right behind Henrik, searching the map.

"According to the fishermen, it was here," he said, indicating a point in the Arkösund archipelago. "Why?"

"The girl had been in the water for about a day. It's not likely that in one day she would have floated all the way out here from land," Henrik said, showing the large distance between the sea and land.

"No, that'd require gusts of hurricane-force winds," Ola said.

"So she must have been dumped at sea."

Henrik pointed again.

"Look," he said. "Pim was found walking on Highway 209, near Brytsbo, and there's coastline both north and south of there."

"Yes, and we've already searched through the whole northern coast. Marviken, Viddviken, Jonsberg, everywhere."

"But," Henrik said, "the drowned girl was found here." He moved his finger down, to the southern area of the map. "What's in the middle?"

Ola took a step forward.

"Kälebo," he said. "Right on the water."

"Exactly," Henrik said. "Pim said that the room she was in was near the water, and if the woman who drowned was dumped at sea, she must have been dumped from a boat. We have a meeting in an hour. Before that, I want you to list everything along this strip of coast in Kälebo—summerhouses, storage sheds, boathouses, everything—because I think both the room and the boat are right there."

The car door shut almost soundlessly. Jana Berzelius froze, listening, but only heard silence.

Even though it was snowing heavily, the snowflakes didn't reach her where she stood in the dense spruce forest. She took a step forward and felt that the ground was soft. The driveway up to the house was long and wound around two curves.

The map wasn't correct. The cottage was indeed close to the water, but not right on it. It had two windows, a wide chimney and a narrow door. Around the ash tree in front wrapped a circular wooden bench that was altogether too big for the narrow trunk. The bench was clearly used during the summer for when people wanted to escape the hot sun, she thought, looking at the thick blanket of snow that now lay on the bench under the tree's cold, straggly branches.

She stopped ten feet from the old oak front door. She watched it, listening again. No one had shoveled around the doorsill, and there were neither footprints nor tire tracks in the snow.

She went around the house, peering in the windows and confirming that the cottage was deserted. She turned her gaze toward the cliffs and went quickly down toward the sea, searching for a boathouse but finding only a little outhouse that she didn't bother to look into.

Disappointed, she turned back to her car, unrolled the nautical chart and looked at it again, hoping that she would find a boathouse somewhere on it.

Per Åström saw his shadow against the outer door as he waited outside the large villa in Lindö. He straightened his spine when the door opened.

"Hello, my name is Per Åström and…"

"I know who you are," Karl Berzelius said.

"I don't think we've ever met."

"Even so, I know who you are."

Per combed his hand through his blond hair.

"Excuse me," he said, "I'm sorry to bother you, but…"

"Why are you here?"

"I'm here because of your daughter. May I come in?"

Per heard Karl's heavy breaths quicken, intensify.

"May I come in?" he repeated.

The words hung in the cold air. Karl didn't answer, and Per had the feeling he intended to leave him standing in the cold.

"Have you heard anything from your daughter?"

"What do you mean?"

"I'm beginning to think something has happened to her."

"What reason do you have to think that?"

"I've tried to find her at her apartment. She hasn't been to the office or court, any of the places she usually is."

"She may simply not want to see you."

Per met his gaze, but didn't answer.

"I just want to try to find out where she could be. She has talked about a summerhouse and I thought… Do you know if she could be there?"

"It is called a summerhouse for a reason."

"I understand that. But I just thought…"

"Goodbye," Karl said as he began to shut the door.

"So you have no idea where she is?" Per asked, sticking his foot between the closing door and the frame.

"Jana lives her own life, without my interference."

"Strange," Per said. "Because I was just talking with Torsten Granath, and according to him, you like to check up on your daughter."

Karl's eyes narrowed.

"He said that, did he?"

Per drew his foot back and stood with his legs slightly farther apart, collecting his thoughts. "When Jana was here…" he began.

"I have no idea what you're getting at with your questions," Karl interrupted. "The last time I saw her was on Tuesday, May 1 at seven o'clock in the evening."

"It's December now," Per said.

"Thank you for informing me," Karl retorted.

"So you mean you haven't seen her…"

"No, we don't see each other often. There's no reason for it. My wife, on the other hand, prefers more contact. That's why, because you're so curious, Jana was here the other day. But you knew that already. Is there anything else?"

"If you hear something from her, would you let me know?"

"Don't count on it," Karl said, closing the door.

Ola Söderström printed out the compilation he'd made of the properties he'd found along the coast near Kälebo. He had gone into great detail, checked both older and newer maps and in the end compiled addresses, property details and all the other information he could find. Twelve pages. He heard the printer rattle as it started up in the next room.

He drummed his fingers on the desk, then got up to get the printouts. When he was just a few steps away, he saw Anders Wester standing at the printer, flipping through the pages.

Ola felt a jolt of excitement and anxiety run through his body. Chatting with the highest brass wasn't an everyday occurrence. Shit, he really had to think quickly now. Had to seem smart, not make a fool of himself or say something stupid.

"Hi," he said, as casually as possible.

Anders turned around and gave Ola a neutral look he couldn't interpret. Just a look.

"What's this for?" he said, adjusting the collar of his white shirt.

"What do you mean?" Ola asked.

"The addresses."

"They're for the meeting. I've listed all of the addresses in Kälebo. Henrik thinks we've been searching in the wrong area, and after the meeting, I'll give these to the patrols, who will check each one of them. We think that the room might be there... I mean, the room where the Thai girl was held captive," he said, cursing himself for rambling on.

"Why haven't I been told about this?"

"I thought..." Ola said, trailing off.

It became silent, the type of sudden silence that happened when people completely dropped the thread of a conversation.

"I thought you knew," Ola said, scratching his light blue knit cap. "That you'd talked with Gunnar. Or Henrik."

"I haven't."

"Are you sure?"

No, this can't be happening, Ola thought. Of course Anders was sure. How dare he question the head of National Crime?

"Well, now I know, then," Anders said, giving the stack of papers to Ola. "Thank you for the information."

Ola took the papers. What should he say? *Thank you? You're welcome?*

"We'll begin the meeting now, then," Anders said.

"Now?"

"Right now. Gather everyone."

"But…"

"Do you have an objection?"

"No, I…" Ola couldn't get any more out.

Despite wearing a short-sleeved polo shirt, the sweat ran down Gunnar's back, armpits and forehead. The pressure in his chest made him falter and reach for the support of the railing.

Gunnar Öhrn closed his eyes for a moment, waiting, feeling the pain fade away before he opened his eyes again. Slowly, he ascended the stairs to the police station. He had walked from the room where the press conference had just finished and had taken the long way back to divert his thoughts.

Now he was forced to return to reality. They had yet another dead girl on their hands, yet another death. That had not yet been leaked to the press. He was stressed by the thought. He looked at the clock and realized it was 4:30. He hoped more than anything in the world to avoid seeing Anders Wester, his accusatory gaze and disgusting grin, and hearing his sour comments about "defects" in the investigation.

It took four minutes to walk to his department.

He felt out of breath. He stopped, drawing in air as if he had been holding his breath.

Then he continued straight ahead, past his office, and stopped short, facing the conference room.

Not because the team was sitting there waiting,

as he had expected, but because Anders Wester had already begun the briefing.

He hesitated, feeling the overwhelming urge to walk away from all of it.

Let that idiot take over.

In pure rage, he pulled out his cell phone, flipped through his contacts, went back to his office and shut the door, hard.

County Police Commissioner Carin Radler answered on the third ring.

"Are we so fucking slow here in Norrköping that you're letting a Stockholm snob take over the whole investigation?" he said, without even saying hello.

She sighed.

"Nice to hear from you, too… Listen now, Gunnar…"

"I just want to know what you're thinking."

"You know what I'm thinking."

"That the rest of us are incompetent?"

"I've said it before, but maybe I need to say it again. Anders Wester is just trying to help. His experience and knowledge in the area of narcotics…"

"Shut up."

"Gunnar!"

"We're just a bunch of idiots, right?"

"I'm really beginning to lose faith in you."

"Goodbye."

Gunnar sighed. He knew he was hammering the last nail in his own coffin. But he couldn't take it anymore. He put on his jacket, left the office and went out onto the street. He walked through downtown again. He knew every street, every sidewalk, every stairwell. Still, he felt like a stranger in his own town.

He wasn't thinking about the idiot anymore.

He was thinking about Anneli.

He felt furious and upset at the same time.

Scared.

He had never before been so fucking scared.

Through the glass walls of the conference room, Mia Bolander had seen her boss disappear down the hall. At first she thought he was just going to fetch some reports or data for the meeting, but when fifteen minutes had passed, she realized he wasn't coming back. That meant that Anders Wester would continue the briefing. She turned her gaze to where he stood with his jarring posture next to Ola. *He looks like a bag of shit*, she thought, sighing. She felt irritated by everyone and everything right now.

She swept her gaze around the table and realized that Jana Berzelius wasn't there, either. It was her case, for Christ's sake.

Jana had been gone for a few days now, Mia thought. And she had harped on Mia about being *devoted* to her work.

The head of a preliminary investigation who wasn't actively participating should be taken off the case. Maybe even get an official warning.

That'd be unfortunate. *Really* unfortunate if that

happened, she thought just as Anders started blabbing again.

"I won't keep you any longer," he said, "but we have one important point left. Ola has, so to speak, done some reconnaissance."

"Yes," Ola said. "I've compiled a list of all the properties along the coast near Kälebo. It will likely take all evening and night to go through all of the addresses."

"That long?" Henrik said.

"There are twelve pages of addresses to go through," Ola said.

"So it's best that we get started," Anders said.

"Yes. I'll see to it that..." Ola said.

"No," Anders interrupted. "I don't know where your boss is, but I'll take over responsibility here and see that the patrols get their instructions. Give me the list."

Ola fell silent.

"But I can do it. It's no problem for me..."

"Thank you for your concern," Anders said. "But I think we'll be more effective if everyone does what they're best at. You surely have more important things to do, Ola. Or is this going to be a problem?"

"No," Ola said, handing over the stack of papers.

THIRTY-ONE

LARGE, HEAVY SNOWFLAKES FELL from the sky as Henrik Levin drove through downtown. He was on his way home, smiling at the thought that he would now be spending the second evening in a row with his family. He rested one hand on the two pizza boxes stacked on the passenger seat so he wouldn't risk them sliding off when he swung around the roundabout.

The traffic had calmed down. The school buildings were dark. The daycare playgrounds were empty. A couple sat in a bus shelter, arms around each other, both with their eyes toward the sky, watching the snowflakes.

Before he left the office, he had called restaurant Ardor and confirmed that Per Åström had been there with a woman at 8:30 p.m. on Friday. It had certainly put his mind at ease, but his thoughts still revolved around where Jana Berzelius could be now. He was going to ask someone on the force to show Ida Eklund a picture of Jana so they would know for certain whether it was Jana she had seen.

Henrik turned into the driveway, carried the pizza boxes into the kitchen and ripped off the lid.

"I'm home!" he called.

"But we've already eaten."

Emma stood in the doorway, hands buried in the large knitted cardigan she had wrapped around her body.

"I said I was going to bring dinner home."

"Two hours ago, yes."

"What should I do with the pizzas, then?"

"Do whatever you want."

"Should I freeze them?"

"Do what you want."

"I don't want to fight. Just tell me what to do with them."

"And I said you…"

Emma fell silent. Her face, which had just looked so exhausted, suddenly distorted into an expression of excruciating pain. Her body doubled over and she grabbed the back of a chair, bending over it and screaming, "Ohhhh… Ahhhh!"

Henrik leaped forward, putting his arms around her, but she couldn't let go of the chair.

"What's going on? Tell me what's happening!"

"My belly," she said through clenched teeth. "It hurts so much, so, so much!"

"Is it time? Is it already time? Should we go to the hospital?"

"No, it doesn't usually feel like this. It…

Ahhhh!… I don't know what it is, it hurts so much. Please, Henrik…help me!"

It had been a long workday. When Anneli Lindgren opened the front door she could tell that Gunnar was already home and probably fixing dinner, maybe potato pancakes or pan-fried salmon.

Memories of their past flooded her thoughts. She thought back to when it had only been her and him, without children, without their son, Adam, when they were newly in love and just beginning to discover each other, when the first nervous sentences had come out of his mouth, saying that he was in love. And then the first dinner, and when he later had embraced her, taken her, and they had eaten chips in bed, and then they'd had each other again. Everything had been completely new and such a very long time ago.

She lined up the shoes in the hall before going into the kitchen.

Gunnar sat at the table with a glass of whiskey and an open can of corn in front of him. He hadn't laid out any silverware or plates. The fish lay fried in the frying pan, the burner was off and the tomatoes sat uncut on the cutting board.

"Why weren't you at the meeting?" she asked. "Did something happen?"

"I don't know, did it?" he asked quietly, pulling the can of corn closer. He looked at the contents for a moment. Then he picked up one kernel of corn at a time and dropped them into the whiskey. He paused briefly between each one.

"Why are you doing that?" Anneli asked.

"I'm counting."

"What are you counting?"

"Years."

Anneli smiled in bewilderment.

"Years?"

"Yes."

"What years?"

"Guess!"

Anneli tried to smile again, but an uneasy feeling began to creep into her chest.

"Ten," Gunnar counted, continuing to drop corn into the glass. "Eleven, twelve…"

Whiskey splashed onto the table.

"Eighteen, nineteen…"

She saw that he held his hand over the glass, held it there a long time before dropping the last kernel.

"And twenty."

He said it in one long exhalation.

Anneli felt cold, the fear on the verge of changing to panic.

"Twenty years," he said, meeting her gaze.

"I don't understand," she said.

"We've been together for twenty years, you and I. We've lived back and forth, off and on, to and from… Even though it's been like that, I never thought that you'd do this to me. I thought I meant more to you, that you saw us as something worthwhile, something to fight for, but now I know that's not how it is. Now I know that you and I, that what we have, or rather had, doesn't mean anything to you."

"I don't understand any of this," she said.

"Me, neither," he said.

He took something out of his pocket. He hid it in his hand but then flung it onto the table. She stared at the bag.

"My underwear," she said.

"Among the towels. Not a good place to hide things. You should know that. And you put them in a bag, too, like a fucking souvenir."

"But Anders and I... We..."

She fell silent.

"You what?"

"Nothing."

"Yes, explain it to me. I really, truly want to hear all of the details. Please, do tell! Did he take you in the bed? In the bathroom, maybe? Or maybe on a fucking table?"

"Be quiet, please. Think of Adam."

But Gunnar raised his voice.

"Are you happy now? Are you? That you got to fuck him again..."

Gunnar's voice trembled.

"And why him? Huh? Why did you have to do it with him? Can you even imagine how that feels?"

He slammed his hand against the glass. Whiskey and corn kernels spilled onto the table and dripped down to the floor.

Anneli met his furious eyes. She couldn't speak a single word, felt completely weak.

"I want you to leave," he said.

"But listen to me, Gunnar. Let me explain…"

"Just go," he said, loudly. "And take these with you."

He threw the bag with the underwear at her. She caught it, feeling terribly ashamed.

Then she turned and left the kitchen, continued into the hallway. Not stopping to see Adam, she pushed the door open and went straight out into the cold evening.

Emma lay reclined in the passenger seat, screaming. She squeezed the leather of the seat so hard that it folded.

Their young daughter, Vilma, was screaming, too, and Felix was sitting next to her. He was quiet, but his wide eyes said it all.

"I'm going as fast as I can," Henrik said, feeling the car skid on the slippery pavement.

He looked at Emma, who was resting her head against the glass. She took short, quick breaths before screaming again.

He had to stop at a red light and leaned forward as far as possible over the steering wheel to anticipate the very second the light was going to turn green. He kept his foot on the pedal and revved the engine.

"We're almost there," he said, trying to sound

calm, controlled. He wanted to show that he had control over the situation, that he wasn't worried.

But his faltering voice betrayed him.

The road split.

Jana Berzelius chose to stay to the left but was forced to turn around when she came to a barrier. She then drove a mile and a half down the other road, to the right, and parked at a wayside behind a pile of logs.

She checked that the knife was where it was supposed to be, right at the small of her back, before she began walking toward the sea. She moved quickly, feeling the adrenaline surging with every step she took. She looked forward to meeting him again.

You and me, Danilo!

Suddenly, she was blinded by the strong glare. Instinctively she put her hand to her lower back. She followed the light between the trees, until it disappeared. She was sure that she was on the right path now.

Her steps became more and more eager, and she had to force herself to stop, telling herself to calm down, be careful, take no unnecessary risks.

The forest became sparse, and the sound of the sea became stronger the closer she came to the cliffs. She looked all around as she walked but saw nothing other than trees and snow. She ran the last bit, stopped dead at the edge by the sea and again felt disappointment rise in her throat.

Not a single building as far as the eye could see. Only cliffs and sea.

The wind tore at her hair and ripped at her clothing.

She was just about to turn back when she caught sight of a wooden post in the sea. It stuck up among the ice floes, not far from where she stood. She climbed down the rocky cliffs, slipping and sliding several times. She saw poles sticking up out of the freezing water and now realized there was a whole pier between them.

She looked around, trying to find a better way to get closer to the water, but was forced to go back around some spruce trees that had grown misshapen in the constant strong winds from the sea. She pushed away their branches but was repeatedly whipped in the face. Her cheeks were stinging, but she didn't care. All of her attention was fixed on getting down to the water.

When she finally reached her goal, she froze.

She blinked once.

She thought she was seeing things, but she wasn't.

There was the boathouse.

They pushed the doors to Labor & Delivery open. Henrik Levin tried to follow the staff as they pushed Emma in on a gurney, but the weight of Vilma in his arms and Felix's short legs caused him to lag behind.

A nurse was talking to him, but he couldn't listen; his only thought was to follow Emma.

He felt angry and scared. Then the nurse disappeared, but her voice hung in the air.

"We'll take care of her now," he heard her say.

He stopped, trying to put Vilma down, but she clung to him, clutching his neck. Only then did he hear Emma sobbing.

He stood there, frozen, watching as the doors to the examination room closed.

Jana Berzelius grabbed the knife from her back. She crouched, moving silently and quickly toward the boathouse. Her hair danced in the wind— straight back, up, sideways—following the gusts from the sea.

The little boathouse stood right on the water, protected by the steep cliffs and the thin pine trees. No windows, just a double door facing the trees.

There were no tracks in the snow here, either. Either no one had been here, or the tracks had already disappeared in the heavy snowfall.

She concentrated on not slipping, and moved carefully forward, one foot in front of the other. Right foot, then left.

She stood with her back against the structure. She listened, but it was impossible to distinguish any sounds other than the howling wind and the sloshing sea.

She felt the door carefully, the soft, damp wood, and found that it was unlocked. Taking a deep breath, she counted to three, yanked the door open and stepped in.

She gripped the knife handle in one hand, flashlight in the other. She stood and listened again, sweeping the beam of light over the floor and ceiling. It was a large boathouse, with a rotting staircase leading to an upper level.

She continued in. There were gaps between the planks, and it was cold and damp. She could still hear the wind, but it was muffled.

She relaxed her grip on the knife, replacing it at the base of her spine and letting her hand sink down when she realized she was alone.

Danilo was not here!

Rage swelled inside her, and she could do nothing to stop it. She punched the wall several times. Again and again. She had wished, hoped, believed that he would be here, and with every strike, she cursed herself for being so idiotic that she had thought these meaningless thoughts. Why would he have stayed when he knew that Pim could expose him?

She projected all of her rage onto herself, no longer thinking of him. She hit the wall before giving up and sinking down with her back against it, but she quickly stood up again. Her shirt had gotten hooked on something sticking out of the wall. She heard the cloth tear, and she turned to see a plank with a sharp edge. That's when she saw the dried blood that had run down the wall.

She took a step back, looking down at the floor,

and saw the spots of blood that had fallen like rain-drops. They had created tiny puddles, tiny dark red puddles.

Her eyes searched around the boathouse again. One of the planks stuck up from the floor. She shone her flashlight on it, crouched over it and pulled. She suddenly thought that the contents of her boxes might be in there. But it was only a plastic bag.

Its contents astonished her. A shirt, some cash and a dozen passports.

The passports showed different Asian women. The names told her nothing, and she flipped through them quickly. She was about to put them back in the bag when she suddenly saw a face she recognized—Pim was staring back at her from one of the photos.

But the passport didn't say Pimnapat Pandith.

It said Hataya Tingnapan.

Just then, she heard a sound from the upper floor. She stuffed the passport and a few bills in her pocket, turned off her flashlight and made herself as small as possible. She held her breath, listening.

It was someone crying.

She felt her way to the stairs, putting her foot on the first step, which creaked a warning. She forced herself to slowly climb the stairs.

A new sob.

She crept forward as soundlessly as she could. She stopped, listened, but didn't hear any movement on the next floor. She turned the flashlight on again. The light roved across the walls, passed over the floor, was reflected in a chain and then caught a face.

A girl.

She sat very still. Her eyes were closed and her face was as pale as frosted glass.

"Isra?" Jana said quietly.

Thick snow blew over the road and Anneli Lindgren felt the car slipping slowly toward the curb. She braked, released the clutch and grabbed the steering wheel firmly to maintain control over the four wheels sliding on the icy street.

She turned into a parking spot, hid her face in her hands and let the tears fall into her palms.

She felt completely exhausted. Everything had gone to hell. Completely to hell.

She got out of the car and stood in front of it with her arms wrapped around herself, taking deep breaths.

A few yards away, in the light of the headlights, she saw a playground. A single swing hung on a metal frame and moved slowly in the wind over tall snowdrifts. The cold iron gave off a shrill sound. Sorrowful and irritating.

She took the bag with her underwear out of her pocket, walked to the playground and tossed it into a garbage can. Then she got back into the car and continued to the police station.

She tried to focus, but her thoughts just whirled around in her head without creating a single complete idea. Everything was so incomprehensibly simple, but simultaneously so complicated.

Her body was shaking when she got out of the car in the parking ramp. Her car hadn't warmed up yet, and she wasn't dressed for the cold. Her fingers were red and stiff. She hurried across the floor, rubbing her palms against each other, back and forth, in an attempt to return warmth to her frozen hands.

She took the elevator up to her office and sat at her desk, wanting to distract her mind with work. She took out cotton swabs and gloves. Before pulling on the gloves, she looked at the ring on her finger, the inexpensive ring.

She had loved it.

Now she pulled it off, holding it between her pointer finger and thumb in front of her face.

She thought how much she still loved it.

Then she put it back on her finger, pulled on her gloves and began to work.

The girl blinked, her eyes wide against the light. Jana Berzelius lowered the flashlight.

"Isra?" she said again.

The girl whimpered and looked at her with big terrified eyes. She sat on a mattress with her hands bound with rope behind her back. She had tape loosely over her mouth and was chained fast to the wall. Next to her was a sink with no faucet. Her jacket was dirty, the blankets around her damp. Her dark hair stuck to her face.

"I don't want to hurt you," Jana said in English. "I'm going to make sure you get out of here. But I have to get help." Then she went back to the stairs.

The girl began to whimper again and thrashed around in panic. She snorted and jerked, pulling at the ropes to get free. She began to scream in spite of the tape over her mouth, panic in her eyes.

"Listen to me," Jana said, holding her hand over the girl's mouth. "If the man who is keeping you here comes back and sees that you're gone, he'll disappear forever, and then we'll never catch him. Then more girls like you will end up in the same place. You have to stay here for now, do you understand? I'll be back."

The girl nodded, the fear plain in her eyes.

"Nothing will happen to you now that we've found you," Jana said. "But when I take my hand away, you have to be quiet. As quiet as you can. We don't want him to hear us."

She slowly took her hand away, stood up and looked at Isra, who was shaking with sobs.

"Everything will be okay," Jana said before descending the stairs. She stopped on the last step, checking first that she had an unobstructed view of the door, then continued over the planks. She peered out and stood there, listening.

The pier creaked loudly as she left the sea behind her. On the way up the cliffs, she stopped and turned back. She hoped that the falling snow would conceal her footsteps. She looked at the pier and the boathouse, out toward the horizon, and felt a hollow sensation creep up her spine, the icy feeling that everything was approaching its logical conclusion.

"Daddy?" Felix said with a worried expression.

Henrik Levin looked down at his son, pulled him into an embrace and held him for a long time without saying a word.

"Daddy, I can't breathe."

"Oh, sorry, little guy."

Henrik let go. He looked at Vilma, who was sitting at a play table and building with multicolored blocks.

"Daddy?" Felix said again, a little more urgently.

"Yes?"

"What's wrong with Mommy?"

He put his hand under Felix's chin, making the boy meet his eyes.

"Mommy's tummy hurts a little. But it's not dangerous."

"My tummy hurts, too," Vilma said, rubbing her eye with her hand.

"I know what we should do for that."

"What?"

"Get ice cream."

"Yum!"

"Can we have whatever flavor we want?" Felix asked, his eyes wide.

"Henrik?"

The voice came from Emma's mother, Ingrid Carlsson, who at that moment came running in the door.

"Grandma!" Felix shouted, greeting her with a hug.

"What happened? Is Emma okay?" Ingrid asked.

"I'm sorry for calling and worrying you."

"But of course you should call me! I didn't understand at first what you were talking about. How is she?"

"She's okay, just pain in her abdomen," Henrik said.

"And the baby? Did something happen to the baby?"

"I don't know yet. She was just admitted. But I'm sure it'll be okay."

His voice faltered again.

He met his mother-in-law's gaze. He nodded instead of saying any more, knowing that it would be more convincing that way.

"Are you two going to come home with me then?" Ingrid said, taking Felix by the hand and reaching her other hand out for Vilma. The little girl refused to take it, instead hugging Henrik's leg even harder.

"I want to stay with Daddy."

"Oh, honey, you can't. I have to take care of Mommy," he said. "Go with Grandma now."

"But what about ice cream?"

"I promised ice cream," Henrik said apologetically to Ingrid.

"And we get to pick whatever flavor we want," Felix added.

"Let's do that," Ingrid said. "Ice cream and a little hot chocolate before we read a bedtime story."

"Can we get one for Mommy, too? Daddy said that if your tummy hurts, you should have ice cream."

"Then we'll get one for Mommy and put it in the freezer for when she comes home," Ingrid said, taking Vilma's hand. "Wave to Daddy now."

"Bye-bye," Felix and Vilma said in chorus.

"Bye-bye," Henrik said, watching them as they walked out of the ward.

Then he slowly sank down into a chair and closed his eyes for a moment.

Per Åström shifted gears and rode his bike across the field of Himmelstalund toward downtown. He pedaled as hard as he could to keep warm after his tennis match at Racketstadion with Johan Klingsberg, whom he'd beaten three sets to one with a match-point ace.

He would shower when he got home.

He followed Södra Promenaden and passed De Geer High School. He hung his mountain bike on one shoulder and pulled open the door to his apartment building on Skomakaregatan, ascending the stairs to his attic apartment. He set his bike down inside the door before taking off the thin Windbreaker and fleece jacket underneath.

In the kitchen, he drank a large glass of mineral water and peeled a banana, which he ate in five bites. He peeled another and ate it in seven bites.

Still not a peep from Jana Berzelius.

He didn't like it.

He wished he could call Henrik Levin and ask if he'd heard anything from her, but he knew he shouldn't. He should wait, just like he always did with Jana. She liked being alone, and he respected that even if it wasn't always easy.

He thought about calling her one last time. But no, he had already called far too many times.

Was there any way to trace her?

He could talk to someone who knew about cellular technology. But who? He had no idea. In the first place, it was only legal to trace people without their consent using cellular technology in the interest of solving a crime. And second, he risked being laughed off, or even misunderstood and seen as a stalker. In other words, he should talk to someone he knew well, someone who took him seriously. It should be a police officer. But despite working at the police station for so many years, he didn't know all that many officers.

The first person he thought of was Henrik Levin again, but he was far from a tech expert. The other was Ola Söderström.

He should ask him what to do.

Ola would know.

Henrik heard the sound of someone clearing her throat and looked up.

A female doctor with bangs and brown eyes stood in front of him. He hadn't heard her footsteps.

"The patient is doing well," she said.

"Do you mean Emma?" Henrik said.

"Yes. She's doing well but needs to stay overnight for observation."

"What's wrong?"

"We don't know. All of her vitals are normal. She threw up once and said the pain in her belly subsided after that. But because she's so close to her due date, we don't want to take a chance and send her home just yet. But I think that *you* should go home and sleep for a few hours."

"Can I go in and see her?"

"She's sleeping."

"Just to say good-night?"

A quick smile passed over the doctor's face.

"Yes, go ahead," she said.

Henrik got up, stifled a yawn and went in to see Emma, who was lying on her back. She was tucked into bed, her eyes closed, face pale. Her hair lay across her throat.

He took her hand, listening to her breathe, and naturally began breathing in the same rhythm. It was calming. He waited a moment, then kissed her hand and left the room.

Henrik raked his hand through his hair and stepped out of the elevator on the ground floor. The cold air hit him as he went toward the parking lot. He needed the air, the short walk.

The little parking lot for Labor & Delivery had filled up. He drove around the hospital building and waited for two delivery trucks before pulling out onto the road.

Just as he was about to shift into second gear, he saw something out of the corner of his eye. He turned his head and thought he saw a car parked behind one of the buildings on the hospital campus.

A black car. A BMW X6.

He only knew one person who had a car like that. Jana Berzelius.

He straightened up in the seat, looked at the car again and felt a strange feeling pass through his body. He couldn't just drive away now.

He cast a glance in the rearview mirror, put his vehicle in Reverse, made a sharp U-turn and drove toward the building to get a better view of the car. But the road was a one-way street in the other direction, and he couldn't break traffic laws. He drove around the building and braked quickly when he approached the spot where the BMW had been. He looked everywhere, but could see that the BMW was suddenly gone.

He rubbed his palms against his eyes and looked down the street.

It was empty.

"Pull yourself together," he said to himself, convinced that fatigue had played a joke on him.

He knew that he should drive straight home and get into bed. That was the right thing to do. The only reasonable thing.

So he twisted the steering wheel and drove toward the exit.

* * *

Pim opened her eyes and looked out at the dark room. The sound of shuffling footsteps came from the hallway, but that couldn't have been what woke her up.

She listened.

She heard the click as a door was pushed closed.

Beeping from a call button. Then everything was silent.

She'd had a hard time sleeping, had been worried about her little sister, Mai. Then she'd begun thinking about those brutal days in the damp boathouse and promised herself that if she ever got home, she would never go through this again. Never, never ever.

She stretched and yawned. She heard the sheet rustle under her when she shifted to her side. She lay like that for a moment, closed her eyes and tried to sleep, but her pillow suddenly felt uncomfortable. She stuck her hand under it and felt something hard. She immediately sat up and pulled the pillow away.

A passport and a stack of Swedish bills.

She quickly grabbed the passport and opened it, hugging it to her chest, hugging her passport as hard as she could.

She opened it again as if to ensure that it was real, that it was actually her passport.

A little piece of paper fell out.

Someone had written in black ink: "Thank you."

THIRTY-TWO

IT WAS EARLY MORNING, AND HENRIK Levin was sitting in his office. He thought about Emma and felt powerless in a way. He couldn't do anything, couldn't affect anything now. The only thing he could impact was the end of the investigation he was working on. But he felt lost.

His thoughts were interrupted by Ola appearing in the doorway with a rolled-up sheaf of papers in his hand.

"I'm really sorry," Ola began. Henrik didn't understand. Did he know what had happened to Emma? Possibly, yes. The police station was a workplace like all others, and gossip traveled quickly through the halls. But this must be some sort of record.

"Thanks. It is what it is. There's not much I can do about it right now, just cross my fingers and hope she feels better soon."

"I don't really follow you…" Ola said, looking uncomfortable.

"Emma," Henrik answered, in a tone that hopefully signaled that it wasn't weighing on him so much that they had to go deeper into the subject.

"What happened to her?"

"She's…" Henrik began, but stopped.

Ola didn't know.

"Nothing, it's nothing, forget it. I misunderstood. What were *you* talking about?" he said instead.

"Kälebo," Ola said, unrolling the papers and laying them on the desk in front of Henrik. "Overnight, a number of patrols checked every building there, but they didn't find any Thai girls."

Henrik sighed loudly before picking up the papers and flipping through them.

"Eleven pages of addresses, and we didn't find anything."

"No, and it's really unfortunate," Ola said. "It's twelve pages, by the way."

Henrik flipped through them again, counting more carefully.

"I count eleven."

"But I printed out twelve pages, and the patrol cars got all of them. I…"

Ola grabbed the papers and counted them again.

"One list is missing," he said, looking at Henrik in confusion.

She needed to dress more warmly if she was going to withstand waiting him out in the chill of the boathouse. Jana Berzelius was back at the summerhouse and went up to the second floor, looking in her bag for clothes and quickly putting them on.

She hurried down the hall past the library and noticed the binders she had left on the floor. She should put them back, she thought.

One after another, she slid them back onto the bookshelf, putting them in exactly the same places they had been.

Her father wouldn't notice anything.

Just as she was about to close the last binder, she stopped. She laid her index finger on one of the documents and began reading. Her father had commented on the result of a judgment with a: "GB."

She had reacted to those initials earlier and now flipped through more pages, scanning the comments more closely on each page. Sometimes there were three lines; other times he almost filled the margin of a whole page with thoughts:

SC determined that the crime should be tried as a drug offense of standard degree. The sentence for both defendants was prison for seven months (benefit for GB).

Her amazement grew as she examined the comments more carefully.

Key witness Anton Ekstam silenced (GB).

Silenced?

She took a deep breath and pulled out her cell phone. She opened the browser and googled Anton

Ekstam. The first hit was a list of people who had disappeared in Östergötland in the 2000s.

> In October 2002, 31-year-old Anton Ekstam from Motala disappeared without a trace. Police and family members conducted an intensive search for two weeks, but Anton was never found…

Jana looked down at the binders again, trying to understand what she was on the verge of finding out.

When she opened the fifth binder, she arrived at a very unpleasant conclusion. There stood:

> Bolanaki contacted witness Lina Bergvall to "clarify some unclear points from the hearing."

Bolanaki?

Jana only knew one Bolanaki.

Gavril Bolanaki, GB.

She put the binders next to each other on the floor, stood up and looked at them. They lay open in a circle around her. She knelt, flipping through pages, comparing and checking.

She realized the initials GB appeared on numerous pages, relating to many different legal proceedings.

She quickly read more of her father's comments.

Witness blamed "poor memory."

Claimed a lack of proof.

Improper seizure protocol established.

What had earlier seemed to be an incredibly successful career in the Public Prosecution Office now seemed to be something completely different.

She bent down to change the order of the binders when she suddenly froze. Car headlights flashed between the curtains, bobbing lights that created moving shadows on the walls in the hall. She cast an uneasy glance out the window and hoped to see a snowplow. But it was her father's black Mercedes, and it pulled in right next to her BMW in front of the house.

She quickly put the binders back on the bookshelf. She grabbed her bag, ran down the stairs to the kitchen window and stood there behind the curtain, peering outside.

She didn't understand. She was particularly confused when she saw her father get out of the car. She didn't know if it was the shock of seeing him, or the fact that she wasn't prepared for him to be here right now. Her thoughts whirled around in her head, not least because of what she thought she had just learned from the binders on the bookshelf.

He disappeared around the house, toward the entrance.

She craned her neck but didn't see him anymore.

What was he doing here?

She quickly left the kitchen, put on her shoes and grabbed her backpack. She heard steps outside the door and had no choice but to retreat into the house, crouching to avoid being seen, and creep toward the living room.

The fluorescent lights in the conference room awoke, blinking to life, when Gunnar Öhrn pushed the button.

The team had been called in and they gathered in the room, one after another. Five of twelve chairs around the oval table were now occupied by Gunnar, Henrik, Mia, Ola and Per. Only Anneli and Jana were missing.

Gunnar saw the light on in Anneli's office and figured she was coming.

"And where is Jana? Anyone know?" he asked, looking first at Henrik, then at Per. Both shook their heads.

He felt a certain tiredness wash over him and was thankful he'd taken two 500 mg tablets of ibuprofen before he'd left the apartment. It usually helped for hangovers, but now it was helping him with the headache he'd gotten after the argument with Anneli last night. Not to mention the stress of finding out that the patrols had missed searching one part of the area in Kälebo overnight. But he found a little bit of malicious pleasure when he realized it was actually Anders Wester who had taken command of the operation in Kälebo. That damn blowhard could take his "cooperation" and shove it.

"This is an enlargement of the area from the missing list," Ola said, nodding toward a picture he'd pulled up on the projection screen. He stood and pointed to the somewhat blurry photo.

"But we haven't actually missed that much. There are only two addresses within this area, and so that you will understand where it is..."

He moved to the map on the wall.

"This is where the picture was taken," he said, pointing to a place two inches from the X that showed where Pim had been found.

"She was found here, and the drowned girl was found here," he continued, pointing to the map of the Arkösund archipelago.

"And what's at these two addresses?" Gunnar asked.

Ola went back to his chair, sat down and glanced at the paper on the table in front of him.

"At the first address, there's an old summer cottage built in 1940. The cottage is still there, right here."

Everyone leaned in to see better as Ola zoomed in on the picture.

"But the cottage isn't right on the water," Henrik observed.

A collective sigh of disappointment seemed to pass through the room.

"So what's at the other address?" Gunnar asked.

Ola took out the paper even though he already knew what it said.

"I was just getting to that," he said. "There was a cottage there, also an old summer cottage, that burned down in October of 2005. It was owned

privately until 1970 when it was donated to the
Ministry of Defense. From 1971, you could rent it
if you worked for the Ministry."

"And now?"

Ola pointed to the enlarged photo. Henrik looked
quickly at the digital map. Water, cliffs and forest.

"I don't see anything," Henrik said.

"Check again," Ola said, zooming in on the picture step by step. He pointed to a spot just a half
mile from the cottage he had just shown.

Henrik leaned forward even farther.

"A boathouse," he said.

"Yes," Ola said.

"Get a helicopter," Gunnar commanded without
taking his eyes from the screen. He stared at the
little boathouse sitting directly on the water. Now
they really had to go all in on the hope that they
were right.

KARL BERZELIUS OPENED THE OUTER door and stepped into the hall. His feet had grown cold from the chill outside. He didn't turn on any lights, instead walking right into the darkness, listening for sounds. But the house was silent.

"Jana?" he said quietly after he had checked the different rooms. "Are you here? I want to talk to you."

He walked with heavy steps to the armchair, which moved slightly as he sat down. The leather creaked as he crossed one leg over the other.

"You have to come out. Come out so I can talk to you. I know…"

His voice cracked. He took a deep breath and then repeated, "I know you're sitting behind me. Behind my back. Behind the armchair. Come out now."

When nothing happened, he slowly stood and looked behind the chair, but it was empty. He stood in the middle of the floor, waiting, but then began walking over the carpet.

"Jana…" he said, his voice soft. "We have a lot to talk about."

He turned around and looked into the hallway. Farther down, the door to the kitchen was ajar. He turned his gaze toward the stairs again.

But both the stairs and the corridor were empty.

Quickly, he moved from room to room. He stopped at the door of one of the guest rooms. It was a smaller room with a single bed, a desk and a bookshelf, three large windows and a braided rag rug on the floor.

The rug was folded, as if someone had kicked it.

"Listen to me, Jana!"

He spoke with a harder tone; the softness was gone, the guise.

With determined steps, he went into the room and turned on the lamp. He stopped and shivered; it was colder in the room than it should be.

His gaze drifted over the bed, the table, the bookshelf. He took a step toward the windows, noting how the lamp was mirrored in the many panes. He listened and heard the sea. *I shouldn't hear it so clearly*, he thought, at the same time as an icy wind blew over him. Then he understood that one of the windows was open.

He went out in the yard again, trudging through the snow to the back of the house. He stood a few yards from the open window and saw the tracks leading from it, saw the distance between them and knew that she had been running from the house. He ran after her.

Immediately after a pine tree near the cliffs, both the snow and the tracks stopped. He stood and looked out over his property.

On the right, under a roof and well-covered by a green tarp, his two motorboats were usually stored over the winter.

But now there was only one.

Anneli Lindgren walked quickly through the hall, faster with every step.

She approached Gunnar's office, feeling how her hair tie was slipping and slowly releasing her ponytail.

His room was empty, so she continued to the conference room where the team had just broken up. The mood was tense.

She met Henrik, Mia and Per in the doorway and nodded toward Ola, who wore an anxious expression and was holding his cell phone to his ear. Gunnar stood farthest into the room, his eyes on the map. He didn't look at her, but she was positive he had seen her come in.

She went straight across the room to him, stopped and tried to get him to look at her.

"I have to tell you something," she said, panting, trying to catch her breath. She noticed they were now alone in the conference room.

"Stay away from me," he said.

"I have to talk to you now," she said. Her voice

was serious and unfaltering, completely unlike the one he had last heard from her. She waited for him to respond, but he didn't. Gunnar stood silently and looked at the map.

"I know that I've really messed up," she said, "and I don't know if you'll ever forgive me, but I…"

"I don't want to hear your damn apology," he said, turning around. "Where were you last night, then?"

She stared at him.

"I've been here at the office. Gunnar…"

"I don't want to hear any more…"

"No, I understand that, but what I have to say is about the investigation."

She inhaled again and exhaled slowly. But still no follow-up question from Gunnar.

"Now you're being really stupid," she said. "I…"

"Am I the one who's stupid?"

"Now, listen to me! There's something I have to tell you."

"Say it, then," he said, meeting her gaze.

"You remember the sample I took of what Axel Lundin had under his fingernails?"

"That is incomplete? Yes, both Henrik and Mia are on me about it because you won't tell them anything."

"It *was* incomplete," she clarified.

For three long seconds, the ventilation system was the only sound in the room.

"What are you trying to say?" he said.

"That I have a match."

CHAPTER

THIRTY-FOUR

SHE CROUCHED DOWN AND WATCHED the boathouse that lay scarcely fifty yards beyond her. From here, you couldn't see her boat. She had laid anchor in a nearby bay, had hidden it as well as she could and had come the last bit on foot.

Jana Berzelius had been sitting in the same place, hidden behind a snow-covered bush. With sweeping, watchful eyes, she looked out over everything around her.

But she didn't see Danilo.

He wasn't there, not yet.

She couldn't let Isra go yet. Isra was her trump card. As long as she was still there, Danilo couldn't disappear.

She had to move to stay warm. She climbed along the cliffs and tried to find a spot closer to the boathouse to watch from. Just twenty yards from it, she stopped behind a pine tree, turned toward the boathouse and waited.

Suddenly, the door opened.

Someone was coming out.

She saw a figure standing in the doorway and ducked quickly. She slowly looked again, but the figure had disappeared.

Had Danilo shown up? And where was he now? Had he gone into or out of the boathouse?

She couldn't wait any longer. She had to act quickly now that she knew someone was there. But it bothered her that the sky had begun to grow lighter. The gray light made it harder for her to approach the house unnoticed.

She lay down on the ground and began to crawl along, in the cover of branches from shrubs. She moved slowly so she wouldn't be seen, knowing that the brain registered movements and sudden interruptions in stillness. No one reacted to an approaching turtle, but everyone reacted to a leopard at top speed. She worked her way forward calmly and methodically, moving her body forward using her lower arms and legs, with her head down the entire time. She regulated her speed and didn't pause, slowly progressing the whole time until she reached the house.

Then she stood and listened for sounds.

She heard nothing.

She took a few steps to the side, standing with her back against the door.

Inside, she was tense and ready.

On the surface, she was calm and relaxed.

She released the knife from the small of her back

and squeezed it a few times to get the blood flowing in her hands.

She counted to three.

One. Two. Three.

She stepped into the boathouse.

With the knife in front of her, she listened in the darkness. She listened for Isra but didn't hear her.

Jana stood in the middle of the cold floor, smelling filth and moisture, hearing water dropping against something metallic that made the sound echo.

She slowly climbed the stairs, one step at a time, feeling her body fill with adrenaline. She moved in a crouched position over the damp floorboards toward the corner.

"Isra?" she whispered.

There was no answer.

The boathouse creaked and cracked around her and she heard how the wind outside had grown stronger. She couldn't get any closer. She tried to breathe quietly, looking into the corner and discovering the ropes on the floor. That was all she saw.

Isra was gone.

They were small, subtle details that Gunnar Öhrn simply could have missed if he hadn't been so attentive. A bead of sweat on her temple, hands under the table. He assumed corrections officer Anne Lindbom was nervous.

For a moment, he had sat still in front of her and doubted himself. But when he suddenly saw her eyelid jerk, he was more certain that she had something to hide.

He cast a glance toward the door of his room to confirm that it was fully closed before he began the conversation.

"It was you who found Axel Lundin in his cell?" he asked, flipping through a report that Internal Affairs had drawn up after Lundin's suicide.

"Yes, that was my shift."

"Can you describe in your own words what happened when you found Axel?"

"I've already done that. It's in the report."

"Yes, it says here that you checked on Axel every hour through the hatch in the cell door, which you'd also documented in the supervision log. It also says in the report that you were working alone, that you left the detention area for a break to get something to eat and that when you came back, you found Axel dead."

"Yes."

"So you left your post and went through the hallway to the cafeteria?"

"Yes."

"But why didn't any of the security cameras in the hallway capture you, then?"

Anne's eyes darted around the room. Gunnar continued, "And how do you explain that your security card was only swiped from the inside and then out, and not from the outside and in?"

"I left the detention area."

"But you couldn't have. How did you get in there

again without using your card? You have to use a security card to enter, right?"

"Yes."

"And you were alone in the detention area, you said. Did one of the inmates open it for you?"

"No."

"So what happened, then?"

The sweat ran down both of her temples now. Her hands were shaking under the table.

"We've examined the film from the security cameras. We know you weren't alone in there."

He could see her swallow.

"We know who was with you when Axel died."

Her face flushed immediately. She bit her lip hard and avoided his gaze.

"I couldn't say anything," she said, almost too quietly to hear, putting her hands between her knees as if she wanted to force them to stop shaking.

"I understand," he said.

"I had to let him in. He said he was going to hurt my children if I didn't obey him."

She lifted her face and suddenly had tears in her eyes.

"Did you let him into Axel Lundin's cell, too?"

"Yes. I had no choice."

The stress pursued him like a fox chased a hare. Henrik Levin checked his service weapon, a Sig Sauer, and felt the metal grow warm from his body.

The hunt was on.

Mia came into the room, also with a holstered weapon.

"Are you ready?" she asked. "The helicopter will be here in five minutes."

"Coming," Henrik said, pulling his jacket over his shoulders but not bothering to button it.

"Did you hear that Pim has disappeared from the hospital?"

"What?"

Henrik spun around.

"I just found out. Her room was empty when staff came in to check on her. They've searched everywhere, but she's gone."

"We had guards on her."

"Yes, but she tried to run away once before, didn't she?"

"Yes."

"And this time, she was successful, plain and simple."

Henrik sighed, suddenly feeling completely exhausted.

"You should maybe tell Jana that her client is gone," Mia said.

"No, there's no point. I can't get ahold of her."

"So tell me, are you still protecting her?"

"Lay off," he said. "I'm not protecting her!"

"Have you tried to find her, then?"

"She has an alibi for the evening when Robin Stenberg was murdered, and I had someone confront Ida again. She looked at a number of pictures, among them a picture of Jana."

"And?"

"Ida wasn't at all sure that it was her. We're making a mountain out of a molehill. We can't put any more energy into that now."

"So you're just dropping it?"

"Yes, I'm just dropping it. Because in five minutes, more like three now, we have an incredibly important assignment to carry out."

"So why are you still standing in here, then?"

He sighed.

"So that I could answer your dumb questions."

Mia laughed and disappeared into the hallway. Henrik was just about to follow her when Gunnar yelled, "Wait!"

"We have to go. The helicopter is here…"

"No, we have to stop. The helicopter will have to wait," Gunnar said. "Anneli has something to share."

"About what?"

"It's about Anders Wester."

First she just heard a sound that quickly disappeared in the wind. But when it came again, she understood fairly quickly that it was the sound of panic, of someone screaming.

Jana Berzelius went around the boathouse. The wind buffeted against her as she went with quick steps out on the pier. She heard splashing from the ice-cold water, filled with chunks of ice. She turned, looking around, but couldn't see anything. She ran over the slippery planks, saw the threatening water under her, slipped, regained her balance and continued in the stiff wind. She ran farther out on the pier.

Rusty iron chains hung from the poles. Water had frozen on them, and small icicles hung down from the links.

She rubbed the snow from her eyes with the arm of her jacket, leaned carefully forward and looked down into the black water.

Suddenly she saw a face break the surface. It was Isra. She flailed her arms around her, fighting for air.

Jana sank down to her knees, bent forward and reached out her hand.

"Take my hand," she said.

She felt Isra's ice-cold fingers through the leather of her gloves. She tried to get ahold of her, but the girl's fingers were limp and Jana felt how they slipped out of her grasp.

Isra flailed her arms wildly, the water splashing around her.

Then Jana heard steps on the pier and slowly turned around.

She saw him.

He stood with his head down and his eyes dark. His hood was over his head, his fists clenched, his jaw set.

"Hi, Jana," he said. "I had a feeling you'd show up eventually."

Anneli Lindgren fell silent and looked at Henrik, Mia, Ola and Per, who sat around the oval table with their mouths agape. They were again gathered in the conference room. Gunnar stood next to her and nodded.

"So you mean," Henrik said, "that Anders Wester's DNA was found on Axel Lundin's dead body?"

"Yes," she said, nodding. "His skin cells were under Axel's nails."

"So…" Mia began, but then fell silent as if she needed to think the thought through one more time. "If he weren't the head of National Crime, I would believe what you're saying, but now…well, I don't know," she said. "What is it you think, really?"

"I don't *think* anything. I'm just saying the facts. Axel Lundin was visited by Anders Wester right before he died."

"Did Wester have something to do with Lundin's death? Is that what you're thinking?" Mia said. "I don't get it."

"But *I* think I'm beginning to understand," Henrik said. "Especially why Anders Wester has stayed in Norrköping and wants to be so involved in the investigation. This bit about cooperating is just a façade."

"That idiot is mixed up in all of it, too," Gunnar said, as if he didn't really understand the magnitude of what he had just said.

"Is he The Old Man, then?" Mia asked. "But what the hell? What's happening to this police force? First Axel and now Anders."

Silence fell around the table. Anneli listened to her own breathing, felt her heart pounding.

"I've wondered this whole time why we've always been one step behind," Gunnar said, stroking his hand over his chin. "But this explains why we didn't find Danilo Peña in his apartment. Anders must have warned him."

"The worst is that now we're still a step behind, too," Henrik said. "He's probably already warned Danilo that we're on our way to the boathouse."

"Oh, hell!" Gunnar said. "We have to get there right away!"

"But we have to find Anders," Henrik said. "Does anyone know where he's staying at?"

"No idea," Gunnar said.

"So what do we do, call him?" Henrik said.

"Yes," Gunnar said.

"What's his number?"

"How the hell should I know?"

"I thought you had it."

"I erased it."

"Ola," Henrik said. "Can you get his number quickly, do you think?"

Ola nodded and started to stand up, but Anneli reached out her hand and stopped him.

"Wait," she said. "I have the number. And I think that it's actually best if I call."

"You?"

Gunnar's voice revealed his clear desire to find that he had heard wrong.

The room fell silent again.

"Yes, let me try," she said, standing up and taking her cell phone from her pocket.

"But we have to have a plan for what you're going to say," Henrik said.

"I'll try to set up a meeting with him," Anneli said quietly.

"Just find out where he is," Gunnar said, "and we'll haul him in."

She took a deep breath, went to the window, turned her back to the others, dialed the number and listened to it ring. She shifted her weight restlessly from one foot to the other. She knew that she was going to have to explain things to Henrik and Mia, but she pushed away those unpleasant thoughts. She was stressed enough over the fact that she was calling Anders. Five rings, then his voice mail picked up.

"He's not answering," she said without turning around. She took the phone from her ear. It felt heavy in her hand, much heavier than it was.

"Call that idiot again. He'll fucking answer," she heard Gunnar say.

He more or less spit out the words. The chair scraped loudly on the floor as he got up. Anneli heard his frustration and wanted to turn around, go to him and put a gentle hand on his shoulder.

Then her phone rang and interrupted her thoughts.

She didn't recognize the number, but she recognized the voice.

"Anneli?"

"Yes."

"It's Anders. I saw you called me."

His voice sounded so close that she had to look around to confirm that he wasn't standing somewhere watching her. But she didn't see him.

"I want to see you," she said, her heart pounding harder now.

"Do you miss me?" he said.

She felt herself beginning to flush, and even though she stood with her back to the others on the team, she turned her gaze to the floor.

"Can I see you now?" she asked.

"Why?"

"I want to talk to you, and I think that you want to talk to me, too."

There was a pause.

"Okay," he said finally. "You'll have to come to me."

"I will," she said. "Tell me where you are."

Isra disappeared under the surface of the water. Jana Berzelius only saw the waves washing over the broken ice. She turned her gaze to Danilo again.

"How did you find this place?" he said.

"It wasn't too hard."

"But you must remember what I said. If you follow me…"

"I'll regret it forever. Yes, I remember."

"Yet you came here?"

"For many reasons. Mostly personal, actually."

She scanned the area, evaluating the situation. She looked at him, trying to see if he held a weapon.

He usually drew his weapon immediately, without waiting, wanting you to see it, to see how it shone, to fear it from the very first moment. But now she only saw his clenched fists.

Then she heard Isra again, a weak yell, and understood that she wasn't going to be able to hold out much longer. Soon the water would swallow her up for good.

"Is this what you do? Drown them?"

"Not all of them."

"But you bring them all here?"

"Yes. Here they can whine as much as they want. Scream as loud as they want. No one can hear them. Who cares about a dilapidated boathouse in the winter?"

"Yet you tape their mouths?"

"Yes, but not too tightly. Mostly for the fun of it. There's always a risk that they'll break down and go crazy or that they'll get it into their heads to try to escape."

"One did escape. It's thanks to her that I'm here."

Danilo's eyes became darker. "I should have taken the capsules out of her myself, drowned her immediately. Shouldn't have waited."

She heard Isra again. Jana turned around and stretched her hand out to her, finally reaching her thin, stiff fingers and pulling her toward her.

"Let her go," Danilo said.

But Jana kept pulling, not releasing her hold on Isra's cold hand.

"I said, let her go!"

The kick came so suddenly and was so violent that Jana landed on her side. Pain shot through her rib cage.

"I'm not letting go," she said.

But after the second kick, she had no choice. Her chest was burning and she lost her grip on Isra.

Jana forced herself up on all fours before standing. She heard his dark, rumbling laughter. It filled the calm that spread through her. She had longed for this moment, longed to stand face-to-face with him. There were no rules between them. Just her and him.

She released the knife from her back.

"No weapons," he said.

When she saw his outstretched, empty hands clench, she dropped the knife. It stuck upright in the pier.

His eyes had narrowed and he took a step forward, holding up his fists. She didn't let herself be fooled into following his fists with her eyes, instead focusing on his feet. She tuned out everything else around her and went straight at him.

He hit her full force, straight at her kidneys. She took the blow, looked for her opportunity and seized it. She kicked him in the ribs, whirled around, switched her legs for the next kick and made contact with his face.

He looked at her, surprised, before he struck back. She saw the blow coming through the air as if in slow motion, ducked and parried with her left shoulder, but she couldn't parry the third and fourth blows, which seemed to come out of no-where. She collapsed onto the pier and immediately felt blood streaming down her face. She had to close her eyes, trying to understand what had happened. She smelled frosty wood. She heard ice crystals falling with a faint patter into the water. With her cheek pressed to the cold planks, she saw him coming toward her. She heaved herself to the side, got her arms up and avoided his fists. He backed up three, four steps.

"Get up," he screamed.

She stood and assumed a defensive position, but before Danilo lurched forward with a new strike, her foot was on the way toward his kneecap. She made contact from above, but not with enough force to knock it out of place. She kicked again, but this time he was ready. He grabbed her foot and wrenched it around. She followed with the rest of her body. She twirled around, landed, rolled and struck out. She no longer kept her rage inside. The adrenaline was pumping through her veins, making her hit even harder. Right, left, right, right again, duck, turn, kick, turn, kick. One of the blows connected with his chin, and she backed up a step, noticing her gloves were bloody.

Suddenly, he was upon her. She ducked, held out her elbow and aimed at the bridge of his nose, aimed again, striking straight into his stomach, and he was forced to double over.

She laid her palm on the back of his head and

pressed his face against her raised knee with violent force, then shoved him away.

Danilo cupped his hands around his nose. When he saw all the blood, he laughed loudly.

She turned, looking in the water for Isra, but she no longer saw her.

"Time to get serious," he said, taking three steps forward and pulling the knife from the pier.

"I thought we agreed no weapons," Jana said.

"The rules of the game just changed," he said.

"I didn't think you liked knives."

"There's a lot of shit you can do with a knife. *That's* what I like," he said, advancing.

PER ÅSTRÖM WATCHED HENRIK AND Mia run through the hallway and disappear into the elevator. Gunnar and Anneli had gone into their respective offices.

Per turned around, looking at Ola, who was gathering the papers that were lying on the table, and thought what a strange turn the investigation had taken. If Anders Wester was one of the people leading this narcotics mess, it would be a scandal of extreme proportions. He could see the newspaper headlines now, hear the special report announcements on TV… It was a bit unbelievable.

He caught himself missing Jana. He wanted to discuss the investigation with her—he'd been right, their respective investigations had indeed merged—but where was she?

Ola tapped the papers against the table three times and Per noticed they were alone in the conference room. He glanced furtively out into the hallway, which was deserted, then looked at Ola again. They didn't really know each other. They'd really just seen each other now and then, in situations like this, when their paths crossed for work.

"So…" he began, adjusting his dark blue jacket. "I'm a little worried about Jana Berzelius…" He opened his mouth to continue, but hesitated again.

Ola looked up from his papers with a confused expression.

"Oh?" he said, and waited.

"I'm just wondering, do you know how to trace a cell phone?" Per asked.

Henrik Levin held his jacket closed with his hands so it wouldn't flap as he and Mia dashed to the helicopter.

He helped Mia get on board first and saw the focused look on her face as she sat down and fastened the seat belt. The pilot and another man were sitting in the helicopter cockpit. The pilot pushed a lever and turned a key on the instrument panel.

Just as Henrik stepped into the helicopter, his cell phone rang again.

"Gunnar?" he said loudly.

"No, this is Labor & Delivery."

Henrik froze.

Labor & Delivery?

No, not now.

"I just wanted to tell you that the contractions have begun and that Emma needs you here now."

Not now.

"Is it possible for you to come?"

He pulled his hand across his mouth and looked at Mia, then at the police officer sitting in the car at the railing, lights flashing.

He wanted to say that he couldn't come, that he was sitting in a helicopter, but he knew deep down what his answer should be. He would never forgive himself if he disappointed Emma now.

"I'm coming," he said, hanging up and turning toward Mia.

"What is it?" Mia asked.

"I have to go to the hospital. It's time."

"She's in labor now?"

"Yes."

"Right now?"

"Yes!"

"Well, get out of here then. Hurry!"

Henrik got out of the helicopter, saw the pilot turn yet another control and push down a pedal. The man next to him picked up a map and laid it on his knee. The engine began to thunder, and after a moment, the rotor blades began to move, spinning faster and faster. It made a deafening roar. The pilot gripped the throttle and lifted off. The helicopter went straight up, slowly and softly, then tipped forward and sped up. It flew past the railing, up over the city.

Henrik stood alone, trying to understand what he was looking at, why he was standing there. Worry spread through his body, and he told himself to be calm. But his body wouldn't listen.

Focus, he thought.

Focus on Emma, the baby.

His heart was pounding as if it was having a hard time moving the blood through his body.

He buttoned his jacket and began running.

Danilo was already upon her.

Jana backed up, knowing that the best defense against a knife was distance. The best counter was a barrier. But there was nothing on the pier that she could hold up against him.

He attacked again. His hands were low, and he swept the blade in small, dangerous arcs.

Jana backed up again.

She was near the edge. Just a few more steps and she would end up in the water.

He began coming toward her, moving side to side in a crescent moon–shaped path as he approached. The knife in his hand mirrored the movement.

A memory came to her. The two of them, in another place, in another time, when they were children, maybe seven or eight years old. They'd moved in half circles around each other, practicing, training, fighting for survival. Just like they were doing now. The memory impacted her so strongly that she became completely still. Her thoughts whirled around while she attempted to collect her strength and appraise the situation. But instead of stepping backward, she let him come even closer.

He feinted with his left hand and swung with his right. The knife blade sliced through the air. She moved, following his movements. Snow whirled up around them.

The same attack again, the knife blade dangerously close now.

He struck out with his hand, and although she ducked, his hand caught in her necklace. Her neck stung when he pulled it loose.

"Look, a trophy," he jeered, letting the necklace dangle from his fingers.

She saw him shift his weight, saw that he'd lost his concentration. In the same second, she took a step forward and made a violent attack, wrenching the knife from his hand, spinning around and striking his abdomen with full force.

The knife slid in, remained buried in his flesh.

Danilo was no longer smiling.

He froze.

She kicked with all her strength, hitting the bottom of his thigh. She mobilized her muscles and kicked again, yelling as she did so to summon all of her strength.

He staggered backward.

For a moment he stood absolutely still.

Everything was completely quiet.

Then he fell to his knees, holding both hands to his stomach, around the knife. He tried to brace himself against the pier but fell, crawling into the fetal position and coughing. Jana saw a streak of blood.

She was trembling from the exertion and forced herself to regain self-control. She went around him in a half circle, standing over him, and pulled out the bloody knife. He coughed up more blood.

"I hate you," she said. "And I have longed for this moment, to finally say that to you."

He tried to say something, his gaze toward the sky, but could only cough. Then she saw what he saw, a beam of light coming over the trees.

"Fuck, they're already here," he panted.

The muscles in her face tensed up and she vacillated between rage and controlled calm as she followed the light.

She left Danilo and went to the side of the pier, looking out over the waves, toward the bottom, but couldn't see Isra anymore.

Then she heard the sound cutting through the icy air.

She knew she had to hurry, had to leave the pier and hide. She couldn't be discovered. Not here, not with Danilo.

But he couldn't stay, either.

It was possible that a lot of officers were approaching, that they were just about to occupy the area around the boathouse.

She turned around, squinting to see him.

But the pier was empty.

She didn't see him anywhere.

She quickly went back toward the boathouse, running through the deep snow. She saw a string of blood and knew that Danilo had disappeared the same direction into the forest.

Only then did she think about the cold. It permeated her marrow, her legs, and made her reluctantly pull her shoulders up.

She stopped, holding her breath, and heard deep, rattling breaths, then a cough.

Then she saw him, just a few yards ahead of her, sliding down a cliff with one hand pressed to his stomach.

Right there, below the cliff, was a wooden boat.

She rushed to the cliff but stumbled and fell, landing on her back. She regained her balance immediately and ran even faster. Her feet drummed against the slippery stones, and he couldn't withstand the force as she rushed at him from behind. She gripped his throat and pulled him along with her.

They fell.

She landed badly, hitting her head on the cliff and feeling a terrible stabbing pain. He lay next to her. She forced herself to her knees and pressed the knife against him, but he had more strength left than she had counted on. He got his hand up, pushing hers back, and she felt the strength running out of her arms. She knew she couldn't resist much longer. She saw that the bloodstain on his shirt was large and seemed to grow. His rib cage moved slowly up and down.

The tip of the knife turned 180 degrees, from his throat to hers. He tried to hold his hand still, but it shook so much that the sharp blade scratched against her skin.

"Do it, then," she said.

Her heart was pounding. She could hear it. It sounded like an angry blacksmith striking the anvil with his hammer twice per second.

"Do what you want to do. Push the knife in," she said again.

She closed her eyes, waiting.

He looked at her and then shook his head almost unnoticeably.

Then he relaxed his arm, tossed the knife aside, let his head sink down to the rock, held his hand to his stomach and panted.

She looked at him in surprise.

"I know you don't understand," he said. "But I can't kill you."

They had traveled quickly over the bare treetops and fields that were white as frosting. They had passed isolated roads and large farms.

Now they were flying at low altitude along the coastal cliffs. The sound was thunderous, and the rotor blades flashed in front of the windshield. Mia Bolander held her hands to her earmuffs and thought about the investigation, everything that she had done to show that she was worthy of a place in the new organization. Everything Gunnar hadn't seen. Or had chosen not to see. Or maybe he'd seen but had already decided.

He hadn't said it directly to her, but she knew. Unspoken opinions were the worst. Ones that weren't articulated but could be sensed.

Gunnar's body language had told her everything

she needed to know. She had summed up all of his looks, heard his sighs, seen his clenched teeth, and understood everything he actually wanted to say, but that he hadn't yet dared to say straight out to her. That she was no longer one of them. One of the team.

She sighed and leaned forward, looking over the sea and strip of coastline. The pilot had radio contact with someone and they talked about turning back.

She felt the helicopter make a sharp turn to the left. It sunk down, rocking gently.

"We're here," she heard through her headset.

The helicopter's spotlight illuminated a boathouse. Mia turned in both directions, looking out through the helicopter's windows, but she saw no movement on the ground.

They climbed up again.

Then she saw something near the pier, someone moving in the water.

"There," Mia yelled. "I see a person there! We have to land!"

"But we can't land here. We have to find a better place."

Mia heard the rumbling from the engine. As they ascended again, she felt suddenly alone. All of the other operations she'd been part of had been with Henrik. And it was always Henrik in command. Now the responsibility was on her.

And maybe now was the time for her to take the opportunity to stand out.

Show what she was made of.

Especially if she could close the whole case. Especially if she could do it entirely herself.

She got ready as they sank down on a white field. The snow was swept away. The helicopter hovered, sinking slowly and then standing still, softly rocking. She immediately unlatched her seat belt, but she was told to stay in the helicopter until the engine had stopped.

Then she ran, crouched against the wind, ran as fast as she could over the cliffs and down to the boathouse.

CHAPTER THIRTY-SIX

THE SOUND FROM THE HELICOPTER had stopped, and silence enveloped Jana Berzelius and Danilo Peña.

For a second, it seemed to her that they were alone in an icy emptiness. Panting and trembling, surrounded by whirling, whipping snow.

"Why are you saying that? Why can't you kill me?" she said, feeling the pulsing pain in her head.

"Haven't you figured it out yet?" he said, coughing. A string of viscous blood ran out of his mouth.

"What do you mean?" she asked.

He coughed again. Warm, steaming blood ran from his body. He was breathing far too quickly, and Jana knew he was close to losing consciousness.

"Killing is the only thing you can do," she said.

"Killing isn't particularly hard. What's hard is not doing it."

She saw the streak of blood trickle along the

veins that were tight in his neck. She saw that he was suffering.

"I still don't understand," she said, forced to close her eyes for a moment because of the pain in her head.

"Everything I've done...has been to protect you."

She shook her head and looked at him.

"No," she said. "Don't even try. You're lying."

"Think about it, Jana!"

"No," she said. "I don't want to hear it."

But he continued.

"I could have killed you in Knäppingsborg, do you remember? But I didn't do it, did I?"

"No, you couldn't. There was a witness, whom you clearly were forced to kill."

"I could have killed you long before...before he showed up..."

She looked straight out toward the rough sea and thought about their encounter at the entrance to Knäppingsborg. Was he telling the truth?

His body was shaking and tears were running down his face. She knew he wasn't crying; the tears were from the pain.

"Where are my boxes?" she asked quietly.

"Boxes?" he repeated.

"You took my boxes, left a sketch so that I would know that it was you who'd been there."

He was blinking constantly, as if he were trying to focus his eyes, and she felt a terrible chill when she suddenly realized the truth.

"You don't have them?"

"Who the hell cares about some fucking boxes?"

"I do."

"They must be valuable."

"No, but the contents are."

She was breathing quickly. The question was on the tip of her tongue, but she hesitated, not knowing if she wanted to know the answer.

Danilo's body was still. From his mouth came small, quick bursts of air.

"So why are you protecting me?" she asked.

"I'm not the one protecting you."

He moved his arm, clenching his jaw, and took something from his pocket and stretched out his closed fist. She held out her trembling hand and accepted her glittering, glimmering necklace, read the initials and slowly began to understand. Everything that had happened to her fell apart, piece by piece, in small individual events, illuminated by an icy, cold blue light.

She stood with great effort, feeling the pain in her head.

"Jana," he said. "You can't leave me here…"

He spoke slowly and quietly. His face was covered in beads of sweat, his lips blue and stiff.

She raised her eyes and saw small beams of light creeping between the tree trunks. She bent down, picked up the knife and fastened it at the small of her back.

"Jana! You have to help me get away from here."

"You knew that the police were coming here. Someone tipped you off, right? That's why you pushed Isra into the water. You wanted to hide your tracks and run away."

Danilo clenched his jaws.

"Help me into the boat," he pleaded.

"No. I can't let you disappear again," she said.

"I'm not going to make it. Help me."

She looked at him for a long time, thinking that he didn't have much time left, that maybe it was better to end everything, right here and now.

But he was in an out-of-the-way place, and when the police found him, it'd already be too late.

She began to walk away.

"Jana," he said. "Wait!"

"No," she said.

"I protected you!"

"I know," she said, turning around. "But I'm a prosecutor. I protect victims, not perpetrators."

She increased her pace, heard him yell something, but his voice disappeared in the wind.

She kept her gaze on the shaking beams of light that were approaching. She held her hand to her head and again tried to will away the unbearable pain pulsing through her temples. She tried to run, but it made her head spin in pain. She took another step and then another. She went faster, ignored the pain and the yellowish light that flickered in front of her eyes. She approached a fallen tree, charged directly toward it and jumped. She landed hard, rolling in the snow, and came to her feet. She saw her own and Danilo's white tracks and ran in them, not looking back, concentrating on counting her steps, trying to gain some idea of how many yards she had put between herself and the police.

When she came to one hundred twenty, she couldn't run anymore. The ground ended and the pier began. She approached slowly and stepped up onto it with silent steps. She didn't want her drumming footsteps to reveal her presence. She went the whole way out to the end of the pier and saw Isra. She had been able to get up out of the water and was huddled there, shaking and crying.

Jana turned around, intending to run back to the boathouse, but she now heard steps approaching. The police were here already and their voices were coming closer.

There was no possibility of coming onto land and hiding. She had to turn around and go back out on the pier. She rubbed her frozen hands together and knew she had only *one* option for getting away without being seen.

She took a deep breath and dove straight down into the water, which surrounded her with a sharp, paralyzing pain.

Mia Bolander moved quickly, her pistol drawn, past the boathouse and out onto the pier. She felt the small pricks of ice-cold snow against her cheeks. She stopped, looking over the water, around the forest behind her, and toward the water again. Squinting, she saw someone lying in the fetal position far out on the pier. She aimed her pistol in that direction and continued, hearing the planks creaking under her shoes.

She tried to hold her weapon still as her breaths came more quickly. Ten yards away, on the frozen planks of the pier, was a girl she assumed was Isra. Her clothes were wet and her dark hair had frozen hard. The scar on her forehead shone white.

Mia holstered her pistol and shouted to her colleagues at the boathouse.

"I've found her! Call an ambulance! Now!"

She felt the icy cold creeping in through her shoes and gloves. Isra lay on her back, her eyes still open, but she barely reacted.

Mia sank to her side, took off her jacket and laid it over the girl. She felt for breath and searched for a pulse before beginning CPR.

Jana Berzelius tried to open her eyes in the icy water but saw nothing but darkness. She swept her hands in front of her in hopes of being able to swim, but she felt nothing but the cold. The water wasn't very deep, but it felt like an eternity as she let her body sink down to the bottom. She dreamed of white daisies dancing in the wind, but came to just as a burning sensation shot through her body. She had bumped against something. She felt around with her hand, but she had no feeling left.

Her lungs were aching. Her head screamed at her to take her last breath, but she sank even farther down in the paralyzingly cold water. She again saw the white daisies dancing before her eyes, quicker this time. They begged her to dance with them. Around, around.

Her head was spinning. She was ready now, to let go and dance around, around.

Another shock. She had bumped against something again.

It was a rusty iron ladder, drilled into a cliff to let swimmers in and out of the water in the summer.

Her clothes heavy, she slowly pulled herself up.

Finally, she broke through the surface of the water, trying to keep herself calm, drawing air into her lungs. With rigid arms, she held tight to the ladder. Small chunks of ice tumbled around her as she began to climb. She coughed, trying to control her breathing, but her body screamed for more oxygen. She breathed in the cold air and felt like it almost cut her throat. She swallowed and inhaled again.

Sharp snowflakes blew in her face. Moaning, she rolled up onto the rocks, stood on shaky legs and began to walk.

Gunnar Öhrn knocked on the door, which opened immediately. He had a hard time not smiling when the man in front of him stiffened at the sight of him.

"Hi, Anders," Gunnar said.

"Gunnar?"

"You look surprised."

"I *am* surprised to see you here at my door, yes."

"Am I disturbing you?"

"No, no. Come in."

Anders closed the door, and led Gunnar into the hotel suite, into a room with two sofas. There were two wineglasses and a bowl of fruit on the coffee table. The lamps had been dimmed; the light was soft. The bed in the bedroom was neatly made, the striped white-on-white silk comforter was flat and the pillows were perfectly arranged.

"Are you expecting someone?" Gunnar asked, nodding toward the table where the two wineglasses stood.

"What do you want?" Anders asked, sitting down.

Gunnar sat across from him, leaned back and looked out the window, letting his gaze sweep over the frosty rooftops.

"We've solved the case with the Thai girls," he said. "The whole narcotics mess, actually."

"Oh, really," Anders said.

"But it's also put me in a very difficult situation. You see, Anneli has analyzed the skin cells she found under Axel Lundin's nails and got a match. She did a quick search in our records and found that they belong to one of us. Someone who works in our building, close to the case, and who has access to the holding cells."

Anders looked at him.

"That doesn't sound so strange to me," he said.

"You don't think so?"

"No."

Gunnar smiled.

"What were you doing," he began, leaning forward, "yesterday when Axel Lundin decided to kill himself?"

"Why are you asking that? Are you suggesting that I murdered him?"

"I'm not suggesting anything. It's just a simple question."

"Axel Lundin committed suicide. Why would I want to murder him?"

"That's what I'm wondering. Go on, tell me."

"You're on thin ice, Gunnar," Anders said.

"I'm just trying to figure out why you visited Axel in jail."

"Did you want anything else?"

"Yes. During the investigation, we've come across two names: Danilo Peña and The Old Man. What do you know about this Old Man, really?"

"Just as little as everyone else."

"Funny," Gunnar said, "because you've gotten rid of most of the other drug dealers, but not The Old Man."

"I don't understand what you mean."

"You're supposed to be so knowledgeable about this area. Carin Radler is always saying what an expert you are. How is it that you don't know anything about The Old Man?"

Gunnar cleared his throat.

"And furthermore, it's a little strange that Danilo Peña went up in smoke at the same moment we got ahold of his name. That can't just be a coincidence."

"I thought you were working on the hypothesis that Peña and The Old Man were the same person."

"Not anymore."

Gunnar leaned forward again and studied Anders's facial expression. But he still looked unaffected.

"I would be cautious if I were you," Anders said.

"Why is that?"

"It's very possible that I will be the next National Police Commissioner, Gunnar."

Gunnar leaned back again, taking a deep breath.

"There are different ways to get power. One is to work really hard for a long time and ambitiously work your way up the hierarchy. Another is to pay others to get the position you desire. That's called bribery."

"Are you claiming that I'm corrupt?"

"Are you?"

Anders laughed scornfully. Then he truly began to laugh, a loud, hollow laugh.

"You're a sorry bastard, Gunnar," he said.

"But honorable. I've already contacted Internal Affairs, and I'm sorry to say it, but I think your dream of becoming the National Police Commissioner was just shattered."

Anders drew his hand over his balding head and stood up, his hand reaching toward the pocket of his pants.

"Don't do that," Gunnar said as he stood, quickly drawing his pistol.

Anders laughed again, and Gunnar saw him raise his weapon.

"Put the weapon down," Gunnar commanded.

"Congratulations," Anders said.

"For what?"

"On the glory you'll have from having cleaned up."

"Drop the weapon. I have officers…"

But Anders moved his finger to the trigger, took a step forward and shot.

Gunnar stumbled backward, tried to catch the arm of the sofa, but fell backward to the floor. Despite the bulletproof vest absorbing most of the impact of the bullet, his chest hurt. It was a superficial wound, he knew, yet his hand went to his rib cage.

He watched as the door opened and two uniformed policemen rushed in, weapons drawn. Anders was quick, though, and turned with his pistol aimed at them, firing a series of three shots so rapidly that they didn't have time to react. Gunnar saw that the first bullet hit one of the men in the shoulder. The second hit him in the stomach, but the third missed.

Just as Anders aimed at the second officer, Gunnar shoved a cartridge into his gun, raised the weapon and fired. There was a loud bang and he felt the hard thrust of the recoil in his hand. The bullet left the weapon and went straight into Anders's leg, through cartilage, bone tissue and muscles, and out the other side. Anders sank to the ground, looking at Gunnar in astonishment, and raised his pistol waveringly, but he didn't have the energy to aim.

Gunnar was already on him, pushing the mouth of the gun away and slamming the pistol into Anders's face. It was a forceful strike right over the bridge of his nose and glasses. The blood spurted across Anders's right cheek all the way to his bald head.

"For Anneli," Gunnar said.

Then he staggered backward, sank into the sofa and saw yet another armed officer come in through the door and toward Anders.

Gunnar closed his eyes, his hand on his chest, and listened to the rattling sound of handcuffs.

THIRTY-SEVEN

THE ROTOR BLADES RATTLED LOUDLY as the rescue helicopter swayed in place in the air. Snow blew away from the ground in a circle, and Mia Bolander put her arm up to protect her face from the whirling flakes as the helicopter came in to land. From behind her arm, she followed the work from the crew as they helped Isra on board. The girl was suffering from severe hypothermia.

Multiple units had responded, and through the trees, the blue light was reflected. One hundred yards from the boathouse, they'd found a dark Volvo with the license plate number GUV 174 and had begun their initial search of the car.

The noise from the rotor blades increased as the helicopter lifted above her. It made a turn in the air and set course southward. It lowered its nose, accelerated quickly and disappeared over the sea.

She followed it with her eyes. She stood with her feet together and felt unsure for a moment whether she was warm or freezing.

"Mia," one of her colleagues called, waving to her. "We've found a man."

"Where?"

"He's lying not far from the boathouse, on a cliff. It could be the man we're searching for, Danilo Peña."

"Is he alive?"

"It doesn't seem like it."

The falling snow glimmered blue and landed like powder in front of her. White and untouched. Behind her, it was colored red. Like a necklace, the blood had left the wound on her neck.

Jana Berzelius went over the cliff toward the forest, knowing that the snow couldn't conceal her—that at that moment, she was completely visible from the boathouse.

But she had no choice.

Five more yards and the trees would be her shield.

The water that ran from her hair down to her neck had already turned to ice.

She focused on how she would take off her wet clothing as quickly as possible, but then her thoughts became cloudy and she experienced a scary confusion from being so violently freezing cold.

She wasn't even conscious of the rescue helicopter flying overhead with its flashing lights.

Her boat was still there, softly rocking on the

dark waves. She had to summon all of her strength just to get on board.

She tried to open the storage seat, tugging on the padlock that wouldn't budge. She lifted her foot and kicked one, two, three times, and finally it opened.

Fleece blankets lay inside. Jana stripped down and wrapped the blankets tightly around her body as she looked out over the bay.

Everything was quiet and still.

She started the engine, held her hand on the gas and felt her body being pressed backward by the accelerating force.

There was blood on his face, his stomach and his throat.

Mia Bolander walked slowly forward and looked at the man lying on the cliff in front of her, all the while holding her weapon aimed at him.

He was lying on his back, his eyes still open, but he didn't react when she knelt beside him. He didn't seem to be conscious.

"Can you hear me?" she said one last time.

But his dark eyes didn't move. They were as black as coal, she thought. When she tried to find his carotid artery with her fingers, she realized that the hunt was over; they'd gotten Danilo Peña. She smiled at the thought.

Her smile disappeared when she suddenly realized that it was important to bring him in alive, that he was the link between the victimized drug mules and the corrupt VIPs.

She pressed her fingers to his cold skin and felt a very weak pulse.

She knew they had little time to get him to the hospital.

Very little time.

CHAPTER

THIRTY-EIGHT

HE SAW THE INDIVIDUAL LETTERS BUT didn't comprehend what they meant. Everything flowed together before his eyes.

Karl Berzelius sat in his house in Lindö with the newspaper before him, and thought about his visit to the summerhouse the day before. He had ordered Jana to stay, to talk, but she'd disobeyed him. Instead she'd run away and disappeared in one of his boats.

He went over it again and again, cursing her more every time.

Then he heard a sound. He slowly put the newspaper down and listened to the sounds of the house. He saw the orange hue of the streetlights shining through the windows and casting striped shadows on the wall. It had already begun to grow dark. The days were short now.

"Margaretha?" he called out, but he knew it was in vain. She had run an errand and wouldn't be home for at least a half hour.

Then he heard the sound again. It sounded like footsteps. Someone was in the house.

He carefully got up from his armchair and walked through the living room toward the hall. He listened to his own steps as he continued over the floor. He looked toward the window and almost screamed—a person was standing there.

He held his hand to his heart and exhaled quickly when he realized that he was looking at his own reflection.

He stood closer to the window and looked out into the yard, at the snow-covered branches of the apple trees. He persuaded himself to stay calm and continue walking. He came to the stairs and was met by a ray of light. A lamp was on upstairs. He held his hand on the railing, taking one step at a time, always with his gaze locked on the light. He started walking more quickly. The closer he came, the more nervous he was.

The door to his office was ajar. The lamp on his desk was on. Now he was convinced that something was wrong—he never forgot to turn off the lamp on his desk.

He stepped into the room, sweeping his gaze around.

It didn't take long before he saw the red box on the desk.

It was under the lamp, the lid open.

But it wasn't empty anymore.

The necklace lay in it.

* * *

Per Åström stretched his arms up, feeling too warm in spite of having taken off his jacket.

He stood looking over the shoulder of Ola Söderström, who had his cell phone to his ear. Ola had contacted the mobile network operator and given them a three-digit number and a password that proved he was with the police. After three minutes, he received the IMEI number he was looking for.

"Thank you so much," Ola said, ending the call.

He pulled the keyboard to himself and punched the fifteen digits into the computer.

"There are a number of ways to trace a cell phone," Ola said, "but this is the most reliable. If Jana has it on, that is."

Ola leaned forward and continued working on the computer.

"Yes," he said, clapping his hands together.

Per leaned over his shoulder and saw the blue dot on the screen.

"Can you see where she is?" he asked.

"You can see where her cell phone is, at least."

"And where is it?"

Ola turned the screen toward him, and a map slowly appeared bit by bit.

"It's still in Norrköping," he said.

"But where?" Per asked impatiently.

Ola pointed to the screen, drawing a little circle around the blue dot with his finger.

"In the Lindö neighborhood," he said.

* * *

She watched him walk to the desk. His wrinkled hands trembled as he picked up the necklace and let it swing between his fingers.

Jana Berzelius stepped forward from the shadow behind the door.

Karl looked up at the reflection in the window and she knew that he was conscious that she was there in the room.

"You've always known who I actually am, haven't you?" she asked.

"Yes," he said without turning around.

Slowly, he walked around the desk and sank into the chair, which rocked slightly. He laid the necklace in front of him and leaned his head back. He closed his eyes and breathed calmly, as if he was saving his strength but was aware enough if something should happen.

"Why have you never told me?" she said.

"Would you have believed me? You didn't know yourself who you were or what you'd been through. You don't even remember Gavril Bolanaki."

She looked at her father, at his old, deeply lined face.

"But you've clearly known him a long time."

He opened his eyes but didn't answer.

"I found binders in the summerhouse," she began, waiting then for his reaction.

But he continued to remain silent.

"I know that you've deliberately influenced the

outcome of over a hundred court cases," she continued.

"That's how it had to be. I had no choice."

"You let innocent people be sentenced to long prison terms on false grounds. You acquitted guilty people for lack of proof. You created false police reports and seizure receipts, even silenced witnesses…"

"I had no choice, I said!" He brought his fist down on the desk so hard that the necklace jumped. His eyebrows had sunken down near the bridge of his nose.

"Everyone has a choice. What did Bolanaki give you in return? Did he give you money? Power?"

"I was a good prosecutor, Jana."

She shook her head slowly, doubtfully.

"I don't understand. How has no one discovered what you've been doing all of these years?"

"Maybe I should blame poor oversight. But in actuality, it wasn't the least bit poor."

"What are you saying? You mean that other people were aware of these illegal activities and let them continue? I don't believe you."

"You can believe whatever you want. Not everything is as simple in this world as you seem to believe. Not everything is black or white."

"Explain it to me, then!"

Her father raked his hand through his hair so hard that his eyes narrowed. "The explanation is called Anders Wester."

Jana bit her lip. "I should have known…" she

said. "Anders Wester. He was here with you on Saturday."

Karl let his hands slowly sink down.

Jana took a step forward, not taking her eyes off his hands.

"When I was here to see Mother," she continued, "I saw Anders's shoes." Not giving him time to answer, she continued, "So how did the three of you meet? Anders, Gavril and you?"

"How do you think people in positions of increasing power meet?"

"That's what I'm asking."

"Anders and Gavril met when they were doing their compulsory military service in Södertälje. I came in long after, in the early eighties."

"That much I understood from reading the contents of the binders. You've seen to it that Gavril dominated the narcotics trade since the late eighties, that he avoided prosecution."

"Gavril wanted to have me on his side. So that's what he arranged. But he's gone now."

"And when he disappeared from the market, you stepped into his place. You became The Old Man. The mysterious man that no one has met, that no one can identify in the slightest."

Her father shrugged his shoulders.

"You can't influence what people choose to say behind your back. But you can influence rumors."

"Why you and not Anders?"

"Society needs a hero. Anders likes the public eye."

"And you don't?"

"I've begun to see the end of my career. He hasn't."

Jana fell silent and looked at her father, met his gaze. "If you knew who I was the whole time, why did you choose to adopt me?"

"There was no other alternative. Or, I should say, the alternative was to remove you. We couldn't just let a little nine-year-old go. You were a difficult child. You knew too much and you ran away. Do you remember that?"

"I remember being taken care of by social services. They told me I was in a train accident and that was why I didn't know my name. So you adopted me to protect the operation?" Jana said in disbelief.

"Don't take it so hard."

"How else should I take it, then?"

He avoided her gaze.

"And the containers…?" she said, feeling herself beginning to tremble with rage, frustration.

"Well…" he said, suddenly seeming to be lost in his thoughts. "Yes, the containers are an unfortunate chapter…that happened without my knowledge. It was Gavril's idea…but that doesn't matter now that he is dead."

"Do you know how he died?" she said, not waiting for his answer. "It was Danilo who shot him, executed him in cold blood so he could take his place…"

"You don't know anything about that."

"Yes, I do," she said, smiling weakly, then becoming serious again. "And Anders, does he also know who I am?"

Her father looked tired.

"Anders?" he said, looking up. "Yes, he knows… but he doesn't know that you've begun to remember."

"And Mother? Does she know, too?"

"Your mother doesn't know anything."

"She knows that the adoption is closed."

"But not why. No one knows."

"Danilo knows."

"Danilo…" He said the name in a single long exhalation.

"He made his mistake by attacking you that night in Knäppingsborg. He should have stayed out of it."

"He made a lot of mistakes, didn't he?"

"By that you mean…?"

"Robin Stenberg, among others."

"Yes," her father said thoughtfully. "He was too eager, acted impulsively. That brings consequences."

"You admit that?"

"I admit that Danilo was a risk, and businessmen like me have to minimize risks."

"You had many reasons to do away with him, and you knew that I wanted to get revenge on him."

"No," he interrupted. "I *assumed* you wanted revenge. But it took a sketch to get you to act."

Jana found it difficult to stand there and hear his words. "You made me kill him."

"Well, good. Then you don't need to worry any longer that he's going to reveal your true identity... and we can both be at ease."

"Danilo said he didn't have my boxes. Where are they? And my journals? I want them back now!"

"How do you know I have them?"

"Where are they? Tell me where they are!"

Karl smiled again.

"You shouldn't hold on to the past," he said. "Everything changes."

"Not people."

"Maybe not people, but times change."

Jana's eyes narrowed, her fists clenched. "Tell me where my boxes are," she said slowly.

"In a safe place."

"Where?"

"Why would I tell you?"

"What are you going to do with them?"

"I may need them very soon."

She took a step forward, both fists still clenched. "How did you know they existed? That I hid them?"

"You've been part of my household for over twenty years, Jana. You should know by now who I am, that I have eyes and ears everywhere."

"Was it the property owner? Did he tell you?"

Her father shook his head.

"Much simpler than that, Jana. Axel Lundin frequented the building on Garvaregatan. He saw you."

She felt her muscles tighten, her breath quicken.

"It's unbelievable," she said. "If Axel was working for you, why would he give Danilo up to the police?"

"Why isn't your problem."

"But it has become yours."

"More of Anders's problem."

Jana took a step forward, tried to relax her body, but the aggression held her in an iron grip. She lowered her head.

"You know it's over now, Father."

"Why is that? What are you intending to do?" he asked calmly.

"You know what I *have* to do."

His look darkened. "If you report me," he said, "you'll never see your boxes again. You'll never touch your journals. Never. And you'll never know whose hands they might end up in."

His voice was clear and distinct. She saw how he clenched his fists and felt the room fill with his suppressed fury.

"Do you hear me?" he said loudly, rushing her, grabbing her arm and shoving her into the wall. He stood so close to her that she could feel his breath on her face.

Jana nodded and whispered, "Yes."

"Answer so I can hear you!"

"Yes."

Then he struck her. The blow landed on her cheek.

"Answer me!"

When he held up his hand to hit her again, she raised her arm and blocked the blow. He first re-acted with surprise, then increased rage. He raised his hand again, but now she gripped his wrist, twisting his arm, twisting hard.

Without blinking.

"Yes," she hissed at him. "I understand."

He tried to say something. She saw it in his eyes. *Let go!*

But she squeezed even harder.

Let go, let go!

He said it, pleading, begging, but she wouldn't let go.

He doubled over, huddled up, sat there, miserable, old and gray.

Only when the doorbell rang did she let him go. Then she looked away from her father.

All this took only one single second. But it was enough.

He heard the doorbell ring inside the house and pushed the button again and again. He took a few steps backward, looking up at the window of the upper level. She was in there—Per Åström was sure of it.

He had seen her car in the driveway. He'd got-ten out of the taxi and asked the driver to wait, then walked cautiously through the snow. Now he tried to calm himself, tried to breathe rhythmically, tried not to seem like a crazy person who had been searching for her, stalking her.

Nothing was actually suspect or out of the ordinary, really. Jana's car being parked at her parents' house was completely normal.

Yet he felt very anxious for her. He pressed the doorbell again.

Snowflakes landed on his face and jacket, making his bare hands cold.

No one came to open the door.

He left the front door and walked around the house, surveying, searching around the yard and patio and looking in the windows again.

Back at the front door, he tried the door handle, but it was locked, as he'd suspected.

"Jana?" he called, thinking that now he really did seem like a complete idiot. But he didn't care, not anymore, not now that worry had gripped him in all seriousness.

He stood completely still, focusing his gaze on a single point in the white snow, and listened. Not a single movement, not one sound from inside the house.

It was a mistake to have come here, he thought, turning around. He went back.

At the same moment, he heard a pistol shot from inside the house.

The echo of the report bounced quickly between the houses on the street.

At first he didn't understand what had happened.

Then he heard yet another shot, followed by two more. The sound was loud and came so quickly that

Per crouched at the gate and put his arms over his head to protect himself.

It rapidly dawned on him.

Shots had been fired inside the Berzelius house.

"Jana!" he yelled straight out into the falling snow.

But now everything was completely silent.

No pulse.

Dr. Amanda Svedlund worked quickly. She had cut through the clothes on the patient lying on the stretcher before her and placed an oxygen mask over the patient's mouth. They had turned up the heat in the rescue helicopter.

Still no pulse.

Nurse Sofia Enberg took out the defibrillator, dried the patient's wet chest and positioned the electrodes.

The patient's heart was in chaos. It was trembling, unable to pump blood through the body. An electrical current could get the heart beating again, but the time factor was crucial. The time between when a heart stopped beating to defibrillation was the most important factor impacting the chances of survival. For every minute that passed, the chance of survival decreased by up to ten percent.

It was crucial that they get the patient's heart beating as soon as possible.

Amanda listened to the computerized voice.

"Analyzing heart rhythm. Do not move the patient."

A beat of silence.

"Defibrillation recommended. Charging now."

The intensifying howling sound permeated the helicopter cabin. Amanda held her finger over the red blinking light on the machine, waiting, and then pushed it.

The current went through the patient's body.

"Defibrillation complete."

The first attempt had no effect. Amanda started the machine again. No pulse.

"Come on, now!" she said aloud, pushing with both hands on the patient's naked chest. She counted to fifteen, tried a third time.

The patient's heart had now been still for thirteen minutes, and the chance of survival was minimal.

Amanda felt a sinking hopelessness, but she didn't show it.

She continued working.

The world rushed past beneath them. They flew over narrow ribbons of waves, towering treetops and powerful electrical lines. The streetlights were like tiny fireflies as the helicopter headed toward Linköping. The engines roared as they came in for a landing at the university hospital.

The emergency room staff was waiting for them. Their clothes flapped in the wind.

Just as the helicopter made contact with the ground, something suddenly happened.

The patient moved.

It was a weak movement, but Amanda saw it.

She looked at the machine.

She saw the rhythm of the EKG monitor.

She saw that Danilo Peña's heart had begun beating.

Per Åström was tense. He stood still for a few minutes before daring to go back to the house. Instead of knocking on the door, he went through the snow to again attempt to get into the house from the back. He stopped at an apple tree twenty yards from the veranda. He went up to the veranda and picked up one of the clay pots. It was heavier than he'd anticipated, but that just made the glass in the veranda door easier to break.

He stuck his hand through to the inside of the door handle and heard a sound from inside. It took him a second to realize it was coming from upstairs. It sounded like someone moaning.

He moved quickly up the steps, very conscious that it was risky to be in the house, but it was a risk he had to take.

When he got to the landing, he could see that a lamp was on in what seemed to be a home office.

He listened and heard someone move.

When he pushed the door open, he immediately saw her on the floor. For a brief moment, he stood there frozen, looking at her bloody face. At first he thought she was dead, but then he saw a small movement in her chest followed by a rattling breath. He took a step forward and saw the pistol in her hand.

Then he saw her father, Karl Berzelius.

"Holy shit," he said out loud.

Karl sat with his back to the wall, his eyes closed, head hanging. Above his left ear, his gray hair had been colored red, and blood dripped onto the floor.

Per walked slowly forward to Jana and sank to his knees. He began carefully loosening the pistol from her hand, but her grip tightened. Suddenly she opened her eyes, looked at him hazily and began to mumble, "I tried…" she said. "I tried to stop… him."

Then she closed her eyes and released the gun.

Hands trembling, Per took out his cell phone to call an ambulance.

CHAPTER
THIRTY-NINE

THE AIR WAS FULL OF COLD FOG AS Henrik Levin pushed more coins into the parking meter at Vrinnevi Hospital. With his hands in his pockets, he crossed the parking lot to the main entrance.

"Henrik?" Emma said when he opened the door to their room in the Postpartum Ward. "I have the TV on. The only thing they're talking about is what happened at the boathouse."

Henrik sat next to her, holding her hand. He looked at their newborn son, who lay snuggled up to Emma's breast.

"So you caught him," she said with a small smile.

"I don't know about 'we'—it was Mia who caught him at that boathouse. She'll be celebrated for her efforts," Henrik said, beginning to think about the young Thai girls who'd been victims of all this.

"You're tired…" she said.

"People don't understand. They were forced to swallow these capsules and..."

He didn't realize he'd trailed off.

The news channel showed a picture of Danilo Peña. They both turned their eyes toward the young journalist telling the dark story of Peña and about the surviving Thai girl who, considering the circumstances, was doing well. The doctors were optimistic.

"Thank God," Emma said, stroking her hand over her son's back. He was lying next to her naked skin under a warm blanket.

Gunnar Öhrn appeared on the screen. He looked exhausted, but he smiled when he said that they would soon be able to put the investigation in the pile of solved cases. Then they showed a picture of Anders Wester, and Henrik heard the words *bribes* and *scandal*.

"What really happened?" Emma asked.

"What can I say," Henrik said, sighing, "besides that this investigation led to something much larger."

"I've heard you say that once before."

Henrik nodded and turned his gaze back to the window. He could sense the sun through the dense fog and saw for himself the first pictures of the police operation taking on Anders Wester. His office at the National Crime Squad and his private residence had been cordoned off. Forensic technicians had spent hours collecting documents, papers, affidavits, receipts and other items that could be used as proof against him in the coming trial. It would take time for the police to register every piece. Everyone who had ever been involved with him would be tracked down.

"You'll have to tell me another time," Emma said with smiling eyes.

He met her gaze and took a deep breath.

"Do you want to hold him?" she asked.

"Can I?"

"Of course you can."

Henrik got up. Emma pushed the blanket away and carefully lifted up the little guy. Henrik took him, standing for a long time just holding him. He breathed in his son's scent and felt his fragile arms and tiny legs against his chest. He felt complete happiness at finally holding his youngest son in his arms.

"I've been so worried," he said. "That's what it was all about the whole time. That's why I've avoided everything, focused on work."

He swallowed, looking at Emma.

"But I love you," he said.

"I love you, too," she said.

"And I love this little guy. I'm just so scared that something will happen to him."

"What's going to happen to him?" she said, smiling.

"He's so little."

"But he's healthy."

"I hope so," Henrik said quietly, falling silent.

* * *

Jana Berzelius pulled her hat farther down her forehead as she stepped out of the Public Prosecution Office with Per Åström. She held her head high and her gaze was steady.

"Are you upset not knowing?" he asked.

"Not knowing what?"

"If she made it or not."

"You mean Pim?"

"Yes. She was your client, after all."

"I know she made it."

"How do you know that?"

"I just know."

Per looked at her seriously.

"How are you feeling, really?"

"It's just a superficial wound."

"No, I mean how are you *really* feeling?"

She didn't answer. She just looked at him, knowing that he was looking for answers, and knew that she had a whole lot to explain. She owed it to him. She owed him a lot, actually. But some things he didn't need to know, neither about her nor her father. Or the boxes that she still hadn't found.

She had searched through the whole house in Lindö and the summerhouse, but she still hadn't found her journals and all the other belongings that meant so much to her. Only her father knew where they were. Her secret, her whole life, now lay in his hands. And his secret lay in hers.

"You haven't said very much about what happened," he said as if he could read her thoughts.

"My father became sick, confused. He was a danger to himself, tried to commit suicide."

"Okay, so that's just it?"

He sought her gaze again.

"It's called a delirium state," she said. "Generally speaking, every illness, no matter whether banal or serious, can cause it."

She held his gaze, thought it was more convincing if she did. She repeated to herself that she had done the right thing lying about her father's mental health. She had said that he'd been so psychologically broken down that her mother could no longer take care of him. As a result, she'd agreed to stay at their house and help her mother. It forced her to neglect her work and her personal life. She couldn't answer the phone or emails.

"He had acted strangely when I was looking for you."

"So you understand."

"He said you hadn't seen each other in more than six months."

"He was clearly lying."

"That's not the Karl I know."

"Maybe you don't know him well enough."

She wrapped her new black scarf around her neck an extra time.

"Will he return to normal again?"

"I don't know," she said, turning her head away. She thought about how one of the bullets had gone straight into the left half of his brain. The injury could mean that his psychological functions could be impaired or even permanently damaged. No one knew yet how seriously injured he was, if he would be able to return to a normal life or not.

"So you knew that he was suicidal?" he asked.

"I knew that he was carrying a deep sadness."

"A deep sadness?"

"You aren't going to give up, are you?" she said, meeting his eyes.

"I love family secrets."

"So I'm guessing you're going to overwhelm me with questions now."

"One might think you know me," he said, laughing.

"And I do. In two minutes, you're going to ask me if we should get lunch."

"Not if—*where* we should get lunch."

"Okay, *where* we should get lunch then."

"And what are you going to answer?"

"That I know a good place called The Colander," Jana said, starting to walk.

The snowflakes landed on her face as she passed a snow-covered park bench. A man pulling a little girl on a sled went past her with a scraping sound.

She continued forward, not needing to turn around, because she knew that Per had already begun following her.

* * * * *

ACKNOWLEDGMENTS

I want to thank everyone who helped me with this book. Everyone who read and gave their opinions, who answered my questions and helped me gather facts, who gave me their time and energy. Many thanks to my editor, Jacob Swedberg, for his careful editing and invaluable cooperation. Thanks to Sofie Mikaelsson and Joel Gerdin for information on general police work. To Johan Ahlner and Lotta Fornander for factual information. And to my sister, my parents and my parents-in-law, who continue to relish my successes and who so happily celebrate them with me.

I want to say a particularly warm thank-you to my mom and dad for all of the hours you have spent reading, supporting and encouraging me. You've always been there for me. Few have the gift of such devoted and loyal parents.

Thanks to Jonas Carlsson Malm, Jonas Winter and the late Tommy Johansson. You were the first to believe in *Marked for Life* and Prosecutor Jana Berzelius.

Thanks to my readers for fun meetings, wonderful conversations and many laughs in boutiques, bookstores, book fairs, libraries and on social media. You give me the happiness and inspiration to write.

This story is fictional. Any similarities between characters in the book and real people are coincidental. The settings are generally described as they are in reality, but I have occasionally distorted them or added certain details to serve the needs of the story. Any errors that have crept in are my own.

There is one person whom I want to thank more than anyone. But what can I say to a man who knows what I'm thinking? Who asks questions that help me find the way? Who is always at my side? Who is my best friend, colleague and life partner? What can I say to you, Henrik Schepp?

I know.

Something I say often, and far too infrequently.

Three little words.

To protect her real identity, prosecutor Jana Berzelius must destroy all evidence connected to her sordid past. But only the criminal Danilo Peña, with whom she has shared a dark history, knows where that evidence is kept. Jana is forced into a risky and ultimately untenable position—agree to hide Peña in her home in exchange for the incriminating files. Meanwhile, she is in charge of investigating a series of gruesome, interconnected murders in which the bizarrely mutilated victims all have some tie to the local hospital—the very place her adopted mother was en route to recently when she suspiciously died in the ambulance. As police search for the killer, Jana pieces together who the murderer is, then must rush to intervene before another victim dies.

Read on for an excerpt from Emelie Schepp's third novel, SLOWLY WE DIE, available summer 2018 from MIRA Books.

PROLOGUE

THE WOMAN OPENED HER EYES AND *looked straight up at me. Her hands began clawing desperately at the air, as if she'd just realized what was about to happen.*

I could see her surprise, her confusion, and I whispered to her that there was no alternative, that it was too late, she had already seen too much in the back of the ambulance.

She should have kept her eyes closed, shouldn't have looked around with her meddling gaze, shouldn't have seen me take the ring.

"I'm sorry," I said, pressing my hands against her nose and mouth, "but what would you do if you were me?"

She didn't answer. How could she?

She struggled again to pull her face away from me, making one last desperate attempt. Her thin body thrashed up and down on the stretcher. She tried to grab my hands, but instead her fingers just grabbed at my arms with increasing panic. Her nails tore at my skin, but I didn't stop. I pressed harder. Harder.

She tried to scream, and I heard a gurgling sound. She couldn't keep it up any longer; her strength began to wane and she blinked a few times without any tears falling.

And then, finally, it came. The awareness. This was the end. Her brain let go of all other thoughts, taking in the reality—crystal clear and horrifying.

There was no sound, only a tiny gasp as she surrendered, as her body finally relaxed and became completely still.

I took my hand away from her mouth and listened to the silence. I smiled. It felt so simple, so undeniable, so complete.

This was a deviation from the plan, yes, but nevertheless it was a beginning. I was filled with excited anticipation, with revenge.

Childlike excitement.

CHAPTER

ONE

Wednesday

PHILIP ENGSTRÖM LEANED AGAINST the black kitchen counter at the ambulance station in Norrköping. Cool spring air wafted in through an open window. He reached for the cup in the coffee machine, wrapped his fingers around it and enjoyed its warmth. Then he walked through the room, sank down onto one of the sofas and took a couple of sips before putting the cup on the nearby coffee table.

He had one hour left before his overnight ambulance nursing shift ended. He had to fight a strong desire to close his eyes and drift off, if only for a few minutes.

He knew that he shouldn't give in to his exhaustion; he needed to pull himself together after the shift's stressful events, but he couldn't help himself. He nodded off and was dragged down into sleep, where he dreamed of a whirling, rushing waterfall. Then he heard someone yell and jerked himself awake, his hands fumbling over the table and knocking over his coffee cup.

"Philip!"

"Hi, Sandra," he said drowsily.

Sandra Gustafsson stood six feet from him, one hand on her hip. Her hair was blond and her eyes the same green as their work clothes. She was the newest ambulance driver, the most recent in a series of recruits. She was twenty-three, competent, worked hard and seemed to care about her colleagues.

"Still tired?" she asked.

"Not one bit," Philip said, getting up and wiping the coffee from the table with a wad of paper towels before sitting back down on the couch.

She looked at him as he attempted to stifle a yawn, then went to the coffee machine, picked up two cups and filled them.

He couldn't resist smiling when she held one out to him. He took a quick sip and glanced at his watch.

"Time to go home soon," she said.

"Yep," he said.

"Do you want to talk before you go?"

She sat in the armchair across from him. Her body was trim and fit.

"About what?"

"About the patient who died."

"No. Why would I want to do that?" he said, taking another sip, still feeling drowsy and thinking that he really should start taking better care of himself. The nature of his work meant his sleep was often broken and as a result he didn't sleep enough. He knew he needed more than an hour or so here or there.

"It was an unusual situation," she said.

"It was your everyday heart attack. What is there to talk about?"

"The patient could have survived."

"But she didn't, okay?" Philip listened to the hum from the coffee machine as he thought about the woman who had died on his shift. He noticed his hands trembling.

"I'm just wondering how you feel about it all," she said.

"Sandra," he said, putting his mug on the table. "I know you're just trying to be supportive, but that psychology nonsense doesn't work on me."

"So you don't want to talk?"

"No. I already said so."

"I just thought…"

"What did you think? That we would sit in a circle and hug each other? Should we all put on our comfiest pajamas, too?"

"According to protocol…"

"Let it go. I've worked as an ambulance nurse here for five years. I know exactly what the protocol is."

"Then you also know it's not okay to fall asleep on a call."

Silence filled the room.

"Just think if someone found out," she whispered.

"No one will find out," he said. "As far as I'm concerned, it falls under work confidentiality."

"What?"

He looked around, checking that no one was within earshot.

"You heard what I said."

"What the hell, it can't be like that!" she said.

Philip met her gaze. "Why not?"

"You're not sane," she said. "You're completely…"

"I know it sounds strange."

"Strange? It sounds wrong…"

He looked at the door and thought about how much he wanted to leave work right this very moment. He wanted to feel calm, hear silence, above all be rid of Sandra.

"I'm sorry, Philip. I can't let it go. You're the one who messed up, not me."

"I never mess up, just so you know. And that's not why the patient died."

"Do you really believe that?"

Philip stared at her as he raked his hand through his hair and took a deep breath to calm himself.

"Okay," he said after a long moment. "This is what we'll do. If, contrary to my expectations, anyone finds out that I happened to fall asleep briefly on a call, I promise I'll report myself."

"What about me, if that happens?"

"You can blame everything on me. Claim you

were afraid to say anything because you were new on the job and all of that. Make it all my fault."

She just looked at him.

"Do we have a deal?" he said.

"Yes, this one time," she said quietly. "But you should really get a handle on things. One more incident and I'll report you."

"Thanks," he said, leaning forward and laying a hand on her shoulder.

"I'm serious," she said.

"I know," he said, getting up.

Prosecutor Jana Berzelius sat on one of the chairs in the broadcast studio with her legs crossed. She was waiting for her turn to be interviewed by Richard Hansen, the host of the morning program for Channel P4 Östergötland on Swedish Radio.

When she saw Hansen's signal, she walked silently to the seat opposite him and put a pair of headphones on. She listened as Hansen smoothly changed topics and announced that next up was Norrköping lead prosecutor Jana Berzelius, here to talk about a rise in criminal gang activity.

"Extortion, robbery and violent attacks with hammers, knives and automatic weapons. Gang violence continues to increase. Jana Berzelius, you've been the lead investigator in many cases of serious organized crime here in Norrköping for many years. What do you think is the reason for the increased violence we're seeing?"

Jana cleared her throat. "First of all, we have to

remember that we're talking about the number of *reported* crimes, that an increase in crime, statistically speaking, isn't the same thing as an *actual* increase in crime…"

"So you're saying that the numbers lie?"

"What we can see is that gang violence all over Sweden is increasing, at the same time as violence in society in general is decreasing."

"And what is causing the increased gang violence?"

"There are a number of possible explanations," she said.

"Name a few."

She leaned forward. "You already named the most important ones in your introduction, and I can only agree that increased access to firearms, along with an increase in social and economic segregation, are contributing factors in this context."

"As you know, we've been tracking the criminal gangs in Norrköping," Hansen said, looking down at the papers in front of him. "Our stories about gang activities regarding the illegal trafficking of weapons, narcotics and people are our most-followed stories. It has been a year since that coverage originally appeared, and there's hardly been any improvement in this area. Very few jail sentences have been handed down, few cases have even ended up at trial, and many people are saying that the Swedish legal system is failing. Should we be concerned?"

"There is always a risk of error in the criminal justice system, which in unfortunate cases can lead to wrongful convictions or even a failure to convict."

"Can a biased prosecutor pose such a risk?"

"Yes, just as much as manipulated police reports, misleading expert witnesses or false testimony. No one, not even a prosecutor such as myself, can deny that these are the dangers that sometimes result in wrongful convictions," Jana said.

"And what do you think about those voices calling for harsher sentencing for violent crimes, for example?"

"We can't prove that harsher sentencing results in fewer crimes. However…"

"In the United States, they have prioritized stricter sentencing and it has resulted in…" Hansen began.

"But we're talking about Sweden. Norrköping, specifically," Jana clarified.

Hansen looked down at his papers again. "Stricter sentencing is an important objective of the opposition's legal policy."

"The foremost duty of criminal policy should be to work for increased opportunities for crime prevention."

Hansen looked up at her and said, "In so-called Policegate, police brass and businessmen have been accused of interfering with justice, accepting bribes and smuggling narcotics, and they will very likely receive long prison sentences, if convicted."

"That's correct."

"From what I understand, Policegate is both complicated and unusual. Besides the obviously reckless elements of violent crime, this is also about a state-appointed official of the highest level who abused his authority, and very gravely so."

"You're referring to National Police Commissioner Anders Wester," Jana said. "But we don't have the whole story yet and not all of the suspects have been questioned…"

"That's true, but you can't deny that harsh sentences are needed in such a unique circumstance to set a precedent for how seriously our society views this type of crime, can you? This is about our trust in the police force."

"I can't comment on that case," Jana said.

"But don't you agree that the penal system is a way for society to see how seriously different offenses are taken?" Hansen said.

"Yes, but as I said, there is no proof that harsher sentences result in fewer crimes, in the short term at least."

"So if I understand you correctly, you think that instead, we should invest more resources in policies that focus on prevention, and this is the only way to lower crime?"

"Yes. Of course."

"And what has led you to this conclusion?"

Jana looked him straight in the eye.

"Experience."

Nurse Mattias Bohed was walking through Ward 11 at Vrinnevi Hospital with his colleague

Sofia Olsson. Outside Room 38 sat a high-security guard named Andreas Hedberg, his back straight and hands folded. As the two nurses approached, Hedberg smiled shyly in Sofia's direction and stood to unlock the door.

Once they had entered the room, Hedberg closed the door behind them and locked them in.

Murder suspect Danilo Peña had been receiving care in this private room, with a security guard stationed outside the door around the clock. Mattias didn't know much more about the patient than what he had read online—that the guy was a criminal who had been mixed up in what had come to be called Policegate. He was suspected of having killed several Thai girls caught up in drug trafficking. The nursing staff that had been handpicked to take care of him had received a strict warning: absolutely no one was allowed to be alone with the patient in the room.

"Did someone forget to turn off the light?" Sofia asked when she saw that the lamp near the bed was on.

"No," Mattias said. "I don't think so."

The private room was small and, aside from the usual medical equipment and monitors, contained only a bed, a nightstand and a chair.

Sofia took out a small glass bottle and swirled it carefully before drawing the fluid into a syringe.

"Oh, by the way, you heard that the patient woke up yesterday, right?" she asked.

"You're kidding."

"Yes, I am," she said, smiling.

"Are you trying to scare me?"

"No, I just want you to be careful."

The patient lay quietly in the bed, except for the rhythmic motion of his chest as it rose and fell with every breath. He was flat on his back with his eyes closed and arms tucked under the blanket.

Mattias kept his distance even though he knew that the patient was in a drug-induced sleep.

"What's up with you? I was just joking," Sofia said, noticing Mattias's nervousness. "He's never shown the slightest sign of waking up when I've been here. He's hardly even moved—he's been lying just like this every single time I've come in."

"But theoretically he could wake up if the medicine isn't strong enough."

"Oh, just relax." She sighed.

"But really, what would happen if he did?"

"He's not going to wake up," she said.

She walked over to the bed and spoke to the patient in a calm voice, telling him that it was time for his shot.

"Why are you talking to him if he can't hear you?"

"Force of habit, maybe?"

She held the syringe full of sedative in her left hand and lifted the blanket up with her right.

"Could you give me a hand?" she asked.

Mattias went over and stood beside her, then reached over and wiped the skin of the patient's upper arm with an alcohol swab. Danilo Peña's body looked thin, he thought. He had probably lost a lot of muscle mass while lying in that hospital bed.

Mattias walked around the bed and tossed the swab into the wastebasket as he watched Sofia move the syringe closer to Peña's upper arm.

"Sweet dreams," she said.

Just then, Peña's hand twitched and his eyes opened. Sofia jumped back and dropped the syringe onto the floor. It rolled under the bed.

"Is he awake?" asked Mattias, who had backed up several steps toward the door.

"No. Look, his eyes are cloudy, unfocused. He's still unconscious. But I wasn't prepared for him to… I mean, I was just so surprised."

She leaned over to pick up the syringe and stretched her arm under the bed, but it had rolled out of reach.

"It's on your side. Could you pick it up while I prepare a new one?"

Mattias looked nervously at the patient before kneeling down on the floor. He could see Sofia's feet and legs as he searched under the bed.

The syringe lay far back against the wall; his name tag and the pens in his shirt pocket scraped against his chest as he wriggled in to reach it.

Just then, he heard a thud above him. He looked around but couldn't see Sofia's legs anymore.

"Sofia?" he said, getting up quickly, his hand gripping the syringe.

His body flooded with adrenaline when he saw

that the blanket had been cast off and the bed was now empty.

Draped across the chair next to the bed was Sofia, her arms hanging limply and her eyes closed.

Mattias stared at her, his heart pounding so hard that it thundered in his ears. Not until then did he realize that he should press the alarm button and call for help, or call for the guard. But his body refused to obey him.

He took a step back, turned slowly and discovered Peña standing completely still behind him, just two steps away, his fists clenched and his eyes dark.

Mattias gripped the syringe harder and raised it, as if to defend himself.

"Don't even think about it," Peña said hoarsely, stepping toward the nurse.

Mattias tried to jab the syringe into Peña, but his arm movement was too predictable. Peña caught his arm instead and twisted it, causing a sharp pain to shoot through Mattias's body.

"What do you want?" Mattias whimpered. "Just tell me what you want, I can help you…"

The pain in his arm rendered him unable to say anything more. He couldn't stand it any longer, and the syringe slipped from his hand and fell to the floor.

"Take off your clothes."

"What?"

"Take off your clothes. Now!"

"Okay, okay," Mattias said, but he remained

standing. He felt paralyzed, as if completely incapable of moving.

Only when Peña repeated the words a third time did he finally understand. As he pulled his white shirt over his head and dropped it to the floor, he noticed Peña's monitor wires. A pen came loose and dropped to the floor.

"Pants, too."

Mattias glanced toward the door.

"Are you stupid? Hurry up."

The blow to his face came so quickly, Mattias didn't have time to react. He touched his mouth gingerly and felt warm blood between his fingers.

Peña leaned over and picked up the syringe.

"Please," Mattias said, "I'll do whatever you want…"

"Your pants."

Mattias quickly undid the drawstring on his white pants and pulled them down past his knees. He tried to yank one leg out, but his white gym shoe got caught in the fabric. He lost his balance and fell sideways. He felt a sharp pain in his hip as he landed on the floor but continued tugging on his pant leg.

He finally got his shoes and pants off and noticed the goose bumps covering his skin. He thought about his son Vincent, who always undressed so slowly. He always had to nag the boy when it was time to take a bath or go to bed. Now he promised himself that he would never nag him again.

Never again, he thought, feeling a lump forming in his throat.

"You forgot your socks. Come on!"

Mattias pulled off his socks and looked at Peña.

"I have a family, a son…"

"Get up," Peña said. "And get into the bed."

Mattias stumbled forward, lacking nearly all physical control, but he managed to stay on his feet and climb up onto the sheets. He waited, panting and trembling.

"Now what?"

"Lie down," Peña growled.

"Here?"

"In the bed."

Mattias noticed the sheets were still warm as he laid his head on the pillow. He was uncomfortable but didn't dare move. Next to the bed he noticed a heart monitor machine and IV fluid pole.

Peña bent over and attached a heart monitor clip to Mattias's finger, then picked up the shirt and pants from the floor and put them on. The pants hung loosely from his waist. Then he turned back toward Mattias, pushed aside the sheet and held the original syringe over the nurse's naked chest, a half inch above his heart.

"It's time for your shot," he said with a sneer.

Mattias saw the needle pierce his skin. Then everything happened so quickly, he didn't have time to react as a coldness spread through his veins.

A red dot appeared from the puncture wound and soaked into the white sheet.

He should have felt scared, but he didn't feel anything. All he could do was observe and register.

Peña said something, but the words echoed as if they had been uttered in a tunnel. Mattias saw him adjust the white shirt, pick up the pen that had fallen on the floor, put it in his breast pocket and look at himself in the mirror. He smoothed both hands over his dark hair before turning again toward Mattias.

"Sweet dreams," he said.

He walked toward the door. Mattias heard it unlock, open and close again.

This can't be happening was his last thought.

Then he felt it come. The silence.

Followed by the chill. It began in his feet and hands, spreading slowly from his legs, arms and head in toward his heart.

And finally, darkness.